Other Books by Bill Ransom

FINDING TRUE NORTH
Copper Canyon Press*

WAVING ARMS AT THE BLIND
Copper Canyon Press*

THE SINGLE MAN LOOKS AT WINTER
Empty Bowl Press

LAST CALL
Blue Begonia Press

LAST RITES
Brooding Heron Press*

THE JESUS INCIDENT (with Frank Herbert)
Putnam/Berkley

THE LAZARUS EFFECT (with Frank Herbert)
Putnam/Berkley

THE ASCENSION FACTOR (With Frank Herbert)
Putnam/Ace

JAGUAR
Ace

*Out of Print

VIRAVAX

BILL RANSOM

ACE BOOKS, NEW YORK

This Ace Book contains the complete text
of the original hardcover edition.

VIRAVAX

An Ace Book / published by arrangement with
the author

PRINTING HISTORY
Ace hardcover edition / September 1993
Ace paperback edition / August 1994

All rights reserved.
Copyright © 1993 by Bill Ransom.
Cover art by Marvin Mattelson.
This book may not be reproduced in whole or in part,
by mimeograph or any other means, without permission.
For information address: The Berkley Publishing Group,
200 Madison Avenue, New York, New York 10016.

ISBN: 0-441-00083-5

ACE®
Ace Books are published by The Berkley Publishing Group,
200 Madison Avenue, New York, New York 10016.
ACE and the "A" design are trademarks
belonging to Charter Communications, Inc.

PRINTED IN THE UNITED STATES OF AMERICA

10 9 8 7 6 5 4 3 2 1

for Nathalie, Gabe, and Dominic
Easter, 2015

ACKNOWLEDGMENTS

Karen and Steve Hart, microbiology, physiology; Peninsula College, Port Angeles, Washington.

Gue Pilon, studio space.

Johanna Marquis/Richard Marquis, studio space.

Ardeth Dunne, P.A., and Philip Kirby, M.D., Viral Disease Clinic, Harborview Hospital, Seattle.

Dr. Larry Corey, AIDS Vaccine Project, University of Washington, Seattle.

Frank Herbert, whose memory is still an inspiration.

Thanks, Lupita, for the moral support.

ASH WEDNESDAY

18 February 2015

1

NANCY BARTLETT STAGGERED away from her husband's body on their living room floor, gun smoke trailing the air behind her like a guardian angel. Her right hand cramped from its grip on the stubby Galil. Nancy used her left hand to pry the right free, then she let her shaking knees drop her to the couch. A winking red light at her Watchdog console signaled that security was on the way.

The mess in front of her on the living room floor did not resemble Red Bartlett any more than the monster he had become had resembled the shy genius, the pride of ViraVax. Red Bartlett had attacked her, his own wife, with a fury that she had not imagined possible. Her devastated apartment was testimony to that fury.

Nancy Bartlett set the hot Galil next to a chunk of skull and hair on the couch, then willed her trembling body into the kitchen, where she wouldn't have to look at what was left of her husband.

Thank God, Sonja's not here!

Their daughter was spending the weekend and her fuel ration coupons at an airstrip out of town, garnering all the flight and simulator time she could get.

Nancy and Sonja lived in the capital of Costa Brava, near the U.S. Embassy compound, where Nancy worked and Sonja attended American School. Red Bartlett lived and worked at the ViraVax facility in the Jaguar Mountains, but visited his family most weekends and holy days at their security apartment in the capital. Today was Ash Wednesday, and Red's forehead wore the smudge that told her he had stopped off at the cathedral for the late Mass.

Nancy Bartlett wanted to hold her daughter with a pain she could hardly bear, but she would rather die the most horrible death than have her daughter see her now.

I might still get that chance, she thought. *Maybe I should call Rico.* . . .

A tone sounded from her Watchdog and she heard the doorlocks *snick* aside. Security would notify Colonel Toledo soon enough.

Four people stepped inside, all wearing full contamination gear. Two carried the shorty assault Colts made for entry into closed spaces, and they prosecuted a quick search. One lugged several cases of equipment and, when the all-clear was signaled, muscled the bulky cases into the room with the body. No one spoke. The only sound in the room was the *whisk-whisk* of their bulky suits and the rasp of their respirators.

Nancy Bartlett had never cared for ViraVax, nor for the Agency's security games that surrounded the labs, but tonight she was thankful for it. She was liaison between the United States and the Confederation of Costa Brava, so the Defense Intelligence Agency investigator would keep ViraVax, the Costa Bravan police and newshounds at bay. She had to tell her story, but at least it would be private. At least, in its ugly way, it would be to family.

2

MAJOR RENA SCHOLZ arrived at the Bartlett apartment at half past midnight, just eight minutes after dispatch. She wore civilian dress under the hazard suit so that she could establish rapport with Nancy Bartlett as soon as possible. The major was already drenched in sweat and cursed the suit's faulty circulator. It seemed to the major that she spent all of her time in Costa Brava drenched in sweat, swatting bugs, daydreaming of home in Colorado. Tonight there would be no daydreaming.

The major toted a drab gray briefcase in her right hand, and over her left shoulder the rape kit hung like a bulky purse.

She posted MPs at front and back doors, activated her helmet camera, then attended to Nancy Bartlett.

"Nancy, I'm Rena Scholz," she began. "Do you remember me?"

Nancy sat at the dining room table without looking up. Splintered chairs and broken glassware littered the floor. Behind her, the dead man's mottled legs sprawled beside the overturned coffee table. One bullet had passed through the dining room wall and punched a hole the size of a quarter through the refrigerator door.

She put up a helluva fight, Scholz noted. The major tapped her gloveware and framed Nancy Barlett in a close-up.

Dried blood caked Nancy's blonde hair black. A grotesque swelling dominated the right side of her face, which was also smeared with blood. The silk housedress that she clutched around her was marred with bloody handprints, and her hands wore their dried blood like brittle gloves. Other than the facial swelling, Major Scholz saw no wounds on her patient.

Nancy nodded, a barely perceptible nod.

"You're the captain who briefed us before Costa Brava."

Monotone, the major noted. *Affect: flat.*

5

Nancy's swollen lips obviously made enunciation difficult.

"That's right." Rena said, "only it wasn't called Costa Brava then, and I'm a major now."

"Time flies," Nancy said.

Her voice remained flat and she didn't look up, she didn't move.

"Can I get you something? Coffee?"

"A shower," Nancy said. "I'd like to clean up."

The major's helmet speaker crackled and her tech sergeant's voice rasped, "Fluid and tissue tests negative, Major. He's not a hot one. Not anything we know, anyway."

"Thanks, Sergeant."

The major stepped out of her hazard suit with relief, and not just from the heat. Setting a traumatized person at ease was hard enough, but being dressed like an alien made it damned near impossible.

Major Scholz disattached the recording device from inside her sweat-soaked jacket and set it on the table between them.

"I'll have to examine you first," the major said. "It's the same exam you would get at the clinic."

"No! You know what he did, you know who he is. . . . Can't you just let me get clean?"

Major Scholz was relieved at the flash of anger in Nancy's blue eyes. If she had continued staring impassively at the tabletop, then she would be a tougher nut to crack. Rena picked up an overturned chair and took a seat across the table. She folded her hands in front of her and spoke softly, her modulations practiced and precise.

"I got into the service as a nurse," she said. "I'm here to help you. We can get this done quickly, right here in private, and get you cleaned up right away. We have to document everything, you understand why. Then you can clean up and we'll move you to another apartment while you get your bearings. We don't have to stay here for the interview. The exam will take ten minutes. I'm not going to hurt you and I'm not going to embarrass you."

Nancy sighed and pulled the bloodstained silk tighter to her throat.

"All right," she said. "Let's get it over with."

Major Scholz found no major wounds on Nancy Bartlett, though her vulva and vagina revealed multiple tears and her body was a mass of bruises. Bite marks that broke the skin, silent screams, tattooed both breasts and the back of her left thigh. Her nose had bled profusely.

Besides the usual body-fluid samples from the vaginal vault, the major was careful to take samples of dried blood from Nancy's hair, fingernails, hands and abdomen. She asked Nancy Bartlett whether she wanted a morning-after pill, which the woman accepted. The major was relieved. It meant she didn't have to slip it to her by subterfuge.

She must know what they've been doing over there, the major thought. *He's had nearly sixteen years to tell her.*

That was something she'd have to find out, on behalf of the Agency, but it could wait until the secondary exam.

The major sealed her gloves and samples into a sterile bag and sent it off by courier, then she helped Nancy into the shower.

Now the tough part, the major thought.

She set up her camera, donned a new pair of gloves and began her examination of Red Bartlett's nearly nude body.

He lay prone with his legs crossed as though he had spun around as he fell. One white athletic sock, his only clothing, clung to his left foot. Rena noted the obvious: two exit wounds beneath the left scapula, which probably took out his major vessels and left lung; one centered at about T5 that must have paralyzed him immediately from the waist down and blown up his aorta. An unidentifiable number of rounds had turned his cranium to brain goo.

The major moved Bartlett's head enough to make out three blood-filled holes in the carpet underneath. A new Galil 10mm handgun sat as though on display on one of the couch cushions. She counted eight shell casings on the floor around her.

She hit him three times in the kill zone before he went down, she thought.

The rest was insurance.

Red Bartlett's lower face and jaw were intact, and what she saw when his jaw dropped open forced a sharp intake of breath. Gobbets of flesh were caught between his teeth.

She tweezed them out and placed them into a sterile bag.

What she saw when she turned back to him never would have appeared in her report, if it had all stopped there. No one would believe her and, indeed, she would have questioned the observation herself.

Bartlett's flesh slumped and settled before the major's eyes. She would never forget the slightest rustle against the carpet, the foul odor of perforated bowel. Had it stopped there, the major could have completed her exam and noted nothing of it.

But it didn't stop there.

His skin sagged off its bones onto a bloody patch of carpet separating her from the body. Major Scholz had to work fast to get any samples at all. This action, though for naught, would earn her a commendation for bravery but not a promotion.

Complete rejection of tissue, she noted, *everything suppurating into a brown sludge, leaking out of splits in the skin.*

A horrible odor, with the heat.

Worse than gangrene, she thought.

Tests said he wasn't hot, but the major wasn't taking any more chances. She sealed herself back into her suit, then gave the appropriate orders. It was very hard for the major to concentrate, to control her breathing. She did her job, and did it quickly before what was left of him was gone.

She tweezed a few bone samples into a bag, then documented her best memory of the more serious gouges, cuts and scratches that covered most of his upper body. Later she would note, on the Watchdog's visual replay, a dozen infected mosquito bites that dotted his lower legs.

The major sealed her gloves inside a second bag along with the rest of her samples, and the tech sergeant *whisk-whisked* out to the van with them. She spent a few minutes mentally scrubbing her hands over the kitchen sink, trying to think of something ordinary or something pretty, something that didn't remind her of blown-up flesh and blood.

The major downloaded police reports on the other victims from her Sidekick and scanned them briefly before returning the device to its case. Murders of two young men and three vicious rapes had been reported in the past six hours, and her machine told her that Red Bartlett was a ninety-nine percent match as the perpetrator.

He could have broken under the pressure of his work.

Bartlett lasted longer than many who had worked out there. But ViraVax was private business and those were rumors, murders without bodies, a Costa Bravan problem.

That would be nice, Rena thought, *but this one's messier than that.*

Red Bartlett was Colonel Rico Toledo's best friend. And Colonel Rico Toledo was Major Scholz's boss.

She ordered a quarantine, which guaranteed Nancy Bartlett six days of heavy drugs, tests and significant memory refinement. When Nancy stepped into the embassy limo for her ride home at the end of the sixth day, she would know whatever the newspapers knew—whatever the colonel wanted them to know, whatever ViraVax taught her to know.

In six or seven days, Nancy Bartlett would remember that Red Bartlett had been tortured and murdered by several intruders, one of whom left behind a weapon traced to the Peace and Freedom Party, the predominantly Catholic guerrilla underground. Probably no one would ask Nancy Bartlett if she found it strange that Red Bartlett was the only Catholic employed by ViraVax, yet he was murdered by Catholics. At least one suspect would be shot while resisting arrest.

In Costa Brava, as in Northern Ireland or the Middle East, religion was a serious business, a very big business. In Costa Brava, the face-off came down to the Children of Eden versus the Catholics. ViraVax was built and operated by the Children of Eden, as was the current Costa Bravan government.

Besides, the major knew that nobody except the missionaries, who were rotated every two years, had ever transferred out of ViraVax no matter what their religion. Nobody who worked there for real would ever go home.

Red Bartlett sculpted artificial viral agents out of bits of protein. The major knew that Red did not invent the technique, but his steady, freckled fingers perfected it. His tiny agents manipulated genes, switched hormones and disease on and off, and he was good at it. He fought famine, and won. The company that employed him was not nearly so kind.

Like many other passionate researchers, Red devoted twelve- and sixteen-hour days to the lab. He would have worked seven days a week as well, if ViraVax management did not insist on everyone observing their Sabbath. His presence at the family apartment on Fridays and Saturdays often was fraught with frustration and impatience. He spent more and more time drinking with his Agency friend and the major's boss, Colonel Toledo.

Records indicated that Bartlett's caution at the lab was exquisite, particularly following nearly simultaneous contagion incidents in the Philippines, Japan and Brazil. The tech sergeant's tests had indicated that this was not one of those incidents.

Somebody has gone to a stage two study without authorization!

The major wondered whether it could have been Bartlett himself. Even Jonas Salk had injected himself first, proving the polio vaccine safe for others.

Who could have done this to himself?

Data on one of this night's murder victims scrolled through her Sidekick. Major Scholz felt a chill, though there wasn't a draft. The victim was twenty years old, approximate age of the other victim. The other had died the same way. Their throats were chewed out. Their genitals were mutilated after they died. She thought of the strips of flesh she had picked from between Red Bartlett's teeth.

Colonel Toledo isn't going to like this, she thought.

Major Scholz did not relish the inevitable trip to the embassy to break the news. Neither did she relish convincing Mrs. Bartlett to remain in Costa Brava.

The ultra-secret ViraVax facility in Costa Brava's Jaguar Mountains would demand free access to the poor woman for their "tests."

The Defense Intelligence Agency probably would offer Nancy Bartlett the job of her dreams, created specifically for her in Costa Brava. Nancy Bartlett was a Latin America specialist who spoke fluent Spanish and who happened to be the daughter of the U.S. Speaker of the House. She was tired of volunteer work through the embassy auxiliaries and the Church. The colonel and his people would have their hands full.

Whoever's going to write PR on this one had better be a Nobel laureate.

Major Scholz sighed and helped herself to a glass of water. She told herself she was very glad she had quit drinking; it was going to save her a tremendous hangover.

Red Bartlett's tissues gave off a little squeal, as of escaping gas, and the major glanced up to see the rest of Red Bartlett collapse on himself and liquefy, like hot wax. An intense blue flame engulfed the body and in moments burned it down to a bubbling tar.

Her squad's fire suppression was good enough to save the room, but nothing recognizable of the body remained. That was when her tech informed her that the tissue samples in her case had also ignited and burned themselves up. The Agency's van sustained a scorching and some smoke damage.

Damage to the dreams and physical well-being of Major Scholz would be considerable, ongoing and unrelenting. She sensed it that night from the start, and noted it in her personal report to the colonel, and she was right.

3

TWO HOURS AFTER Red Bartlett's death, his teenage daughter, Sonja, was committed to a landing of the new Bushwhacker jungle fighter. The Bushwhacker, the enemy and the jungle were simulations but her glove and helmet controls were not. Just as she rolled under enemy fire to rocket their bridge, her visuals blacked out of her visor display, the pitch and yaw of her seat returned to straight-and-level and Sergeant Trethewey's voice echoed in her helmet receiver.

"You have company," he said.

His voice was flat, cold, nothing like his usual self.

"Who?" she asked.

Sonja's stomach went cold. She had her private pilot's license already at fifteen, but she had no authorization to be in this simulator seat, nor inside the military half of the airfield, for that matter.

Before the sergeant could answer, a harsh voice asked, "Are you Sonja Bartlett?"

Maybe it was the sudden change in Trethewey's usually jovial demeanor, but she had a bad feeling about this one. She caught a glimpse of herself reflected on the blank screen of her visor: disheveled blonde hair coming out of its braid; sweat that her suit couldn't keep up with stung her blue eyes. A red impression from her helmet's visor seal would frame her freckled face.

Not very presentable, she thought.

Sonja lifted her visor and caught a glimpse of two armed figures dressed in black entering the sergeant's control booth in the north wall. Her stomach lurched again.

Sonja had been well educated in the hostage-taking politics of Costa Brava. The embassy held workshops on hostage survival on a monthly basis, and Sonja's parents saw to it that she attended.

Her friend Harry Toledo was also a regular.

At their first session, Harry had joked, "Rule number one: Don't put yourself in a situation where you'd make a desirable hostage."

Then Harry had nodded at the children of ambassadors and bankers and high-level military surrounding them in the auditorium.

"This is exactly the kind of situation they tell us to avoid," he said. "We're supposed to hang out with invisible people, *normal* people."

"Normal?" she'd joked back. "What's that?"

Tonight, two men in black fatigues filled up the control booth and four more strode into the simulator room with their hard breathing and their stubby rifles. None of them pointed their weapons at her. She framed each one in turn as though they were inside the targeting square of her visor. At least one of them was a woman. Sergeant Trethewey, who had garnered her the simulator time, was gone.

"It's an EP drill, isn't it?" she asked.

No one answered.

Always before, during one of ViraVax's Extreme Precautions drills, they never actually contacted her. This part of their drill, securing personnel and dependents, was always simulated, mainly because she and her mother were the only dependents living away from the facility. For several years, they had been the only dependents, period. These days, ViraVax didn't hire anyone encumbered by family or friends. Usually they simply called her mother to tell her the result and issue the "all-clear."

This time was very different; the men's presence and their down-to-business eyes told her that.

"Yes, I am Sonja Bartlett," she admitted with an exasperated wave. "Is this a drill?"

She pulled off her helmet and looked the leader in the eyes. They were light blue, like her own, and their gaze, ice-cold.

"No," he said. "This is not a drill. We are here to account for your presence and to hold you until further notice, nothing more."

Sonja secured her helmet and control gloves to the console, and stepped down from the simulator.

"What happened?" she asked.

"I can't tell you that," the leader said.

The second, a woman, came up to stand beside him. Her gaze was all inspection and concern.

"Well, then, who?" Sonja asked. "If you can't tell me what, at least tell me who. Is it my father?"

She had always been afraid of this moment, knowing even what little she did of her father's work and the kind of place that employed him. This she got aplenty from Harry, since his father had been chief of security, and from the web. The guerrillas fed plenty of stuff into the web for her to pluck off, and it wasn't all propaganda.

The leader glanced at his second, then back at Sonja.

It was the second who spoke.

"Yes," she said, "it involves your father. Your mother is safe."

"It's serious, isn't it?"

"Yes."

They showed no sign of escorting her to another room, so Sonja sat on the simulator step, her body edging close to panic.

He must be dead, she thought. *They wouldn't be so close-mouthed if he was alive.*

She thought of her mother, alone in her apartment, and of her grandfather, who had fought to keep them out of Costa Brava.

"You can't raise a family there," he had said. "It's a stinkhole of a country, even if it is new. I should know, I see the reports."

That was a smoke screen, Sonja knew. Her grandfather was Speaker of the House back in the U.S., and he saw their unwillingness to relocate in America as a cowardice.

"Everybody wants out!" he'd shouted over the speaker at Christmas. "The good people of this country can't just bail out and leave it to the goddamn criminals. . . ."

But they hadn't fled America. Nancy Bartlett was a Latin America specialist who had followed her love and her dream. She'd married the virologist Red Bartlett, who also followed his dream, and they had converged on Costa Brava. Sonja knew no other place and, like her closest friend, Harry Toledo, she called Costa Brava home.

A squawk on the leader's Sidekick indicated an incoming message. He glanced at the screen, then nodded at Sonja.

"We're authorized to move you now. We'll be taking you to Colonel Toledo's. He will inform you of the situation. Do you have anything here that has to go with you?"

Sonja pulled her flight log out of the rack beside the simulator.

"Just this," she said, hoping she didn't show any of the fear that shimmied in her knees and bladder. "Let's go."

4

MARTE CHANG'S BLACK hair whipped her face as she stepped onto the gangway and into the downdraft of the unmarked Mongoose's huge twin rotors. The exhaust stink was worth it; the rotor wash cut the smothering humidity trapped with her on the valley floor. Marte shaded her eyes with one hand and shifted her underwear with the other. ViraVax spread out before her, nothing like she had expected.

No roads, she thought, and suppressed a shudder.

The only way into the remote facility was by air, and air travel was not her strong suit. From her vantage point atop the lift pad, Marte noted the triple fencing tipped inward around the perimeter, the precipitous valley walls, the tangle of lush jungle. Occasionally, over the exhaust smell, she caught a sweet whiff of floral perfume. She didn't see a lot of people top-side, but the few she saw seemed very busy and spoke very little.

A crew of red-clad workers unloaded supplies from the Mongoose while another crew refueled. They *whirrrrred* along in little carts with fat tires and followed dotted lines painted into the concrete. Marte Chang's eyes became accustomed to the glare, and she saw that all of the workers displayed the moon-faced, close-eyed, thick-tongued features of Down's syndrome.

"Innocents," she said.

No one could hear her over the noise of the rotors, and it wouldn't matter if they did. That was what the Children of Eden called them, "Innocents."

Because they don't have souls, she thought.

This she had heard often during her undergraduate days at the Universidad de Montangel, the high-tech school in Mexico owned by the Children of Eden. They had no souls because, according to

15

the Children of Eden, these people weren't truly human.

Trisomy twenty-one, she thought.

Her genetics instructor at Montangel called them "Triples," "Trips" and, because he was a recovering gambler, "Blackjacks." Genetic analysis identified the dominant type as having three sets of chromosome twenty-one instead of two.

You would think they would get more *of something.*

What they did get were more heart surgeries and abdominal surgeries, more openness, more need for reassurance and touch. The Children of Eden made up the world's leading experts on Down's syndrome, and funded hundreds of foster homes for them in Costa Brava alone. The latinos called them *deficientes.*

Their medical students get a lot of surgical practice, Marte thought.

ViraVax housed a complete surgical suite, clinic and emergency room staffed by missionaries on their two-year rotation. This was one of the things that Joshua Casey's preliminary briefing had not told her, but her briefing from the Agency had.

Marte Chang turned back towards the black hulk of a plane, hoping for a reflection that would help her tidy up. The only glass in the top of the doorway sucked up light and threw back a distorted image, one that gave her a fat jaw and a pin head. She had instructions from Dr. Casey to wait atop the gangway until someone came for her. All of these *deficientes* hurried about their business, but none of their business seemed to have anything to do with her. She presumed that it was Joshua Casey's way of putting her in her place.

A couple of missionaries, identifiable by their white baseball caps, directed the lift pad crews and, in the fields below, brown-suited crews tended the agriculture. Every available surface yielded to the tillers. The tops of all of the ViraVax building—*bunkers, really,* she noted—teemed with fruits and squashes and blossoms. The fenced-in farmlands surrounding these bunkers made up more than 350 square kilometers of cultivated soil.

They feed their entire facility, plus the foster homes and outlying missions.

ViraVax could be wealthy from its fruit production alone.

Artificial viral agents made the difference. Compressed and packed inside a retroviral shell, AVAs entered a target organism and carried out certain engineering tasks there—usually insertion or deletion of a single protein, a single amino acid, or a regrouping of chains within the nuclei of the cells. Crops flourished, diseases fell to the microsword.

Even the microsword has two edges, Marte thought.

If the Agency was right, ViraVax engineered a series of famines in Moslem nations and was experimenting on its Down's syndrome charges, proving that any top has its bottom.

"Ms. Chang!"

Her name was a mouthful for the red-haired young man who waved to her from one of the carts. He carried all of the characteristic trisomy features behind a huge smile, and expertly swung the cart around to meet her at the bottom of the step.

He flapped his stubby fingers at her in the Latin gesture that meant "hurry along." Her two bags already lay in the back.

"I'm David," he said, and offered a hand as she stepped in.

"Thanks," she said. "Pleased to meet you."

"Hold the bar," David said, indicating a handhold on the dashboard.

Her understanding of what he said was a beat or two behind his saying it. He waited until she had a grip, then wheeled her towards the flight-deck elevators. They rolled aboard, cart and all, and rolled off at ground level. Colored lines in the pavement guided crews between barracks and work.

Marte noted that worker jumpsuits and overalls were color-coded to match the lines on the pavement.

They passed about a dozen *deficientes* watching a bald-headed man run an obstacle course built entirely of rubber tires. The young people laughed, and clapped, and several mimicked his performance as best they could. Nothing here pointed towards the danger she felt, a distinct pressure between her shoulder blades like a warning finger or a gun barrel.

"We'll see Dr. Casey now," David said.

He pointed towards a huge bunker overgrown with banana trees. A welcoming party of two awaited her behind the foyer doors, a tall, blonde woman and a balding young man.

"I'm Shirley Good," the blonde said, "and this is our attorney, Noah Wheeler."

Marte shook hands and the others did not waste time with small talk. They escorted her inside the facility proper. She glanced over her shoulder just before the hatch swung closed, and saw David waving at her. She waved back, the hatch closed and Marte had the terrible feeling that she had just seen the outside world for the last time.

This mission would accomplish three things for Marte Chang. It would pay back her education expenses and her obligation to the Defense Intelligence Agency, guarantee the production of her revolutionary new power plants worldwide, and it would make her a very wealthy young woman. Marte Chang was a scientist, not a spy, and she was eager to prove her science, even in the heart of the enemy.

The enemy, to Marte Chang, was anyone who practiced bad science, or excellent science to bad ends. The Agency had positioned her to find out firsthand how bad the science and the ends might be at ViraVax. They suspected the worst.

Marte was surprised at the sudden and complete sadness that washed over her. She flicked a tear out of the corner of her eye and took a deep breath.

Poor, poor, pitiful me.

Her parents had met in the United States while on student visas from China. Both had been hunted down and killed in the streets of Seattle by Chinese death squads when she was four. This vendetta was carried out as a reprisal for their part in the civil war which bloodied the Chinese streets and led to the ongoing, expensive conflict with the U.S.-Russian-Japanese alliance. She was no stranger to betrayal and fear.

The U.S.-Russian-Japanese alliance had just accomplished a Middle East "police action" that turned into a Pyrrhic victory at best. The alliance gained control of the surviving oil fields, but they had perpetrated a genocide that had brought Marte to the verge of renouncing her citizenship. It was this sentiment that had led her to look for work outside the United States.

Marte wanted to crush these agents of death, wherever their headquarters. They gave science a bad name, and she didn't like that. Marte had never suspected that her search would lead her to the threshold of her benefactor, the Children of Eden. Like the old friend who had betrayed her parents, the Church blasted a big hole in her fabric of trust.

She had uncovered the source of "warfare by drought and pestilence," a charge leveled at the United States by over a hundred nations. That source was ViraVax, under the umbrella of the Children of Eden.

ViraVax PR experts helped the government dismiss these charges as paranoia, group hysteria, irrational rantings of a heathen elite.

Marte Chang would trust herself now, and no one else.

Casey and another half dozen of his staff awaited her in the Thinktank, Casey's brainstorming parlor complete with a scale-model topo of the entire valley asprawl in the center of the room. At the top of the topo, three kilometers north of ViraVax, a dam blocked the tiny Río Jaguar and tapped it for power.

"Marte Chang's work, the Sunspots, will make this dam obsolete," Casey began. "It frees the rest of the valley for agriculture and removes a dangling sword from over our heads. Her viral agents form sheets of intricate microcircuits, and this discovery may win her the Nobel Prize. Meanwhile, she is ours. Please welcome Marte Chang."

The applause and enthusiasm were genuine. Casey's loud-voiced introduction had put her off at first, but now she felt excitement taking over where fear left off. She brushed aside her initial disorientation.

"Thank you," she said. "I look forward to working with all of you. I did not expect to start quite so immediately. . . ."

"This is the Litespeed age," Casey boomed. "Your data arrived on the network and preliminaries were completed two days ago. We've discussed everything, drawn up agreements. . . ." He nodded towards the folder in Noah Wheeler's hands. "We've been waiting for your body to complete the journey. Perhaps someone will engineer us a teletransporter one day, who knows?"

Marte smiled politely to reflect the polite laughter in the room and thought that, with all this preparation, she could have spent less time out there on the lift pad under Costa Brava's merciless sun.

Joshua Casey introduced her around, confirmed assignments, and they all shared a pitcher of ice water to cinch the deal. It was a custom of the Children of Eden, like their foot-washing custom. She hoped that they wouldn't have to go into that here.

Joshua Casey's little eyes glittered as he tolled the lab's virtues.

"Fire fighters, security, all medical-technical, lab-technical or shop apprentices are missionaries on a two-year rotation, practicing to be mayors, generals, farmers," he reported.

Marte would sum up later for her own report—to the Agency—through a network drop known only as "Mariposa." She needed to establish contact immediately through the facility's satellite burst system, something she had had a dry run on only once back in the States. She had much more confidence in her skills as a virogenetic engineer than in her abilities as a spy.

I wish I'd been able to clean up, Marte thought, between smiles and nods.

She presumed that Casey was proving a point about his work ethic—freshening up was not nearly so important as a lesson in control.

A tall blonde, the only other woman in the group, received a hushed message from a frightened-looking young man at the door. By the time the blonde reached Casey to relay the message, everyone had fallen silent, the weight of her burden apparent in the grim set of her mouth. What she told Casey ended Marte Chang's orientation for the day.

"Let us pray," Casey intoned, and all except Marte closed their eyes and bowed heads. The rest was a few moments in coming.

"Our brother, Red Bartlett, has been murdered at his home," Casey said. His voice held the tight, low quality that Marte associated with anger, and it quivered. "He was struck down in his own home by forces of the idolators, by the betrayers of Christ, and his wife was gravely injured. Lord"—Casey lifted his hands—"we pray for her complete recovery, and solace from her terror."

A pause.

"Aren't Bartlett and his wife Catholic?"

The voice came from behind her and Marte was shocked at the audacity of the question. Casey, however, registered what she would describe as pleasant surprise. He let the question hang in the air like humidity, unanswered.

"Shirley," Casey said, his voice measured, in full control, "show Miss Chang her quarters. I want Mishwe in my office." He turned to address the group. He never glanced her way. "The rest of you, reflect on the consequences of living among the gentiles. Had Red Bartlett made his home exclusively among us, he would have had the pleasure of meeting Miss Chang today. That is all."

That night, before sleep, Marte Chang summed up her observations, orientation and her briefing. Once she mastered sending messages out on burst, she wanted plenty to send. Marte wanted to be sure that her Agency obligation terminated here, once and for all. Keeping a lab notebook was second nature to her. She tried to think of this that way—observations of an experiment jotted into a log.

"Personnel here go through physical conditioning as well as their scripture study," she wrote. "They share food preparation and housing chores, and those who stay on for an additional tour come out with a degree in hotel management or public management or personnel management. This is the Children of Eden's practical university and the degree means you know how to run at least part of a world. A Gardener world.

"They manage the model village above the ViraVax labs— health care, farm operation, shipping/receiving, transport. The Innocents are called domestics or laborers, but to the Gardeners they're just biomechanical servants, slaves and spare parts. There is a pair of missionaries for every dozen Innocents, and the Innocents are closely bonded with them. The missionaries are all males between the ages of eighteen and twenty-two. They are devoted, enthusiastic and horny. Half of the Innocents are female. The problems inherent in that arrangement conflict mightily with the strict sanctions imposed by their religion. The sergeant-at-arms for these sanctions is someone I haven't met. He's in charge of the mysterious Level Five labs that will be providing the medium for my Sunspots—Dajaj Mishwe."

5

DAJAJ MISHWE WAS slightly out of breath when he entered Joshua Casey's inner office, and his bald head glistened sweat. This, and the casual smile he wore, angered Joshua Casey even more.

"What have you done?" Casey demanded.

"I was teaching my Innocents to run the tires."

Casey slapped the desktop and scattered a stack of transparencies.

"Don't play with me!" Casey shouted. "You know what I'm talking about! Red Bartlett!"

Mishwe stood a little taller, and to Casey he seemed relieved, satisfied—certainly not penitent.

"He stumbled on the Nullfactor AVA and a shipment of parts," Mishwe said. "I told you to keep him above Level Five."

"So you *killed* him?"

Mishwe shrugged.

"It was an experiment," Mishwe said. "How did I know he would go to town for his ridiculous ash-rubbing?"

Casey strode around his desk and poked a finger into Mishwe's chest.

"Better that he did," Casey said. "Better that he killed anyone here, because now he's killed us all. Colonel Toledo is his best friend, and a Catholic, and he hates my guts. . . ."

"But he is not a problem," Mishwe said. "We have seen to it that he is out of control. A drinker. A womanizer. His own Agency has confined him to his office for two years now. He commands no respect, not even from his family. . . ."

"His best friend went berserk, then melted down and burned up spontaneously in front of a half dozen Agency witnesses," Casey said. "Whatever the Colonel says or does is irrelevant.

The Agency itself will mount an investigation and demand an accounting. My God, man! Bartlett's father-in-law is Speaker of the House. . . ."

Joshua Casey ran a hand through his thinning hair, then sat on the side of his desk, trembling. He tried to calm himself. He was embarrassed. He had taken the name of the Lord in vain in front of a subordinate. It eroded his authority, his personal integrity. He didn't permit it in others, and he couldn't tolerate it in himself. He had to get a grip.

"There is more to this," Mishwe said.

Casey pinched the bridge of his nose, gathered himself and said, "Go on."

"The AVA that took Bartlett down, I linked it to that aggression package that Toledo's Agency wanted."

"That never worked." Casey said. "We dropped it. I don't—"

"The Agency dropped it," Mishwe corrected him, "because the subjects turned on anything, including their own troops. Their sole purpose was to kill rivals and reproduce. Bartlett worked on that project for a while, and the Agency wants to keep it quiet. Tell them that he continued studies on his own, and this is what it got him. Complain about the damage he did here, about the work he's left undone, about how hard it will be to replace him. Tell them he showed bad judgment, and we were lucky it wasn't worse. Tell them you'll keep it quiet if they will, and they will."

Casey noted that Mishwe's voice was unexcited, smooth, with just a hint of mirth around the edges.

"You call yourself the Angel, Dajaj, I have heard you say it myself. But what you have done . . . you have killed a man—no, three men, including his victims. . . ."

"You have said yourself that the Catholics are breeding the world to death," Mishwe said. "Your father has preached that they who worship idols are lost; not soulless, like the Innocents, but *lost*. You were not squeamish about Project Labor. Why do you squirm over this?"

"There will be an investigation," Casey sighed. "The new woman . . ." He turned his palms up in helplessness.

"The new woman may very well take Bartlett's place," Mishwe said. "Her work is meticulous, and her Sunspots, the product of genius. If she sees too much, she'll simply have to stay with us forever."

"Get out," Casey croaked. "Get below where you belong, and don't let me see you topside unless I call for you."

Mishwe's only response was an underbreath chuckle as he walked out the door.

6

COLONEL TOLEDO STOOD aside from the handful of mourners at Red Bartlett's funeral, his full-dress uniform tighter and hotter than he'd ever remembered. It was a cloudless afternoon, and the Colonel watched overhead as Sonja Bartlett circled the little biplane from the El Canadá coffee plantation into position. She carried a canister of her father's ashes along with her.

Sonja's the same age as Harry, he thought. *They're like brother and sister.*

Sonja loved Red Bartlett, that had been clear. Her father had been Rico's best friend since before Harry and Sonja were born. Sonja and Harry grew up together. Their parents had spent hundreds of weekend evenings together, playing pinochle, barbecuing. Red stayed at the ViraVax facility during the week and came home most weekends.

Maybe if I'd worked it that way, Harry and I. . . .

The Colonel didn't like thinking about maybes. It had been clear for some time that Harry hated him, and there wasn't much the Colonel could do about that. Not any more than he could control his own anger, or the drinking that brought it on.

Rico Toledo reflected on his son's antagonism—the embassy counselor called it teenage rebellion syndrome. Rico recalled their many Saturdays in the gym, how he taught the boy to fight and to navigate the embassy's elevators. They were good memories, but not recent memories.

The Colonel stood alone and reviewed his failing marriage, his drinking, his bad standing with the Church since the ViraVax fiasco years ago.

It all started with the mission that led him to meet Red Bartlett in the first place. The Colonel—a lieutenant then—created a character with the guerrillas in what was then Belize. This character

27

lived on now in legend throughout the region, even to the Rio Grande and Texas. "Jabalí," they had called him then: "Wild Boar."

Colonel Rico Toledo watched Red Bartlett's ashes puff for a moment and disappear behind the yellow biplane. The dead man's wife, Nancy Bartlett, had returned from her hospital stay just this morning. Her blonde hair framed that classic, oval-faced beauty, but her blue eyes were unfocused. The Colonel's wife, Grace, supported Nancy Bartlett on one arm. Nancy's step was unsure and her mind confused, but no sign of her beating remained.

No one from ViraVax came for the service. It was the Sabbath for them, and Colonel Toledo, a notoriously bad Catholic in a country where it mattered, knew their customs entirely too well.

ViraVax was none of the Colonel's business now. This he had been told clearly and repeatedly, and it was with that understanding that he initiated his own investigation of Red's death. The Colonel knew that it wasn't a *who* that did his friend Red Bartlett, it was a *what*. He wanted to find out who made the what, and how it got into Red Bartlett. Somebody was making sure that he didn't.

Just yesterday the Colonel had stood apart from mourners at the funeral of Henri Vasquez, known member of the Peace and Freedom underground and one of Colonel Toledo's principal contacts with the guerrillas. Henri Vasquez was the man that the García government accused of Bartlett's murder. The Hacienda Police offered ample opportunity for the press to photograph the rebel's body. They had cut off his hands before they shot him, and it would have made a convincing story if Rico Toledo had not already known the truth.

But he didn't know details, like the part about how Red Bartlett had become the Agency's first documented case of spontaneous human combustion.

Spontaneous, my ass!

The Colonel wanted a drink from the bottle of Flor de Caña in his glove box. He did not walk the twenty meters to his car because he was proving to himself that he might *want* a drink, but he didn't really *need* one. Red Bartlett would've called "bullshit" on that but Red Bartlett had never been much of a drinker and, besides, he was dead.

Rico Toledo kept his eyes on the sky even though the plane was gone. That way, he didn't have to watch his wife console the shattered Nancy Bartlett. Soon enough he would have to face the press and announce what the United States intended to do about Red Bartlett's death.

Bury it was the statement that the Colonel wanted to give but, like the matter of the rum, he had to sort out want from need.

The Colonel had met Red Bartlett just before the turn of the millennium and a month after Guatemala finally took Belize. The U.S. ambassador, a black man, was being held with three other U.S. citizens by elements of the Guatemalan Tigres, a particularly lethal battalion that also employed an extensive death squad arm in the civilian sector. The ambassador had suffered a heart attack on the third day. On the fifth day, he had suffered another.

Lieutenant Rico Toledo had volunteered for this mission because he spoke Spanish and looked Hispanic, and it was his opportunity to prove he was as American as anyone else in the U.S. Army.

His mission was specific—locate and free all four Americans, trapped somewhere in the Maya Mountains. He was a wild card, an experiment. If he was killed, they sacrificed a lieutenant to save an ambassador. If he was captured, not killed, the Guats gained an indefinite period of excellent propaganda out of him.

Rico Toledo came out of it with a promotion, a reputation and guerrilla contacts that would serve him well for nearly two decades. "Wild Boar," they had called him in the bush. It was nothing like what they called him now.

The virologist he saved was Red Bartlett, the only married employee of the fledgling but wealthy ViraVax. At the time of his capture he had been attending a week-long orientation sponsored by his new employer.

Rico got out, he got the ambassador and the virologist out and he effected the execution of Colonel Matanza of the Tigres in his wake.

Bartlett settled into a peculiar life at ViraVax. His wife had an apartment in town, to be close to her work at the embassy and Sonja's school. Red traveled there every Friday at sunset and returned every Monday at sunrise, while ViraVax observed its Sabbath. They permitted him to observe his holy days, but with reluctance. Some weekends it was not safe to fly, because the airspace was not always secure, and ViraVax forbade anything from coming in or going out by land. That had been upon recommendation by the Colonel himself.

Grace Toledo and Nancy Bartlett became friends, confidants, made plans of their own while their men ground down their lives like pencils. Sonja and Harry attended the same American School but both were loners. The constant turnover of embassy personnel had taught them at an early age that it was no use to make friends who would just transfer out. They were both bright, graduating nearly three years ahead of their age group.

Colonel Toledo had kept his family in Costa Brava because he liked the information business and because living in Costa Brava was safer for them than living in the States. Things were going to get ugly here, that was for sure, but he had hoped they wouldn't get *that* ugly.

Today his son, Harry, also stood apart, watching the lazy circles of Sonja's yellow biplane from the opposite side of the garden.

He's a dead ringer for me at fifteen, the Colonel thought, *but I'll be goddamned if I can figure out how he thinks.*

Both Harry and Sonja were uncommonly bright and beautiful, but they lived in a world completely shut off from his own. It was his own doing, a drawback of the intelligence business but one that he'd always thought he could work around. This was the Colonel's year to discover just how wrong he'd been about a lot of things.

When he thought back on his lifetime of warfare, personal combat and fistfights, his memories danced across a lighted backdrop, softened by distance and time. He remembered that job in the bulb fields, the last of his petty fights that a small-town judge would allow. He was given a choice that was a favorite of judges of that time: military service or jail.

Couldn't get much further from embassy work than that, the Colonel thought.

Three years before Boss fell into that bulb digger blade and they'd tried to blame it on him, Rico had fought for his life for the first time.

It was late summer of the year that Rico Toledo began seventh grade. At twelve, and in spite of his spectacles, Rico Toledo was a fighter with a no-holds-barred reputation.

I sure don't miss wearing glasses.

He smiled at the memory of those antique lenses, those relics of the machine age. Rico Toledo did not like to rely on machines, not at all.

The Agency's gift of radial keratotomy had perfected his vision years ago, as it had his son's, and age hadn't caught up with him yet.

Chuck had been a big tenth-grader who had just walked up to Rico and hit him. Rico didn't remember feeling the punch, but he remembered the burst of blood in his nose, and being surprised that he was sitting on the sidewalk. The bridge of his nose hurt where his glasses had rested, and, before he could react, Chuck was astraddle his chest.

Rico remembered the blurred silhouette of Chuck, holding a rock high over his head, ready to strike. He hefted the rock high for leverage, and Rico twisted to the left, curling up as tight as he could. The heavy rock threw Chuck off balance, so when he tried to catch himself Rico lifted both legs and tipped Chuck over. All he heard was their breathing, wet and popping, and the scrabble of gravel underneath them.

Rico's shin caught Chuck a good shot in the crotch as he tipped over. Rico grabbed him by the hair with his left hand while he punched Chuck's face with the right, as hard and fast as he could. Rico quit when Chuck stopped moving. He left him there in the driveway. Rico's right hand was useless for a week and he didn't get a good night's sleep for months. Of course, there had been hell to pay, starting with his father.

Now his wife motioned for him to bring the car around. The Colonel nodded, mumbled a private prayer for whatever soul Red Bartlett might have remaining and signaled the embassy driver. He glanced up at the biplane again, but there was no more sign of Red Bartlett on the wind. The Colonel sighed and straightened his tie.

There's a shitload of work to do, he thought.

Getting even for Red Bartlett wouldn't be easy. He knew, without a doubt, he would be doing it alone.

7

MARTE CHANG KNEW that she would be observed, constantly and closely, and she tried not to resent it. Resentment would get in her way, and anything that got in her way meant she would have to stay that much longer. She would confront Casey when the time came. Meanwhile, she vowed to work day and night to get herself out of this box.

She watched the light on his Sidekick behind him, winking its collusion with her as it transmitted her first message to Mariposa. She would know within moments whether their system worked. If it didn't, if Casey could detect her piggyback message, then she would be through, her project would be through, and there was an excellent chance she would be dead.

Marte anticipated the first morning of switchover, less than a month away, when the most superficial portion of topside operations would be transferred to her Sunspots for a test run. Marte would be honored in a brief ceremony, and Casey would likely admit her to his inner circle. She had hoped to be out of ViraVax long before her contract was up, but she was beginning to doubt it. Casey was paranoid beyond her imagination, no doubt due to regular proddings by Dajaj Mishwe. He protected his facility as she might protect it if it were her own, but not for the same reasons.

The lake above the dam above ViraVax appeared nightly in Marte Chang's sleep. At first it was tranquil, the blue-green calming place for her soul. Lately it had been the stuff of nightmares, a pot of acid dissolving anything it touched. For her, living downstream in earthquake country, it was the dam of Damocles. The sooner she activated her new power source, the better she would feel. The only thing that scared her more than that thousands of tons of water was Dajaj Mishwe, genovirologist.

Mishwe had been topside again and this caused quite a stir among the Innocents in Marte's sector. The twins who cleaned her room, Rafaela and Renata, considered him some kind of angel.

"Why do you call him 'Angel'?" Marte asked.

" 'Cause he guard the garden. He come topside and no burn up."

"People come up and go down all the time," Marte said. "Nobody dies just because they came from below."

"We stay up here," Rafaela explained, "they stay down there. If we go down, we die. If they come up, they die. Dajaj, the Angel, go anywhere."

Marte thought this must be part of some fairy tale that they told the Innocents to keep them in their proper sectors.

"How do they die?" Marte asked. "Does security kill them?"

"All burn up," Rafaela said.

"The sun," Renata added, "it burn them all up."

"No," Rafaela contradicted, "the Lord burn them. Sword of the Lord."

With the Innocents, Marte found it difficult to separate fact from fantasy. Much of the ViraVax control over them depended on teaching them fear.

"Have either of you actually *seen* anyone come topside and burn up like that?"

Both heads bobbed and their eyes glittered.

"Yes, yes. We saw. Right there. Right there."

Renata pulled Marte's sleeve and pointed to the open area between the supply warehouse and the B complex, where Marte had noted a scorched patch of earth, neglected in an otherwise well-raked compound. Obviously, none of the groundskeepers, all Innocents, cared to go near that spot. Even now, as she watched, a group of them laden down with garden tools shuffled aside so that no one had to walk on that place.

"Why not Dajaj?" she asked.

Renata shrugged.

"He is an angel," she said. "Angels do not burn."

"Do you like him?"

Again, the enthusiastic nods.

"He wash my feet. He give me the water, the bread."

"He show me run the tires," Renata said.

She high-stepped a demonstration, gripping the handle of her cart.

Marte Chang found that surprising.

Mishwe, of all people!

It was the first time she'd heard of anyone at ViraVax treating the Innocents as anything but good-natured pack animals, and Mishwe was the last one she would have expected to do it. And he washed their feet, which implied that he thought they had souls.

Who knows what Mishwe thinks?

The one time she'd seen him running the tires, she had had the impression that it was not sweat running out of his pores, but evil itself.

It's strange, she thought. *He's in great shape, got a great tan, yet it's a four-hour decontamination cycle each way to Level Five.*

"Does he run the tires with you often?" she asked.

"Every night," Renata said.

"No, no," Rafaela contradicted. "You don't know nothing. You wait every night. Some nights he don't come."

Every night, Marte thought.

Something clicked for her, the way it happened in the lab sometimes.

Even Casey had to cycle through decon to go below Level Two, which was why he spent most of his time topside conducting business and receiving the few necessary outsiders.

But Mishwe lived at Level Five. He was labmaster, second to none in sheer hours of work each day, and it was common for him to work days without sleep. He was legendary for this. So, how could he afford the eight-hour round trip to cycle topside and return?

He doesn't.

Mishwe must have a private, direct access topside. It was probably a supply shaft or something left over from the original construction.

And he would have to have an agreement with someone on watch, she thought.

She pegged Mishwe as someone who would keep his agreements to a minimum, and he would not waste favors on a midnight exercise program. The bargain that he had struck was most likely a threat rather than an agreement, a threat that at least one security guard believed to be good.

If he could get in or out of the bunkers at will, so could any virus he carried. So could Marte Chang.

If I had the nerve.

Marte had one overriding reason for being at ViraVax. It was not because they had bought her Sunspots. There had been plenty of offers, even though her papers and patents had not yet been made public. She was here because the Agency was convinced that something extraordinary was happening at this facility, something very dangerous that her expertise could identify. She had explicit instructions to take no action herself, and they didn't have to worry about that. The only action Marte Chang wanted to take was a flight home.

"Why is he topside today?"

Marte had caught a glimpse of him just moments before the twins came inside, heading towards Casey's office.

The sisters giggled and shrugged, hiding their mouths with their hands and making only a pretense at housework.

Marte's lab setup was split between Levels One and Two and she had cycled into Level Three only once. What she had seen even at the upper levels had horrified her, and she'd included those findings in her first burst to Mariposa and the outside world.

She felt like a traitor.

Because I am one, she thought.

A large series of donations to the Children of Eden coincided with Marte Chang's scholarships to the University of Montangel. She had lived among the Children of Eden for six years, shared a dorm room with four other girls who had become her best friends.

Hers had been a hand-me-down favor: her parents died because of an Agency error, the State Department acted as go-between to get the tax burden of a church called Children of Eden eased by targeting select minority loners to bring the university's population base up. Someone high up in the Agency owed this Mariposa a favor, and their interest in a share of Marte's product was +3. Marte Chang was the equivalent of a space shot or an ICBM and the time had come to use her.

This was not so unusual. Such careers had been groomed since the existence of universities, monarchies, religions and other closed systems. What was unusual was how perfectly Marte Chang's interests coincided with their own, and how bright she was.

She showed it right away at fourteen when she gave ten percent of her scholarships back to the Church as her tithe, a very nice touch. That kept most of the missionaries off her back, and the few who persisted were awash within moments in her enthusiasm for practical applications of genetics. This enthusiasm was genuine and passionate.

Trenton Solaris, the albino director of the Defense Intelligence Agency, bought in for a share in manpower and matching. Marte Chang received a donation of a new Litespeed so that she could cut her teeth on the technology. Her facility with hardware got her bids from the best: Genentech, Cold Springs Harbor, Three Wells and ViraVax itself. The Agency had its reasons for taking a clandestine peek inside ViraVax. Rico Toledo had made the original recommendations for action and requested a fully dedicated operative. Now that Bartlett was dead, Solaris had some personal reasons for getting an op inside ViraVax.

Red Bartlett's death was one, personal safety was another. Any death at or implicating ViraVax demanded a "shoot first, ask questions later" posture of seizure, containment and quarantine. Extreme Precautions drills ran, on the average, once a week, never during Sabbath, sometimes standing down for as long as three weeks. Extreme Precautions protocols were initiated on the evening of Red Bartlett's death. Those protocols ran their course in the field, in the news, at the embassy and inside the lab. As far as Marte Chang could determine, nothing had changed except Red Bartlett was dead and she sat on the hot seat.

8

SONJA BARTLETT IGNORED the little kissing sounds from the sopheads lining the street and picked up her pace to keep their quick hands off her butt. She had spent all of her fifteen years in Costa Brava, but only this year had she managed to get into downtown La Libertad alone. Being female in Costa Brava had its price, and Sonja had no patience for it.

The doorway of the Pan American slid open with a burst of conditioned air that teased her long legs underneath her cotton skirt. A waiter in traditional Mayan dress escorted her to her mother's table near the fountain. She knew that the waiter was an embassy informer, and that her mother knew, but the noise of the fountain made eavesdropping difficult and they never talked about anything important, anyway.

"I've asked you a thousand times not to walk," Nancy said. "People disappear here."

"Hi, Mom," Sonja said, and kissed the offered cheek. "I'm glad to see you, too. What's this about you going to work for that raving dzee, Colonel Toledo?"

"For a genius, you certainly limit your vocabulary," Nancy said. "Sit down to a civilized lunch and let me—"

"Explain? Convince? Bribe? I hate him. He put that place down here and it killed Daddy."

"Sit down!" Nancy ordered.

Their waiter set a tray of sliced fruit between them, lingered for a moment and then scurried away at a flick of Nancy's wrist. His slick-soled sandals *slap-slap-slapped* the marble.

"Rico Toledo did not put 'that place' here, the government did. And you know damned well it was a guerrilla who killed your daddy and . . . and . . ."

Nancy Bartlett blinked back tears, took a deep breath and let

39

it out slowly. Her right hand began a tremor that she controlled with her left. She looked more confused than hurt, and it took her a moment to get her bearings. Sonja saw once again how, except for the length of their blonde hair and the age now showing at her mother's eyes, mother and daughter could be twins.

"I'm sorry, Mom, I was really out of line that time." Sonja took her mother's hand and gave it a squeeze. "But you know what I mean . . . they worked him and worked him and sometimes he didn't leave that lab for two weeks, three weeks at a time."

"They didn't *do* anything to him," Nancy interrupted. "He was a grown man. He didn't have to work there. . . ."

Sonja squeezed again.

"Well, I still don't see why you want to work for Toledo. He beats his son and chases women. . . ."

"How do you know he beats his son?"

"I see Harry at exams. He schools it through the webworks now, because he doesn't like people to see him all beat up. It's one of those things that everybody knows but nobody talks about."

"How long has that been going on?"

"Just this year." Sonja speared a slice of mango and nibbled off the end. "Harry doesn't talk to people anymore. Spends all his time on the webs."

"I'll be working for the embassy, honey, not the Colonel."

"Don't you think it's strange, Mom? There's a civil war in this country between the Protestants and the Catholics. ViraVax is backed by the largest evangelical movement in the hemisphere, yet it was installed by the one U.S. colonel who's a Catholic."

"I asked you to stay out of the politics here," Nancy hissed. "That kind of talk could get you killed. And stay out of the gossip, too."

"I'm serious, Mom. What's going on out there?"

"Sonja!"

Sonja sighed and pulled her napkin onto her lap. She didn't trust Colonel Toledo before her dad's death, but now, after spending a week at his house, she despised him. The Colonel was seldom home, but when home he was always drunk and belligerent. It only took two days of the Colonel's hospitality for Sonja to realize that he was having an affair with a woman half his age, an embassy woman just a few years older than Sonja.

He did Mom a favor, she thought. *Even if I despise his motives, I have to remember that.*

In the aftermath of Red Bartlett's shooting, the Colonel had released an official statement declaring that Red Bartlett, virologist, had been killed when he came home and surprised an intruder. The Colonel's release made no mention of the assault on her mother, one that was evident in yellowing bruises even after a week in the hospital.

Maybe he wanted to spare her the embarrassment, she thought. If that were the case, she could respect him for that much.

But what if he's covering something? Something that Mom can't remember?

The intruder had been killed in a gun battle with security and that was the end of it.

Except nothing violent ever seems to end in this country. It only escalates.

News from the webs said the same thing about the United States these days.

Sonja sighed, and focused on the water sound of the fountain to calm herself. It was a real water fountain, not a Gardener hologram with a fractal sound track. This waste of a resource subtly assured the clientele that the proprietors were Catholic, not Gardener.

Their waiter brought the chicken smothered in green mole that Nancy Bartlett always ordered, and two coffees. This time he did not attempt to linger.

Sonja reached for the coffee, and the end of her thick blonde braid plunked onto her plate. She wiped it off with her napkin and flipped it over her shoulder.

"I wish you'd get that cut," her mother said. "I don't see how you can stand it so long in this heat."

"The Maya women do just fine."

"I know that you're fascinated with them, dear, but no matter how hard you try you cannot be a Maya Indian. It's a simple matter of birth."

"You mean genetics, don't you?" Sonja asked. "Daddy could have made me a Maya if he'd wanted to. He did things that were harder than that."

Sonja studied her mother for her reaction. She had never known how much her mother knew about her father's work, and until this past year, Sonja had not bothered to wonder herself. This year she had heard rumors, and after her father's death strange messages interrupted her research on the webworks. These messages linked ViraVax with the dramatic plunge in Costa Brava's birthrate.

Nancy Bartlett's pale complexion paled even further, and a fire kindled in her blue eyes. Her full lips, so much like Sonja's, were drawn tight. She spoke with an intensity that Sonja had not often seen from her mother.

"ViraVax invented the AIDS vaccine," Nancy said. "It was the last medical breakthrough of the twentieth century and it won Joshua Casey the Nobel Prize. You think of all that as ancient history because you weren't born yet."

"Mother, I'm not saying . . . I know important things happened there, and I know that Dad's AVAs, or whatever he called them, have fed a lot of people. But he changed. I saw it myself, and you've known him longer. . . ."

"He didn't change," Nancy interrupted. "They changed him."

"That's what I'm saying. . . . That's why I don't want you to go to work for that Colonel Toledo."

"It's *not* Colonel Toledo," Nancy insisted. "They took him off ViraVax two years ago. I'm not even working for the embassy this time. I'm a private consultant. Essentially, I'm getting paid for going to dinner with interesting people."

Nancy Bartlett's face took on a hardness that her daughter had not seen since her mother's release from the hospital.

"Who, then?" Sonja whispered. "I don't believe the guerrilla story, it's too easy. Who did this to him?"

Nancy twisted her napkin around her fist, untwisted it, twisted it again. Her pale right hand resumed its tremor and her left hand held it prisoner under the napkin.

"The Colonel doesn't know everything that happens at Vira-Vax," she said, her voice hoarse and strained. "He doesn't know half of what Casey is doing up there. His job was to keep the compound secure, and nothing more. They took that away from him when the Children of Eden started training their own security. He's the one who got you all of your flight simulator time, by the way."

Sonja's mind was racing. She was surprised that the Colonel had helped her, that was true. But the mysterious messages coded to her drop on the webs had told her about the changes in ViraVax security, and more.

How much does Mom know? she wondered. *How much torment has she lived with all these years?*

The messages were signed "Mariposa," which shocked her at first because Sonja had learned to fly nearby in a biplane that the owner called *Mariposa.* She wondered how much the underground knew about her life. She suspected that it was quite a bit, if they could access her on the webworks without leaving a footprint of any kind. Harry had tried tracing them for her, but got nowhere. If Harry couldn't find them, they were good.

Mariposa accused ViraVax of a multitude of sins, one of them being the plummeting birthrate in Costa Brava and the extremely high incidence of Down's syndrome babies born in the last five years.

Costa Brava is your government's testing ground, one message said. *They are breeding a robot work force for the future. That is why ViraVax has higher security than the Galil weapons plant across the ridge—its weapons are infinitely more powerful, more insidious.*

Two years ago, Sonja would have dismissed the messages as a propaganda ploy by the guerrilla underground. They saw the news of her father's death and wanted to recruit her. They knew she was vulnerable and they were famous for capitalizing on vulnerability. But Sonja Bartlett was extremely bright, and she had already formed her suspicions about ViraVax and the Children of Eden before the first letters marched across her screen.

ViraVax already killed Daddy, she thought. *I'm not going to let them get their hands on Mom.*

Sonja thought that Colonel Toledo might be the answer, after all. His new offices would be in the embassy, not at the Double-Vee compound. Her mother would remain free of that place, and Sonja would have the opportunity to find out exactly what they were up to.

I wonder what their hospital did to her out there?

Nancy Bartlett pushed her plate aside and signaled the waiter for her customary glass of wine.

"You're being awfully quiet," Nancy said. "Are you all right?"

"Just thinking."

"About your father?"

Sonja nodded.

"I was just thinking of him, too," Nancy said. "I was surprised he remembered Valentine's Day and brought us those chocolates."

"All melted."

"But they were real chocolate, straight from Belize."

"It's not Belize anymore, Mom."

"I know. I know," she said. "I just remember our vacations there when you were a baby. The locals still called it Belize and that's how I remember it."

"Isn't that where Colonel Toledo takes his girlfriends?"

Nancy frowned, and sighed. She started to say something, stopped, then started again.

"Time for a change of subject," she said. "There *is* good news in the world, you know."

"Good news? Like what?"

"I've found us a place. A real place."

"You mean all to ourselves? Out of the city?"

"Exactly like we planned," Nancy said, and raised the last of her wine for a toast.

Sonja felt her pulse race with hope. She had shared the security apartment with her mother for ten years, and she hated it only slightly less than she hated the ViraVax compound. She attended college now on the webworks, like Harry did, rather than use one of her scholarships to a school in the States.

Red Bartlett's death had shocked Sonja into the realization that she could not remember him as a live-in father, only as someone who visited her mother's apartment on weekends and holidays. She did not want the same thing to happen between herself and her mother.

"Chill, Mom! What zone is it in? Is it a real house . . . ?"

Nancy laughed, and Sonja realized that it had been months since she'd seen her mother laugh.

"Better than that. You know the place El Canadá?"

"You mean . . . El Canadá the coffee *finca* with the little airstrip that I fly out of every Thursday?"

"That's the one."

"Chill, are we going to rent the guesthouse?"

"Better than that," Nancy said. "I put a down payment on it yesterday. We're buying it."

"You *bought* it? But how . . . ?"

"We're rich," Nancy said. "Actually, the company bought it for us. Part of an insurance agreement. Your father always put his money back into the company and his research. I've cashed most of it in. I . . . I like this country, honey. It might be a mess, but it's better here than in the States. I want to stay on here. I hope that doesn't disappoint you."

Sonja was stunned. El Canadá was one of her favorite places on earth. An elderly Canadian couple, Mr. and Mrs. Marcoe, owned it. They spoke an antiquated French between them. Mr. Marcoe taught flying until his eyes went bad, and Sonja had been his last pupil. Every Thursday for three years he had taken Sonja up in the little Student Prince biplane while her mother visited with Mrs. Marcoe, a hardworking woman with an exuberant sense of humor.

"Mom, I just want to be with you. But it's a big jump from the apartment to a coffee plantation . . . how will we do it?"

"The Marcoes are staying," Nancy said. "They'll manage the place. This consultant job is something I've always wanted for myself, not for the money. I can do most of the work from home and send it in over the webworks, like you kids do." She sipped her water and widened her smile. "There's more."

"More? How could there be more?"

Sonja was so excited that she could barely keep her seat.

"I bought the plane, too," she said. "*Mariposa* is yours."

Sonja's plate slipped out of the waiter's hands and crashed to the tiled floor, sending bits of blue porcelain skidding into the lobby. Sonja scooted her chair back and let him clean up. She noted that her mother still looked happy, really happy, not only for the first time since Red Bartlett's death but for the first time that Sonja could remember.

Sonja conjured some happiness herself and smiled at her mother, wanting to savor their newfound closeness, wanting to perpetuate this sense of happiness and hope forever. But secretly she worried about their waiter: who he was, what he heard and who he heard it for.

She would get to the bottom of her father's death, even if it meant taking on Colonel Rico Toledo, or an alliance with the guerrilla underground. Sonja knew her strengths: she was patient, persistent and bright. Someone had attacked her family. Someone was going to pay.

9

CHIEF EXECUTIVE OFFICER Joshua Casey received his father, Calvin, in the mahogany-paneled suite that fewer than a dozen people had seen. Casey knew that his father disapproved of the luxurious appointments of this inner office, but Joshua insisted that it reminded him of quality, of excellence. Neither he nor his father would settle for less than that. Not for ViraVax, and certainly not for the Lord.

Both father and son served the Lord in their fashion: Calvin Casey's television ministry, *The Eden Hour,* brought the Word into a quarter of a billion homes each week; Joshua Casey's ViraVax provided them the freedom from disease and the agricultural bounty that was befitting the Children of Eden.

Joshua Casey helped to weed and prune the Garden, making the Children of Eden acceptable in the hard eyes of the Lord.

Today the Master looked drawn, older than his sixty-five years, and Joshua Casey frowned his concern. He knew that his father, like himself, observed the strict dietary guidelines of their faith. Both men were vegetarians, and they augmented the benefits of their diet with daily hydrotherapy as outlined in the *Handbook for Health* written by his father nearly forty years before. Neither had missed a day of the Lord's work in his lifetime.

"Hello, Father," Joshua said, extending his hand to the elder Casey. "What brings you back to Costa Brava?"

"The Lord's work, of course," he said. "And yours." His voice was gravelly, strained. "I decrypted your report on the Bartlett matter. It worries me."

"It's unlike you to worry, Father," Joshua said. "Please, have a seat."

Joshua patted the headrest of one of two leather recliners and, once his father was seated, he relaxed in the other. A silver serving

47

table between them held a small loaf of bread, a pitcher of ice water and two glasses. Joshua poured each of them a glass and broke each of them a piece of bread, as was their custom. Calvin nibbled the bread, sipped the water, then set the glass down with a barely audible "Amen."

Each took out a handkerchief and brushed the other's shoe—a ritual foot-washing.

"Bartlett's work helped us make great strides in controlling the Papist menace," Calvin said. "I wanted to be sure that he had not fallen prey to their treachery."

"I appreciate that, Father." Joshua Casey shifted under the Master's demanding gaze. "He did not fall to the Catholics. He fell prey to something more mundane—an artificial viral agent, presumably of his own design. It must have been a private project, there is no mention of it in his log."

"Then I presume the intruder story was provided by the Agency."

"Correct."

"Whatever possessed the man to experiment on himself?"

Joshua Casey sipped his ice water, decided against lying.

"He didn't. It was an accident."

"Accident!" The older man rose out of his chair. "Well, then, what if the whole compound's infected?"

"Relax, Father. Sit, sit."

Calvin Casey sat, but he didn't relax.

"It was a simple influenza vector, designed to operate out of the DNA of the mitochondria rather than the cells themselves. . . ."

"In plain English, please," Calvin said. "I'm a preacher, not a virologist."

Joshua Casey ran a hand through what was left of his hair.

"Several things are set up to happen, based on different signals," he said. "In this case, the body's immune system was ordered to attack itself. The entire body became a raging, irreversible infection."

"You mean, he rotted alive?"

Joshua Casey couldn't meet his father's gaze.

"In a manner of speaking. The body digested itself and rejected itself at the same time."

His father's face showed the expression of utter disgust that he usually reserved for Catholics.

"And how did he get it?" Calvin asked.

"Mosquitoes," Joshua said. "We thought it was impossible, at first. An enzyme in the mosquito's stomach must have reorganized the virus instead of destroying it. It shows the delicate balance we operate under here."

Joshua Casey did not offer his father details of the ghoul that Red Bartlett had become in his final hour. Whatever raged inside him had demonstrated a tremendous drive to replicate. Joshua's preliminary investigation pointed to an unauthorized study at Level Five, but Dajaj Mishwe was the principal investigator, not Red Bartlett.

This one might lead us to the right one, Casey thought. *Mishwe can add it to his candidates for the final scouring of the gene pool.*

Joshua Casey did better than prepare for Armageddon—he scripted the plan. Dajaj Mishwe carried it out.

"Any other casualties?" his father asked.

"Everything was contained and sterilized," Joshua said. "Nothing else got out. You heard the official statement."

"Yes."

The Master, Calvin Casey, pursed his lips so that his little gray mustache looked like the edge of a blade under his ample nose.

"Is there anyone here who would have wanted him dead?"

"No, Father, it was nothing like that. . . ."

"I want you to get rid of that Colonel Toledo."

"Get rid of . . . but why?" Joshua protested. "The Agency keeps him on a short leash at the embassy. Since his people trained our security and turned it over to us, he's stayed out of our hair. He's provided the ultimate security and cover—even the AMA believes we're in Puerto Rico. Why get rid of a good thing?"

"He has not provided the ultimate security," Calvin said. "If he had, that madman's wife would never have been permitted to live outside this compound. His daughter would have been schooled here, like the rest. He's a Catholic. I want this incident to disappear. Call in a favor from the Agency, if you have to."

Joshua Casey wrung his hands and felt the sweat on his upper lip betray his fear.

"Father, it's not that easy. First, the widow is the daughter of the Speaker of the House. We have bought her a house and property nearby as a gesture of goodwill. She will stay. Second, no one goes to the Agency, the Agency comes to you. Now, the Colonel's news release was accepted by all parties as the truth. . . ."

"The wife shot him, you say. How long before she develops a very inconvenient recurring nightmare and tells someone?"

"One of our best people conditioned her during her hospital stay," Joshua countered. "We backed up her conditioning with the usual hypnotic and one of our new AVAs that permitted her to 'remember' more correctly. I assure you, she and the child are not a problem. His work with us was well worth—"

"The Colonel himself, then," Calvin interrupted. "How long before his intelligence organization informs him of your experiments on his fellow idolators? What will you do when he turns on you with all of the resources at his disposal? It is better to take care of this now."

Joshua Casey smiled. It was not often that he acted in anticipation of his father's wishes, but each time he had, it had served to bond them closer. Pleasing his father was like pleasing the Lord, something that was a supreme satisfaction in and of itself.

"The Colonel has been one of our subjects on several occasions," Joshua said. "He was one of the first sperm vectors. Dajaj used him for a successful genetic duplication trial the year we opened here, almost seventeen years ago. We had the opportunity to reinoculate three years later and successfully sterilized his wife through the AVA delivered in his sperm. As you know, the embassy physician is our man, so we have had good follow-up on her. . . ."

"Can you predict exactly what this Colonel will do at any moment?" his father asked.

Joshua Casey was stung into silence. He waited in respectful silence to hear his father's suggestions on the matter. Apparently, there would be none.

"Then get rid of him."

Calvin Casey worried about his son. While Costa Brava was the perfect proving ground for the armory of the Lord, it was still a bastion of the idolators, the Catholics, and they did not take challenges to their centuries of power lying down. And his son's company built viruses, artificial viral agents. This made Calvin Casey uneasy. He had designed the perfectly healthy regimen for the Children of Eden, a regimen that was touted as exemplary by none less than the American Medical Association and the World Health Organization. He did not relish the idea of some Catholic or some laboratory spill wiping out all that he had wrought in his forty-five years of service to the Lord.

"Father? Are you all right?"

Calvin Casey forced himself back to reality.

"Yes," he said, "I'm fine. Just tired, that's all. And worried about you, of course. No need to press this subject further, you know how I stand. As for the lab, I presume that you are taking proper precautions and caring for yourself. Your mother would be proud, bless her soul. But there is one thing that would worry her."

Joshua Casey smiled. "I know, Father. You want me married."

"It's not that I want you . . . well, perhaps it is. Your mother and I were one organism, if I may speak your language for a moment. I know that now, because I am half a being without her. It is something that I can't explain, because you've never had the experience."

"It's unlikely that I'll meet the perfect woman here, Father." Casey smiled again. "Isolation is a must, you know that. I'm married to my work. . . ."

"Hogwash. Besides, you're the sole surviving Casey. Do you want everything that we've worked for to fall into the hands of strangers?"

"I'll work on it, Father. I promise."

"Commit to it," his father ordered. "Your assistant, Shirley Good, has demonstrated promise, I believe, and uncommon loyalty. There has been talk. You, of all people, must be above talk. Take care of it."

"We'll see," Joshua Casey said, reassuring his father with his best smile. "We'll soon see."

Joshua Casey excused himself, then returned to his overcluttered study and the complicated problem of Red Bartlett's death.

Mosquito bites.

That had been in the report. Mosquito bites, scratched up and still inflamed, probably five or six days old. Red Bartlett hadn't been topside in nearly two weeks, so he had to get them inside the facility, somewhere between his labs at Level Two and Mishwe's supply labs at Level Five.

Now, how could a mosquito get in here? Casey wondered.

Everyone below the topside level was fumigated, stripped, cleansed, clothed in sterile jumpsuits. Every molecule of air and water was filtered, cleansed and sterilized in a four-hour ritual. The lab complex was just that, complex, and most of it lay underground, bunkered against an uncasual glance or a neutron bomb.

Now Casey held the histology return on what was left of Red Bartlett: "Tissue rejection reaction/purulence; complete cellular breakdown."

Bartlett had never had a transplant of any kind, nor transfusion, yet his body had disintegrated, burned with a blue flame, just like several Innocents from Mishwe's section. Red Bartlett melted and stank and so did the whole damned scene.

If a mosquito transmitted this from one of Mishwe's experimental subjects to Bartlett, then all of us could be in danger.

The only other answer was equally frightening—Bartlett had been deliberately infected with an experimental AVA, one with which Mishwe had taken other liberties, of late.

If Red had worked at the brassiere factory in La Libertad, Major Scholz would be content to read about it tomorrow on the web. But Bartlett was her boss's best friend, and he worked for ViraVax, and Casey knew that she knew as well as he did that the odds for spontaneous human combustion were slim no matter what the tabloids said.

Rico Toledo's situation was another reason for Agency involvement. Falling so swiftly on the Colonel's sudden decline, his best friend's suspicious death would look even more suspicious.

As it looks now to me, Casey thought.

Suspension, suspicion and more drinking took Rico Toledo down . . . or did it? The Agency chief, Solaris, claimed Toledo was better than that, and the albino was never wrong.

Toledo's conduct towards his family had been unconscionable, and a formal censure had been in the works for a month when Grace Toledo cut him. Catholics were such barbarians. Something like this would be unthinkable in a Gardener family.

It worked out quite to Casey's satisfaction, however. Now Toledo would be far too busy with his personal battles to snoop into corners at ViraVax.

Too bad she didn't kill him, he thought.

Casey took a deep breath and let it out slowly.

That's the way Mishwe thinks.

In truth, it was a strong reason for keeping Mishwe on. A lot of Casey's wishes became fulfilled because of his right-hand man's ability to intuit them, get them done without a lot of aggravating questions, ethical decisions or publicity.

Suddenly, a lot of nasty arrows pointed to Mishwe. He had always been the facility's most valuable player, even though he chose to play alone. With Bartlett gone, Casey was free of the only

Roman Catholic on his staff, but he was seriously short-handed, as well.

Maybe Marte Chang will work into something permanent, he thought. *That is,* willingly *work into something permanent.*

Meanwhile, there was the matter of Mishwe. Casey decided it was time to put a leash on the man, but it would have to wait until Marte Chang's project was finished. Then she would either be one of them or gone, and that would determine what kind of leash to put on Mishwe, and how short.

10

HARRY TOLEDO CLEARLY remembered the bright lights of his birth at the turn of the millennium fifteen years ago, he remembered the blood-stink and the noise. The blessing of his extraordinary memory had turned on him as often as it had given him comfort. The stink came back to him now as he nursed his broken nose. The lights and the noise had been with him all along.

"Your father used to hate to fight."

Grace Toledo raised her voice loud enough so that Harry could hear her over the running water.

He always did a good job of it, Harry thought.

Grace Toledo was washing her hands for the fourth time in an hour. Harry studied his battered face in the hallway mirror and didn't say anything. If it weren't for the cuts, bruising and the swelling, he would be a dead ringer for the Colonel at fifteen. They shared the same gray eyes, dark hair, high cheekbones, full lips. The Colonel wore his hair short and crisp; Harry's curled over the back of his shirt collar.

We sure as hell don't share attitude, Harry thought.

He listened to the *whirr* of his terminal down the hall as it copied his personal network and files into his Sidekick for travel.

Harry saw that he would resemble his father, too, in the break that pushed his nose just a hair to the left.

Great, he thought. *Another tender reminder of paternal affection.*

It was too early for Harry to tell what kind of beard he might have. At fifteen, it was normal that he would hope that it would fill out more. Nothing much in Harry Toledo's life was normal. He was an information junkie who finished high school two years early from his home terminal. For a year he had shown up at

American School only to take his exams and fill out paperwork. He didn't miss having to explain his constant bruising.

The water stopped.

"Do you think he'll die?"

"I don't know," Harry said. "They had to strap him down to get him out of here. . . ."

Now that he and his mother were alone, they could consider such things. The house Watchdog system had notified security and the embassy, who responded with their own people. The Costa Bravans would be brought in first thing in the morning.

That will not be pretty, Harry thought.

Costa Brava's Hacienda Police would not bother themselves over a coffee worker's wife who stabbed her husband, even if he died. But when the stabbed husband is a famous North American colonel, someone's head must roll. Harry looked at his watch.

Five-twenty.

He keyed the Watchdog scanner for the departure of the last of the embassy's investigators.

05:04:58.

Harry's mother didn't have much time.

It doesn't pay to be famous, he thought.

Some of the time it paid. Being a liaison for the new Confederation of Costa Brava had brought Colonel Toledo and his family this mansion of a house in the Colonia Escalón neighborhood, one of the most exclusive in all of Central America. It came with a full security system, including guards, who might be good at defending against outside attack, but so far they had not saved Harry from his father's unreasoning wrath inside.

"Are you sure I'm clean?" Grace asked.

Harry looked at her outstretched hands, red from their scrubbing.

"Yes," he sighed, "they're clean. Have you read *Macbeth* lately?"

"Humor me," she said. "I just wanted him to stop. He would have killed you this time. I didn't expect . . . There was so much blood."

She patted his shoulder and checked the Watchdog.

"How many did they finally leave?"

"Two out front," he said, "and two behind. And the binoculars in the apartment beside the power station."

The security contingency for their protection also meant they were prisoners. His terminal ceased its telltale hum. He pocketed his Sidekick, then ran a large magnet over the drive section of his terminal. He pressed "format," gave its warm top a pat, and turned back to the mirror and the antiseptic.

His mother turned on the faucet again.

"We can't wait," she whispered. "I don't trust any of them. I'll tell you what we'll have to do."

Harry listened with the detachment that comes with fatigue and an adrenaline letdown. He and his mother had been up all night while the Agency reviewed its protocols on "extreme domestic incidents involving Agency personnel while in-country." People who had sat at Grace Toledo's table for dinner now debated whether she would be arrested, deported or dragged back to Washington for an inquiry.

Harry felt a little giddy from no sleep and from the beating his father had given him. His nose stopped bleeding before daybreak but his right eye kept swelling until it puffed shut. This time, antihistamines didn't help. Every time he sat down it was harder to get up.

Harry couldn't remember what he'd said that set his father off. His parents had started off arguing about vaccinations. It turned to Harry and his time spent at the terminal and on the webworks.

"It's the only way he can get privacy," his mother had argued. "He's bright, he's doing fine."

"He's *not* doing fine," his father shouted. "It's not *normal* for a boy to stay inside, alone, at a terminal."

"*He's not normal,*" Grace shouted back. "He grew up here and this country's not normal. *We're* not normal. It's not *his* fault that you don't do anything with him anymore."

"Oh, I suppose it's *my* fault."

Harry had interrupted, but he couldn't remember what he had said. It hadn't been the first time, but he was sure that it would be the last. He stood in front of the bathroom mirror and pried open his right eyelid. No wonder his mother avoided looking at him: his iris was a gray cameo framed in blood.

"Raw-hamburger sandwich," he muttered.

That was what his eye looked like, one of his father's raw-hamburger sandwiches on white bread.

Grace Toledo was still on the phone to Washington, so when the intruder alarm sounded, Harry hurried down the hall to check the screens. It was their neighbor, Yolanda Rubia, and not the Hacienda Police. She was actually no longer their neighbor, since her recent divorce, but her family still held the property, along with the largest coffee plantation in the country.

Nobody stopped her at the gate, he thought.

Neither guard was in sight.

Yolanda was one of the "embassy wives" that he and his mother both liked. She had a three-year-old boy with Down's syndrome and three teenage daughters who attended private Catholic school. Harry had nursed a terrible crush on the oldest, Elena, who was two years his senior. Since the divorce and Yolanda's subsequent employment at the Archbishop's office, they had seen very little of her or the children.

Her driver, a black, middle-aged North American, mopped his balding head with a huge white handkerchief. All the drivers carried big white handkerchiefs in case of cross fire. At fifteen, even Harry knew that this war had no etiquette.

The security scan verified that it was this Gilbert Williams who had driven Harry and his father, the Colonel, from the airport one night.

Colonel Toledo, Harry thought. *He's not my father anymore. He's just Colonel Toledo.*

If rumor proved true, he wouldn't be a colonel much longer, either. If the Colonel survived the scissors slash that had saved Harry's life, he would be very lucky to stay out of jail. A fearful nausea washed over Harry at the thought of his father, so he swept that thought aside.

Harry pressed the bolt release himself and opened the front door. Francesca hadn't shown up for work but Harry had taught himself the security drills. He had seen Williams only the one time, three months ago, and he'd looked so much younger.

"Jesus, kid!" was all Williams said.

Grace Toledo met them at the door and Yolanda Rubia handed her a plain envelope, the kind that might hold an invitation to one of the embassy parties.

"The Colonel, he did this?" Yolanda asked, nodding at Harry.

Neither Harry nor his mother answered. Grace Toledo glanced around the courtyard as she pocketed the envelope.

"The men?" Grace asked.

Her blue eyes indicated the unlocked gate behind the Archbishop's car. Harry saw no sign of either of their guards, and neither did his mother. His part of the plan had worked. The kids that Harry had signaled were shooting off firecrackers down the block, and Williams wiped at his sweat as his quick brown eyes sought snipers on the rooftops.

Later, Harry would remember this as the day no roosters crowed, the day the crippled parrot in the mango tree did not bark at the cats, the day the cats and Francesca and even the fruit flies disappeared. He could never be sure about the truth, but that's the way he would remember that last sunrise in Colonia Escalón with his mother.

Two concussions shook the house. Harry recognized the *whap-WHUMP* of *"un tigre,"* an antipersonnel mine that the army set up around power transformers, substations and relay towers. Harry flinched, though he'd been practicing not to. Gilbert Williams flinched, too. Harry's mother didn't, and neither did Yolanda.

"The gate was open," Williams said. "I didn't see anybody."

"They're throwing us to the wolves, the bastards."

"There is much that you do not understand," Yolanda said. "Whatever happens, I am with you. You must hurry. I will be in touch."

Yolanda hugged Grace Toledo and kissed her cheeks, then shook Harry's hand.

"Ciao," she said, and hurried down the drive to disappear around the wall.

Williams had the door open for Harry; Grace was already inside. Harry limped quickly over to the car and slid into the backseat beside his mother.

She has a plan, and it doesn't include the law.

Harry felt better already.

Another *tigre* blew on the block behind them. Neighborhood children taught Harry to find where they were buried. They lobbed water balloons made from the government's free condoms to set them off. The substation behind them had been taken out three times this month by guerrillas. This time they did it as a favor to him.

"What about the kid?" Williams asked. "Nobody said anything about a kid."

Harry suppressed a smile. Williams was getting very exasperated. Transporting the Colonel's wife after she'd cut up the Colonel was not the most secure duty of the day.

"You're a driver," his mother said. "Drive."

Harry said nothing and looked straight ahead. His mouth tasted like pennies and he could barely control his breathing. He concentrated on not touching his eye, which throbbed deeply with his pulse.

Someone would have to pay. The embassy had distanced itself from them overnight, the usual political precautions. Harry was surprised that his mother had a plan, and not one of the embassy's contingency plans, but one of her own. The darkened windows of the Archbishop's car helped Harry to relax.

His mother removed the envelope from her pocket and read the first line, and smiled.

"Do you have an address, Mrs. Toledo?"

Harry saw the hint of a smile twitch the corner of Grace's mouth, something that Gil probably would not notice. Harry did not know what to feel, but he knew he didn't feel like smiling. Besides, it would probably hurt his eye and his split lip.

"Show us the guesthouse."

Harry watched Gil's eyes reflected in the rearview mirror. They widened in disbelief, then Gil turned to protest.

"Guesthouse," his mother repeated.

There were a lot of code words in Costa Brava, this Harry well knew. He knew several for use with security or the embassy and they all carried standing orders that did not require confirmation. Their driver might not like whatever Grace just told him, but he wouldn't dare take a chance and disobey.

Before turning back to the wheel, Gil gave Harry's mother a long, appraising look. Then he grunted, punctuating some personal decision, and drove. He kept his white handkerchief on the seat beside him, draped over a pistol. He attempted conversation only once.

"Mrs. Toledo . . ."

"Call me Grace."

"Yes. Well, I had something personal to say and now it looks like there won't be time."

"Tell me now."

"I don't want to disturb the boy."

"Harry knows everything."

"I see."

Harry saw a tic of disapproval in Gil's cheek reflected in the rearview mirror.

They were leaving the posh suburb of Colonia Escalón and entering the first of several shantytowns that lined the roadway circumnavigating the capital. Skinny pigs dozed in potholes, veiled in the blue smoke of a thousand charcoal fires. The scent of fresh tortillas breached the car's air-conditioning. Williams cleared his throat and continued.

"I wanted you to know that a lot of us know what you went through with your husb—with Colonel Toledo. You did what had to be done."

Harry watched a barefoot boy and girl his own age pushing a cartful of broken metal towards the city. The curbside tire wobbled under the weight and made the going tougher. A piece of chrome trim nailed to the side said "Mitsubishi." A makeshift cage with two scraggly chickens teetered atop the load. The dark boy bent to his traces, his bare back a study in tendon and bone. Two Down's kids, *deficientes,* followed behind, holding hands and the tail end of a rope.

The swell-breasted girl glanced up from her chore and their gazes met. Harry waved and she flashed a smile and waved back. The brother never looked up. The Down's kids compared tongues and laughed at some unspoken joke.

"Yes," his mother said to Williams, "thank you."

Her voice sounded weak, detached, unlike her.

Harry had not seen much of his father during the last few years, and what he had seen he did not like. His father didn't take him to the gym for karate on Saturdays anymore, and Harry was too old to play hostage-and-escape. Harry's father had spent most of his military career in Central America, first as an advisor and then as chief of intelligence. Costa Brava was a new country, rising out of the ashes of four old ones. Colonel Toledo had made that happen, at the expense of his family.

The Colonel kept two households, the one in Colonia Escalón and an apartment across from the embassy. Grace Toledo, young and lonely, lately had outmaneuvered the advances of a half dozen junior officers who paid casual visits, but seldom when the Colonel was home. To her, and to Harry, this was a sign that his father's affair with the red-haired embassy staffer was more than rumor.

Finally, the Colonel's increasingly bizarre and violent behavior brought her to an ultimatum: they would live together as a family or split up for good. Grace Toledo, like her husband, was a Catholic, and this was a decision that she had not made lightly.

Costa Brava seethed with secrets, with codes within codes. Harry's movement within the country had been tightly restricted all his life, which was true of all dependents of embassy personnel. Still, he had versed himself in the hot fluidity of the politics and he had learned a decent Spanish, though only English was permitted at the private American School on the embassy grounds.

Harry had just graduated at fifteen and looked forward to never going back.

Grace Toledo told Harry everything she knew because Harry was still her most constant companion. Still, there was a black hole of secrecy in Costa Brava, and Colonel Rico Toledo stood in the middle of it. Neither Harry nor his mother had been able to penetrate its veil. She had alerted him to the usual security precautions as they were passed to her.

"See how our cannibals dance" meant that all personnel were restricted to embassy grounds or to quarters, due to an undisguisable incident involving the internal law of the country. It was also a warning of imminent action against Americans, accompanied by increased fighting within the city itself. Harry was sure that this message had already flashed among embassy personnel due to the incident between his parents.

According to the official embassy releases, there was no guerrilla activity within fifty klicks of the capital, yet the power substation on the block behind them blew up with chilling regularity. Harry had stopped believing the embassy, and his father, long ago.

Williams pulled up behind a bunker-like building fronted by a row of shabby garages on the Avenue of the Martyrs. Harry recognized the structure immediately as a "hot-sheet" motel. He understood now the meaning of the word "guesthouse."

This particular motel was a singularly unremarkable place on a narrow street that offered plenty of cover behind burned-out cars but few options for escape. These were things that his father had taught him to observe, and he did so now out of habit. Much of the embassy's intelligence was gathered electronically, but the Costa Bravans still relied on real eyes staring out real windows, on real ears against the right doors.

Grace Toledo dismissed Williams in the street across from the motel garages. Three of the roll-up doors stood open for business. After the Archbishop's car disappeared around the corner, Grace hurried Harry through the leftmost of the three.

Hot-sheet motels provided the ultimate accommodations for the clandestine affairs of a traditionally Catholic nation. Designed to meet the illicit playtime needs of diplomats, politicians and the occasional priest or nun, the hot-sheet motels also hid guerrillas, political refugees and bandits.

They made perfect temporary isolation units for "hot ones," the unvaccinated infected, or "cold ones," the vaccinated but infected.

The unvaccinated and the uninfected, like Harry, they simply called "lucky." The latest vaccine, one that his father's Agency helped the World Health Organization to distribute, was supposed to end the need for vaccination once and for all. His parents' last argument had exploded over the subject of vaccinations.

A hot-sheet motel had no office. The client drove into one of the open double garages. A locked door led from garage to accommodations. To the left of the driver's door a large drawer jutted from the wall. This drawer held a tray for cash and a rate schedule that boasted the convenience of a one-hour minimum fee.

Harry's mother counted out some bills into the tray and closed the drawer. She drummed her fingernails on the handle and Harry heard someone rustling on the other side of the wall. A small red light winked on and the sign next to it said "Listo." She slid it open and took out a stack of towels with a key on top. She handed the towels to Harry and opened the door.

Harry had seen a lot of motels during their vacations around the region, but this one was different. A single window high on the courtyard wall admitted sunlight but prevented casual snooping—or sniping. A huge bed with a thick red bedspread took up most of the space. Weavings of Maya design hung on the walls, resplendent in ancient sexual practices. A peek into the bathroom revealed a condom dispenser next to their complimentary champagne. The bottom of the condom dispenser rested atop the ice in the champagne bucket. It didn't seem to Harry that they would be very comfortable chilled like that.

He set the towels down and picked up a brochure that listed certain personal appliances that could be rented from the management, and an accompanying illustration showed three large penis-like devices. His Spanish wasn't good enough to decipher all of the instructions.

"Put that down," his mother said. "You might be as smart as an adult, but you're still just fifteen."

He sat down gingerly on the bed, more aches and pains reducing his movement to a series of cartoon-like jerks.

"Now," she said, "we'll see. . . ."

His mother opened a bedside drawer, where most motels kept their Bibles. She pulled the drawer completely from the cabinet. Taped to the back was a fat brown envelope.

Harry heard a car pull into the garage. The door rumbled closed and footsteps walked away. His mother, who had been holding her breath, relaxed. She shook out the envelope's contents onto the bed: car keys, Canadian passports, Canadian and Costa Bravan currency, some note cards and computer diskettes. The passport with Harry's picture was registered to James McCarron, a fifteen-year-old from Coquitlam, British Columbia.

The bedspread smelled of cigarettes and chocolate, and the chocolate smell reminded Harry that he'd been too wound up to eat, and his stomach growled. His mother heard it, too, and dug out a candy bar from the bottom of her purse.

It hurt his face to chew, so Harry just let it melt in his mouth. His mother scooped everything into the envelope except the car keys and led him back into the garage.

"I paid for the night," she said. "That might buy us some time."

Their car was a beat-up, pre-millennium Lada taxicab. Harry's mother picked up a Tigers baseball cap from the backseat and tucked her blonde hair inside. There was no passenger seat in front, so Harry got in back.

"Where to, young fellow?" she asked.

"To the airport," Harry said, "and step on it." He tried a smile, but it hurt too much.

"We'll take the scenic route," she said. "I think you'll appreciate it."

She hopped out quickly and closed the garage door behind them. They were a couple of kilometers away when the two embassy staff cars swept past them, accompanied by a jeep with a pair of MPs, led by a Costa Bravan Special Security van.

"Looks like Gil didn't believe we had guesthouse privileges," she muttered. "It'll take them a while to get into that room—the President or the mayor could be in there with one of their wives, for all they know."

She drove them south, out of the city, through the lowland farms and into the hills. This was coffee country, protected from guerrilla attack by the private security forces hired by the growers, and by small monthly payoffs. It was Harry's opinion that many of the security forces worked both sides of the fence, a notion not all that uncommon in embassy circles.

His mother turned off onto a well-kept side road and stopped the taxi at a huge iron gate decorated with a giant maple leaf and the words "Casa Canadá."

On other plantations the workers lived in cardboard appliance cartons or under makeshift plastic tents. Here at Casa Canadá each family was provided a two-room cabin with cement floor, a water spigot and a garden plot. Single men and women occupied two bunkhouses that flanked the cabins. Someone had fashioned play equipment for children out of a few dozen old tractor tires.

A long concrete trough under a thatched roof made up the laundry. All of the able-bodied men were in the fields, in the army or with the guerrillas.

"This isn't the road to the airport," Harry said.

"You didn't say *which* airport."

They swept past the huge drying area with its mounds of coffee beans, and the aroma was so thick that it even penetrated Harry's swollen, blood-encrusted nostrils. Three long sheds abutted this area, and past the sheds stretched a concrete runway. A yellow biplane touched down, then climbed back up to come around again.

A red-faced blonde woman walked up from the middle shed to meet them, and only when she stepped out of shadow did Harry recognize Sonja Bartlett's mother, Nancy.

"Hello, Grace," Nancy said, extending a hand that lately had seen a lot of physical work. "I guess it's 'Patricia,' now that we've made you a Canadian."

"Hello, Nancy. I haven't told Harry. . . ."

" 'James,' " Nancy corrected. "At least, for a few days he's my Canadian nephew, James."

Nancy Bartlett shook Harry's hand, then stepped back to look at what his father had done to him. Harry didn't like the darkness that crossed her face, nor the blaze in her eyes.

"The sonofabitch," Nancy muttered.

She shook her head as though to wake herself and smiled. Her moment of fury and disorientation was not lost on Harry.

She's been through a lot worse than I have, Harry reminded himself.

People still talked about the break-in and the murder. Harry heard from one of the junior officers that she'd been raped as well. Her father, the U.S. Speaker of the House, vowed annihilation of the group responsible. No one took this threat seriously. The U.S. had all it could handle right at home.

Harry resolved to stay quiet, wait and watch what his mother and Nancy Bartlett had in mind.

Nancy quizzed him briefly on the information on his new passport and Harry answered her in Spanish.

"He'll be fine," Nancy told Grace. "If you two have to run, your papers are in order, including inoculation cards. Family and business people fly in and out of here all the time, and the Marcoes are always on the up-and-up. You can stay here, then fly out later if that's what you have to do. The customs inspector comes here when they fly the coffee out. He'll sign off your cards, if it comes to that. The coffee's going to Mexico City.

"If worse comes to worst and you have to run, tickets will be waiting for you at Pan Am in Mexico City. Then to Vancouver, Canada, with a change of planes in Los Angeles. Canadian money isn't tagged, so it won't be traced until you change into dollars. My sister will meet you in Vancouver. Don't worry. It's all covered, you can relax now."

Harry's mother had fooled him, too.

She must have arranged this . . . weeks ago. Maybe months.

Nancy and Sonja Bartlett hadn't lived out here all that long. Still, he'd always thought his mother's thoughts and motives to be transparent. Harry was both amused and relieved to find out otherwise.

One yellow biplane drew a lazy figure-eight against the bright blue sky over the airstrip. It pretended to be a falling leaf, then swooped into a slow, spiraling climb.

The three of them began their dusty walk up to the house. Nancy was asking his mother how the fight started.

"This time it was so ridiculous. . . ." His mother faltered, something Harry had seldom seen. "Vaccination. It was time for Harry to get his vaccinations. You've seen the hot ones in that compound at La Ceiba? They're all over this country and it's nothing to fool with. The Colonel refused, and the García government said, 'No shots, no visa.' Rico went into one of his rages. This time he got after Harry, too, and there was no stopping him. . . ."

Harry's mother couldn't finish and Nancy patted her shoulder, her expression grim.

"The rest I suppose you've heard," Grace said.

Nancy nodded, then took Grace's arm and guided them through the screened porch and into the house.

"Shouldn't you handle this back home?" Nancy asked. "Down here, it's his country and anything could happen."

"My life is here, too," Grace said. "Harry's lived here all his life, and I've spent my whole adulthood here. I'm not going to let anyone run me off. Isn't that what you decided, too?"

Nancy poured Harry a cup of the finest coffee that he had ever tasted.

"To freedom," Nancy toasted.

"And to standing up for yourself," Grace added.

Harry took his cup out to the porch and squinted into the sky. The little yellow biplane tipped its wings in a salute, and Harry caught a glimpse of long blonde hair streaming back from the cockpit.

Sonja!

For the first time all day, things were looking up.

11

MARTE CHANG WATCHED the pink wash of dawn highlight a lush hillside that she was forbidden to explore. The triple-fenced perimeter was topped with razor wire, angled both inward and outward. ViraVax looked more like a prison than a lab. She knew now why she had thought of submarines when she answered Casey's questionnaire, and why he had scrambled their communication both ways when it passed through the web.

At least with a submarine you're spared the temptation of the view, Marte thought.

She shortened her focus to her reflection in the glass, lifted a strand of her straight black hair and let it fall. It had been a week since she'd had the enthusiasm to curl it. Marte hadn't touched her makeup in a week, either. She was surprised at her reflection. She had used eye shadow and eyeliner to make her eyes bigger, wider, more . . .

. . . Caucasian?

Yes, she admitted, *more Caucasian.*

It was the pressure of all those . . . *mongoloid* faces, smiling at her in the passageways, serving her meals, plucking at her sleeve and fetching her clipboard.

What am I afraid of? she wondered. *That people will think I'm one of them?*

Marte Chang's intellect had always been her pride. She was embarrassed now because she hated bigots and snobs and she had just caught herself thinking like both.

She took a closer look at herself.

The reflected Marte Chang had a pair of wide, dark eyes separated by a slender nose that punctuated her full lips. She was surprised to find that she liked her eyes without the makeup.

I must be slipping, she thought. *It's the isolation pressure.*

She wondered whether the men in Costa Brava would like her eyes or not. Marte Chang wondered whether there were men in Costa Brava at all. The selections at the lab were completely unacceptable, including Joshua Casey. His ability to second-guess the genetic code bordered on the psychic, but his social skills and his sex appeal were zero. The missionaries were worked to the edge of exhaustion and took out their frustrations on the Innocents. Marte had witnessed many verbal attacks, and stumbled on at least one sexual encounter between a *deficiente* woman and a very embarrassed security guard.

Marte had turned her back and exited the room. The glare from the missionary turned her initial anger into fear.

Like everyone at ViraVax, Marte had been choppered directly into the security complex in the Jaguar Mountains, so she did not have a firsthand familiarity with the political or geographic terrain. She had studied the Agency's briefing packet carefully, and Costa Brava came up in an occasional newsline, but both emphasized the squalor and desperation. Marte's glimpse of one jungle hillside made her ache for more.

"You will be here for a six-month tenure," Casey had said. "All regular staff lives on the grounds. Our missionaries rotate through in two-year increments. We pay the highest royalties on developments, our profit-sharing benefits are unequaled. You might consider staying on."

"I might," Marte had lied. "On the other hand, I've been in school a long time. When this job is done, I'll have some money for a change. I want to travel a little before settling down."

Marte had hoped he would take the hint and release her for a weekend, but the Bartlett incident made everyone at ViraVax tighter than usual.

By the shift of Casey's eyes Marte knew he had expected her to jump at his offer. Six months ago, she might have. That was before Sunspots, and that was before the call from Solaris, the briefing by Mariposa. Yes, it would be a good idea to travel.

"This field moves too fast for you to be gone from it very long," Casey pointed out. "You'll get bored, worried. Look us up, we'll consider you for a two-year hitch. We insist on two things: you have no leave during that time, for any reason; you do not investigate other employment opportunities while you are here."

Marte's head buzzed with the complexity of this thing. She had come here for an installation that might take as little as four months. The extra two months guaranteed that she would have plenty of time to snoop around for the Agency as well.

Casey's voice became louder with his increased enthusiasm.

"Your personal affairs can be settled through the webworks or the mail," he said. "Like everyone who comes here, you have neither lover nor family. . . ."

This matter-of-fact statement stung her, but she did not let it show. He was right. She had nothing to go back to and everything to stay for, so she might as well stay.

How did he know all that?

Some things weren't covered in the preliminary questionnaire she had filled out, yet Casey tossed off the intimate details of her life casually, as though they'd spoken of them many times.

"You know, I indicated on my questionnaire that I did not want to do any weapons work."

"Yes?"

"I might be naïve, Dr. Casey, but I'm not stupid. You wouldn't employ this level of security unless . . ."

"You graduated from a Children of Eden school, did you not?"

"Why, yes, but . . ."

"And what made you choose that particular school?"

Casey's loud voice rattled her thoughts.

"I'm a vegetarian, I like the health aspects of that . . . preference. The Children of Eden believe that earth itself is the Garden of Eden, fallen into disrepair. I wanted to be a part of restoring the earth. . . ."

"And you received full scholarships, true?"

"True."

Marte felt her cheeks flush.

"You said, *that preference,* Miss Chang, not *our religion.* You are a tithing member of our faith, are you not?"

"Well . . . not exactly. I pay tithes because I wanted to give something back, pass on the favor. I have read every book your father has written, and seen his vids. Of course, they're with my things back home. . . ."

"Ah, Miss Chang, this is your home now. The Children of Eden comprise a great family, and the nucleus of that family is here, in Costa Brava. We undertake many projects worldwide for many reasons. All ultimately must benefit the goals of the Children of Eden or we do not accept them. By that token, neither would we ask you to accept any project that you feel compromises your personal principles. Fair?"

Marte Chang felt that her personal principles had not been adequately spoken to, but she did not relish continuing this conversation at such close quarters with such a loud-voiced little man, so she dropped it.

"Fair," she said.

"Good."

Casey smiled, caught himself scratching at his scalp and brushed imaginary lint off his lapel instead.

"Shirley will continue your orientation. She's been with us from the start and is best prepared to answer your questions. She will provide your upgraded access cards within the hour. My office is open if you need me."

Marte breathed a lot easier when he was gone.

Six months locked up with this man, she thought. *The Agency bonus had better be sainthood.*

The thought was a throwback to her Catholic childhood with her parents. She dismissed it, but not without a smile.

Marte Chang waited a half hour for Shirley, then decided to explore the outdoors on her own. She already knew that this building, "A-Lab, Level One," housed her apartment, office, lab and technical-support staff. Her walk down the main hallway did not deviate into the facility, however. Her eyes were on the back door, and every step led her closer to the fresh air that she craved. She stumbled through the back door of A-Lab into one of the sudden tropical downpours that swept through nearly every afternoon.

Marte Chang looked up to see a bald man, stripped to the waist, running full tilt between two parallel rows of tires. He made incredible speed, stepping lightly inside each tire, in spite of the fact that he held a glass of water in each outstretched hand.

He turned for the run back, and his dark eyes flashed as he sprinted towards her.

Dajaj Mishwe!

Marte Chang stood her ground, though every muscle of her body screamed at her to flee. His expressionless face betrayed a thrill at the last-instant widening of her eyes.

He flung both glasses of water at her, glasses and all. She parried them both reflexively and prepared for attack, but he simply sprinted past her into the lab. The glare from his eyes was as infuriating to her as his actions. He was everything that the Agency briefing had warned her about.

The cocky bastard was already dripping rainwater on Casey's office floor when Marte stalked right in. She trembled in her attempts to keep her indignation from fanning into rage. She vowed that she would not cry. Marte Chang sensed that rage was like a perfume to this man, and hysteria a fine wine.

Casey dismissed Mishwe with a jerk of his head. Though it was a small office, and crowded, Marte gave him plenty of room to pass without touching her. Perhaps it was the presence of the boss that restrained the man.

Casey explained in his usual boom of a voice: "He is a survivor of the messianic wars and quite a treasure, in his way. You will work with him sometimes, we all do. He spends most of his time at Level Five."

Casey handed her a towel and she mopped her face dry.

"What do you mean 'work with him'?" she said. "I don't want to be in the same city as that madman, much less the same building."

"He is a magician with genes, particularly the *access* to genes. Besides, all culture media are provided by his people at Level Five, and your project requires more medium than the rest put together, does it not? You will find Mishwe an invaluable tool when it comes to implementation. . . ."

"No," Marte said, her lips pressed into a firm, pale line. "I do not want that man near me, or near my work."

"Well, my dear, that's simply unnecessary. Dajaj despises people, especially women, and bears our infrequent encounters under great duress. The Innocents adore him, however, and what patience he has, he has for them. If you stay away from his little playground back there, then you will likely never run into him by chance. I promise you, he will not seek you out. He seeks out no one."

"He scares me," she said, and dropped uninvited into Casey's easy chair. "Eccentric is one thing, abuse is another. He *assaulted* me. . . ."

"We are different people here, different from the outside world," Casey said. He swept a hand about him in a gesture that Marte was sure he considered dramatic. "Here in our isolation we must develop a tolerance that surpasses what we find on the outside. It is in our best interests. May I show you some of his work?"

"I'm not sure I have the stomach for it," she snapped.

"Calm down," Casey said. It was as close as he had come to giving her an order. "You are not leaving, you have too much at stake. He is not leaving. You share the same roof. You don't have to get along, so you must coexist. He will not harm you, that is not allowed. With information comes understanding, so you need more information."

Marte rubbed her face with the towel, an opportunity to escape Casey's blue-eyed gaze. Something in her body screamed at her to leave, to run, to get as far away from their shared roof as money could get her. But her intellect reminded her that this was not practical. She would find the tools to practice her intricate, expensive art nowhere else in the world, so she must make do here. Hers was the dilemma of the composer/conductor whose instrument is a symphony.

And there was the matter of the Agency.

"Okay," she said, "show me."

"It's a long cycle through decontamination," Casey said. "Several hours down to Level Five, several hours back. We could do it another time . . . ?"

Marte chilled at the thought of seeing Dajaj Mishwe again, but she could not expect too many offers for a look at Level Five, so she accepted, with what she hoped was a convincing eagerness.

Casey led her to a large apartment.

"It's an elevator," he explained. "Everything cycles automatically, illustrated for you by the orientation vid. We are most fussy about procedure on your first cycle. You may nap if you like, or access your system through the console provided. I'll take an express later. You may be thinking, 'Rank has its privilege,' and you would be right. However, I assure you I still have to submit to the basic unpleasantries."

The apartment was boring, the orientation disk was boring, so, in spite of her nervousness, Marte Chang napped through the three-hour cycle to Level Five.

Dajaj Mishwe's lab was meticulously kept. To Marte's relief, Casey had called ahead, and Mishwe was gone. Marte was sure that he watched them from behind one of the two-way mirrors that separated each lab from its living quarters and electronics studio. Three thick ropes hung from the high ceiling, about five meters apart. Free wall space was studded with tiny pieces of rock—movable rock.

"Dajaj likes to climb," Casey said. "It relieves his tension, like the tires. We all have our releases, correct? These are more innocuous than many."

Marte answered with a grunt as she took in the detail of Mishwe's workspace.

Like her temporary setup topside, it was as spacious as a well-lit barn. The decontamination/suit-up room and refrigeration facility were identical to her own. There the resemblance ended. Marte's experiments focused on the placement of metals within retroviral structures during replication. She seldom worked with anything larger than single-cell cultures, but Dajaj Mishwe obviously preferred larger animals, animals of all types. There was no doubt that his favorite was the standard white rat.

Thousands of rat cubicles formed a great rat city around the lab. Hundreds of other rodents were confined to expensive isolettes.

Like Mishwe, she thought.

Dozens of white-suited trisomy helpers shuffled the byways, feeding and watering and cleaning the animals.

"Lab rats," Casey mused. "He does love them, doesn't he?"

Marte understood that Casey meant the trisomies as well. She found it difficult to imagine Mishwe loving anything, so she kept quiet.

Dajaj Mishwe had been a nocturnal animal long before his recruitment by Joshua Casey. Animals were easier caught at night, when they slept or drowsed or stalked, like he himself stalked.

Marte knew that the Agency had turned Mishwe down for their own ranks, years ago, but Casey hired him, anyway. No one knew the practical limitations of mammalian physiology like Dajaj Mishwe. There were certain matters of physiology that only came out of experimentation on human beings, but human subjects were banned, even in Costa Brava. That was where a lab associate like Mishwe could give a company a real jump on the competition.

Dajaj liked live animal studies because he got paid for tormenting and killing his subjects, something that was almost, but not quite, satisfying. His associates used cultures and tormented microscopic creatures. Mishwe stuffed his lab, and half of the transport bay, with cages. And one whole section of topside barn, the one nearest the landing pad, was closed off and silenced.

It was here, in the security of Level Five, as well as in gallerias around the country, that the Agency suspected Mishwe of keeping his special subjects, his live ones. Certain cold-storage houses held the dead.

Dajaj Mishwe was a strong man, and agile for someone who spent his life watching. He injected and watched. He peered at tissues, slides, electron-generated images of glands and brains. He watched.

ViraVax provided a complete gymnasium at its mountain facility, but Dajaj preferred the privacy of his tire yard. In a gravelly area behind Marte's topside labs, he laid out a hundred brand-new tires in two parallel lines. He cleaned the tires before and after each use. Eventually the rubber whiskers formed in the tire-casting process wore off, and Mishwe bought new ones. He would not run his agility drill through used tires.

Three or four times a week he came topside and sprinted through the tires, high-stepping into each one, sweat popping a shine over his bald head. Sometimes, on a difficult day, he ran the tires for an hour or more, stopping only when he could no longer keep his footing.

Sometimes he carried weights, to build his upper body, or glasses of water. Sometimes he balanced the glasses on the backs of his hands.

When Mishwe came below after walking in the rain, dozens of the level-bound Innocents would crowd around him, touching his damp hair and skin and clothes and calling him "Angel." It was as close to rain as they could get, though he permitted a select few the occasional night mission topside. Exposure to ultraviolet would trigger an autoimmune response coupled with a cell-proliferation order. They would melt down to a muck the consistency of an overripe mango. Of this, Marte Chang was sure.

Marte had solved the Red Bartlett mystery on her fifth day on the web. Today, when the Agency transmitted its daily report to Casey, Marte would fire a burst back. There would be a helluvan explosion in certain diplomatic parlors back home as well as in Costa Brava.

Bartlett's tissues and systems had attacked one another, while his body's cells launched into a duplication frenzy. His tissues had fought out quite a battle, and within the hour his body was reduced to a seething mass of putrid organic matter which burst into flame and consumed itself.

Marte had found encrypted data files on six Level Five Innocents that documented the same phenomenon. These files also documented the source of the phenomenon: Dajaj Mishwe. That left her with two questions.

How many people did Mishwe infect? Was Red Bartlett's death an accident or murder?

"Red Bartlett discovered the pilot gene," Casey said, even though he knew that she knew it, "the one responsible for survival and self-replication. Dajaj designed a retroviral torpedo that unleashed millions of tiny sculptors inside the nuclei of a thousand rats."

Casey gestured grandly, as though conducting a symphony, as he explained details to her in his loud, distracting voice. Marte Chang could scarcely believe that Joshua Casey was the son of the Reverend Calvin Casey, father of the Children of Eden. Calvin Casey was a far more charismatic man than his son, much better mannered and far better looking. Calvin was born to the airwaves, Joshua to the nooks and crannies of commercial labs.

"Keeps things interesting," Casey concluded.

Marte had not heard much of what he said. Her mind took up its own protective stance and had stopped listening.

Casey was silent, finally. He seemed anxious to show her everything. She thought she'd better take advantage of the mood while she had the chance. She had a feeling that, should he ever judge her correctly, there was much that she would not be allowed to know.

Find out everything, she thought. *Tomorrow may be too late.*

It would not be easy to get back to this level on her own.

"What's back here?"

"Histology," he said, and relief showed in his smile. She had made the right choice. "We manufacture viruses, antibodies, vaccines," Casey said with a wave of his hand. "We also develop and manufacture culture media. That's Mishwe's baby. You've seen his media catalog, I trust?"

"Of course," she said. "But the company was not called ViraVax. And its shipping address was Basil, Switzerland."

"Right. The usual precautions. No, Marte, Dajaj takes care of all of that right here. Quite a market."

"Show me Histology."

For the first time she saw Casey's shield drop, and in that glimpse she tasted fear in his hesitation. Gone in a blink.

"Why not?" he said. "You're here."

Casey activated the double doorlock, and she followed him through. The doorway became a polished concrete corridor that slanted down thirty paces, then up again thirty. It opened up into one of the five huge bunkers that stretched for a half kilometer, more than a hundred meters underground.

"It's like a little city down here," she remarked.

"Another country," Casey grunted.

She marveled at the deception, the simplicity of camouflage that hinted at none of this from the air. She had already noted

that most flights came and went after dark. The landing pad was
six levels up and a world away.

How handy for him.

Tiers of crates and shipping containers lined the walls and
aisleways. Forklifts, cranes and electric tractors filled the air
with a hum that bordered on whine. Marte noted the heady scent
of ozone in the air. Casey pointed out refrigerated rooms and
positive-pressure storage. Inspectors and shipping clerks, all missionaries, wore full gowns and foot coverings. Retarded helpers
wore loose-fitting, pajama-like clothing. Like their counterparts
topside, Level Five's workers were colored overalls to match their
restricted pathways marked by lines in the floor and by colored
lights in the walls.

Colored lines diverged under the glossy waxed floors to deline-
ate different pathways. The wax made the floor squeak under
Marte's uncovered shoes. The inspector frowned when he heard
it, started to gesture with his clipboard. Then he saw that she was
a companion of Joshua Casey and nodded politely.

From somewhere further back, high-pitched screams.

Marte's flesh prickled.

Casey smiled. "Primates," he explained. "You might as well
see the menagerie."

The menagerie took up most of a hundred-meter-long wing of
the bunker. Racks, ramps and scaffolding formed a convoluted
maze up to the rafters ten meters overhead. Within that maze
lived thousands, tens of thousands, of animals.

"It takes twenty people each shift, around the clock, to handle
it," Casey said. "Still, they receive the Sabbath free, too. As
you can see, the Plexiglas partitions are individual bioms. The
animals are quite comfortable."

"Sure," Marte snapped, "if they like cages."

"Like many humans in this life, they have no choice. They
derive what comfort they can and deny the rest."

Along the wall stood nine cubicles, three atop three atop three
more. Each was fiberglass, about a meter square, with a small
hole high in one side.

What could be in there? she wondered.

An armed security guard stood at one end of the stack of
cubicles.

"What's in there?" she asked. "In those boxes."

Casey frowned, but it was the frown that she had already
learned to recognize as a mock seriousness, at a time when he

would deliver a prepared statement.

"Hot chimps," he said. "Their infection is stabilized and they're awaiting . . ."

"My God" was her involuntary comment.

"Do not blaspheme. They are chimps, after all, and will be destroyed when we've completed the necessary tests."

Marte thought she heard a human voice cry out, but the guard silenced it with a stun butt to the side of the box. She regretted that the box was out of range of her Sidekick's microscan adapter. She wanted to burst as much of this out as possible, but a single visual frame required as much transmission space as a hundred pages of text.

What if I never get in here again? Marte wondered.

Casey must have noted her expression of shock, the direction of her gaze.

"Quite good at mimicry, aren't they?" he said. "In the lab they find adopting human mannerisms often brings them extra attention and food from the Innocents. Shall we move along?"

As Casey took her elbow to escort her back to the decon lift to Level One, Marte Chang wondered, once again, *What in God's name have I got myself into?*

That night, half-asleep in her Level One quarters, she listened to fluctuations from her air conditioner and thought of those meter-square boxes. She imagined herself inside one of them, stooped, unable to either stand or sit. The dreamer Marte Chang listened through a feeding slot while the person in the box above her whispered, "Someone will get us out of this, you'll see."

Marte Chang tossed in a fitful sleep, convinced that, with no one behind her and nowhere to go, nobody could get her out of this. She could only make the best of things while she was here.

Time for a woman-to-woman talk with Shirley Good, she thought.

Marte had learned to filter out the *scuff-scuff* of footsteps in the hallway, their inevitable pause at her door, the occasional touch of the latch or sniff on the air. The Innocents were curious, shy, good-natured. Now she sensed a pause at her door, a presence without footsteps. Not a breath. Not a shadow. Not an Innocent.

Mishwe!

Marte Chang's heart rate got in the way of her breathing for a moment but she kept her respirations as steady as possible. Just as she had sensed he was there, she sensed his absence. The nighttime traffic of busy Innocents resumed.

12

COLONEL RICO TOLEDO closed the slats on his office blinds with a *snap,* shutting out the merciless sun and the weekly demonstration at the embassy gates across the way. These were not Costa Bravans venting spleen against the United States; these were U.S. citizens. North Americans who didn't have the *huevos* to stand up to the White House gates at home shook their pale fists at this air-conditioned box fenced off from the diesel-grimed pesthole that the locals called a country.

The Colonel was in a bad mood because he was in a bad position. The muggy heat prickled the stitches under his dressing, and he nursed a hangover that would have registered a 7 on the Richter scale. Rico snorted unselfconsciously at the sight across the street. Those demonstrators thought that they displayed solidarity with the locals, but were seldom in-country long enough to discover that the locals disrespected anyone who spat on his own flag.

"They do that every week, you say?"

The voice behind the Colonel—a high, nasal voice bordering on whine—belonged to his new assistant, probably an eventual replacement, a fresh major by the name of Hodge. The Colonel was fresh himself, in a way. The Agency sent Solaris down to deliver the verdict: collect vacation, leave the country, possible court-martial. Rico was uninvited to García's celebration of his one-year anniversary as President without a coup. Then, in the morning, the mandatory debriefing, his personal ass-chewing for losing Red Bartlett and for the trouble with his wife. The blade fan overhead growled as it always did in low gear.

The Colonel growled a little himself.

"I thought you were in intelligence."

When Colonel Toledo turned imaginary cross-hairs between Hodge's eyes, he saw a flush wash over the major's cheeks.

81

"Colonel, I appreciate what you've been through. I was just making conversation. You were injured in one of those demonstrations when you first came in-country, I heard."

The Colonel felt a surge in the pulse at his neck, the rise of unreasonable anger. This curse of rage he recognized but he could not throw off. Drinking both triggered the rage and smothered it. The trick was in the timing, and bad timing had plagued him of late. It worried him because he'd lost control, lost some memory. It worried him because counseling meant talking, and talking would mean his job. Not talking now might also mean his job.

Rico needed the vacation, that was clear. He hadn't taken time off in nearly five years. Grace made sure that she and Harry took several vacations a year, which the Colonel encouraged. He always came up with a lot of "product" when the family was out of reach.

Though he was a young forty-five, the Colonel knew that anger had already kicked his blood pressure into the danger zone. He reminded himself that this was something that was happening to him lately. It wasn't Hodge's fault. Hodge just happened to be handy.

"Conversation," the Colonel hissed. "You mean small talk."

The Colonel glanced around the bare office: fan, desk, three windows with blinds, the inevitable mold that bled through a fresh coat of government-issue pastel lime; two olive-drab file cabinets, one cabinet of electronic wizardry capped with two telephones. It was just as he had entered it nearly twenty years ago, except for the holos, the Litespeeds and Sidekicks. He couldn't bring himself to focus on Hodge.

"Conversation . . . okay." The Colonel glanced at his watch. "Conversation."

Easily said, not so easily begun.

Another glance at the embassy and he felt his testicles sucked towards his abdomen—he had nearly lost them out there, seventeen years ago. They took over a month to heal and still gave him trouble. And every Wednesday that they kept him in this office overlooking the embassy, he had remembered. Even though it was a punishment assignment, Rico knew he would feel better facing the weekly demonstrators from the front.

"Adhesions," the embassy physician had told him. "Take a week off so that you can just lie around and we'll take care of that for you. If you wait, it's just going to get worse."

Maybe that's my problem, he thought.

The Colonel preferred to think that his problem was anything but pressure. If it were pressure, he'd have to retire, just when his organization was in place and its position in this country secure.

The Colonel had taken some licks in his time, but that series of kicks to the groin had been so quick and so hard that he couldn't remember it. He remembered gagging on his own vomit, and a crushing, stunning pain that even morphine didn't cure.

Then, in the hospital, he got infected with some tropical bug that didn't even have a name and he nearly sweat to death.

"Fever of Unknown Origin," he said.

"Colonel?"

"What I had, in the hospital. Fever of Unknown Origin."

Rico saw the shade of fear cross the assistant's eyes. There was a vaccine against almost everything these days, but plenty of things left that a vaccine couldn't help.

Plenty of things new.

AIDS had been the first breakthrough, a real money-maker. Now everyone got a multivax the same way the Colonel got one of the last smallpox scratches as a child.

The Colonel had worked with ViraVax, the developer of the multivax, setting up their compound only a half hour away from the capital by chopper. No one had yet come up with a cure for everything. But someone had come up with a few other viruses, every bit as nasty.

Of course, there were always a few who succumbed to the vaccine itself.

The Colonel had been immersed in the world of viruses and vaccines for years now, much against his will. ViraVax had been his cover job here while he infiltrated the local rebels. Then the Colonel had been plucked out of field intelligence just when his networks were humming and his sources secure.

Maybe they know my opinion of which side we're taking, he mused.

He thought it unlikely. Colonel Toledo shared his opinions with no one, not even Rachel.

He had some scores to settle in the intelligence community, and now his government was making that impossible. He had been around too long to think that it was an accident, a toss of the die.

In Costa Brava bullets outnumbered beans by three to one, and the most valuable commodity was information. Colonel Rico Toledo's boss in the Agency back home called it "the product."

Costa Bravans, living closer to poetry, spoke of a "little sigh," or "the whisper," but very few real whispers bent hairs in real ears.

Lots of high-tech tricks had sprung up in the last twenty years. By the time Colonel Toledo had engineered the Costa Brava confederation in 1998, modems and faxes winked their tireless semaphore from pocket Sidekick to satellite to desktop. Colonel Rico Toledo was as old-fashioned as his posture—when it came to information, he preferred to stick with lips.

Real names were as rare as prime rib in the information business, but they were particularly rare in the Central American republics. Colonel Toledo's last assistant had had three informants feeding him reliable product for a year.

"Messy execution will get you a messy execution," Spook had warned in the academy.

As usual, he'd been right.

Now Bartlett and another contact were dead and the three informants had turned out to be one person, also dead. Hodge, the greenhorn, cooled the hot seat and the Colonel was fielding a backhand slap.

The Colonel saw no streetwise, predatory luster in Hodge's clear, blue eyes, just the vapid gaze of a bored statistician.

He won't make it, the Colonel thought, *but he'll probably outrank me in a year.*

Nobody had ever pulled in more product than Rico Toledo, though there had been some cost, some personal cost. The Colonel's marriage, for years exemplary in embassy circles, imploded. He had always been a reasonable man, but lately an unreasonable violence and an unreasonable lust had overtaken him.

Midlife crisis, he told himself.

But in the back of his mind the final report on Red Bartlett nagged at him and betrayed the monster that Red had become.

I knew him longer than I've known my son, he thought. *We had Thanksgiving dinner last year with his family.*

Rico tried not to think about how he'd spoiled the day by getting drunk before dinner, then he'd hurried out for a hot-sheet date with Rachel. And it had been nearly impossible for Red to get away from the Double-Vee for the day—the Gardeners didn't celebrate Thanksgiving, only their Sabbath, which started each Friday at sundown.

The Colonel thought perhaps he'd seen just one too many bodies, an opportunity that Costa Brava presented every morning to anyone who drove the streets. And in twenty years he had done a lot more than just drive the streets. Confederation was supposed to change all that—eliminate the death squads, distribute land and wealth more satisfactorily—but all it had accomplished was arrested development, and a few palms greased with a lot more money.

Recent reports of the plummeting birthrate had been received with relief, at first. Even Catholics agreed that overpopulation was a fundamental problem, so when it began to solve itself there was talk of a miracle, even in the evangelical President's palace. If there were no starving masses, there would be no need for revolution. But if there were no starving masses, who would cook, clean, kill and die for the rich?

Every miracle has its curse.

But in recent months some troubling figures had come across the Colonel's desk. Very few children had been born this year, fewer than the record few of the year before and, of course, the year before that. It was true. But other figures were also true: nearly fifty percent of these births were Down's syndrome, trisomy twenty-one. Rico had made himself familiar with terms like "mongolism," "trisomy" and "chromosome 21." With very few exceptions, these were births to Catholic families.

The Colonel had done his research. Down's syndrome used to be called mongolism. One form of Down's was a congenital condition related to the twenty-first chromosome. Genetic aberrations brought one thing to Rico Toledo's mind, and that was ViraVax.

The Colonel did not like being duped, especially by the likes of that sweaty-palm Casey. He did not want to be pulled out of the field and off this project before he had a chance to complete his own investigation.

"This ViraVax thing is the chance of a lifetime," he'd told his wife, Grace, when they were young and beginning the foreign service life. "It's embassy placement, a government corporation with profit sharing—we get the best of both worlds."

Rico had nurtured a monster, and now it threatened to swallow him whole.

The Colonel had cultivated a lot of rebel contacts through a number of aliases and gathered more viable product than any Agency operative in Central America. He thought it was time to call in some favors.

Hodge rearranged his desktop for the third time in ten minutes. He'd been briefed on Colonel Toledo and probably thought it

was dangerous to listen. The Colonel would have to straighten
him out, because if somebody didn't tell this maggot how things
really were, he wasn't going to be worth the toilet paper it would
take to keep him here.

"You told me you could imagine how it will be, but you
can't," the Colonel told Hodge. "You saw what they did to that
girl Sheffield was seeing in Quezaltenango, I hear . . . and what,
a few others? If you stay at this desk—*if* you stay one *week* I will
promise you that you'll know *your* limit. . . ."

The Colonel caught himself fisting the desktop, took a deep
breath and let it out with a slow whistle.

What's happening to me?

Hodge had scooted his chair back to get some running room.

A rabbit, the Colonel thought. *A goddamn chickenshit.*

Another slow, deep breath.

"Sorry, Major," the Colonel said, and tugged at his jacket. He
wouldn't have to wear his monkey suit for a few months, that
would be a relief. "I really don't want to see you get hurt."

"I appreciate that, sir."

"You're checking your watch, Hodge, how very polite. Well,
I won't make you listen to my story. Your briefings are set up
for your Sidekick, review them at your leisure. Call me anytime,
if you can find me. The desk is yours. The rest is product, and
you won't find *that* in the files."

13

WITH MARTE CHANG'S employment came her "eyes only" access to certain spurs on the ViraVax networks. A few of these spurs led to the webs, the outside world. If Shirley Good were to be believed, an entire satellite went to orbit for the exclusive benefit of ViraVax, and Marte Chang was lonely enough to take full advantage of it. Since she could not explore the beaches and bistros of Costa Brava, she threw herself into the geography of the web, the ViraVax files and her dreams.

The one person to whom she felt connected was Mariposa, on the Agency's burst line. Her social life on site was Shirley Good, known in her New Age days as "Phoenix Rising" before her conversion by the Children of Eden, God's Gardeners. Of the hundreds of people living at ViraVax, fewer than a dozen were normal females. For ViraVax, Shirley was extremely normal.

Shirley Good had been the records clerk for ViraVax since the opening of the Jaguar Mountains facility nearly twenty years ago. Marte guessed her age at forty-five, about the same as Casey's. Shirley was taller than Marte, who was taller than Casey, and her hair was a shock of red wool mushrooming to her shoulders. The top of her head was shaved clean to about three fingers above her ears. A rose tattoo curled over her right ear, its stem and buds trailing down the back of her neck.

Shirley bit her fingernails down to ragged nubs, which she'd tried to dress up with a little clear polish. Even that, for a Gardener, would require a serious meditation on vanity. Shirley's hands, like her face, reflected the death-like pallor of someone who had been out of the sun's light for a very long time.

Marte suffered a sudden, frightening vision of herself trapped, as Shirley had been trapped, by the heady magnitude of their projects and their isolation. Sunspot production was ahead of schedule, and Marte Chang wasn't the least bit sorry.

"Some people call Dr. Casey 'the Mountain,' " Shirley explained. "Since he won't come to anybody, everybody has to come to him."

Something's happening between those two, Marte thought.

It was the lift of Shirley's jaw at the end, her telltale pride. Marte found herself rooting for them, for whatever scrap of a relationship they salvaged out of their severity and their work. Marte had never sustained a sexual relationship beyond a weekend. No man had ever excited her as much as her work.

Marte Chang had been summoned with her idea, and ViraVax converted that idea to reality. Marte's was a new twist on solar technology, a viral process that would make her extremely rich.

Being rich isn't much good if I can't get out to spend it, she thought.

From the moment her chopper touched down on the lift pad, Marte Chang counted the thousands of moments to go in her contract. She was a viral engineer, not a spy. Marte Chang was beginning to think she wouldn't make it.

It's been the most productive month of my life, she reminded herself.

She still felt a chill in her belly, a chill that told her over and over, "Get out. Get out now." But Casey provided the only way out, and she was bound to her contract, which stated that failure to fulfill meant she would forfeit her profit share of any of her patents or developments. She told herself she was just being a baby.

Besides, she thought, *living in the U.S. isn't pretty either, these days.*

Thanks to the dedication of the ViraVax staff, Marte had full setup for production completed in less than two weeks. Her first installation of her Sunspots would empower ViraVax itself within a month, and they could anticipate freedom from the hydroelectric system by Easter. Marte would go ahead and let them believe that she wanted ViraVax to handle commercial production.

Marte had underestimated the enthusiasm of the missionaries and the Innocents alike. ViraVax had leased the rights already, and in two more months some Costa Bravan corporation would start commercial production.

Marte had tailored, then colonized, a very prolific, very sturdy virus. The excellent organic growth medium provided by Dajaj

Mishwe had trebled her experimental outputs. Once she had initiated her changes, the rest was growth and production, a lot of time for research, and snooping.

Marte coaxed the protein shell of the virus to take on silicon, at first, then certain metallic structures. Marte directed her mutation into a suitable architecture of capillaries and tubules, then killed and fixed the viral colony in position.

This task proved simple, since she grew the colony within a durable, nontoxic medium that hardened into interlocking amber hexagons. The annual solar yield of electricity from one acre of Sunspots had a projected worth on the U.S. market of a half million dollars.

Marte thanked the fates that she did not have to face Dajaj Mishwe once during the entire process. His preparation of her various media was brilliant, however twisted his mind, and she posted him a formal thank-you note on the lab's interior net. She thought that it was the Christian thing to do, though she was growing more disenchanted daily with the Christians around her.

She had witnessed several further incidents of sexual contact between the young male missionaries and the young female Innocents. She reported these incidents to Casey, in three cases documenting a positive ID of both parties. Via memo, Casey thanked her for her concern and reassured her that punishment would follow.

She never saw any of the perpetrators or their victims again, and presumed them transferred to another sector.

They'll just keep it up wherever they go, she thought. *They'll just keep getting moved around.*

She was vulnerable now, this she knew. She would have to be strong to keep from turning to someone for security, protection. Even Casey could look attractive if she were scared enough; that was something Mariposa had warned her about. Mariposa, who was so good with computers, seemed to know so much about confinement.

Marte saw very little of Casey during her first month, but the signs of his approval began appearing in her bank account within a week. Casey was strange, and strict, but his profit-sharing system and bonuses were generous beyond her imagination. All researchers received a monthly stipend from ViraVax, but anything that turned a profit for Casey turned a profit for the principals involved as well. A ten percent tithe was automatically deducted as a donation to the Children of Eden, per a clause in her original contract.

Marte realized that it was likely she would never want for money again, no matter how things turned out with the Agency. Now that her financial worries were gone, she was discovering her real wants.

She wanted what was forbidden.

"What *do* you want, girl?" Shirley asked her over lunch.

They sat at a table in one of the facility's teahouses, under some well-cultivated vines. Beside them, a fractal splashed electronic water over real rocks.

"I want walks in the jungle," Marte said, "sun on the beach, a lover who can't spell 'acetylcholine.' "

"Futures on your Sunspots swept the market today," Shirley told her. "The *Star* says, 'For the first time, scientists guarantee liberation from the oil barons.' You're hot property, baby. Just hang on. Stay here awhile, till the flash fades, then go out there and buy your beach, snag you a man."

Shirley repeated Casey's scenario for her: the energy giants would try to block production, they would be squelched by the Agency, then they would scramble to get aboard.

It was a very smooth choreography, and Marte realized that these partners had danced together before. The Agency's name rolled off Casey's lips all too easily for her comfort.

All of this buzzed through her mind as she shared a huge salad with Shirley Good.

"Y'know what I did before this?" Shirley asked.

"What?"

"Phone sex," Shirley whispered. Then she giggled. "It paid okay, and I didn't ever have to let them touch me."

Marte was stunned, then amused. She couldn't suppress either blush or giggle.

"But why . . . ?"

"That's what everybody asks." Shirley bit off a chunk of celery and crunched it unselfconsciously. "I'm agoraphobic. I've always looked for jobs that I could do indoors. Preferably at home, on the webs. That's why this job is perfect. I get all the outside world I need via nets, webs and sats."

"But, Shirley, what about . . . . you know, meeting someone. . . ."

"Falling in love? Having babies? Honey, I got raped at thirteen by the baddest man in town, and that was enough of that for me. These hands might be ugly, but they suit me just fine."

Marte felt her traitor skin blush again, and Shirley patted her shoulder.

"Don't feel bad, honey. I'm happy as can be in this job. This is the perfect place for me. You'll see, it might grow on you, too."

Marte Chang loved her work, too, but she was not in love with this place or its people. She was young enough at twenty-six to love bright lights and company, uncomplicated male company. The Children of Eden had put her through school, but she liked a drink now and then and she considered their observance of the Sabbath to be an obsession and an obstruction to responsible science.

Shutting down the entire lab for thirty-six hours a week is a major pain, she thought.

Casey went so far as to require the on-duty security squad to walk the perimeter every Saturday. He would not allow them to work inside his compound. Marte wondered what they were supposed to do if they found anything suspicious.

Marte had studied everything she could find related to Joshua Casey. She had accepted his invitation with hopes that ViraVax meant a step towards her own lab near some great university in some great city. She had arrived in Costa Brava by private carrier with an overnight bag and the clothes on her back, expecting to install the prototype of her system and get an occasional weekend on the beach—anything to get out of the snake pit that the United States had become. She got her chance and instant isolation at the same time.

Shirley taught her everything about coordinating incoming data files from the eleven satellite clinics that fronted for Casey's research—nursing homes, a couple of VA hospitals, prisons, a trauma victim center, a school for the retarded and one fully active Central American army. The school for the retarded had been a clandestine clinic under Casey's direction for two decades.

"They vaccinate the retarded students into becoming universal donors," Shirley explained. "When transplanted, their organs will never be rejected."

"You mean, it's an organ *farm*?"

Shirley's blue eyes widened. "Oh, no," she said, "it's not like *that*. It's just to demonstrate that this vaccine is extremely versatile and it doesn't harm humans. Did you think we went in there and *harvested* those organs?"

"Oh, no," Marte reassured her. "No, of course not. I'm just . . . unaccustomed to the idea of experimenting on human beings."

"It's not like that," Shirley insisted, "really, it's not. For one, they're kind of like vegetables themselves, you know? And they're none of them Christian souls. . . ."

"But they're *humans*, Shirley. . . ."

"Well," Shirley said, sitting up straighter, "you've been here long enough to see what we're doing. You've never seen *us* doing anything to people, have you?"

"No, but . . ."

"But what?"

Marte thought of the two dozen bunkers and outbuildings that made up the Level One compound. Of that two dozen, she had toured the four that made up the ViraVax labs and administrative sector, and one half of Level Five.

What's in those other levels, she wondered, *tractors?*

Marte laughed a little, nervous laugh. "Nothing. I guess I'm getting claustrophobic here. It's like living in a submarine, or on an Antarctic research station, except outside it's so beautiful."

"Working out helps," Shirley chuckled. Her hand went to her chest when she laughed, as though her small breasts would get out of control. "I use the gym a lot. Sometimes I'm the only one in there and it really helps me work off some of this stress. The missionaries like it, and they're on two-year contracts, too."

"Yeah," Marte said, "but it's always the same people I work with, eat with, breathe filtered air with. I'd give a month's pay right now for a weekend on one of those sunny beaches right over there."

She pointed to what she thought was west, towards the legendary Costa Bravan beaches that were only fifty klicks away.

"There are 'field trips,' as Dr. Casey calls them, for the occasional contractor, like you."

"Right. Same bunch of people, with our security escorts, no contact with anyone from the outside. . . ."

Shirley frowned, put a nail to her mouth and then pulled it away.

"Use the gym," she suggested. "Use the pool, use the counselor. That's what it's all here for. Pretend you're on a drug treatment program and the outside is your drug. You simply have to do without it. You knew that when you signed on."

"I'm sorry," Marte said. "I didn't realize that talking about it would get you depressed, too. You're right. The opportunity I have here with my work is unequaled in the world. I should be thankful for that."

"And to be at the heart of the Children of Eden," Shirley said. "Don't forget that."

"That's right," Marte said.

She gathered some artificial enthusiasm for Shirley's benefit, and smiled. "It's a privilege to be on the ground floor of a new order."

"That's a good one, Marte."

"What do you mean?"

"The ground floor of the Garden of Eden. . . ."

Shirley laughed, and it was an obvious attempt to put Marte at ease.

"My subconscious is quicker than my conscious," she said.

"You don't have to be a hermit, either," Shirley said. "Come to the gym in the morning, after readings."

Marte smiled, glad that someone here had feelings for something more than work. "Deal."

"At one time, there weren't *any* women here," Shirley offered. "Not even Innocents. You would think that would be an advantage for a single girl, but not this place."

"I thought you weren't interested."

"I've had my daydreams. Like you, everybody's so involved in their projects. Besides, Dr. Casey's rules are so strict—no fraternizing, all women in the lab must be on birth control, as if there were enough free time that you might need it."

Marte swallowed hard, then asked the hard question.

"Has there ever been a contamination situation?"

"No." Shirley laughed, but her expression hardened. "No, never." Her glance flicked to one of the ever-present security monitors in the back corner of the room, and she repeated, "Never."

"If there were a contamination, would you know about it?"

Shirley blushed all the way to the rim of her red hair.

"Probably . . . I don't know."

She picked up her tray and inclined her head towards the door.

"C'mon," Shirley said, "I'll show you some special tricks on that computer."

Shirley introduced Marte to some of the social features of Jaguar Mountains' computer system. With the proper set of codes, access to the outside world was unlimited. It was access *in* that was the problem. Shirley herself carried on an active correspondence, much of it frankly sexual.

"You just have to remember that everything coming in or going out is monitored," she said. "But if you want to visit with a real person in the outside world, with a human who doesn't know the first thing about viruses or Costa Brava . . . well, there are millions of them out there."

Marte showed herself to brighten a little.

"I used a couple of networks when I was in school," Marte said. "I wouldn't mind visiting with some of those people again."

"Well, it's not all that easy. You have to be sure they don't know who you are or where you are or what your work is."

Marte laughed. "You're kidding—isn't that what most people talk about? Themselves, their work, their community."

"We aren't most people," Shirley warned. "I just make up a person, a job and a place. Then for an hour a day I become that person. It's like . . . like being in a movie, or something. Try it. I bet it'll help."

14

HARRY TOLEDO JOCKIED the beat-up Lada taxicab across La Libertad's industrial zone towards his father's girlfriend's place. Heavy rain made the going slick across the metal-deck bridges. It was already dark, and the army was setting up the evening checkpoints. He had to be back at Casa Canadá before curfew. In Costa Brava, anybody on the streets after curfew was a target, and the shooting, pretty good. Each morning the bodies on the streets proved that point, though the lesson behind the point was never clear.

Harry had only driven a few times by himself on the back roads of Casa Canadá, and he had never driven at night. The one wiper smeared mud a little thinner on his side of the windshield, and he counted on rain gusts to clear it.

The evening traffic bore him along in an increasingly frantic pace. Some people, including Harry, had a long way to go to beat the curfew home. Besides, if driving took too long, Harry knew that his father would be passed out drunk and this ride to a showdown would be for nothing.

He had picked up a Maya family, hitchhiking to the bus depot. The two youngest children were *deficientes,* carried in backpacks by their parents. The two older children carried large carved crucifixes over their shoulders for the coming Holy Week ceremonies. Since dropping them off a few minutes ago, Harry felt very much alone. Now he had to think about his father.

Harry had been afraid of his father for as long as he could remember, but in the past two years the fear had congealed into terror. This weakness humiliated him, even though he kept the weakness and the humiliation well hidden. Now his anger overrode that fear, and he wanted to face down his father before he lost the edge.

"Someday you'll understand," he tells me, Harry thought. *Like I don't understand already that a home with him in it is more dangerous than the goddamn streets.*

The driver behind him hit the horn and nudged him. The light was red but there were no police, so it was merely a suggestion. Harry held his breath and dashed on through.

Less than a kilometer to go and the traffic didn't let up, not even in the stretch along Central America Park. Harry felt the first fingers of fear scratching at his anger.

Even if he kills me now, Harry reminded himself, *it's better than waiting for him to do it later.*

The Colonel had made it clear from the start that they couldn't hide from him. Today's visit was just a punctuation mark on an old message.

This morning the Colonel hadn't beaten anyone up, but he had punched out all of their kitchen cabinets and ripped a door off its hinges in his fury. Their divorce was nearly final, expedited by the embassy and an eager stateside lawyer. Divorces in Costa Brava were rare and far from easy.

I don't see why he was so pissed-off, Harry thought. *He's already moved in with Rachel.*

Rachel Lear, a receptionist at the embassy's Civilian Services desk, wasn't even ten years older than Harry. Rachel was easy to spot anywhere in a crowd with her red mane of hair, and Harry had spotted her a number of times, always with a different man.

Now the Colonel was on "extended leave" from the Agency and Harry could tell he was getting bored and restless. The Colonel drank a lot—anybody connected with the embassy seemed to do that—but he drank prodigiously when he was bored.

Boredom would frustrate his father, and Harry hoped that Rachel Lear knew what she was up against, living with his father when he was frustrated.

I guess she's got the frustration cure, Harry thought.

Harry wished he could cure his frustration of living so close to Sonja, who stayed so far out of reach.

She lives in that airplane, he thought. *That, or on the webs.*

The Colonel had found Harry as soon as he signed onto the information networks, and followed him no matter how often he changed his password. The message was always the same: "Someday;understand."

Harry didn't understand yet. He saw a counselor three times a week at University of Central America in the city. He spent his days on the university network, through his machine at Casa Canadá, accumulating as many credits as quickly as he could. Life was pleasant at Casa Canadá, and it was made more pleasant by his daily contact with Sonja Bartlett. But he could not hide at home, doing nothing, and wait for his father to destroy them again.

"What do you want to do with your life?" his counselor asked him yesterday.

"I want to erase every border from the map of the world," Harry had answered.

"Well, you're young," the counselor said, "you have plenty of time."

This morning, the Colonel had intercepted Harry on his way up the front steps of the university. At eight-thirty in the morning, in the middle of the sidewalk, the Colonel stood, unshaven, drunk and very loud.

"You listen to me!" he shouted, but then he didn't say anything. When Harry turned to go, the Colonel shouted again.

"You listen to *me*!"

Again, Harry waited. Again, his father said nothing. A knot of curious students lounged on the steps instead of going inside. A pair of Hacienda Police began to swagger down the sidewalk towards them.

"You're embarrassing me." Harry said.

He felt his cheeks blaze red when his father mimicked his words silently, then spat at his feet.

"Someday you'll understand," he slurred.

"You said that before."

"Your mom thinks I'm crazy," he said. "Well, I've had people trying to kill me all my life. That changes your perspective. That's a word you'd like, 'perspective.' I just don't want you to hate me."

Harry didn't answer.

It's too late, he thought.

Harry looked past his father to the heavy metal doors where some of the students had stalled on their way to class. A few of them glanced at Harry and his father, whispering. Harry didn't know anyone on campus except his counselor, Jesús, and César, one of the librarians. He'd learned to take his mind off his father by diving into the terminals. "Putting on the right blinders," his mother called it.

"Do you hate me?"

His father weaved a bit, his boilermaker breath too close for comfort.

"Yes."

It came out with a croak.

The Colonel blinked, pulled his shoulders back and sneered.

"Well, you go ahead and hate me. What you hate isn't even me. It's you. You'll understand that when you get older."

The Colonel's voice had risen again and more students gathered around to see what would happen. The *guardias* had recognized the Colonel and now they whispered between themselves at a distance.

"I think that the problem is, *you* hate *me*," Harry said.

"You get this from your counselor?"

"I've got to go," Harry said, and started up the steps.

"Got a pressing engagement?" his father sneered again. "Or turning your little yellow tail to run?"

Harry pulled free and turned his back again. His father gave him a shove between the shoulder blades that sent him on a tuck-and-roll across the stone steps. As Harry gathered his books and fought down the stinging leap of tears, César rushed out the security doors and hollered, "Hey, you! What's going on here?"

The Colonel simply flipped him the finger and walked away.

Harry had caught the late afternoon bus to the gate at Casa Canadá. When he got home he found his mother in the wreckage of their kitchen, sitting at the table, sobbing.

The sonofabitch did it again!

For Harry, it was as though he'd been asleep for the past few weeks. Now he woke up, and he woke up swinging. He wanted to ride his anger this time, ride it right down his father's throat. He jumped into the taxi and raced back to town, not caring for once whether curfew caught him in the streets.

Harry was sweating heavily when he knocked at his father's girlfriend's gate in Zone Three. A wall of cinder blocks protected Rachel's little house, but it was too close to the door so Harry stood in the street. Rachel's was an inelegant door in an inelegant neighborhood.

A heavy mist laced with charcoal clung to him outside and a rivulet of sweat traced a shudder down the back of his shirt. Harry knocked again, louder, and Rachel opened it. Behind her, the opening theme of *Jaguar* blared from the TV. Somewhere further back, his father shouted "Shut up!" at a yapping dog.

"Come in," she said.

Her smile, though timid, seemed genuine. Her small, round face was pale and her blue eyes framed in dark circles. Her nipples were a distraction against the thin yellow fabric of her low-slung blouse.

"No, thanks," Harry said.

Harry's throat was tight and his message came out in a rush.

"Tell Colonel Toledo I want to see him outside."

"He's not a colonel anymore."

"Tell him his son wants to see him outside."

Harry turned from the doorway and walked to the taxi parked in a slew of garbage. He felt safer with more room and some darkness to run to.

Colonel Toledo filled the doorway and didn't say a word. He wore a fatigue T-shirt with a tear just below the neckline. His gray eyes drilled that famous cold stare into Harry's. The Colonel was most deadly when he was quiet, a lesson Harry had learned young. The glare from the living room light accentuated the jagged scissors scar that Harry's mother had carved into Harry's father's neck that night nearly two months back. Harry took a deep breath.

"Don't try to look us up anymore," Harry said. "You scare Mom so bad she cries for days. It would be better for everybody if you didn't come over."

This was the most Harry remembered saying to his father on a single occasion in years. The last of it came out in a rush because he was trembling so bad that he felt his voice tightening up, ready to crack.

Colonel Toledo shut the girlfriend's door and stepped outside into the yard.

"Who's going to stop me?"

This was the question Harry knew he would ask. Harry's heart beat so hard he could barely catch his breath.

His father's fists scrunched down in their pants pockets, sagging the cuffs around the tops of his bare feet. Harry had seen the lightning-quickness of those feet when his father took him to the base for workouts.

The Colonel's shoulders hunched against the post-rain mist in the slouch of the army boxing champ, ex-totterer of nations, ex-husband, spoiler. He was drunk again, and unshaven, waiting.

There was only one thing Harry could tell him.

"I will."

The Colonel's right shoulder leaned towards him and Harry expected the snake's head of its fist to snap out and sting him right to sleep. He expected the usual beating, but this time he meant to give some of it back before he saw stars.

Harry's father looked him up and down, then cleared his throat and spat.

"Right, then," his father said, and pursed his lips that way that always meant trouble. "All right."

The Colonel stared Harry straight in the eye for a moment, two moments. Those were the eyes that looked back at Harry from the mirror each morning. His father's face had an alcohol bloat, a scraggle of beard, and his hair was thinning. Still, their resemblance was stunning.

"Curfew?" his father asked.

"I'll make it."

Colonel Toledo then turned to his girlfriend's door. He fumbled the latch twice before it opened, lit up a yellow rectangle of street, then he slammed the door behind him without a look back.

Harry breathed so fast that he got dizzy. He listened at the door, but no one moved inside. Their television chattered in the background. The tremble in Harry's body quit when his hands got a grip on the wheel. He raced the old cab the whole way across town, zigzagged back streets to avoid roadblocks and floored it when he hit the highway. The mist thinned out to nothing and by the time he got home he saw stars.

15

DAJAJ MISHWE WASHED Joshua Casey's feet carefully in the large ceramic bowl and toweled them dry. This was a time of daily humility and reflection for all of the Children of Eden, a time when Mishwe felt closest to God. Still, he wished that Casey would do something about the suppurating ingrown nail on his left great toe. It distracted Mishwe from his meditations and further reminded him of the societal pus that he was committed to excising from the world.

Mishwe hung up the small white towel and sat at his own low stool. He removed his shoes in the customary silence and accepted the cursory foot-washing that passed for Casey's ritual. The son of the Master was not a patient man, not a holy man, but he was instrumental in the rightful restoration of the Garden of Eden.

"Amen," Casey muttered.

He placed both towels into the laundry as Mishwe emptied the bowl and washed it out. This, too, was a meditation for him.

"I'm worried about Toledo," Casey said.

"I'd put a hunt on him," Mishwe said.

Casey laughed as he pulled on his smelly black socks.

"You are so eager, my friend," Casey said. "This one got to you, did he?"

Dajaj Mishwe bristled, not at the mention of the unmentionable Colonel, but at being called "friend" by a blasphemy of a powermonger like Joshua Casey.

Beware the kiss, Mishwe warned himself.

"It's not a 'he,' it's an 'it,' " Mishwe said.

"How unkind."

Casey massaged his scalp with his thumb and forefinger.

"You grace your primates with gender, don't you?" he asked.

101

When Mishwe didn't answer, Casey affected a shrug.

"Call Toledo whatever you want," he conceded, "but he presents us with a problem that his death would only complicate."

Mishwe disagreed, but he did not argue. He did not want to give his strongest reasons for the death of Colonel Toledo. The lives of Adam and Eve, their reinstatement in the Garden of Eden, depended on a close control of Colonel Toledo. His death could be made very useful.

"What is this problem that a good death cannot solve?"

"He's well connected to us," Casey warned, "as was Red Bartlett. You have set us into a trap, there. If Toledo dies, a second arrow on an Agency map points here. I will not be able to keep them off. Besides," Casey added, "better the evil we know than a new one."

Mishwe was not really interested. What interested him most was the stimulating daydream of pushing all of Colonel Toledo's buttons and launching him to the breaking point. It had not worked with Red Bartlett, so he'd resorted to the Meltdown solution. But, thanks to Mishwe's foresight years ago, Colonel Toledo was infinitely more susceptible to rage.

"The Agency's dropping it," Casey said. He tugged on his favorite white tennis shoes and laced them up. "They suspended Toledo and sent him out of sight. His replacement shows no signs of interest in anything outside the embassy compound. It's quiet, things are in our favor. I won't tolerate any loss of this advantage."

Mishwe grunted his acknowledgment. He dwelt on the rage-and-aggression unit, one of several that he had added to Toledo's little cocktail. It was a twist on the nausea bug he'd crafted years back—the "vomit virus"—disabling, but hard to trigger on demand. Once triggered, it produced beaucoup casualties.

Very messy, Mishwe thought. *Very messy, indeed.*

Casey was enamored of viral solutions. Mishwe was a virologist but he was also a practical man. He believed that many problems responded best to some old-fashioned solutions.

"Another problem," Mishwe announced. "The Bartlett woman."

"She's wiped," Casey said. "Not a problem."

"She's not wiped, she's conditioned," Mishwe said. "Conditioning breaks down, and we can't afford—"

"Do you want me to throw you a bone?" Casey snapped.

He jabbed his forefinger into Mishwe's chest.

"You want somebody to kill and you won't leave it alone until you get one, is that right?"

Mishwe pushed the finger away. He did not blink.

"You know I'm right," Mishwe said. "Just like I was right that the Toledo woman would take her kid out there. We have both kids in reach, no feathers ruffled. That's an advantage that we don't want to lose."

"So, if the Bartlett woman is killed, they'll move the daughter back to the States. The daughter's family will send for her and the Toledo woman will lose her last tie here and she'll pull up stakes. . . ."

"They're too smart for that," Mishwe said. "Nobody who watches the webworks would go back to the States right now. There are only two sides, in Costa Brava, and our side owns the President and his Cabinet. Besides," he added, "she and Toledo are the only outsiders to leave here alive. We need to tidy up."

Mishwe had already begun his own edge-trimming, but he chose to continue to keep quiet about it.

"Do you see any alternatives other than those you have suggested?" Casey asked.

Mishwe paused, accepted a deep, cleansing breath.

"Yes," he said. "Bring the children here, to Level Five."

"That kind of thing gets messy. It has a way of getting out."

"Nothing gets out of Level Five," Mishwe said.

"You get out," Casey snapped. "Bartlett got out."

"Bartlett wasn't supposed to be there in the first place," Mishwe hissed. "You assured me. . . ."

Casey waved the argument moot. He sat at his desk and addressed his console.

"Intercom, Shirley."

"Connecting," it replied.

A moment later Shirley was on the line.

"Sir?"

"Get Mishwe all that we have on the Toledos," he ordered, "particularly any upcoming appointments we've intercepted. He's vacationing somewhere—let's make sure it's not in our backyard."

"Yes, sir."

"The Bartlett woman, too," he added.

"Their network accesses, too?" she asked. "I could route all traceable entries directly into his console."

Mishwe nodded his approval.

"Fine," Casey said. "Thank you—"

"One other thing, sir," she interrupted.

"Yes?"

"Marte Chang. I think we should have a talk about her."

Casey scratched his head, pursed his lips, and Mishwe caught the hint of a flush rise out of Casey's collar.

Well, well, he thought. *The boss is human, after all.*

Mishwe knew as well as everyone else at ViraVax that Joshua Casey and Shirley Good met for a private lunch and hydrotherapy twenty-one days out of every month. It was not the kind of thing one called to the boss's attention, nor was it the kind of thing one ignored.

"Very well," Casey said, "we can talk at lunch."

"I suggest we talk sooner," she said. "Chang's on the webs with an agent of the Catholic underground, and somehow she's accessed some Level Five logs. She asked Files for records on all lab fires, and recharge schedules for all fire suppressors. She might be on to Meltdown."

Good move, Mishwe thought, with genuine respect.

Mishwe's labs, both at Level Five and topside, used more fire-suppressant than the entire facility. Still, anyone inoculated with Meltdown presented serious problems during routine lab studies. A simple blood draw could be spectacular. Mishwe had infected many of his coworkers as part of his personal fail-safe measures. He'd caught Red Bartlett entering Level Five by his own secret tunnel. Red Bartlett hadn't had time to be an experiment, he was a simple elimination.

"I see," Casey said. His complexion went from blush to white. "My office, ten minutes. Off, now."

The line went dead. Casey turned to Mishwe and his big voice got bigger.

"Nothing fancy here," he said, "like your trick in La Libertad with those communion wafers. Whatever you do, see to it that the idolator guerrillas get the credit."

"My pleasure," Mishwe said, exiting with a bow, and he meant it.

16

COLONEL TOLEDO RECEIVED his divorce judgment the morning the stitches in his fists came out. His hands were stiff and tender from their fury against Grace's cabinets, so his fingers fumbled at the wire seal on the messenger's packet. Inside, Rico found the validation paper and a personal note in Grace's calligraphic hand:

> " . . . really loving someone" (*the yearning brushed the edge of agony*) "means you are willing to admit the person you love is not what you first fell in love with, not the image you first had; and you must be able to like them still for being as close to that image as they are, and avoid disliking them for being so far away."   —Samuel R. Delany, "The Star Pit."
> I can't avoid disliking you anymore.—G.

Rico crumpled it, smashed it, tossed it out the open window and into the rest of the garbage strewn in the street. He made a quick call, two quick sugared rums, and paced off the dingy cubicle of his life.

Twenty minutes later Rachel picked him up in her black Flicker and settled a bottle of Wild Turkey between his thighs.

"This looks like a ticket to trouble," he said.

"Then you're looking at it all wrong, as usual," she snapped.

It was the same thing she said before, after she'd called him by somebody else's name. Considering they were making love at the time, he hadn't yet found a right way to look at it. She white-knuckled the handgrips and did the smoky-tire all the way home. Then she handed him the pouch with the official DIA seal.

"Two in one day," Rico muttered, "a goddamn big shot."

Inside he found his official suspension on Defense Intelligence Agency letterhead, clipped to his severance paycheck. That, in itself, was a clear message that he was through. Solaris's meticulous left-handed signature smudged in the middle of the "o." The smudge looked genuine but that didn't mean squat. Something as simple as a smudge gave a document legitimacy. A smudge said, "This is personal. See, I touched it myself."

ComBase, the DIA brain, employed software that altered each electronic signature of every tight-ass bureaucrat with combinations of over a hundred smudges, squiggles, skips and runs. That permitted a volume business with a personal touch. It had been Rico's graduation project at the academy, so the Agency made millions and he got a commendation.

He tore the bank draft loose from the notice and stuffed it into his back pocket. For the second time in as many hours Rico crumpled a fistful of paperwork into a ball, smashed it flat with his fist and sailed it out the window.

After Rachel's Wild Turkey came hard sex in the bedroom, more sugared rums. With the rum came rage, remorse and a wild Flicker ride to the airport. The two of them stumbled aboard a flight to somewhere before Rico passed out.

Ex-Colonel Rico Toledo woke up tangled in Rachel's arms and legs, their tropical sweat prickling at him where they pulled apart. A muggy heat smothered everything but the familiar aroma of their sex. White sheets contrasted their skins—his, dark and brush-scratched; hers, schoolgirl pale. He sat up against the headboard, another hangover hammering his temples.

The Yucatán dawn made a white glow of his pants where he'd slung them across a chair at the bedside. Rico had stitched a ring into the right-hand pocket of those pants for safekeeping. Such a treasure should not be flashed among men of the children of the large, wormy bellies. Even with his connections, the stone took more of his severance pay than the IRS. Only Rico knew how much went into *that*. He liked the feel of it when he slipped on his pants. Its cool gold never warmed up.

The Agency left him enough to scrape by on for six months, if he stayed in Mexico.

A year, in the States.

But then he would be in the States and that was no picnic right now. He had set out to prove something by flying to the heart of the Yucatán. After at least two days of nonstop drinking, it was time he found out what.

Rachel Lear was half his age, with red hair and freckles the Latins called *pecas*. She had a prodigious thirst for men, and that remained more of a problem between them than their ages.

Unlike the pinch-nosed embassy crowd, the *campesinos* understood that it was not an unnatural thing for a man to love a younger woman. Many *campesinos* had been cut by their women, as well, and all of them drank when the bottle passed around. Colonel Toledo, the chameleon, had held a role so long that he had become like an insect in amber.

Rico marveled over his turn of luck as he sat naked in the lounge chair. He watched Rachel sprawl facedown to fill his hollow in the bed, her right hand tucked under her cheek, her right leg cocked to her waist. A tuft of red hair reached between her legs for the sky.

The Yucatán was truly a place of magic, a place of ripples in the drapery of time. This was Latin America, but not a war zone. Not even a war country. Rico had fled here twice before. In 1998 he was forgetting a war. In 2010 he brought Harry and Grace to see the heart of the Maya empire, and to avoid some ugly but necessary steps that the Agency was taking all over Costa Brava in his absence. Grace had got histoplasmosis from exploring a Maya cave and Rico had spent most of that vacation in a hospital, but, like it or not, it made an excellent alibi when he returned to Costa Brava, and to the political fallout.

Now Rico tried to forget Grace, and that wasn't working. He and Rachel had argued all night. It started . . . well, he pushed it out of mind. That would not discourage him now from enjoying the dawn of the day that everything would change.

A bone-white sunlight seared anything that was not stone, adding counterpoint to his headache. Rico pulled on his rumpled clothes and turned the window fan on high. The bearings howled and ragged blades shrieked against the frame. Not much of a breeze kicked up, and Rachel didn't stir.

Rachel spoke Spanish, but she was shy because she'd learned it in school and most of the embassy staff enveloped themselves in English. She refused to speak it except between them, so Rico did most of the talking. She attracted people, men and women, so Rico talked a lot, but talking came pretty natural to Rico, in either language.

It's sure a plus when you're outspooking spooks, he thought.

Rico Toledo, on the retirement track with the Defense Intelligence Agency, made a helluva tour guide.

Didn't talk much at home.

Bob or Bernice, friends of Rachel's from the beachside bar, flushed the toilet across the hall. They were Rachel's age and on their spring break from college. Neither of them spoke Spanish and they didn't have much time left. Consular flunkies and federal reps checked their registry at the guesthouse twice a day. Lots of good Americans jumped in the last few days, they'd learned that much. They were Rachel's friends and pretty boring, but Rico had tried to deliver them some culture, anyway.

Rico gulped down the warm, flat beer he'd been saving, then poured himself a dark rum. He added sugar and lemon, then carried it to the veranda to sip with the parrot, who asked him his name over and over and over. By the time Rico finished his drink he was restless again and needed to move.

"Get up," he said to Rachel. "Your friends are up and the car's here."

"Don't order me around."

She spoke into her pillow and he could barely understand her.

"Try this, okay? Okay?" she said. "Just tell me that the car's here."

He didn't answer.

"Try it."

Rico poured himself another Flor de Caña, mixed in the sugar and the lemon slowly, then set the spoon on the glass tabletop.

"Okay, okay," she said.

She sat up cross-legged on the bed, her red blaze of pubic hair a challenge for his attention.

"If you'd said, 'Rachel, the car's here and your friends are up,' I could've—"

"Can it," Rico said.

He tossed back his sweet, dark rum and left for a coffee with their driver.

Rico and Rachel argued mostly in Spanish. They affected a conversational tone, so her friends wouldn't catch on. Of course, their driver knew everything and became more nervous by the kilometer.

Their driver, Carlos, didn't speak English. His left arm had been withered by polio and his car overheated crossing the tiny range of sierras between Mérida and Uxmal. He topped off the radiator with water from a wine bottle. Carlos was a smooth, cautious driver.

When the argument with Rachel got more personal than Carlos could bear, he interrupted with a passionate assessment of the

American football playoffs. At one point, with all but Carlos and Rico sleeping, a huge buzzard rose from the shoulder of the road and gyred once around the car, its black eye fixed on Rico the whole time. Rachel slept tucked up against him. Her long red hair whipped their faces in the wind.

Carlos launched into the old tale about the Soothsayer's Temple and the sacrificial ball court.

"The man was birthed from a feathered serpent's egg," he said, "and became a man in one night. In one night he built the Pyramid of the Magician, Temple of the Sorcerer. You will see, it is a night's work."

Rico didn't tell Carlos that he'd been here twice before, that he had lived with the Maya years ago and ghosted most of the jungles of the region. Instead, Rico kept him talking.

"And the sacrifice of the ball court?" Rico asked.

Rico could see Carlos was let down by this question, like he'd expected something more from Rico. Even the casual tourist has heard of the sacrificial ball game of the Mayas. Rico was flattered that Carlos expected better of him.

Carlos shrugged.

"Two teams, with captains. They wear equipment like your football, lots of pads. They try to slap a hard rubber ball through a stone hoop sideways on the wall. The winning team gets to run through the gallery, collecting jewelry and favors from the nobles. If the weather has been bad for crops, the winning captain has the honor of being killed. To save his people."

Carlos didn't seem interested in elaborating and recited this lecture in a bored monotone.

"How did they do it?"

A sigh, a *thump* of the withered limb against the car door.

"Cut throat, cut off head, open chest and take out heart," Carlos said.

He added the appropriate gestures.

"Efficient," Rico admitted.

Carlos shrugged.

"The ball court is nothing," he said. "The Magician's Temple, that is very special." Carlos repeated, with a nod, "Very special."

"What makes it special?"

"The place, the earth that it is on. Its position in that place. The centuries. You will see." Carlos nodded his head at Rachel. "It will be good for you, the temple. You will see."

Then he stopped the station wagon on the shoulder to add his last jug of water to the radiator. The only mountain pass that Carlos had driven was this pitiful saddle, just a hundred meters high at the summit. The only other breaks in the terrain for two hundred klicks were temples.

Carlos explained how sunset and moonrise faced off on the diagonal at the top of the Wizard's Temple, making the inner chambers into alternating geometrics of silver and gold, shadow and light. The staircase casts an undulating serpent of shadow against the walls. This happens once a year, and this is the night.

" . . . and you stand inside, at the top, and let the shadows divide you. Then good and bad will leave your body: good to the light and bad to the shadow. You walk out with your luck for the rest of your life."

His glance shifted from the road to Rico's eyes, back again. Then back.

"Who told you this?" Rico asked. "A teacher?"

"No, no teacher. Uncle. He was a bad one, my friend, and he came back cured of the women and *mezcal*."

"Do you think I can be cured?"

This was the first time Rico spoke of the argument, of his relationship with the young woman. It felt possible in Spanish.

Carlos softened his voice almost to a whisper.

"There is no cure for love, friend," he said, but the word he used for "cure" was "salvation." He rattled his bent left arm against his door and shrugged a twisted fist skyward. "If my uncle is right, if there are these devils, then I will walk away from them tonight."

Rico had no idea at the time that "tonight" meant "midnight" and "I" meant "we."

They drove awhile in the relative silence of the road and the countryside.

Rico felt Rachel's breathing shift. Now she stretched, and looked around, and Carlos aimed his attention straight ahead. Rachel's eyes shone with an ice-light: cold, blue and clear. At dawn, driving the scrub jungle through heavy mist, he noticed her eyes had been a lush, snakeskin green.

By the time the five of them got to Uxmal their eyes were tired from afternoon sun off the hood. Everything seemed hazed in light, a fine white wash. Carlos preferred to wait with his car in a patch of shade, so they cleared the guard gate without him and walked to the foot of the Temple of the Magician. A busload of American college students climbed the steep face in a gusting wind, all shouting to one another in rude, idiomatic English.

To the left hunched a lone Jaguar statue, an altar. Several of the young people gathered around this one. Rico explained the Jaguar and fertility to Rachel and their friends, the Agency's briefing version but a good one. From somewhere on the breeze came a whiff of tortillas hissing over charcoal.

A fat American girl about Rachel's age jumped onto the statue, clasping its head in her dimpled thighs. Another girl shrieked, then turned to the rest and shouted, "Tim, Brian . . . Shelley sat on its face! You guys, it was *so* funny! She sat on his *face!*"

"Must've been too big to get her mouth around it," one boy commented, and they all laughed.

Rachel's friend Bob reached for an empty Coke bottle that leaned against the Jaguar's shoulder, but a little dark-eyed boy snatched it up first.

Rico pulled them away in disgust, sorry that he'd been seen speaking English at all. He and Rachel wandered the stones under a reddening sun and climbed the Wizard's Temple just before sunset. Everyone else came down early, afraid of the treacherous footholds and the rising shadows.

Shadows clarified the open spaces between the sacrificial ball court and the scrub jungle skirting the compound. A few stragglers walked the ball court below. Every word they spoke rang true to Rico four hundred meters away. Every grunt and cry of the ball players must have been heard by all. It was a ceremonial game, a great prayer to cheer on the restoration of happiness and plenty.

Rico toyed with the ring in his right pants pocket. Marrying Rachel would be respectable, and not at all what anyone would expect.

Especially Grace, he thought.

Another buzzard circled twice, then trailed out of sight somewhere towards Costa Brava. The scrub jungle around the temples reminded him of his first meeting with Red Bartlett, inside the border of what had once been Guatemala, and, before that, Belize, British Honduras, the Mosquito Coast. The young Red came down to please his wife and to hone his broken Spanish. Like Rico, he had stayed, seduced by the ultimate opiate of doing what he loved. That was a lifetime ago.

Bartlett's lifetime.

Rachel and the other couple waited on the veranda of the temple, but Rico stood inside, watching them and shooting pictures through the archway.

"What's the matter?" Rachel asked with a childlike shrug. "Can you see through my dress?"

Rico had been staring from the shadows. She stood in the doorway of the temple, her body backlit by sunset and a glorious rising moon that just fit its shoulders into the frame of the entrance around her. A sharpness in the setting of the ring in his pocket bit at an infected hangnail on his finger.

"Nothing's the matter," he said, "just daydreaming. Yes, I can see through your dress."

They stood inside a stone doorway atop the Sorcerer's Pyramid, a doorway that framed tonight's moonrise over sunset perfectly. This room had been the Magician's personal quarters. Bats chittered from the beam holes. Outside, crickets and cicadas quieted with the rising of the moon. When it came time to give her the ring, Rico didn't know why he asked her what he did.

"I thought we were going to drop it," she said. Those soft lips thinned into a hard gray line. Her freckles stood out in the rising moonlight, distinct in a dead sort of way, like bruised scales.

"I can't drop it."

"What do you need to know for, anyway?"

"Because you don't want to tell me."

Rico's heart was slamming along pretty fast, and he had the shakes a little bit. Hunting used to make him feel that way. Slipping around in a war at night made him feel that way.

The shadow of the hooked arm of their driver snaked across the temple wall behind Rico like a great plumed serpent, encircling Rachel's head and shoulders. It was all an illusion of shadow, but in an eyeblink it boosted Rico's heartbeat even more.

"We must go now," Carlos announced. "They are locking up, there will be trouble and a fine."

Rico thanked him. Rachel took Rico's hand and they called the others. When the going got rough, Rachel picked her way ahead of him. He got two great shots of her silhouette against the moonlit stones. Her pale dress fanned out like wings in the breeze, the red splash of her hair the only real color left against the gray.

They met Carlos on the path, and two muttering guards locked the gates behind them.

"Do you know how you're going to get back in?" Rico asked him.

"Yes," he said. "What about the others?"

"I haven't asked them. Everyone is hungry and thirsty, no? Let's go to the mission that we passed. After dinner I will ask."

"For this, for the rest of the night, you are the guests of me and my car."

Rico thanked him, as though he had a choice, but courtesy demanded it.

"There are snakes," Carlos warned. *"Serpientes."*

He repeated the word for Rachel's sake, but to her credit she didn't flinch.

"There are *cenotes,* wells. They drop out from under you in this earth here. It falls in sometimes and swallows you up."

"When was the last time?"

Carlos shrugged. "I don't know. People just say."

Village women glided in with the unsubtle dusk. Their arms resembled great wings, draped as they were with embroidery. Green- and blue-bordered sashes trailed them like fragile tail feathers. They held the dresses to Rachel and smoothed them out, sweeping her blaze of hair where they wanted it for effect in the dim light, *just so.* Their eyes reflected coffee and candlelight.

Rachel bought a white dress, a pretty one that immediately came unstitched, but it was that warm, happy time of evening just as the mosquitoes come out.

They downed a few beers at the mission bar, then dinner. Carlos stuck to Diet Coke and cigarettes that he snapped out of the pack to his lips in a graceful, one-handed flick. The others liked the idea, Rico knew they would.

Then Bob told them about the duct tape in his bag.

"For around the doors in the hotel in case there's a fire," he said. "But we could make a ball out of it and play on the court. That would be a trip."

Rachel and Bernice laughed and toasted, "Yeah, let's do it!"

They had two hours to kill. Carlos paced it off outside.

When Rico stepped outside for air, Carlos showed him the path. A power line strung out from the mission in a straight line to the temple grounds, for the tourist shop. Scrub brush came chest-high to Rico and wasn't hard going except for the bugs.

Chiggers in the grass bit them up around the ankles. They were just drunk enough and the moon bright enough that they made it, still a little tipsy, sweating under the ivory disc of a moon. Bob's duct-tape ball was a silver blur against the stones of the ball-court wall.

"Remember," Bernice called out from some shadow to Rico's right, "winning captain gets sacrificed."

"Only on special occasions," Rachel said.

She let go Rico's hand and slapped the makeshift ball into the wall. It skidded, sparkling up along the stones in a long, smooth arc.

"You have to be quiet down there," Carlos hissed. "The guards will hear."

Rachel tugged Rico's sleeve.

"Where are you going? Don't you want to play?"

"Yeah," he said. "But I want to see the moon now from the top. Then I'll come down and play."

"You won't," she said. "You always say you will, but you won't."

The ringstone in his pocket irritated his right thigh with every step up the steep stairway of the temple. It seemed to grow heavier, colder.

"Play ball!" Bob said in a clear whisper.

Rico turned to watch Rachel run off to the game. He topped the temple stairs, conscious of the beer numbing his feet, toying with his balance. At the top, Carlos faced away from him, standing across a diagonal line of stone inlaid across the floor.

The doorsill at the tips of Rico's feet dropped away down the rough stone face to the ball-court plaza. Now the moon polished the face of the stonework and lit up the countryside. All around them birdsongs started up, sleepy and confused at the light. The scent of allspice and bougainvillaea hung in the humid stillness of the night.

The moon sighted down the diagonal between Rico's feet. He did not feel a particular pull towards either side.

Bob scored below, his duct-tape ball *thwocketing* through the ancient stone goal. They were all excited and a little bit drunk yet, so it wasn't surprising that Rachel called him by the wrong name. It was one that Rico had heard her use by mistake instead of his own.

"*Bob,*" she corrected herself, "I'm sorry. I meant 'Yeah, *Bob,* nice shot!'"

Suddenly Rico stood awash in light. The shadow had swept aside while he was distracted, and now he heard other voices down below, speaking abrupt and agitated Spanish. Behind him, Carlos sighed and shuffled forward. He patted Rico's back with his good arm.

"We'd better go down," Carlos said. "Now we will all be fined. There is trouble. I hope you and your friends have money."

Carlos flexed his left arm a couple of times before they started down.

"The arm," Rico asked him, "will it work?"

Carlos shrugged in his way, intent on the footing. The moonlight's angle dazzled them on their climb down, the way it reflected so brightly off the stone.

"Perhaps with exercise," Carlos said.

When they were nearly down and the four guards approached with the others, Carlos asked, "And your woman? The girl?"

"It is lost," he said. "Perhaps another time."

The guards might have settled for a private sum and the whole matter could have been dropped right there. The chief of the guards delicately insisted that he and his men had standards. Bob indelicately shoved a wad of money under his nose before Rico could intervene. It became a long night.

The next morning in the city Rico sold his plane ticket and paid off the fine against Carlos and the station wagon.

Carlos drove Rachel and the others to the airport while Rico sold his ring to a thin, unhappy-looking jeweler above the courthouse. It came to quite a pile of pesos. By the time Carlos pulled in with his radiator steaming Rico had already moved into the spare room, the small one out on the porch with all the light.

Solaris walked in a week later, claiming a personal call. The remarkable albino left behind everything there was to know about Red Bartlett, or anyone who showed interest in Red Bartlett. Solaris implied that Rico could be back in the saddle soon. Meanwhile, they both had some whispers to drop and personal markers to call in, and it would start back in Costa Brava with a party at the embassy. Solaris even bought him a suit, a white one like the old boys wore in Guatemala, when there had been a Guatemala.

Rico was unofficially employed. He sweetened a rum to celebrate.

17

LA LIBERTAD OOZED like a great brown sore from the crusty foothills of the Jaguar Mountains to the sea. Sonja banked *Mariposa* around as gently as she could to give Harry an all-points view. Harry was getting better about flying, but he was still far from comfortable.

Industry met the sea at La Libertad, fouling the lucrative bathing beaches and the mandatory air alike with its thick, brown scum. Pollution was the Satan that President García had sworn to smite when the Children of Eden won him his office.

Fouled air framed the elegant, emerald islands of plenty in a sea of despair. The private grounds of the haciendas of the wealthy had long ago sucked the surrounding beauty dry.

No wonder the Gardeners are winning over the rich, Sonja thought. *Greening the earth is noble. Feeding the poor is a threat.*

The Gardeners promised the poor more food. While there was no more food, there were fewer people, so it was beginning to work out much the same.

Birthrate down to zero in some neighborhoods, she thought. *But never a word on the news—the* Gardener *news.*

Two large buildings that were not private stood out from the rest: the National Palace, home of President García; and the United States Embassy. Sonja's mother would be attending a reception at the embassy this afternoon and that made Sonja nervous. The reception would end after curfew, and her mother would have to spend the night.

I don't know what's worse, she thought. *Curfew roadblocks or drunk politicians.*

In the past couple of years she'd had a few bad experiences with the drunk politicians, their backhand brushes against a breast, a

117

bump against her butt. Sonja thought she'd take her chances with the roadblocks.

The palatial and embassy compounds were made more green, more beautiful, by the scabby contrast of the surrounding poverty that they fed upon.

Sonja watched the guns of the outdated Phalanx system on the embassy rooftop tracking her little biplane. The Phalanx was outdated, but blow-by alone would disintegrate her Student Prince. If she continued her course for a few more moments, a red flare would warn her off. If she did not change course within thirty seconds of the flare, she and Harry and her little biplane would be confetti.

Sonja throttled up and banked towards the Park of Justice and Mercy, and as they lost altitude she heard clearly the horns of morning traffic blare over Harry's groan and the clatter of her engine.

La Libertad was not a peaceful city, even from the air.

A Holy Week procession intersected a political march, and between icons Sonja could read signs like: "Alphabets not Bullets," "Beans and Liberty," "Arrest the Death Merchants." She wasn't quite low enough to recognize faces. Sonja was sure that both she and Harry knew some of the demonstrators. Students all over Costa Brava chose this spring vacation to march the streets with their signs and masks.

Three truckloads of soldiers positioned themselves ahead of the marchers and to either side. One soldier pointed up at Sonja's plane, and another spoke into his Sidekick. A Mongoose vertical takeoff jump jet had been hovering near the crowd; now it turned on axis and rose to Sonja's altitude. She changed course again, heading back home via the long loop up the valley.

"What's going on?" Harry asked, pointing towards the crowd.

His voice sounded distant over the FM headset, though he was only an arm's reach in front of her.

"Peace and Freedom Party march," she said. "Mostly high school kids. Death squads executed three teachers yesterday."

"I didn't hear about that."

It wasn't in the papers, Sonja thought.

She had read it on her console, one in a string of mysterious messages that appeared under the signature "Mariposa."

What do they want from me? she wondered.

The Peace and Freedom Party was Costa Brava's legal arm of the guerrilla underground, and they had to know that she was watched constantly. Anyone with an aircraft, even an old biplane, was monitored. Her flight log could be faked, but the rationed gasoline could not. Her hours of flight per liter of gas had to match her logbook entries precisely, or the García goons would simply cut out her gas card. Worse yet, they could impound her plane and shoot her.

Of course, I could just use gas from the car, she thought. *That's the beauty of an old machine. But it's a hassle.*

And they would catch her, anyway. There were precious few airplanes in Costa Brava that did not belong to the young officer corps, and the last Student Prince in Latin America was particularly visible.

Harry pointed off to their right.

"Company," he said.

An old Dragonfly had taken watch over the crowd. The black Mongoose remained behind them, though far enough back to be nearly invisible against the sun.

One klick back? Or three?

Then Sonja realized that it didn't matter. The jump jet could be on top of her in a blink, either way.

"I saw one paleface in the jump seat," Harry said. "Couldn't tell about the pilot because of the helmet."

The gunship was too far away for her to make out detail now.

"What do you suppose they want?" he asked.

"Careful," Sonja warned him. "This FM's good for almost a kilometer."

She flew on in silence, skirting the Jaguar Mountains to take advantage of the lift. This route took her to the edge of the protected airspace around the ViraVax facility. She skirted that edge in a semicircle to get a better look.

From the air the compound looked like any other large, successful farming operation. All the barns and sheds were immaculately kept and lined up in order. The main complex looked like a simple packing plant, though she knew from what her father told her that it took up several stories underground.

It was only on close inspection that she noted the subtleties of the chopper pad, gardens atop camouflaged bunkers, the three separate perimeters of razor wire.

Dad worked there longer than I've been alive, she thought, *and I still don't know what he did for them, or why.*

Red Bartlett had worked there all her life, yet there were levels in that compound that he couldn't access.

It seemed strange to Sonja to know so little of the place that took up so much of her father's life. She felt resentful that he chose to spend his life there instead of with her, and doubly resentful that no one from ViraVax ever called to see how they were doing.

A group of *deficientes,* dressed in blues and reds and browns, turned their faces skyward and shielded their eyes from the sun.

He spent nearly twenty years there, she thought, *and now it's like he never existed.*

Sonja's reverie was shattered by the flyby roar and back draft from the Mongoose. The biplane lifted as though by the hand of God, then nosed over. Sonja yanked the throttle, dropped the nose even more to gain speed, then leveled out at about ten meters from the treetops.

"Jesus Christ!" Harry yelled. "They tried to kill us!"

The Mongoose wallowed to a stop, turned slowly on its column of air and closed the gap once again. Sonja tried lifting the nose but that just sucked her further into the turbulence of the jet wash and battered her eighty-three-year-old plane nearly apart.

This time Sonja didn't have the altitude to spare and she nearly clipped the treetops. The hillside below dropped into a canyon and Sonja dropped with it. Maybe she could save them, after all.

Sonja's attention came back to Harry, who kept repeating "Shit!" over and over behind her.

An officious-sounding male voice drowned him out on the FM.

"Shut up," the voice said. "Land on that pad to your north-east."

The voice spoke unaccented English. The pad he indicated was in the middle of the ViraVax compound, and the Mongoose hovered between them and freedom. She didn't know who these people were, but if they wanted her they were going to have to earn her.

Sonja pulled her FM off, leaned up in the cockpit and yelled at Harry.

"Hold on!"

Sonja wasn't going to put down at ViraVax. She wanted to get as far away as possible before they forced her down, hopefully far enough from ViraVax that someone would see what was happening. The Mongoose came in from her left and fired a cannon burst across her bow. Sonja opened her throttle wide and headed straight down-valley.

18

Ex-Colonel Rico Toledo prepared for the embassy's afternoon party and tried not to be ashamed at the sight his bathroom mirror showed him.

Ten kilos overweight, he thought.

Rico noted the circles and bags under his eyes, the hint of yellow around the blue irises, the flab at his throat that exaggerated his scissors scar. His T-shirt did not ride up on his belly anymore; at least his short vacation had cured *that* much.

Dropped about fifty kilos of girlfriend, too, he thought.

He hadn't been taking applications, either, and this would be another evening alone among the jet set. Besides, attending a formal function solo would make him look properly repentant.

Rico washed his face again, the water as hot as he could stand it. He had been invited to the embassy party for a reason, but so far no one would tell him that reason. His gut told him that he had better be on his best behavior, something that got harder for him every day. He tossed off the last of his Wild Turkey and rinsed with a mouthwash.

I'll switch to beer, he thought. *That smooths out my wrinkles pretty well.*

A shudder chilled him to the quick in spite of Costa Brava's heat and humidity.

The Colonel's drinking had kept his socializing down, but it dampened the cycles of unreasonable lust that overwhelmed him lately. Alcohol had not kept down the terrible hot rage that also seized him at odd moments. In fact, the drinking took him to the edge of rage where the Colonel rode its crest like a champion surfer. Only his greatest effort reined this rage in. After the incident with Red Bartlett he had more to fear than his unbridled tantrums.

I get fevers, he thought, *and night sweats. Fevers come with bugs, and I've been bodyguard to the bugmaster.*

Rico had started charting his fevers, rages and lusts the way a woman might chart her ovulations. He wanted evidence undeniable, evidence that would prove his need for drink to be out of his control and not his fault. He wanted any responsibility except his own and, what was worse, he knew that.

His log revealed that his cycle was dictated by the cycle of whatever woman he was with. When he was with two women, when his affair with Rachel began and overlapped his marriage to Grace, his drinking and bullying became erratic. But the intensity was increasing, and he didn't know how much more he could take.

Rico checked the mirror again, and his face looked better, flushed to color from the hot water. He saw the color, ignored the webwork of broken vessels that made it. He was struck, again, by the similarity of his son's features to his own. Even dissolution and flab couldn't hide that.

Harry looks so much like me that it scares me, he admitted.

Rico thought that whatever had come between them had been a result of this mysterious rage. Staying away was the safer bet—Harry was right—but Rico felt cowardly staying away and he didn't like that as much as he didn't like the rage. He would have to do something about that. Meanwhile, he would put out new feelers on Casey's operation, and the embassy party would be a good place to find out whether El Indio was still willing to work with him. His work had saved him before.

When? he wondered. *When could they have slipped me a bug?*

His military inoculations came long before Casey's time. Casey's people tampered with inoculations, IV solutions, even irrigation water these days, fully authorized from Rico's command. The Colonel had been a good soldier, he had kept his mouth shut.

The hospital, then?

That was the likeliest time. Rico shuddered again to think how long he'd been in Casey's grip. It had to be that time at the embassy hospital, after the beating he got at the gates. Now he questioned everything, even the coincidence of the beating.

What else did they do to me there? And who in the Agency knows about this?

He and Grace had been newlyweds when he had been drawn into the weekly ruckus by the taunting from some demonstrators. After what he'd been through in Guatemala, Rico didn't take confrontation quietly. Grace had been in-country less than a year and he was already a hero, something he'd wanted her to see for herself.

Immediately following his hospitalization, Rico and Grace had a baby due. He'd wanted Harry born back home in Seattle, but Grace disagreed. She'd insisted on making the best political position possible in Costa Brava, and that had included a show of faith in local medicine. Besides, embassy personnel always had the ViraVax medical team available for emergencies.

It paid off, he thought. *I'll give her that.*

If it hadn't paid off in a big way, Rico wouldn't be heading to the embassy tonight. In spite of his recent indiscretions, and in spite of the turn of this government towards the evangelicals, Rico Toledo owned a lot of favors, thanks to Grace. He vowed to use those favors wisely.

His thoughts flashed on Red Bartlett, on the real story that even Nancy Bartlett hadn't been allowed to remember. Another shudder iced his spine and he shook it off.

Is some of my memory altered, too? he wondered. *Am I going to end up like Red?*

The Colonel had played the superspy game for nearly twenty years. All that he knew for sure about that time was that Harry was his son. That much he could see for himself.

The little shit's got balls, I'll give him that, he thought. *He looks so damned much like me, I can't believe it.*

The Colonel's sour stomach churned and his palms leaked a constant, clammy sweat.

If they did give me something, I sure hope it wasn't passed on to Harry.

Something horrible inside Rico fought to get out, and alcohol would spring it loose. He rinsed out his glass and downed a few swallows of water. This embassy party would be the acid test.

Rico had some scores to settle, and he needed some help. He would go right to the top, to El Indio, the one man Rico had never seen, whose voice he had never heard. All communication with El Indio was by whisper or on the web. Rico resented the web and considered anything electronic compromised, but he would resort to the web to find El Indio.

Rico would need something to trade. Right now, he didn't have much of anything but an attitude and a bad reputation.

His drive from his rooming house to the embassy was interrupted twice when army patrols blocked traffic and dragged people from their cars. This had become so much a part of his life that it was nearly invisible to him now, except that he was becoming conscious of his new vulnerability as a civilian.

At one traffic light a skinny *indio* washed his windows and offered to sell him a roll of toilet paper. The sun over the boy's shoulder was blocked by the evening flight of hundreds of green, shrieking parrots. The boy wore a dozen rolls of toilet paper strung on a rope necklace, and warned Rico that the shortage would only get worse. Rico bought two rolls and tipped the boy two darios for the windows.

Four marines passed the Colonel through the gate, and a Costa Bravan corporal parked his car for him. When he exited Search and Sniff, Rico saw the divorced woman Yolanda Rubia talking with Major Scholz. Señora Rubia had been his neighbor in Colonia Escalón, and the neighborhood's only divorcee. Her ex-husband, Philip, was one of the coffee cartel's richest merchants. A family feud with the Garcías kept him out of the country most of the time.

Rico had rescued one of their daughters from a death squad years ago, the operation clandestine, quick and lucky.

Yolanda's family disowned her when she divorced, but her children stuck by her. The Colonel stepped in one time when soldiers came to the house. The Colonel's position with the Agency made things easier but still they were far from easy. One sister kept touch by whisper through the Colonel until her husband got the black roses at work.

Having someone killed was not a problem in Costa Brava, but a divorce reflected poorly on the system. The remaining Catholic aristocracy meted out punishments for the sins of its own in costs which had little to do with money. Rico had experienced these hidden costs himself. He had a hunch about Yolanda, a hunch he still carried, and a debt that he now wanted to collect.

In the language of the pamphleteers of the left, Costa Brava's coffee *fincas* rooted themselves in the pungence of the poor. Above the root line it was orchids, toucans, parrots and coffee. When the world wore dust and tattered cotton, Yolanda's family wore silk.

The Colonel reached out to shake her hand and suddenly her silk was spattered with blood—the Colonel's blood.

The Colonel woke up under a table, against the wall, with Yolanda Rubia pushing herself out from under his legs. Somebody had bombed the reception, and Rico stood between Yolanda and the bomb. The unfortunate Lady Piedras had shielded the Colonel from the blast. His legs didn't work and he tumbled Yolanda to the floor again in a heap. That, too, was lucky. Someone started shooting at someone else outside and several bursts of rifle fire stitched the wall just centimeters above their heads.

"Come!"

Yolanda helped him up by the armpits, then he crawled across broken glass behind her through the reception pantry to the alleyway. The wounded started to scream and the Colonel's ears throbbed to an invisible beat. Yolanda pulled him along with her, displaying a physical strength that he never imagined her to have.

He was ashamed, later, that he had not thought to look for Grace or Nancy Bartlett. The Colonel's thinking was scrambled right after the blast, and it was a few hours before he recovered.

As Yolanda recalled later: "It was fortunate for the Colonel that Lady Piedras was of a size."

The Colonel remembered very well the pavement litter, the aftersmell of tropical rain, the urgency. He followed because of the hypnotic quality of Yolanda's large brown eyes.

Rico realized soon enough that she hadn't been staring longingly into his eyes. It was all the blood from his scalp and face. The Colonel understood, finally, that he had been hit. He thought that the pain gods were sporting for putting the message off as long as they did.

A yellow Mercedes sedan pulled up where the alley opened onto the Avenue of Liberty or Death. Yolanda pulled the Colonel down in the backseat while her driver zigzagged through the city and past the coffee *fincas* a few kilometers south. The pain intensified to the percussion of back road chuckholes.

"I am 'Elena,' " Yolanda confessed simply as she helped him out of his bloody shirt.

The Colonel was too stunned from his wounds to respond. That she was Elena, his contact with the guerrilla underground, seemed logical to him. It had been his hunch, after all, and this hunch had let him intervene in her country's machinations against her.

Presidents had died on this soil for less.

Two impressions stayed with the Colonel as he tied his shirt tight to his scalp: the rich smell of new leather upholstery and Yolanda's thick perfume.

"What do you call it?" he asked her. "The perfume?"

" 'Poison.' "

Fitting, no? the Colonel thought.

It was his man, El Indio, who got them into cover that night at a country retreat of the French Embassy. A French physician stitched him up while Yolanda worked the angles. Three hours later, they headed for the mountains on Irish papers.

It wasn't until they got to the mountains that the news came through that two Irish nationals had been killed attempting to bomb the Archbishop's office.

"The government says they were hired by the Peace and Freedom Party to make it look like a piece of government work," Yolanda informed him, "and the bomb was identical to the one that hit us at the embassy."

"So, they're saying that your people bombed the embassy *and* the Archbishop, and that you tried to pin it on García?"

"Yes."

"Somebody wants you, me, the Archbishop, the embassy *and* García."

"Who would see all of us as the enemy?" she asked. "Those who hate the Archbishop side with García."

"Unless García's a sacrifice," Rico said.

"On whose altar?"

"On the altar of the Children of Eden."

El Indio's contact at the French Embassy had filled them in via a network scramble that smelled strongly of Agency work. High-level Agency work.

"Somebody else to blame," Rico said. "Casey is stirring up all the hornets. Trouble is, mad bees sting everybody, Republicans *and* Democrats."

"Israeli agents captured two Irish nationals in New York," the report said. "Britain had paper out on them, but the Israelis were persuaded to make delivery to a clandestine jail in the Confederation of Costa Brava for 'a big whisper.' "

The two Irish were dead; the Colonel and Yolanda held their passports.

Everybody's getting into the act, Rico thought.

He scanned the rest of the Frenchman's briefing.

"Costa Bravan authorities fingered the dead Irish for the embassy job, claiming they were assisted by two agents of the Peace and Freedom's guerrilla arm: Rico Toledo and Yolanda Rubia."

The government came out smelling like *plumeria,* he and Yolanda didn't. It was too pat. No mention yet of Grace or Nancy.

Company waited for them in the mountains.

It wasn't El Indio meeting them in the highlands, but El Indio had covered everything. A Korean doctor checked out the Frenchman's work on the Colonel's head and face. Rico had hoped to meet El Indio face-to-face, but he was vain enough to be thankful it wasn't today.

For twenty years he had had contact with El Indio, very indirect contact which always traced back to thin air. He knew that El Indio had to be rich, because there was a quality, a classy touch, to everything he did that the Colonel couldn't quite explain.

El Indio sent a woman who traded their Irish passports straight across for Canadian paper. It was the best anyone could make of a truly smelly scene, and it turned into one of those impromptu alliances that paid off on all fronts, against the odds.

The odds started churning again.

Their hideout in the highlands was a four-bedroom town house, with complete office and satlink consoles set out like the mints on their pillows. The rebels operated a restaurant two blocks towards the lake, across the highway from the mechanic's shop, which they also owned. Yolanda pointed out more.

"That's Adan's carpentry shop," she said, "and the gas station . . . there, the whole streamside up the valley is the farming and water-supply co-op. So you see, we are not really a political party," Yolanda explained. "We are an economic confederation, like Costa Brava."

"That's El Indio's touch," he said to Yolanda. "A practical elegance."

Yolanda's gaze shifted at the mention of El Indio, and she stared past Rico towards the mountains.

"I, too, have never met him," she said. "Only messages on the web, and he leaves no footprints."

"Good business," Rico mumbled.

The housekeeper had put up plenty to eat, but the Colonel felt nauseated. The in-and-out hustle of people and equipment around him intensified that nausea. He excused himself to shower and change clothes. His face and head throbbed, swollen against the stitches. Soaking off the caked-on gauze was the hardest part.

The shower door slid open and Yolanda's voice interrupted his soap cycle.

"Video news, we're on!"

Rico pulled a towel around himself and followed her down the hallway. The soap drying in his scalp and the bristly stitches didn't help the reawakening throb. Staring at a flickering TV without so much as a beer aggravated matters. Rico's stomach flipped, but what they said at the last put everything on ice, including his belly.

Big news after Tuesday's bombing and the convenient shooting of—now it was *four*—Irish assassins was the disappearance of a small plane with two teenagers aboard. They were Sonja Bartlett, granddaughter of the Speaker of the House of the United States, and Harry Toledo, son of ex-Colonel Rico Toledo, whose car was the source of Tuesday's bomb at the embassy. Presidential sources speculated on whether father and son were involved in some wild-cat political scheme, or whether the bombing was Rico's personal vendetta against his ex-wife.

Preliminary reports said that both mothers were safe in an undisclosed location. Embassy security allowed no interviews, but implied that the women were being held at the embassy compound for their own protection.

A caller purporting to be from the Knights of Malta took credit for the kidnapping and for the bombing. The Archbishop's office reported that the call was a hoax and charged the García government with staging both the bombing and the kidnapping. García predictably blamed the Peace and Freedom Party.

Colonel Toledo's name came up in all three scenarios as the perpetrator. A lifetime of his personal and professional laundry flapped across the airways.

"I've got to go back," he told Yolanda. "I have to find those kids."

She placed her hand on his arm. Yolanda's touch excited him and this weakness caused him to blush; he felt it prickle over his throat and cheeks. Since Rachel, Rico had slept with no one and had slept very little.

"Don't go," Yolanda said. "Casey's people know you can't stand by while your child is in danger. Your own fear becomes the bait that snares you. Those *maricones* won't come up here and look for themselves."

Rico knew she was right. It didn't make a difference: this was his son, and the daughter of his dead best friend.

"I'm going."

"They want *you*," Yolanda said, gripping his arm. "You would warn me not to fall for it. . . ."

"You don't fight like I do. . . ."

"Don't underestimate me any more than you already have," Yolanda said. "They want us fighting ourselves," she reminded him. "They want you on your own, they want us to turn on you. All of this you know. You have used this technique yourself."

It was true. He had used all of the techniques now arrayed against him. That was a plus, and it was why he felt like a good fight. This was familiar turf. With luck, Rico could narrow his field of fire to a single target.

It would be unlike those monsters at ViraVax to make things so simple.

Meanwhile, Rico's worst fear, the worst fear of any parent, was also true. Someone had his child.

The two dead Irish nationals had already become four dead Irish nationals. Since the next figures in question were Harry and Sonja, the Colonel wanted to ensure no juggling.

Rico, headache in hand, used the rebels' hardware to pry a few old debts off the webs. He triggered his coded distress burst to Solaris and requested Agency support. It was a long shot, but Solaris had known him from the start.

"Solaris, you better be with me," Rico muttered.

"What was that?" Yolanda asked.

"Just thinking," he muttered.

Then, when her eyebrow asked for more, he growled, "Anybody not with me is against me. Anybody against me in this one will not survive."

Yolanda made an impatient snapping gesture with her hand.

"There's the *yanqui* sense of justice," she hissed. "Kill one hundred thousand people to rescue two hostages. What are we fighting for, if only to become *them*?"

"Get off the high horse," Rico said. "I've seen what you do when you have to do it. I will accept your support, but not your judgment. That is a waste of time."

Yolanda shrugged, a Costa Bravan gesture that Rico found particularly endearing at that moment. He shrugged back, and she giggled, the tension between them broken.

"My preliminary assessment of network support will be ready

in a few minutes," Yolanda said. She smiled at him and added,
"We are not enemies, remember that."

The Colonel knew by now that El Indio happened to be
Yolanda's original contact even before the confederation, and
he was disappointed that she, too, had never seen his face or
heard his voice. Rico's identity had been double-covered with
both of them as well, though now it didn't matter.

El Indio had been Rico's pioneer contact from the Peace and
Freedom people, and his invisibility became a matter of prin-
ciple. Rico got the diamonds on his Agency cuff links for being
persistent, but this time persistence hadn't paid off. Experience
had taught him to survive by knowing what mattered before it
mattered.

Slow, irregular, meticulous—the Colonel, Yolanda and El Indio
were of the old school, though young enough, and these aliases
within aliases were badges of honor. Like prisoners isolated in
their holes, they lived for their communications, for the secret
message. What armies it might stir didn't matter much compared
to the challenge of reliable product verified and reliably delivered.
That is, until now. Now it was personal.

A conference had been scheduled in the dining room of the
open-air restaurant. Yolanda and Colonel Toledo walked with
impunity through the cobblestone plaza of this rebel village to
their reserved seats. Bugs fluttered the few hot lights and buzzed
in the thick night air. Rico was bleary-eyed after four hours in
meetings, but he scanned everyone in the place and at no time
did El Indio give him the sign.

The Colonel's wounds itched in sweaty bandages, and standing
all day had made him light-headed. The village barber did a
pretty good job of trimming stitches and restructuring his hair to
minimize the damage. Rico had just assessed himself in the rest
room mirror. The face cuts couldn't be helped, and his scissors
scar throbbed a pink pulse into his collar.

Pretty, he thought.

He returned to their table and began to sit when Yolanda tugged
his sleeve and stopped him.

"Here's Philip," she said.

Yolanda's ex-husband rose to greet them, displaying the strength
and grace of a man of his station.

What hair Philip Rubia had was gray. Though just fifty, he
looked considerably younger than the Colonel. His suit and tie
cut him the figure of a chief executive officer, which, though

in absentia from Costa Brava, he still was. His red-rimmed eyes never left Yolanda's, never met the Colonel's.

The Colonel swept the room for a sign from El Indio, but saw only Philip Rubia's bodyguards and a few political assistants busy with their own game.

Yolanda stepped aside. Philip Rubia gripped the Colonel's hand tight and affirmed his determination to help with Harry and Sonja. Then Philip whispered to both of them, "I am the old friend you have been seeking."

"You!" Yolanda growled, a hand to her chest. "You mean that *you* are El Indio? All the time we were married, it was *you* . . . ?"

"Yes," he said with sad eyes and a bow, "all that time. I couldn't say anything, it was too dangerous. . . ."

"Think what we could have done *together*," she hissed.

"What? Get caught?" he asked. "Died? Look what we've accomplished this way. . . ."

Rico was surprised at Philip's revelation, but not shocked, like Yolanda.

But I wasn't married to him, Rico thought. *I didn't divorce him for spending so much unexplained time away from the family.*

Yolanda drew herself up, her brown eyes brimming, and took a deep breath before she spoke through her clenched teeth.

"There *was* another woman," she said. "I was not mistaken about that."

"No." El Indio admitted, his sadness tight in his throat. "No, you were not mistaken."

Yolanda's face flushed and her eyes glittered with fight. Rico couldn't tell whether it was anger or sadness, or both.

"Thank God you admit it," Yolanda whispered. "It is better for both of us, for our work. . . ."

"That woman," El Indio said, "she, too, was a matter of our work. . . ."

"Don't insult me, or her, with that story. And don't feel so bad, Philip. You are so much inside yourself, so intellectual, it is refreshing that you listened to your body at least once in your life."

At that, Yolanda and Philip became aware of the silence around them. This silence dissolved in a couple of coughs, the squeak of a chair, a question from one waiter to another across the room: "Do you think Reyes will play in the World Cup?"

Rico sensed, more than heard, the incoming drones. This time it was he who saved Yolanda with a shove.

"Down!" he yelled.

A fireball challenged the sun, and the concussion stripped the thatch from the restaurant roof.

"Look!"

El Indio pointed out a roiling column of black smoke about three blocks away. Another round exploded in the street and peppered the fleeing patrons with shards of hot spring steel.

"It's the town house!" Yolanda shouted as Rico pushed her down.

"How did they know?" Philip asked.

His gaze that met Rico's was cold, accusatory.

García's boys had found them, after all, and the guerrillas' mountain stronghold was not nearly as secure as they wanted to believe. This had to be an Agency tip-off.

But how?

Rico's hand went instinctively to the scissors scar on his neck, and then it became clear: how the albino had found him so easily in Mexico, how García's inept army suddenly gained a new efficiency.

They'd planted him with a Parasite, a minuscule transmitter that used the body's own electrolytes as a battery. Rico felt along the scar and found the tiny lump that he'd thought was a little cyst or an undissolved stitch. He squeezed it between the nails of his thumb and forefinger as hard as he could bear. Finesse would have to wait.

"Come on!" he growled, and grabbed Yolanda's hand.

Once again, they stumbled through smoking debris and the screaming wounded, Philip and his men providing cover and following close on their heels.

19

SONJA BARTLETT WOKE up naked, bound and gagged inside a hot plastic bag. Hot gravel outside the bag scorched her left cheek and shoulder. She squirmed in her own sweat, slick as a fish in the bottom of a boat, and tried to free her feet and her thumbs where they were bound behind her back. The air inside the bag was so hot and thick she could barely stay conscious no matter how hard she gulped it in.

It's a body bag, she thought. *They think I'm dead and they're going to bury me!*

A slug of adrenaline threw her back into her struggles, then her muscles spasmed until she was helpless. She concentrated on slowing her breathing. Gradually, the colored lights faded and her vision focused on black. When she got control of her breathing, her mind cleared.

If they thought I was dead, they wouldn't need to tie me up, she reasoned.

Her muscles twitched all over her body, little ripples of random electricity. She felt well-bruised, but not broken.

She was a prisoner, then.

Whose?

Sonja remembered lying in her bed, drifting towards sleep. Her Knuckleheads poster, a peel-and-peek holo, shimmered down on her from the wall. Dimly, other images materialized. She remembered flying *Mariposa,* shots, the Mongoose. . . .

Hacienda Police, she thought, *or one of García's death squads.*

It was clearly not guerrillas. They flew ultralights on suicide missions, crude-framed kites powered by lawn-mower engines stolen from the rich. A Mongoose meant money, and money meant a government, or ViraVax.

ViraVax!

133

That place scared her more than any government could. They probably wouldn't kill her, but that thought scared her, too.

Sonja was soaked from the unbearable heat inside the bag, and her lungs could not gulp enough stale air through her gag to keep her from suffocation. A large zipper cut her nose when she twisted her face and worked at the gag. She strained upward to get her nose closer to the zipper and managed to suck a little air through its teeth. Someone pinched her nose through the plastic, and when she jerked away in breathless panic she heard a muffled laugh.

Sonja lay still for a hundred heartbeats, listening, but heard nothing except her own desperate gasps for air. The pressure at her temples and the tingling in her fingers let up. The gravel hurt her spine and shoulder blades, but she worked the thick plastic against it, trying to abrade herself a breathing hole.

A muffled command barked from nearby. A flurry of kicks and blows pelted her body, but they did not seem enthusiastic and she was somewhat protected by the thick plastic around her. Sonja stopped fighting when those agonizing spasms clutched at her muscles. She ran out of air, and once again the darkness inside the bag met the white light behind her eyes.

Sonja woke to her butt dragging along the ground. Someone carried her under the armpits, someone else grunted at her knees. The one at her shoulders had his arms far enough under her armpits so that his hands gripped her breasts. Sonja squirmed away, but he just laughed and renewed his hold.

Her bearers jog-trotted, grunting and huffing, then slung her up, up, and let her drop to a metal deck. She'd heard the whine of turbines overhead and the clamor of boots.

The ship lurched and sideslipped. Sonja leaned against another body, also in a bag, unmoving. She nudged it with her foot once, twice, and it was a body, all right. Nothing nudged back.

Oh, God, it's Harry! she thought.

She remembered the shots and prayed that they hadn't killed him.

Nobody would gain anything by killing him, she thought. *Like the hostage trainer taught us, we're worth a lot more alive than dead.*

Sonja remembered a warning from the Mongoose, and the crash.

She remembered racing *Mariposa* to the edge of a burned-out cornfield before the Mongoose overtook her. A dirt road entered the jungle just ahead and she had strained the little biplane to its limit trying to make it. The Mongoose settled just a few meters above her and its turbines robbed her of all her lift. *Mariposa* dropped unceremoniously the last ten meters to the ground, the stick completely loose in Sonja's fierce grip.

When Sonja woke up, someone sprayed her in the face from a small canister before she could climb out of the cockpit. The person who sprayed her wore breathing apparatus and a black flight suit without insignia.

Stunned by the impact of the crash and by the spray, Sonja was fightless when her assailant pulled her T-shirt over her head and stripped off her pants and underwear. Another dzee held her up from behind. Her vision faded as they bound and gagged her, and she did not remember anything more until she woke up in the bag.

There were men and women in the outfit that took her. They were talking now, and had to speak up so that they could hear each other over the noise of the rotors.

"Casey says she's safe," a man's voice said, "but he said that her old man was safe, too, and look what went down with him."

"I don't like any of this," a woman said. "Casey didn't tell us the truth about Bartlett, or Bartlett's wife. Now this, for no reason. . . ."

"No," the man corrected, "it's the reason that we all live for. To serve the Master Gardener in his restoration of the earth. You could be the one headed for Level Five, you know. Watch your mouth."

The woman snorted. "Yeah, well, I've had my fill."

"What are you going to do about it, sweetie? Quit? . . . Shit!"

The plane pitched forward and dropped, the pilot a few beats late on the uptake. Sonja's stomach churned.

What has Casey done with my mom and dad?

She swallowed hard past the lump in her throat.

And what has he done to me that makes them worry about whether I'm "safe" or not?

The Mongoose lurched and slewed, lurched again.

"Won't that shitbird ever learn how to fly?"

"He must have relatives in high places."

"He does," the woman said. "His father's president of the JIL chain. Started by the Master himself. . . ."

The bird dropped so suddenly that Sonja cleared the floor. When the pilot corrected, the deck came up fast and knocked what little wind she had out of her. The bag next to her groaned, then kicked against her back.

"Hey," the woman said, "now our other puppy's waking up. I thought they were supposed to stay out for four to six hours."

"Have you ever known anything that was military issue to work the way it's supposed to?"

"No," she said, "but if these *payasos* beat themselves up, there'll be hell to pay when we deliver."

"They haven't been that fussy in the past."

"There'll be hell to pay," she answered, "and you know it. Buster, we are in a no-win situation."

"You better watch your mouth. Casey doesn't much care for rough language."

Then the military frequency came on, reporting that Harry's father had bombed the U.S. Embassy, that he'd used his familiarity with security personnel to get it past the sniffs and into position.

"This attack is believed to be a personal, not political gesture," the dispatcher reported. "Officials believe the bomb to be an attack on Colonel Toledo's ex-wife, who wounded him in a domestic dispute recently. No U.S. citizens were reported killed in the blast. Three Costa Bravans were killed. . . ."

Thank God, Sonja thought, *Mom's okay.*

A frightening thought came to mind.

Maybe the Hacienda Police think Harry and I had something to do with it.

Their landing was a hard one and Sonja heard the head next to hers hit the deck just before her world exploded in a burst of white light. She woke up moments later as someone wheeled her somewhere on a very smooth gurney. The air was cooler here, at least, and she no longer felt like she was suffocating inside the bag.

She remembered the hostage training that repeated, "Don't worry about what you can't control. Concentrate on what you *can* do."

Right now, she couldn't even muster a scream.

The electric motor whined to a stop, and Sonja heard a strange language gather around her, full of thicknesses and grunts. At first, she was afraid. Then, when she realized where she was, she was terrified.

20

JOSHUA CASEY WAS a big-voiced little man with a swagger to match. This afternoon the voice was louder than usual, the swagger more subdued. Even the dullest of the Innocents who had been around him longest knew this to be a deadly combination. Joshua Casey was often angry, but this time his anger was white-hot, and the object of that anger was Dajaj Mishwe.

"I wanted subtle, Daj," Casey growled. "Bombing is not subtle. Kidnapping, that's not really very subtle, either."

Casey paced, his fists tight as he ranted.

"I fear those who might discover our hard-won secrets," he said. "You don't understand that world out there, Daj, so *stay out of it!* We must never trust even our family or our dearest friends out there. They share the power of betrayal. We are wedded to these secrets, till death do us part, you and I and everyone here. This is *your* world, *your* family."

Casey shook the tension out of his fingers and faced Mishwe.

"Now," he said, "tell me your version of what happened outside, and your part in it. Convince me that it does not threaten us here as I believe. Answer to me, Daj, or before the Sabbath ends you will answer to the Master."

Mishwe stood at the doorway to Casey's topside office, his wide smile undiminished by the outburst. He knew how much Casey hated the comparative vulnerability of his topside offices. Forcing the meeting topside actually gave Mishwe the edge. Casey would be angry, this he knew. But fear would be the basis for this anger—fear that what Mishwe had done would be discovered, and the greater fear that a disaster would catch Casey topside, exposed, out of the safety of his bunkers.

Mishwe knew his own limitations in social intercourse, and he knew Casey's moods. He would not leave the doorway until he

137

was ordered inside or until he was sure that he wouldn't need it. Dajaj Mishwe did not fear Joshua Casey personally—he knew he would snap the man like a pencil when the time came—but Mishwe always kept a back door open, even at Level Five. It was the discovery of that back door, and its secrets, that became the death of Red Bartlett.

"Some valuables that belonged to us were in danger of being misplaced," Mishwe said. "I brought them here for safekeeping."

"It's not as simple as that," Casey growled. "Don't insult me. There are the matters of a rather messy *U.S. Embassy* bombing and a kidnapping of two children of high-level Americans, both with ties to *this facility*. . . ."

"The bombing?" Mishwe shrugged, nonplussed. "It is blamed on the Colonel. He was a problem for us and now his own people will drive him out. The children? We want to assess our results with them, no? Take them to stage three? We have them here. We want the Colonel? He will come after them or his own people will drive him to us."

Casey stepped closer and his breath bathed Mishwe in the odor of raw garlic. Casey ate whole cloves of garlic to combat his precipitous blood pressure. Judging from the flush on his face, he wasn't having much luck.

Casey pointed a finger at him, and Mishwe resisted the urge to snap it off.

"And you used the Mongoose in an unauthorized operation," Casey said. "You went over my head to use a highly visible tool that is not supposed to be in our hands. Now, the Colonel. The embassy lists him as missing. What will he do? Lie still? You don't know this man."

Casey's neck began to tremble and he breathed deeply twice to calm himself. "I warned you after the Bartlett incident—stick to your lab rats and leave the strategy to me. Is that clear?"

Mishwe tightened, his smile faded. "But you don't see. . . ."

"I see that you've endangered a dozen sensitive projects." Casey's fury sent droplets of spittle flying. "I see that you've endangered this very facility, our organization. The Master believes that you have endangered the Children of Eden as well."

"But they are *mine*," Mishwe said. He pointed his finger at Casey's chest. "I *made* them, I have the right . . ."

"This facility arranged those children," Casey said, "the way a grandmother might arrange a marriage. *God* made them. Do not equate yourself with God, that is blasphemy. And I am this facility. If they *belong* to anyone, they belong to me. As you belong to me. You gave up your rights when you came here, barely a step ahead of the law. We work as a team here. I will not have you or anyone else making decisions that affect our security. The squad who operated for you has been transferred to your lab. I want everything you can get from them; make sure nothing is unturned. Then disappear every one of them down to the cellular level, clear?"

Mishwe offered no response. He had expected a reprimand, but he also had been sure that Casey would understand completely once he'd explained. These particular children were successful products of the first viral-assisted human conceptions. They were clones. To let them go unstudied would be scientific neglect of criminal proportions. And to people the Garden of Eden with anyone less than Adam and Eve would be the truest blasphemy. . . .

"You're confined to deep quarters," Casey said. "I can't trust you topside, and if there's trouble I don't want you available. You have some atonement ahead of you. Meditate on that, and ask God to show you the way."

"You can't . . ."

Casey turned to his console and addressed his machine.

"Code Q, Suite 1-A. Code Q, Suite 1-A."

"You didn't have to do that," Mishwe said.

He let his face show neither anger nor fear, only disappointment.

"You didn't give me a choice," Casey said.

Two security guards carrying Colt Bullpups appeared behind Mishwe with no more noise than fog over a riverbank. One placed a precautionary muzzle to Mishwe's head, but Casey waved it away.

"I need your cooperation, Dajaj," Casey said, his voice a growl. "I need your *voluntary* cooperation. But something of this magnitude cannot go unanswered. I suggest you spend this Sabbath in prayer and reflection. Only you can come up with the perfect atonement for this indiscretion."

Casey nodded once, and the guards started Mishwe on the decontamination route to his lab.

"Dajaj!" Casey called after him. "Do those children no harm whatsoever or I will feed you to your rats myself."

I have the perfect atonement, Mishwe thought, and smiled.

On his way to Level Five, he daydreamed of the great cleansing coming soon, coming very soon.

21

HARRY SMELLED THE familiar burst of blood in his nose and thought for a moment that he was home. Something snapped his head back, and a facemask shoved itself into his field of vision. Blue eyes flicked a quick, assessing glance over him.

"Hey!" Harry yelled, releasing his harness. "What the hell . . . ?"

Someone popped a spray at his face, and someone else shouted at Sonja, but the helmet speaker was off, so it sounded like a child at the bottom of a well calling for its mother.

"Freeze!"

A spatter of blood brightened the cockpit's leather liner, but he couldn't move to find out where it came from. He had no sensation at all in his arms or legs. Blank spots swam across his vision, like great black amoebas, and time slowed way down. His pulse and respiration also slowed, and his body broke out in a profuse sweat.

Sonja moaned just a few meters away and Harry agonized because he could do nothing for her.

"Look at me!"

The spacebitch's voice commanded, though muffled through the seals of her hazmat suit, and Harry's body tried its best to obey. She, too, was sweating: the suit's conditioner could barely keep her faceplate clear. He tried to focus, but all that came to him was the blur of her blue eyes. His eyes twitched uncontrollably from side to side. When he quit trying to control them, the spasms stopped.

He knew from the blue eyes and the bio suit that she was ViraVax security, Night School trained and equipped. No natives were allowed in the Night School or in ViraVax security, though

141

the Colonel had admitted applicants from other nations as long as they became U.S. citizens. Precious few were willing to do that these days.

Harry was not surprised that his father didn't trust the locals. Maybe that was part of why they took him off the Night School and stuck him in the embassy. The Colonel didn't trust anyone, even his superiors, and he had made that clear. They saw it as paranoia aggravated by booze.

Spacebitch and her partner wrestled Harry out of the cockpit and dumped him unceremoniously onto the ground. The next time he saw those blue eyes in the bio suit look down on him, they spun down a long dark tunnel just out of reach, and Harry fell in after them.

Harry woke on his back, hot and under lights, bright lights. His musculature rippled with uncoordinated twitchings. He managed to get his legs and arms to work well enough to roll himself onto his belly. This way the glare didn't pain his eyes quite so much. Harry's mouth was very dry and sore and tasted like an old handkerchief.

"If you move too much you'll get sick."

The voice was Sonja's, off to his left. The pulse in his ears was his own. He couldn't focus on Sonja; the effort hurt his eyes and started them twitching again.

"Pull up your sheet," she told him, "you're naked."

Harry scrabbled his hands against a pillow, mattress, bed frame. He found the corner of a sheet and pulled it over his shoulder. That was much too hot, so he shrugged it off to his waist. The tremors came and went. When they mostly went, his vision began to clear and the lights didn't seem so bright. Sonja was asking him something over the loud rushing in his ears.

" . . . hear me? Harry?"

Sonja spoke to him from a bunk across the room. She had her sheet pulled up to her chin, and she sat upright against an institutional-pink wall. Wet blonde hair tangled around her face and shoulders, dampening her sheet. Harry's own hair was wet, too, but not from sweat. He could not tell whether she'd been crying.

"Yes," he answered, "I hear you."

His voice squeaked a little in his dry throat.

Harry sat up and looked the room over. There wasn't much to see. Windows at the far end, very bright light, lots of plants outside. Refrigerator, cupboards, sink, door. Sonja's bunk, a fold-out type, nearly touched his in the center of a room empty of embellishment or inspiration. Another door, table with two chairs. Back to the windows.

"Are you okay?" he rasped. "Is the plane okay? She was hit . . . ?"

"I'm okay. Sore and sick. *Mariposa* wasn't hit, but the crash definitely killed her."

Sonja spoke in a monotone, her knees pulled to her chin and her lips buried in her sheet.

"I'm glad you're okay," Harry said.

He wanted to reach out and touch her but he didn't trust his trembling muscles. He blinked his eyes rapidly but his vision didn't clear any faster.

"Did they bring anyone else here?"

"No," she said. "Just you and me."

"What's behind the doors?"

"We're monitored," she cautioned, and lifted her gaze to a thumb-sized wide-angle bubble overhead.

"We don't want them to know what we know," she said. "It's in the handbook under 'Don't let them know what you know.' "

Harry's stomach untightened a little in relief at her wry humor. *Her monotone must have been for the camera's sake.*

Harry chilled suddenly, and when the chill passed he felt more in control of his arms and legs.

"Where are we?" he asked, indicating the foliage outside their window.

It looked like Mosquito Coast country around Monkey Boy Creek.

"Decontamination," Sonja said.

She answered the question in his gaze.

"It's not a window," she said.

At that, the scene shifted and reshifted to become the cinder-ridden tree line of the volcano Izalco.

Harry tested his legs, then stood up, clutching his sheet like a lifeline.

"Is one of these doors a bathroom?" he asked. "I'm sure that's not a national security question."

Sonja raised her voice and nodded at the door. "The end of my bed." She moved to the foot of her bed so that she could whisper as he walked by: "I saw shadows moving behind the mirror. Two of them."

Harry pulled his sheet into the bathroom with him, regarded

himself in the mirror and used the toilet. The room was small with just a basin, shower and toilet. Walls and floor were made entirely of one piece of porcelain with a large drain in the middle of the shower area.

Not large enough to get through, he thought.

His father had taken him through a warehouse drain once, as part of one of Harry's hostage-escape lessons. Harry showered four or five times a day for weeks afterward, and he was glad for the excuse not to go that way.

Little packages of soap, shampoo and conditioner sat out on the counter just like in the hotels. Someone had already scrubbed him clean, but they hadn't bothered to dry him off very well.

Harry tried to position himself so that his back was to the mirror. He had to lean against the wall that the mirror was on, directly across from the door. He knew that they probably had a wide-angle that would pick him up, anyway, but he tried not to think about it.

He turned, adjusting his sheet, and studied the mirror from an angle.

There!

A sliver of light on, then off, as someone slipped through a door in a darkened room. Sonja was right. When he relaxed his gaze, he saw dim features on the other side of the glass, two faces reflecting the red wash from their controls.

"Of course it's the Double-Vee," Sonja went on, loud enough for him to hear through the door. "Who else would allow that idiot pilot in anything but a bad suit? You call that flying?"

He faked a dizziness and leaned against the mirror. It was good old glass, not metal or petroleum. Through his palm and forehead he detected a flurry of activity behind the mirror, then a high-pitched machinery whine.

This time the dizziness was real, and his stomach lurched towards his throat. Like anyone reared in Costa Brava, Harry had experienced his share of earthquakes. This movement was not the characteristic jolt-and-roll of the local temblors, but a prolonged sinking. . . .

Decontamination, Harry thought. *We're starting down.*

He didn't know much about what happened in the bowels of ViraVax, but he had heard a lot of stories. The sinking feeling in his stomach wasn't all the fault of their elevator.

He opened the bathroom door and stood under its frame, any-way. Harry didn't feel so nauseated standing up, and he got a better view of their room. The peel-and-peek that he had mistaken for a window now hosted a clean-cut young Gardener, pointer in hand, explaining decontamination precautions.

Sonja was not paying attention to the canned spiel coming from the viewscreen, even though she had the volume as high as Harry could stand it. Both she and Harry pretended interest in the safety instructions, though Harry knew that they didn't have to worry about that. It was clear that wherever they went would be under escort.

Harry leaned over and whispered, "They'll split us up, sooner or later. They probably only had the one decon elevator available. If you get the chance to run, don't think about me, just go."

Sonja laughed. "Where to?" she asked. "Even the Pentagon isn't as secure as this place, you told me that yourself."

Harry shrugged. "Something might come up," he said. "Just be sure you're ready for it when it does."

Harry tried to think of a few somethings that might come up, but his thinking was mushy, like running in molasses.

" . . . at first I thought they were after your dad," Sonja was saying.

"What?" Harry snapped his attention into focus. "What about my dad?"

She reached up and squeezed his hand.

"Something blew up at the embassy," she said, her voice still noncommittal. "They say your dad did it. I didn't hear anything about . . . about anyone else, except that no Americans were killed."

Grace was at the embassy. Nancy Bartlett was there, too.

He wouldn't be that crazy. . . .

Harry wouldn't bet his Litespeed on it.

"Where did you hear this?"

"On board the Mongoose, when they were bringing us in. It was on the radio."

"The sonofabitch."

Sonja squeezed Harry's hand again, twice, and he remembered they were being watched. The Gardener on-screen directed them to several faithlines that they could access via satlink.

Harry changed the subject.

"What do you mean 'at first'?" he asked. "Who do you think they're after now?"

"They're after us," she said. "Your dad's just icing on the cake.

Doesn't the book say they usually separate prisoners?"

Harry shuffled from the bathroom, careful to close the door behind him. They were undoubtedly observed in either room, but it made him feel like he'd shut out something noxious. He paused to examine the second door at the foot of his own bunk before answering.

Solid. No latch on the inside.

"Maybe we aren't prisoners."

"What else would we be, then, locked up here like this?"

Harry didn't even have to think about that one.

"The other's over the peel."

Harry felt like he was smothering, for a moment, then his ears popped and he felt the *whish* of conditioned air.

"They exchange and sterilize the air completely at every level," she said with a nod at the screen. "The dzee on the peel just explained it."

Through the sweaty sheets, Sonja's naked hip touched his own. He had dreamed of her touch more than once, but never this way. Still, he did not lean away. Neither did she.

"So," he said. "They're probably not holding us hostage. That would be stupid, even for them. We could describe the Mongoose, this place—course, they could send us out of here with completely new memories."

"They can do that?" Sonja asked.

Her pale face paled even more.

Harry shrugged. "It was part of a study the army did out here," he said. "My dad objected to having a civilian company involved. ViraVax claimed that he was a Catholic and prejudiced against the Children of Eden. I never heard of anyone actually *using* what they developed here. . . ."

"They brought my mother here after my father was killed," Sonja said. "It was much closer to get her to the hospital at La Libertad but they said this was more secure. . . ."

Once again they struck a silence between them. Harry half listened to the missionary explaining the timesaving features of their cubicle. His attention pricked up when the dzee said, "When this orientation is complete, a console will be provided to maximize your time here in the bosom of God's plenty. Praise Jesus, for He is the Vine and we are the branches. . . ."

A console!

"Did you see the spacesuits they wore?" Sonja asked. "They were afraid to touch us until they got us in here."

"Maybe they did something to your dad and to my dad, and now they want to see what it's done to us."

"That's the way the guards talked."

Harry felt chilled again.

What if I get like my dad?

That thought scared him as much as his capture.

"Mariposa warned me, too," Sonja said.

"The mysterious woman of the web," Harry said.

His mouth still didn't work right and it came out like mush.

"Mariposa could be a man or a woman, or several people," Sonja said. "But I have the sense that she's a she, and one person, and she's trying to help."

"A key would be nice. . . ."

The peel-and-peek washed itself clean with a sweep of intense white light. A dark-skinned, bald-headed man came into focus, naked to the waist. He bowed and grinned at them through the backlight glare.

"Welcome," he said. "I've been looking forward to this for a long time."

The camera pulled back and the bald-headed dzee gestured two *deficientes* into view.

"Matt and Deborah will assist you through decon," he said. "Please do not hinder them or confuse them in their duties. They become anxious when things don't go as planned."

Baldy patted each of them on the shoulder, and the couple, who looked to be about Harry's age, smiled broadly.

"What *is* your plan?" Harry blurted.

"Your console will be available shortly. I will speak with you again at that time."

The screen blanked, then displayed a rain-forest waterfall with the caption "Another piece of our Garden won back!"

Harry couldn't sit still. He had to pace the tiny room in a jerky stumble, trailing his sheet behind him. He noticed that not just their walls, but the ceilings, bunks, and doors were all shades of pink.

We're either on another planet, or I'm still rummy from the spray.

He focused on Sonja's blue eyes. Finally, she smiled.

"ViraVax," he said. "Chill."

Sonja nodded.

"I was hoping maybe I was hallucinating. . . ."

"My dad talked about their decon," she said. "The first time it takes hours, and they do it in a pink room because pink calms people down."

"Great," Harry said. "The only facility in the world guarded by security developed by my father. That was before the Agency pulled out, and we can see they've gone downhill. All five levels underground can survive a direct hit by a nuke. This place has a private army better than most countries. Our odds of getting out of here are not good."

A human figure filled the screen. It was the bald-headed dzee, picking up as though they'd been in the middle of a conversation.

"You've been rattled," Baldy said. "We're keeping you here for observation."

"I guess that's right, since you did the rattling," Harry said. "For how long? Twenty-four hours? Twenty-four years?"

"Until we have what we need," he answered.

"You promised a console the next time you saw us," Sonja said. "Where is it?"

Baldy blinked a couple of times, looked off camera and then back.

"Yes, that will be provided."

"What about my mother, and Sonja's mom?" Harry asked. "They were at the embassy. . . ."

"The embassy has them under protection," Baldy said. "They are not harmed."

The man's voice was soft, modulated, accented from a region that Harry couldn't place. His gaze was intense, chilling. Baldy didn't budge, and neither did his smile. Harry cautioned himself to believe nothing, like the textbook said.

Consider everything a lie which is not an order, Harry recalled.

He hoped, at the very least, that his mother was not here at the Double-Vee.

"And where are we?"

"You are not home."

"Tell us something we don't already know," Sonja muttered.

"If I did that," he said, "we wouldn't have any fun at all, would we? I would tell you things, then you would tell me things, then we would just sit around, bored and crabby, picking on one another. We have all the time in the world, and this is much more interesting."

Harry caught a glimpse of several mongoloid faces staring at the camera from a white room behind Baldy. One of them

pointed and laughed around a huge tongue. Right at the edge
of his awareness he perceived a very high, very faint mechanical
whine.

"My name is Mishwe," Baldy said. "You are under my super-
vision. Your health is excellent and will remain so. Any communication to or from the outside comes through me. A handset and
console are provided for this purpose. This is a biological hazards
area, so your door will remain locked for your own protection.
'Patrolled by guard virus,' you might say. Exploration discour-
aged, should you find yourself outside."

"What about our clothes?" Harry asked.

"For now, you're wearing them. Think of yourselves as Adam
and Eve for the moment, and be unashamed."

The door *snicked* open and Harry jumped towards it. His vision
flickered, winked, and he woke up in a heap on the floor, weak as
water. Mishwe smiled at him from the peel.

"A test and a demonstration," Mishwe said.

"Eat shit and die," Harry mumbled through jaws locked tight
in spasm.

The dzee appeared not to hear.

"Your bodies will not tolerate sudden moves," Mishwe said.
"Whatever you do, I suggest you do it slowly."

The doorlock whisked shut. The whine deepened, then picked
up with a noticeable lurch.

"They're cycling us down another level," Sonja said. "That's
two so far."

The deeper they went, the worse their chances.

Sonja helped Harry onto his bed and pulled his sheet up for
him. Uncontrollable trembling in his legs and arms rendered him
helpless. She draped part of her sheet over his own and lay down
beside him. She began a vigorous rubbing of his arms.

"I'm not cold," he told her. "Whatever he did, it wiped out my
muscle control. I'm not cold, I just can't stop shaking."

Even as he spoke, the shakes let up. Harry stretched each arm
and leg carefully, then tried to rise. Sonja gently pushed him back
down. Her lips brushed his ear.

"Don't let them see how fast you recover," she whispered.

Of course! Harry thought.

He had been taught hostage protocols many times by the embassy and by his father, but his thinking was fuzzy. The glare was
gone, but it was replaced by a sweet-smelling something on the
air. Even if these were their normal precautions, it wasn't making

Harry feel any more comfortable. ViraVax was the size of a small city underground. How would they ever find their way topside again?

Harry faked the shakes for as long as he could, but finally he had to stop out of exhaustion. Sonja draped his sheet over him as he lay, half-somnolent and sweating, able to whisper only "Thanks."

Sonja paced, naked and silent, in front of the screen. The scene remained the same, with the same caption. Sonja continued to pace unselfconsciously with her arms folded under her breasts, head down, her tuft of blonde pubic hair backlit in waterfall silver.

Harry thought her incredibly gorgeous, and unwise to display herself that way—no telling what these people would do to them. He always believed, way down deep, that she was a lot braver than he was. Maybe it was the flying.

"Stop staring," she said. "I can't think."

"I can't think, either, with you marching around naked."

"Work on it" was all she said.

Harry reviewed his dad's hostage drill and computed their odds.

"Most casualties occur in the first few minutes of capture," the embassy pamphlet said. "Under no circumstances should a hostage argue with or resist the captor, unless ordered to harm another hostage. Expect to be killed if you argue or resist."

Harry's breathing settled down. They'd made it through that stage, and it was supposed to be the toughest.

Dad's right, he thought, *I have a lot more luck than smarts.*

It had been a long time since he'd had a fond thought of his father. It was a good feeling.

We've come this far, he thought.

Though aware that he didn't know how far "far" might be, Harry knew that hours, perhaps even a day, had passed and they were alive. That meant that they would probably stay alive, barring a mistake on his part, or an accident.

These people might want to know what else his dad taught him, what else he knew of his dad's work with the embassy. He would have to watch for that.

Meanwhile, Sonja continued her back-and-forth prowl of their room. A squirt of adrenaline headed for his groin, and suddenly Harry had a bad feeling about why he and Sonja were locked in together.

They want us to get it on, he thought.

Harry wondered whether the "Adam and Eve" remark meant that Mishwe had arranged this for the cameras, for his personal pleasure or for science.

Probably all three.

As if on signal, the whine stopped and their outer door *snicked* open. Mishwe stood in the glare, a bundle in his arms. His face was shadowed, unsmiling. Behind him, the unmistakable rattle and cry of monkeys in cages. Two more mongoloid faces peeked around the door.

No more bare-chested stuff—Mishwe wore a white cotton shirt with long sleeves rolled back to the elbows. He placed his bundle on the floor at the foot of Harry's bed.

"Clothing for you. I am to apologize for my treatment of you. Soon your accommodation will be made more suitable."

"Suitable for what?" Sonja asked.

Mishwe paused, then went on without looking at her.

"A meal will be served in fifteen minutes. I have Nullfactor for that muscle tremor. . . ." Mishwe held up a capsule and demonstrated for Harry. "Crush capsule, inhale."

"What else does it have?" Sonja asked. "What else have you given us?"

Mishwe's gaze never left Harry. It was an appraising gaze, as a father might look over a long-lost son.

"If you don't take it," Mishwe told him, "the tremors continue for days. Some people become more sensitive each time. For them, something as small as a heartbeat will set them off. Very unpleasant, sometimes fatal. One for each. Don't swallow them."

Mishwe placed a paper cup with two pink capsules atop the stack of clothes. He backed to the doorway and Harry stopped him.

"You didn't apologize," Harry said. "You said, 'I am to apologize,' but you never did."

Harry's throat was dry. He wanted to see how tight a leash Mishwe was on. The instructors always said, "Don't antagonize your captors, particularly in front of their friends. They will kill you to maintain authority."

Harry was gambling that authority was being maintained, and that included an authority over Mishwe.

Mishwe's bare head flushed.

"I apologize."

Harry was amazed. The claw in his belly relaxed a bit. Mishwe was on a tight leash. They would not be killed. At least, not immediately. They apparently had a high value that they were not aware of.

Maintain dignity to the best that your resources allow.

"No," Harry said, "that's the same thing. To apologize, you have to say you're sorry."

Mishwe sucked a deep breath and let it out slowly. His gaze met Harry's. His voice did not hesitate or falter.

"I'm sorry," Mishwe said, and he added a nod. "I treated both of you without dignity."

He left without looking up.

"Well, what do you make of that?" Harry said.

"That you're an idiot," Sonja answered, "who's bound and determined to get us killed."

"I think he's hurrying this 'win over their trust' phase just a little, don't you?"

Sonja picked up a white pullover top and clutched it to her chest while she sorted through the clothes. They each got towels, pink blankets and a pajama-like top and bottom of white, baggy cotton. Harry laughed at Sonja, clutching the clothes to her chest.

"What's so funny?" she asked.

"You," he said. "Suddenly you're Ms. Modesty."

Sonja started towards the bathroom, then changed her mind and dropped the clothes on her bed with a sigh. Harry picked up his things while she stepped into the pants and pulled on her shirt.

The loose-fitting shirt and pants reminded Harry of the gi he wore during a hundred Saturdays in the gym with his father. For years, the two of them spent Saturday mornings kicking the mirrors, bags and each other to old rock and roll tunes. That had stopped a couple of years ago, when the Colonel's anger and his drinking got out of hand.

The lights modulated in their room, slowly, and the glare from the peel dimmed to the same flat pink as the walls. A skinny young Matt and a very fat young Deborah wheeled in a cart that smelled of food. Both of them wore the same pajama-type clothing that he and Sonja wore. Matt and Deborah set up their meal quickly, placing everything meticulously on the table without so much as a gestural conversation between them. Harry noted that there were no knives or forks, only spoons.

"Do you two work here," Harry asked them, "or are you prisoners, too?"

The young man worried his tongue in and out of his cheek and frowned deeply, as though he wanted to say something, but Deborah's stern gaze kept him quiet.

"This stuff isn't poison or anything, is it?"

Nothing.

The two left as they came, silent, the woman leading and the man pushing the cart. This time Harry pushed out the door behind them, but immediately he was shoved back inside by another guard dressed in a hazard suit.

"What do they think we have?" he wondered aloud. "Why do some of them have to wear those suits around us?"

"Maybe they're protecting us from them," Sonja said. "No telling what *they* have cooking inside."

Harry was feeling a little better, a little more like he and Sonja might live through this, after all.

"Will you join me?" Harry asked, and offered her his arm.

"I'm not so sure," Sonja said, her voice low.

"Aren't you hungry?"

"Aren't you worried about something in the food?" Sonja whispered.

"No," Harry said. "If there's anything in there, it's probably to kill whatever resident bugs we've got that they don't want. So far, everything has had a reason and they haven't really *hurt* us since we got here."

"That comment about dignity," she added. "It didn't sound right, coming from him."

"Are you saying that because you've known him so well for so long?"

"Stop it," she hissed. "I'm not the enemy."

"We've got plenty of them to choose from," Harry whispered. "That Casey guy who runs this place, for instance. My dad hated him. I don't know whether it was this place or the religion, but he hated him. And I got the impression that his assignment to ViraVax and away from the field work was some kind of punishment, some kind of lesson the Agency was teaching him."

"Anyway," Sonja said, "we're still being recorded and studied and I'm positive that they will never allow us to leave here alive."

Harry sat at the table and inhaled the fragrant steam from the food.

"Don't worry," he said, "the food's probably safe. They'll want to keep us in good shape during this experiment, or whatever. I'm not doing those, though."

Harry indicated the two pink capsules in their paper cup.

"That's transparent. If they want me to take their bogus antidote, they'll have to give it to me the same way they gave me the original. I'm here, but I'm not helping."

With that, he raised a middle finger to one of the lenses and dug into his bowl of hot milkrice and honey.

22

JOSHUA CASEY WAITED in his spartan outer office and monitored the arrival of his father at the lift pad. As usual, the facility's work stood still while staff and Innocents alike turned out for a glimpse of the Master in the flesh.

"Look there," Casey said.

He zoomed the monitor to focus on a large dark stain under the chopper's left-hand skid.

"Is that what I think it is?" Shirley asked.

Casey grunted acknowledgment.

"Another Meltdown," he said, and glanced at the time on his screen. "The Sabbath starts in three hours and no one out there is working!"

"The Master always lifts morale," Shirley reminded him. "Next week's production will make up for it."

"The sooner he's secured in here, the better," Casey said. "If there's a Meltdown while he's here, the whole world will know about it."

Casey tapped the peel to indicate the Master's entourage—personal secretary, bodyguard and historian. Everything he did or said was documented for his next book or film or sermon. Documentation, for Joshua Casey, was the enemy. No one in this entourage, including his father, had been permitted below Level One. Only the Master knew that the facility went deeper than Level Two, and even he did not know details of what transpired there.

"See the others to their quarters," Casey said. "Have the Master brought directly to me."

"Yes, Joshua."

Casey refocused on his father's craggy face, its lean lines belying his thick thatch of gray hair. It was a face of authority and wisdom, one that television had imprinted forever into the awareness of nearly three quarters of the population of the globe. No pang of conscience, no guilt at all, shadowed that face or those clear, blue eyes.

It's because I do the dirty work and keep it to myself, Casey thought.

Keeping the children to himself, keeping the Meltdowns to himself, would be nearly impossible. His best bet was sequestering his father for a briefing as quickly as possible.

The customary bowl and towels were laid out on the side table for foot-washing, and a beaker of fresh ice water stood ready on the serving tray. The Master would stay over for the entire Sabbath, which was an honor and a joy for the ViraVax staff, but a source of great apprehension for Joshua Casey.

Calvin Casey was a tough act to follow, and Joshua had been following him all his life. Calvin started in Christian industry with JIL—the "Jesus Is Lord Gas Station and Mini-Mart" chain—in the mid-1980s. By the turn of the millennium his Children of Eden had put a leash on the oil companies through their distribution bottleneck. Other gas stations burned in a decade of civil embroilments, but the Jesus Is Lord Gas Stations and Mini-Marts stood firmly in the grip of the faithful, who subsidized their protection and low prices with their tithes.

Joshua Casey grew up with faith healers, vegetarianism and high colonics. His long-simmering scorn for traditional medicine had not been tempered in the least by his experiences in the bio-engineering field. He delighted not a whit when they accepted the products of his research. Medicine was always behind research, tugging at its coattails, bogging it down. Joshua Casey was ahead of the best and he intended to stay ahead. He knew what his assistants whispered about him, he knew everything that transpired around him. Information was his forte, whether gossip or codons.

Now there was this matter of Dajaj Mishwe, and an international political disruption that threatened to turn the spotlight on ViraVax, the Children of Eden, on Joshua Casey himself.

These incidents must be made to disappear.

What Mishwe had done to create these two children was nothing more than a genetic midwifery, and Mishwe flirted with blasphemy when he indicated otherwise. Indiscretion was forgivable, blasphemy was not.

Mishwe's passions, such that they were, needed to be redirected into his work.

His assigned *work.*

Dajaj Mishwe still had great value to Casey, to ViraVax and to the Children of Eden, in spite of what he'd done. Removing him altogether would not be an irreparable loss, but without a ready replacement it would cause a major inconvenience. And Joshua Casey suspected that removing Mishwe might leave certain experimental programs undirected, programs like Meltdown, which was dangerously close to going rogue.

I have been distracted lately, Casey admitted. *I was careless to let Mishwe act on his own.*

Marte Chang was Casey's distraction. He had restricted her to offices and quarters on Level One, and to the lab/production facilities allotted to her on Level Two. Still, there was the chance of an accidental encounter with the children or with Mishwe's other handiwork, and that would ruin everything.

Casey placed himself at stalemate: he needed Mishwe, he wanted Chang and he was stuck with two kidnapped teenagers.

He windowed out the lift pad monitor and rotated holographics of a half dozen likely viral structures at his desktop workstation. It was the kind of thing that helped him think out more than one solution at once. He marked out linkage points and coded in the proteins that he wanted placed there. He sought a viral construct that would reverse the Meltdown response once it was initiated. Nothing here looked especially promising, but Mishwe could try them out on that squad that picked up the children. There would have to be an explanation, of course, but he had time for that.

So soon after the Bartlett case, too, he thought. *This will require considerable thought.*

Red Bartlett had been careless, therefore a great waste. Casey did not want to throw good money after bad.

He caught himself scratching at his scalp.

Somebody could coax a virus into tinkering a gene to regenerate hair, he thought.

It was actually a simple task, one that he could visualize easily. He noted the sequence in his Sidekick and vowed to give it to one of the techs as a bonus one day. On a slow day, it might even get the Agency off his back.

But Joshua Casey would not tease it out himself. He had bigger fish to fry than engineering a living line of cosmetics. Even if it were ready today, he would never allow himself to receive any inoculation, knowing what he himself had perpetrated on the unwitting laboratory of the world.

He shook his head, trying to rid it of distraction. Those two children quartered in decon posed the greatest threat ViraVax ever faced, thanks to Mishwe.

He just couldn't wait, Casey thought.

He knew, as Mishwe knew, that they had already waited plenty long enough.

This was not the way!

They could have gathered the materials they needed a thousand other ways, then raised a covey of fetuses in the privacy of Level Five, in the wombs of the Innocents, and no one would be the wiser.

But Mishwe had never wanted this to be a lab procedure. He'd wanted to see how the children would fare in the real world. He wondered whether their offspring would be viable. Offspring of the first AVA-initiated clones would be stage three of the process begun years ago with a viral infection that significantly altered Colonel Toledo's and Red Bartlett's spermatic structures.

Casey had to admit that his heart rate rose significantly at the prospect of stage three. He could imagine the kids now, drugged and naked in their quarters, under the voyeuristic electronic eye of Dajaj Mishwe. That would be changed immediately, of course.

Joshua Casey tried not to scratch at his scalp.

Primitive, he thought. *Disgustingly primitive.*

His recent hair transplant represented to him all of the inelegant butchery of modern medicine, the pompous witchcraft that had tried to charm him into its fold. The baldness represented something that was out of his control, and Casey needed control. This matter with the teenagers was proof enough of that.

These particular adolescents were clones, products of only one "parent" via the machinations of artificial viral agents. Therefore, it was possible that, like the Innocents, they had no souls and whatever became of them required no pang of conscience.

But the storm over their disappearance demanded an intricate defense.

Casey's attention shifted to the cool, sensuous image of Marte Chang. She would be here forever, he was sure of that now. So much the better if it were voluntary, and enthusiastic. Anything less would bring the Agency down on him, and he was not yet far enough along in his plan to risk that.

Shirley Good would have to be dealt with in time, he could see that, too. She belonged to ViraVax and her accommodation would be simple. Shirley was one of the saved, however, and that made Casey squirm a little.

The answer will come, in time, he thought.

If things didn't work out with Chang, he would give her to Mishwe as his "special assistant." Special assistants did not last long in Mishwe's care, but they inevitably proved an invaluable source of hard data.

Casey turned his thoughts to Mishwe and his young subjects. Dajaj Mishwe had been, unquestionably, the most valuable tool in the ViraVax facility. In the beginning, when Casey had the idea of ideas, Mishwe had been the technician to make it happen. Casey had marveled then at his father's foresight in seeking out and training intelligent loners and orphans.

Everything that Joshua Casey had wanted to accomplish in bio-engineering depended on one thing—reliable and repeated access to the body, an immune system override.

Or a disguise.

Casey needed something set up inside, something resident in the body itself, undetected by the immune system and ready to be called into action at his bidding.

It had been a crude kernel of an idea, formulated at a time when big-money grants focused on immune disorders. Casey had been ahead of them all along in theory, but when his father delivered him the virogeneticist, Dajaj Mishwe, idea became substance.

Hackers, Casey recalled. *It all started with hackers.*

He'd known what he had wanted to do for the world long before he knew how to do it. He'd wanted to engineer a humanity that was worthy of repopulating the Garden of Eden, and on the way to that goal he wanted a humanity that would either work to restore Eden or get out of his way. To do that, he needed a key to the body's various mechanisms without triggering its immune system. Then he needed the right pair of hands to carry it off. Mishwe had those hands.

In those days Casey thought of himself as a hacker—not a computer hacker, but a gene hacker. The most important thing to a hacker was "getting in," gaining entrance to a system. Casey was smart enough to conceptualize a viral sequence, an artificial viral agent, he called it, that could be introduced into a body through common procedures—flu shots, communion wafers, childhood inoculations. Casey called this stage formatting.

The Formatting AVA prepared the body to receive any further materials that Casey might prepare for it. He was a man who thought ahead. He and Mishwe invented the rest at leisure, knowing that his gateway was clear and his security perfect.

Casey acknowledged that pride was one of the more dangerous sins. Nevertheless, he allowed himself pride in knowing more about virology and gene-shifting than most professional virologists, and as a chief executive officer he had a lot more power. Money, filtered through the Children of Eden, was no object.

Casey was the first to consider monoclonal antibodies as stepping-stones rather than stumbling blocks. By engineering the proper hybridomas that produced the proper antibodies, he came up with a multistage biological lockpick that could also become a time bomb, at his whim.

And now Mishwe had surprised him, just when things were moving so smoothly that he'd thought surprise impossible. Mishwe's experiment with the teenagers had never been authorized, had been a whim, albeit a successful one, and Casey knew now that he should have ended it fifteen years ago.

Casey spoke to his console.

"Shirley."

"Here," she answered. "What is it?"

"Get me the status of the two packages that Mishwe brought in, please."

"On-screen or in person?"

There would be plenty of data in the system soon enough. He knew that the Agency did its share of eavesdropping, and he wanted to be sure that everything within the system was secure, even from them.

"Better bring it here," he said. "Priority."

"Will do," she said. "And, Joshua, there's something else."

Shirley never called him Joshua except in their most intimate moments. He scratched his scalp again.

"What?"

"The Chang woman. She's very unhappy, and she spends all of her spare time running search programs on our system."

"She's young, bright, bored and lonely," Casey said. "We have to prove to her that we're her family now. Her Sunspots will be up and running soon, then she'll be gone. We've been over this—"

"Why are you so quick to take her side?" Shirley interrupted. "I'm telling you that my flags are up. We don't know what she'll find. Bartlett's log is somewhere in the system, and we haven't been able to find it ourselves. . . ."

"You're right," he said, more to shut her off than out of conviction. "I'll watch it. Meanwhile, tag everything that her system finds."

"I already have," she said, her voice a little too smug to suit him.

His Sidekick beeped and his daily report from the Agency began its scroll down his viewscreen. He routed it to the mainframe in his inner office for review later. He preferred to tackle the Agency's prose at night, when he tried to wind down for sleep. Casey did not take medicines, chemicals or inoculations of any kind, but he had found that the Agency's doublespeak experts could lull him to sleep in moments.

Two Innocents shuffled through his doorway, Daniel and Louisa. They pushed their small cart over the threshold and nodded. He acknowledged them but did not speak—it merely encouraged their chatter and distracted them from their chores.

Mishwe spoke with them often. Indeed, the little emotion that Mishwe squandered on the world went out to these soulless ones. Mishwe was their champion, and Casey had to admit that he got good work out of them.

Daniel poured two glasses of ice water and unwrapped Casey's tiny loaf of hot bread while Louisa emptied his wastebasket of its one crumpled page.

"She's naked," Daniel said, giggling, and Casey looked up.

"Who's naked?"

"The girl." He pointed towards the decon elevators. "Naked, naked."

Louisa chimed in, hard to understand around her thick tongue. "Naked boy, too," she said. "Bad boy."

Her expression, like Daniel's, was all smiles. "Bad boy" was merely rhetorical, what they expected him to think of it. They were right.

What the hell is security doing? Showing them off to the whole world?

Perhaps this was Mishwe's idea of insurance—not everyone who saw them could be disappeared, and neither could the children.

"You will not speak of what you have seen to anyone," he ordered. "Forget the boy and girl. I want both of you to set up the Master's quarters immediately. Repeat."

Daniel repeated the orders, counting on his fingers. "Forget the boy and girl. Set up for the Master."

Daniel's expression showed that he was very pleased with himself, and Louisa looked equally pleased, though all she had done was dust the same spot on his desk over and over.

"Very good," Casey said, and dismissed them with a wave of his hand.

He hoped that these two were the only ones to have contact with the children. It would make the inevitable upleasantness to come much, much cleaner.

Mishwe put the children into decon without consulting Casey. This infuriated Casey at first, but he saw the wisdom and the inevitability of it now. At least there would be minimal chance of cross-contamination.

All traffic took place topside, from the lift pad. Limited as that traffic was, it still provided an exposure, and any glimpse of those kids would be the end of ViraVax.

Yes, Casey nodded to himself, *we're committed.*

Mishwe would pay, one way or another.

Mishwe knew he'd never let them go, he thought. *He knows that I can't let them go, either.*

Mishwe had his indiscretions, but in his fifteen years at ViraVax they had always occurred down below, threatening no one.

He must feel strongly about these children, Casey admitted.

That was when he realized that Mishwe felt strongly about the Innocents, too. He treated them like his own children, and they flocked to him wherever he walked in the facility. Casey was surprised at this revelation, surprised to the point of alarm. Mishwe seldom showed interest in anything beyond his science.

Dear God, he prayed, *make the solution to this problem clear and quick so that Your work can proceed unhindered. . . .*

"Dr. Casey. . . ."

Casey started at the woman's voice behind him, then flushed as he hurriedly donned his cap to protect his scabby scalp from view.

"What is it?" he snapped.

He projected his voice, already louder than most, and paralyzed Marte Chang in his doorway. Casey produced a reassuring smile and motioned her inside. He noted her glance at the holographics and dismissed them with the flick of a key. He cleared a stack of enlargements from the only other chair. His outer office was small, meant for clutter. Clutter said you were busy, took up space, kept people from staying long. Level One was the only place that Casey was concerned about appearances.

"I'm sorry," she said. "I know you don't like to be disturbed here. . . ."

"I *refuse* to be disturbed here," he corrected. "Therefore, you are not disturbing me, you are merely interrupting my work."

Casey manufactured another smile and waved her towards the chair. She had the potential of being his most talented viral engineer, and he did not want to alienate her. Her power project was nearly finished; he'd strung that one out long enough to get a good feel for her work. She could make a satisfactory replacement for Red Bartlett, should she be persuaded to stay. When he was convinced of her loyalties, he would introduce her to some of their more interesting projects.

"Sit," he insisted. "As long as you're here, let's both be comfortable."

Again, the complete smile.

Marte Chang crossed to the chair, and Casey watched with undisguised pleasure. Two years ago Shirley had snared Chang's transmission of her paper "The Virus as Industrial Robot" on its way to a network presentation. The paper had been precipitated by, and quoted heavily from, the seminal work of Dr. Joshua Casey on manipulations of viral architecture. He had received the paper closed-circuit, bypassing the web, through an expensive but valuable arrangement that he had with several carriers around the world. He was out of country, but not out of touch.

Marte's paper had proceeded in the direction of Casey's own research, and its practical applications could well surpass it.

How convenient that I own the means to practical application, Casey thought.

In six months Marte had made up ground that had taken Casey six years to cover. And he thought she was beautiful, in a reptilian sort of way.

Casey was lustful of her beauty, cautious of her intellect, and he had yet to sound out her motives.

Why us? he wondered.

Hundreds of facilities and a dozen small countries would have paid lavishly and treated her like royalty if they'd had the chance to produce her Sunspots.

But she chose us.

He would like to believe it was divine providence, but something in his spine said otherwise.

Of course, she had received her bachelor's and her master's at the University of Montangel, built by his father and owned by the Children of Eden. She had been young, brilliant, graced with more scholarships than she could use, but she had never accepted the Children of Eden as her faith. This he could not understand. She did everything alone. Some saw this as a sign of fear. Casey thought she must have great courage.

It was not public knowledge that the university had been built by Casey's donation of his annual royalties from HIVAX, his AIDS vaccine. Let the world's eye be on his father and the university—Casey preferred the comfortable anonymity he had built for himself in Costa Brava.

Though much less important than his breakthrough with oncogenes and the subsequent control of cancer, the AIDS vaccine carried with it a suitable drama. His work with oncogenes handed the medical boys their breakthrough on a platter—the AIDS vaccine he accomplished on his own. But the Costa Brava installation of ViraVax and its employees, for all practical purposes, did not exist.

When Joshua Casey realized the implications of his first artificial viral agent, he turned to the Agency for a multilayered security package. He wanted to disappear before he could ever be discovered, and it had been the wisest move of his life.

If Marte Chang found out about half of the operations at ViraVax, she might be trouble. But if push came to shove, he would use the national security argument to get what he needed. It was an unassailable argument, since it was nominally true.

And Casey's ultimate plans far exceeded the petty concerns of national security.

He would need to test her out, sooner or later.

So far, it appeared that she thrived on her project to convert the facility from their hydroelectric source to her Sunspots. He'd thrown small problems at her, too, and found her both curious and quick to solution. Winning her over would require a certain delicacy, a delicacy which Casey knew all too well was not a part of his natural makeup.

He had made her wait while he pretended to examine one of the transparencies.

"What is it?" he asked, and noted her undiminished agitation.

He steepled his pale fingers and frowned in an approximation of concern.

"You have experimented on Costa Bravan citizens without their knowledge or consent," she said. "That's unacceptable."

Casey felt the tiger in him preparing to spring and relaxed. He opened his posture and rested his hands on the arms of his chair. Aggression was what she expected, what she prepared for. He would give her something of the tar baby.

"I have done nothing of the sort. . . ."

"ViraVax has," she said, "and you are ViraVax."

As usual, his first inclination was to lie. He suppressed it. Taking her into confidence would bring her closer. Besides, he had nothing to fear and she had nowhere to go.

"Where did you get your information?"

"It's all around me," she said, pointing out the window at a group of retarded youngsters returning from the gardens. "This country went from the highest birthrate in the world to the lowest within the last ten years. All since you came to town. Coincidence?"

"All individuals who have been recipients of any program here were duly represented by their government," Casey said. "We developed the biology, but it was their choice to administer it. Bear with me one minute." Casey put up a hand to stop her protest. "You were not here for the longest-running civil war in the Western Hemisphere. *That* was their means of birth control, along with bad water and infant dysentery. It makes what's going on in the U.S. right now look like a picnic. There's an old saying in population control: 'You've got to shut off the faucet before you reach for the mop.' We enabled anyone who wishes it to shut off that faucet."

"But how . . . ?"

"Simple and elegant," he said, and smiled. "We added a vector to the routine inoculations, a vector that renders the membrane of the ovum impenetrable by the sperm."

"No, I mean *how could you*?"

Once again, Casey silenced her protest with a gesture.

"I know how you feel," he said. "I have feelings about this sort of thing, too. But we are *toolmakers*. If we manufactured pipe wrenches and some plumber bludgeoned his wife to death with one, would we be obligated to stop manufacturing our wrenches? Should we throw all of our resources into the development of a softer wrench? I think not."

"But this is *terrible*. . . ."

"Well," Casey said, and leaned forward, capturing her gaze, "we can't think about that. Regrettable, perhaps. Terrible, perhaps. But that is the past. It is out of our control, and we must go on. We must continue to provide humans with the best possible tools to improve their quality of life. You are here because you have the skills to do that. I guess I must ask you now, are you willing to go forward with us and help us with things we can control? Or will you leave us, dwelling on the past and on things over which we have no control?"

"There is more."

Casey sucked in a breath and blew it out in a display of great impatience. He waved her on.

"Does the term 'trisomy twenty-one' mean anything to you?"

His gaze did not waver, but he was beginning to have doubts about the efficacy of hiring Marte Chang. The prospect of marrying her, he could see, had been an adolescent fantasy. If he was not fully satisfied of her loyalties by the end of this interview, he would have to find another suitable use for her.

"This country also has the highest incidence of trisomy births in the world," she added. "Does that mean you've decided what *kind* of children people will have?"

"Yes," he said flatly, "and it means that, once again, you are dwelling on the past. Psychologists will tell you that it is not a healthy habit to pursue."

The hint of threat appeared to be lost on her. She went on.

"The children that these people are allowed to have . . . an extremely high proportion are high-functioning Down's syndrome children. With a side effect like this . . ."

"It's not a side effect," Casey said. "It's a whole different matter."

"You mean . . . the García government *wants* this? But why?"

Casey shrugged, and sighed his best frustrated sigh.

"Again, they've misused one of our tools," he said. "They attempted to create for themselves a manageable labor force. . . ."

"They're just biological industrial robots, that's what you've done here!" Marte snapped.

Casey put all of his conscious effort into maintaining his calm.

"Once again, Ms. Chang, I assure you that *I* have not done this. *We* have not done this. But, yes, it has been done. And it is in the past. And in the future we shall do our best to see to it that this kind of technology cannot be misused. But to do that, we need responsible personnel. It was no accident that we chose to implement your own technology to power this facility. You are exhibiting right now the very forthrightness and honesty that we hope to cultivate here. That is our investment in the future. Do you want to be a part of that future?"

Her gaze wavered, and it was her turn to sigh. She twisted and untwisted a strand of her long black hair around her finger.

"I'm not . . . I mean . . . I think so. I had to talk to you about this. I couldn't just go on as though I didn't know."

"Of course not."

Then Joshua smoothed his tone.

"The truth is," he cooed, "I've been expressly forbidden to pursue any follow-up that would interfere with this program."

"But if you're not concerned about the welfare of the test subjects, surely you don't want to endanger others, maybe ourselves. . . ."

"That's why we take precautions here, Ms. Chang. We have been in business for more than fifteen years, and not one of us has come down with so much as the sniffles."

This was a lie, and the reason he spent as much time as possible in his private bunker. But he knew that there was no way she could prove otherwise. He had taken care of that. This time it was Marte who put up her hand.

"This is not an attack," she said. "I came to you with something important when it came to my attention. I will continue to do that so that we can continue an excellent working relationship. What you do about it is your concern."

Casey leaned back in his chair. His instinct had been right when he hadn't told her that most of the Agency's field subjects were not in Costa Brava, nor were they inmates and prisoners.

Is she with us? he wondered.

He didn't like having to wonder. If she deduced two of their projects, she might deduce more. This one didn't seem to bother her, which was a plus in her favor. He would like very much to replace Mishwe, whose psychosis had finally placed them all in jeopardy. But to replace Mishwe, she would have to be loyal and without conscience. Still, she had come to *him* with her suspicions, not to the outside world.

Maybe that's the sign, he thought. *Maybe she's the right one, after all.*

Regarding other matters, Casey was confident that the security squad had covered their tracks too thoroughly for even the Agency to follow, much less a wet-behind-the-ears graduate.

He smiled his most winning smile.

"I appreciate that," he said. "I am embarking on a new project that is most fascinating. I could use your expertise. How about discussing it over dinner?"

"It's a dangerous policy to date the boss."

He hung on to the smile.

"This isn't a date," he said. "It's a meeting. Trust me."

At last, the smile that he'd angled for crossed her lips.

"Promise it won't be the cafeteria?"

He promised.

23

COLONEL TOLEDO RODE inside a special compartment in the back of a refrigerated van, heading further into the Jaguar Mountains. Tío wrestled the wheel around the usual washouts, chuckholes and debris. Rico eavesdropped on Tío's steady stream of innovative profanity through the earpiece connected to his Sidekick. Yolanda rode shotgun in the cab.

The Colonel wanted Yolanda and he wanted a drink, but he wanted to find Harry even more. He stuffed the unflattering cravings of his body as far down into the dark as he could, and concentrated only on those things that worked towards his son's release.

Eight men had died when the drone dropped on their command center. The precision of the strike was rare in Costa Brava. It indicated that someone had good data, and the guerrillas speculated that that someone was higher-placed than the García boys, perhaps someone in the embassy itself. Some said that they were striking at the guerrillas out of frustration, using product from Agency files compiled by Rico himself. Rico didn't tell them about the Parasite, and he hoped that the unit he cracked was the only one they'd planted.

"They really don't want you," Yolanda had reminded him. "They only want what you can bring them. You are the bait for a great fish. Who would come to help you, Colonel, if you were trapped and alone? Who would be held hostage if you were held hostage?"

He had the dark ride in the truck to think it out, and he was sure she was wrong. They already had what they wanted—the kids.

Peace and Freedom is far bigger than anybody guessed, he thought. *Even if I told everything I knew, it wouldn't destroy them.*

Within a half hour of the strike, guerrillas assembled new equipment at a rendezvous twenty klicks up the road. There seemed to be no end to their supply lines, and their equipment was the best. All brand names had been removed, but Rico recognized the satlink modules and Litespeeds as Japanese. They were superior to the embassy's equipment, and the embassy had a trade embargo to blame for that.

One thing Rico knew was that he had no disagreement with the guerrillas. He had monitored them, infiltrated them and occasionally fought them over the past twenty years. Now they were stronger than ever, and they clearly didn't see him as a threat. The guerrilla movement that he had been fighting had been a sham, street theater set up to keep the Agency and its cousins busy while the real work went on uninterrupted.

Japan needed land, and obviously the Peace and Freedom people had struck a deal.

But Colonel Toledo's secrets could fill many a grave and empty a lot of pockets. ViraVax, for sure, would go down. The Agency, like Peace and Freedom, would be nicked but not out. Different butts would polish different chairs in a few governments, but the Children of Eden would remain the wealthiest single entity in the world, with or without the two Caseys.

The Colonel reflected on Project Labor, the trisomy twenty-one project, and the fact that the process was a ViraVax patent that his protection made possible. He should have known that a paranoid like Casey would cover all bases. Everything kept coming back to Joshua Casey.

Those goddamned Gardeners are going to own the world.

Catholics believed unbelievers to be unsaved, but Children of Eden believed them to be unhuman. Cattle. Tools or chaff.

The Colonel, like many Agency personnel in Costa Brava, was a lip-service Catholic, in it for family and the network. Rico thought of himself as an Old Testament Catholic. The New Testament didn't allow the flexibility of expression of the Old Testament. He empathized with someone who would turn water into wine at a party, but from a soldier's point of view, eye for an eye made much more sense than turn the other cheek.

Good guys carried swords in the Old Testament, he thought.

In the New Testament, only bad guys used their swords. Rico Toledo was not ready to offer up his sword upon anyone's altar. The Colonel smiled. He was a good guy who carried a sword, like the archangels Gabriel and Michael, and it was high time he used it. Rico had a gut feeling that he would heft it against either El Presidente Rigoberto García or Joshua Casey.

Within an hour of the Colonel's arrival, a condo four-plex outside a sleepy highland village became Command Central, a duplicate of their bombed-out quarters down-valley. Reports of the kidnappings varied wildly, and for the first time Colonel Rico Toledo felt blind, deaf and dumb in the heart of a crisis. Yolanda and El Indio brought in twenty people and a vanful of electronics. So far all the Colonel had been able to muster was a whopping headache.

The government hadn't bothered to send troops to mop up after the drone. It told Rico that they were confident of their strike or scared shitless of a face-to-face with the guerrillas. His money was on the latter.

El Indio assured him that all of their new equipment was shielded and transmissions double-scrambled, but some villager still could pop them for a favor or a job.

"Still, you do not understand how black their hearts are," El Indio lectured him, as though Rico were a greenhorn. "You are like me, more interested in the network, the information, the game. I respected you, your work. I respect you now. I do not respect your government's complicity in my country's misery."

The four techs who were setting up were very good, and very fast. Rico and El Indio stood in the middle of a living room snarled with cables, gloveware, terminals, printers, satboxes and Litespeeds.

"Blaming the bombing on me, that's to be expected," Rico said. "I'm suspended, a wild man, so even the U.S. can speculate on this one and come out a winner. But the kids . . . I don't get the connection."

"Perhaps there is no connection," Yolanda said. "Maybe whoever did the bombing didn't know about the kidnapping plan. Somebody saw the opportunity to get some press out of linking the two, perhaps even a third party. You have made such deliberate misconnections to the press yourself in the past, no?"

Rico nodded, and felt his shoulders sag in spite of himself.

"Yes," he sighed, "more than once. But we usually *knew* the reality even if what we released was fiction. Somebody, somewhere, knows what's going on. I sure wish I had access to the Agency."

"We're getting our eyes and ears connected now," Yolanda said. "This place is secure, but we will jump all of our electronics through at least three steps as a precaution. . . ."

A lot of good it did last time, he thought, but he kept it to himself.

A young woman waved at Yolanda from across the room and gave her the thumbs-up sign.

"Satellite's hot," Yolanda said. "I'll have a report for you in just a few minutes."

"Thanks," Rico said. "I feel so . . . useless. . . ."

"Don't worry," she said. "There will be too much to do very soon. You could rest. . . ."

"No, I couldn't," he said. "Not until I get my boy."

She hugged him in silence, and left. The smell of the sweat in her hair lingered after her, and Rico felt a rush of desire. Just as suddenly, he felt the upswelling of rage.

"My son is snatched, my ex-wife unaccounted for, I'm blamed for an embassy bombing and there is *nothing* I can *do* about it. . . ."

The Colonel caught himself pounding on the desk. El Indio, the technicians in the room, their two teenage guards, all stared at him, stock-still. To most of these people he had been one of the enemy for years, and an Agency man, at that. He was a Catholic in name only and he had installed the Children of Eden in this region and in this government. Only El Indio knew how many times he had acted on behalf of the Peace and Freedom Party.

"I'm sorry," Rico said, breaking the tension. "I'm sorry, but I have to do *something.*"

El Indio shook his head. "It's better that you don't," he said. "We don't want anyone out there on your trail to find us here. Don't worry, we have everything here, everything. You have underestimated us all along, as was our desire, but now you will see what we can really do."

Rico Toledo settled in to wait, but he had never waited well and didn't intend to start now. He was angry and hyper so he had a few rum and sugars. Then he wanted Yolanda. He tried to write it off to their bonding under fire, to cabin fever, but his body wouldn't listen. He concentrated on the important things.

Why weren't there any reports about Grace, or Nancy Bartlett? he wondered. *Not a word about them from the press or the network.*

Rico well knew the penchant the press had for interviewing grieving family members at uncomfortable times.

The bomb was really in my car, he thought. *Who was the target? Who wanted everybody to think it was me?*

Rico couldn't think of any time that his car had been out of range of his Watchdog, the alarm adjunct to his Sidekick. Whoever had got to him had been good, or simply inside.

The corporal, he thought. *The one who parked my car. . . .*

So far, the only pronouncements coming across the newslines were from the García government, and they clearly used the incident to discredit him. Anyone up-and-coming in the García government was going to do it through the military. Anyone up-and-coming in the military would be a Gardener, trained in the Night School, founded by Colonel Rico Toledo.

The U.S. wasn't talking and the Agency was out of touch. Rico couldn't be completely sure about the Peace and Freedom people except that they saved his skin, and were now amassing their resources to help him find Harry and Sonja.

Maybe they planted the bomb so that they could get me here, get me on their side.

He didn't think that was likely. Bombs were too nonspecific, too messy. Their own people would have been at risk.

If not García, and not Peace and Freedom, then who?

One of the guerrillas brought a pot of coffee and set it between El Indio and Rico on the desk. He was the truck driver, Tío, about Rico's age, potbellied. His jeans rode low in the back, and his T-shirt said: "So What If That Horse Was Blessed by the Pope. Can He Plow?"

Out of the back pocket of the jeans Tío pulled an envelope, folded many times. He nodded at Rico, his eyes cold, then unfolded the envelope and handed it to El Indio. He passed the list of numbers over reverently, clearly honored to be in the presence of such a legendary pair as the Colonel and El Indio.

Rico tossed back his rum and sugar. El Indio's attention was wrapped up in the headphones he wore and the viewscreen he studied.

"Jabalí," Tío said with a respectful nod. "Jabalí."

Rico's skin cooled at the sound of that name, the one he hadn't heard except in his sleep for the past twenty years. Yes, he had been Jabalí, Wild Boar, but that was two decades ago in a country that, like so many, no longer existed.

Again, he looked the fuzzy-haired guerrilla over and tried to place him.

"Belice?" he asked.

"No, señor, not so far as the ghost of Belice. The networks. I
followed your strategies on the web. We have used them here, as
you know."

"I know," Rico said. "You've used them against me."

Tío covered his mouth when he laughed, a custom of the
mountain folk.

"Not until now did I know that you were also the North
American Colonel Toledo. But you know, we used your strategies
against your government, not against your esteemed self."

"I was representing my government, and it was my butt out
there getting itself kicked and looking bad."

Rico tried to calm himself down. He was looking for a fight,
he could feel that now, and this man was not.

This man is not the enemy, Rico reminded himself. *Back off.*

Tío straightened, his expression hardened.

"Yes, your country was distracted then, as it is now," Tío said.
"They forgot you down here. That was when you learned to live
here, and quit coming after us."

Rico did not want trouble with this man, or these people. He
fought the unreasonable urge to rip Tío's throat out. He practiced
being casual and measured out his voice.

"What do you do here?" Rico asked him.

"I break codes and access the webs," Tío said. "Getting us onto
the networks is easy. Covering the trail is another matter. Tell me,
señor, why did you not go back to your country?"

"I've lived here most of my life, I know this country," Rico
muttered. "I don't know the United States anymore. It's a jungle."

"A jungle, yes," Tío said. "They are animals up there, it is true.
And in Costa Brava, of course, we are civilized."

Both men laughed.

"Welcome," Tío offered, and shook Rico's hand. "I have five
children myself, and three grandchildren. We will find your son."

Tío stepped back, snapped a half-salute towards El Indio and
left.

Rico's hands shook just a bit.

Booze? he wondered.

Hubbub in the room picked up once again as everyone turned
to their chores.

"Have you heard of Project Labor?" El Indio asked.

He twisted one of the earphones aside so he could hear Rico's
answer.

"I have," Rico said. "It's no longer viable."

"What is it?"

Rico sighed, then said, "I can't tell you."

"You won't tell me, you mean. Remember, you yourself taught me the subtleties between 'can't' and 'won't' in English."

"Why can't you be grateful for all of the things I did tell you, instead of harping on what I didn't?"

The Colonel's dander was up again, and his head throbbed.

"Grateful?" El Indio's face flushed, and he stood. "Grateful?"

"Yes," Rico said. "That's been our relationship. Grateful for what we got, no pressure elsewhere. It was not an Agency operation. It was Costa Brava, direct from Minister of the Interior. Where did you hear the term?"

"Something from the networks," El Indio said. "Mariposa and Tío got us into a Night School system. I have a memo here that says you registered a protest over Project Labor. I gather that it was implemented behind your back, and that it was something vital. Your embassy job began the next week. You never mentioned it."

Well, El Indio's people were better than he thought if they could crack even one box on the Night School web. It was true: with Project Labor they had gone around him. It was also true that he had elected to keep quiet once he found out. The inoculation had been done with an appropriate sense of blasphemy—through communion wafers. The outcry, even now if it became public, might turn ViraVax, the Costa Bravan government, the United States government and the Children of Eden into political rubble.

The Colonel did not feel the violation or the guilt that he usually felt when faced with the fact of Project Labor. Right now he felt only anger, even though he himself had commanded similar operations once they had saddled him with ViraVax.

Project Labor had meant he was marked as a rabbit. They had thought he might run, defect, turn rogue. They knew he was Catholic, and they did not trust him to oversee an operation aimed at Catholics. He would not have supported this program aimed at any human being. He had been an old-fashioned soldier even when he was young, one who gave and valued loyalty.

Would they have done it if I'd fought them, or if I'd gone public?

It scalded him that they had been right about him. He was a good soldier, he kept his mouth shut. The results overburdened his loyalty.

Yolanda and El Indio's youngest child, La Fey, was retarded. There were many more retarded children in Costa Brava these days. They were all trisomy twenty-one, Down's syndrome. Project Labor did it, and even after he saw it implemented, the Colonel had kept it quiet.

But now, how could he tell El Indio, or Yolanda? It would be easier to load the story anonymously onto the networks, addressed to the Church. That way he wouldn't have to face anyone.

But now he had to face El Indio.

"I can't tell you about that operation right now," Rico said. "I wish I could. It does not threaten us here. I promise you that I will give you every detail when this is over."

Rico swept his hand around the room, indicating the dozens of electronic communications devices that the guerrillas had moved into the room during the past hour. Other rooms and other condos were equally full.

"I guarantee you, if we get my boy and that girl out, I will give you enough information to keep all of this equipment busy for a long time to come. . . ."

"So," El Indio challenged, "you would use your son as the hostage now. We lost eight good men to that drone. Now, you say, *if* we get your son back . . ."

"Dammit," Rico snapped, "you know what I mean. Whether we find him or not, whether we get him back or not, I will still load your system. I owe you that. I owe a lot of people that. But that is then and this is now."

"You are not my enemy, Jabalí," El Indio reassured him. "You are overtaxed, and in pain. You know I will help you in this, no matter what."

Rico squeezed the bridge of his nose and rested his eyes for a moment. He breathed slowly, deeply, and relaxed himself. He wanted another drink but poured himself a coffee instead. He knew that he was headed into one of his hair-trigger moods, and it wouldn't take much to detonate him.

"I know that," Rico said with a sigh. "Thank you."

24

EACH TIME MARTE CHANG left her quarters, a pair, then six, then a dozen round-faced, Asian-eyed, pear-shaped people pressed around her. They approached cautiously, patting one another and jabbering up their courage to touch her. The Innocents lived for touch, and their stubby fingers explored her hair and her skin. Only one of them, David, had noticed her Asian eyes, so similar to his own.

"Look!" David said when she climbed aboard his cart.

He pointed to her eyes, then to his own, and laughed.

"We're almost the same," he said.

"What do you mean 'almost'?" Marte asked. "We're both human, aren't we?"

Marte had been curious for some time to see how the Innocents viewed themselves. There were classes of Innocents, based on relative ability or disability, and David was definitely upper-class. He read maps and memorized all the topside routes. He exhibited no rocking behavior, no self-destructive tics that many of the Innocents suffered.

"We're both human, aren't we?" Marte repeated.

David contemplated her question for a moment, staring at a knot of workers gathering at their lockers. Then he smiled.

"Tongue?" he asked, and stuck his own out for inspection.

"What?" Marte said.

Her ear wasn't tuned yet. Shirley had told her it would take time, but that had been nearly two months ago. Even when she heard a keyword from one of them, she had trouble unless it was in context.

"Don't respond to the keyword unless it's an emergency," Shirley had told her. "We're all supposed to encourage them to speak the whole idea out."

177

"See your tongue?" David asked.

He grabbed his own by the tip and pulled it out of a big grin to show her.

Marte was taller than any of the Innocents, and when they looked up to her, their faces eager, hugging one another, she wanted to gather them up in her arms. She did not think about what was happening to them in Practical Medicine on Level Three, or in Mishwe's lab on Level Five.

She stuck out her tongue and David squealed at the sight, at once amused at the spectacle and aware that there was a difference.

That was what the group pressed around her now was doing, laughing and sticking out their tongues. They pushed one another to get closer, but none of them clung to her, as they sometimes did. That was the hardest for her: she hated to let them go.

Marte shut her door against the gentle press of their bodies. She leaned her forehead against the cool steel and listened. They went about their version of small talk, which took a moment, no more, and they left.

Marte remembered the morning, after her glimpse at Level Five, when she had shouted at the Innocents around her. She had frightened them terribly, and they fell over one another, howling and crying, in a stampede of soft flesh and sobs.

Marte Chang let her own tears roll, now that her door latched behind her and she had tissues in hand. She knew it had been coming, tears for all those hundreds of thousands of betrayals perpetrated against innocent humans. Tears for herself, trapped here in something way over her head.

Destroying this facility won't even be enough, she thought. *In fact, we may need the facility to stop the spread of damage already done.*

It frustrated her that Dajaj Mishwe, the worst of the worst, probably would be spared just for access to his brain. She had done what Mariposa had asked: she had stirred things up, challenged Casey, siphoned off huge gulps of data. Casey seemed completely unintimidated by her queries, her accusations, and he went so far as to volunteer further information supporting her charges. The implication was clear.

He does not intend for me to leave.

Marte wiped her eyes and blew her nose, and saw that the wait-state display on her Sidekick had changed from a tiny holographic rainbow to a butterfly.

Mariposa!

Marte felt relief and a rush. Contact with the outside world had become her drug, as Shirley had warned. Now Marte readied her packet on Project Labor, a long tale of involuntary sterilization and insidious conception. Marte hated this part of the burst—the wait, the final two-minute countdown to transfer. Marte wanted it to be time for the Agency download the minute she found something new, and she was finding something new every minute.

"Go ahead," Mariposa would say, "wish your life away."

The butterfly began to wink off and on.

Yes!

Marte set her hands into the glove-like controls of her system. She keyed the protocols and waited.

Mariposa had set Marte up for her position inside ViraVax, which had been the black hole of information. Not only did nothing come out, but probes that went in were followed to their source. That source and its operator were destroyed, physically and completely.

From Mariposa's coded instructions and protocols, Marte helped her weave a carrier resonance pathway into the dispatches between the Agency and Casey. During that time, Mariposa and Marte could converse in bursts, as the data was fed, or they could load and unload prepackaged cargo. Either way, their messages piggybacked on the data bursts flung between the Agency and ViraVax.

Marte prepared a packet of files and synopsis of her meeting with Casey to transmit to Mariposa, and did so when the butterfly's wings began to flap. Simultaneously, her instruments indicated that she was receiving a similar load from Mariposa.

The load was a return on her inquiry about Mishwe. It did nothing to set her at ease.

Mishwe was born in Jerusalem twenty years sooner than she would have guessed. He saw four countries razed around him as a child. His father was an interpreter and middleman, and his mother a terrorist. Both died young. They left him in care of an uncle, who figured out how to get Mishwe's inheritance without having Mishwe. The uncle signed him on with a Children of Eden boarding school.

"Though this was a politically and environmentally correct choice," the load narrated, "certain cousins labeled it a contravention of their religion and beat the uncle to death with tire irons."

The Children of Eden already had Mishwe, and his money.

It was here that the video ended, images of that painfully beautiful, dark-eyed boy. Marte knew all too well the peculiarities of the Gardeners' beliefs. Photographs constituted graven images to the Children of Eden. Having a graven image made for oneself transgressed vanity and precipitated self-worship. One mirror was allowed per household, solely for grooming purposes, above the bathroom sink.

Mariposa had one of her best people inside the Records Department of the Children of Eden. There were awards for Mishwe, certificates of intelligence, scholarships, but no more pictures.

"Dajaj had always been a bright, intense child," the load went on. Her screen displayed a file dramatization of a schoolroom among the Children of Eden. "He blossomed intellectually under their various testings and placements, but he never opened up as a person."

It was obvious to Marte that Children of Eden became his parents. They nourished and purified his body, Temple of the Lord, and showed deep respect for his mind. This respect, by all appearances, was genuine.

If the Gardeners were his parents, then Calvin Casey was Grandfather. The PR people explained to Mishwe that he had received a scholarship, directly from Calvin Casey. They said that the great man, the Master himself, had saved Mishwe from certain death in the streets. At age seven, it's unlikely that Mishwe knew any better, but it was good bonding material.

No one showed more devotion in his tenure at EdenWood than Dajaj Mishwe. Besides tithes, the Gardeners gave the fruit of their mandatory recycling—paper, glass, plastic and metals. Once a week Mishwe reported to the sorthouse to bundle newspapers and magazines, and to prepare the glass and plastics for the weekly meltdown. Marte imagined that Dajaj loved this part, watching the pots of glass redden, twitch and liquefy. Before supper, he stacked the finished ingots for tally and shipping. Nothing was wasted, everything belonged to the Lord.

In Mishwe's first term at second-level, the dean of science informed the headmaster that an inordinate number of laboratory animals died at the hands of his prize student. When challenged, Mishwe defended himself by stating simply, "I study the physiology of life. To accomplish that, things must die."

The PR people hurried in to smooth things over, and Mishwe never made a public statement again.

Before he was seventeen, Dajaj Mishwe wrote illuminating papers on the moment of death, already having dispatched thousands of animals in his thirst for data. Animal shelters provided most of his victims, abandoned dogs and cats. Humans came soon enough.

He was questioned, in his ninth year at EdenWood, over the death of a seventh-year female, but he was never arrested. Gel was found on the body, of a type for and on the sites of EKG and EEG electrodes. Puncture wounds were found, too, where core samples had been taken of right thigh muscle and tibia, and blood from the left femoral artery. One group of locals blamed the murder on alien scientists from a UFO scout ship. That was as close as they got to Dajaj Mishwe.

On each of Mishwe's three unsuccessful missions for the Church, bodies with similar wounds were found in the nearby communities. He was recalled by the Church, then assigned to serve out his two years as a missionary for the brand-new research component of ViraVax. Mission work became a standard recruiting practice for ViraVax. From the very beginning, ViraVax preferred brilliant, malleable loners from among their own ranks, young men who bonded with their mission team for life.

No non-Gardener who accepted a ViraVax contract has ever been seen alive again, Marte recalled.

It made Casey's offer of permanent employment look frightening, indeed.

"Because of his high intellect," the load revealed, "Mishwe has always selected environments and conditions that offered him privacy and a ready supply of animals. He's the kind of psychotic who would walk into a feed store with a tennis racket under his arm and buy a bucket of baby chicks to go."

This last was live, but on a burst-delay and encrypted.

Marte had no time to reply before the Agency briefing ended, their pathway severed behind it. The visual went blank for a moment, and the rainbow motif returned.

Marte was shocked when Mishwe's face filled her monitor. The camera pulled back, and he stood in the neutral zone between the transport station and her Level Two labs.

Mishwe was no longer allowed to intimidate her in person, so he had to settle for electronic methods.

"So now we are both confined to our areas," he said. "There is much to be done in this lab, and you have curtailed my freedom to accomplish my projects. Your scurrying about and your tattling backfired on you, so now two of us are working under unnecessary limitations. This will not do."

"You frighten me," she said, finding it easier to admit to his image than to his face. "I cannot work if I'm afraid to be alone with you, or to encounter you in the hallways. You would harm me, given the opportunity, wouldn't you?"

Mishwe did not laugh, but a dry wheeze escaped his throat and he shook his head.

"Harm you?" Mishwe's emphasis was on the "harm," not the "you."

"You misrepresent me, Ms. Chang. I might study you to death, but to *harm* you . . . no, not harm for the sake of harm."

"You should be locked up. . . ."

Mishwe cracked the first genuine smile she'd seen from him.

"You are seeing how I belong here," Dajaj said. "We are fellow prisoners in the grasp of science."

"You don't belong anywhere." Marte's voice was a bare whisper, a rasp on stone in the dark. "And I've got a contract, I'm no prisoner."

"No?" Dajaj smiled, and shook his head. "Try to leave. Especially now, after your . . . revelations to Dr. Casey. You don't belong anywhere. I belong here. I'm perfect here. I can live forever here."

The sickness in her stomach did not come from the danger, from Mishwe's perfect smile. It came from the truth. She belonged nowhere, to no one, and Dajaj Mishwe did. If she stayed here, even to fight him, she might become him. She had nowhere to go; he had only to bide his time. Mishwe, Casey, Shirley . . . none of them expected her to leave ViraVax alive.

They would channel her where they wanted, take what she put out, milk her for more, then sell her to the slaughterhouse where Dajaj Mishwe was chief butcher. They had known all along that, one way or another, she would be here *forever.*

I cannot look away from his eyes, she thought. *I must not be seen to run.*

She smiled, though her stomach churned again, then smiled wider.

"I may not belong anywhere, but I'm where I belong because I'm here," she said.

"Zen shit," he said. "Chill."

Mishwe's calm, contemplative exterior contrasted greatly to his usual frenetic self. Marte thought that he looked like one of his iguanas in the wet morning grass, cooled down enough to slow even an eyeblink to languor.

Yet Mishwe was no reptile. He stood, solid and quiet and unbowed, with his back to one of the positive-pressure intakes for the lab's air supply. The slight breeze fanned the air nearly to flame around him. She imagined the heat from his body to be unbearable, and the passageway narrow.

Twice before in their encounters in the passageways he had thrown off a transitory, tangible heat that forced her back a step. Just as quickly, it had died. Now Mishwe rubbed his arms as though to warm them and stepped out of the viewer without so much as a nod. He was more subdued than she'd ever seen him. *Somebody tossed some water on his campfire,* she thought.

She shuddered to think what Mishwe could have done, in the light of what the load revealed, that made him this contrite, penitent and subdued. Then she sighed, screwed up her courage and started her plan—find her way out of "lab arrest," determine what had the facility in such an uproar and get the hell out of ViraVax any way she could.

25

RICO TOLEDO SKETCHED out pathways of embassy data, and one of the techs fed them into El Indio's buffers, providing the guerrillas with everything he could muster that related to Harry and Sonja. Electronics was not his forte, but he had picked up a few tricks over the years. Riding piggyback on someone else's message was one of them. He scribbled clumsily, his rage held at simmer, and he cursed the alcohol monster that squeezed his temples and belly. The rage was tinged with lust, now that Yolanda had reentered the room.

"Well," Rico told her, "so far they have nothing. It appears I am the red herring."

He pointed out a memo to his replacement captured from the embassy screen: "Find Toledo and you'll find the kids."

He had said *"arenque rojo"* for "red herring," and she corrected him.

"Arenque ahumado," she said.

The Colonel's senses picked up every nuance of her presence— the scent of her powder mingled with the volatile plastic scent of her old-fashioned eyeglasses that perched in her hair. Yolanda's presence was so powerful that he could not meet her gaze right away. While she stood beside him, scanning some paperwork, he sat, staring at his console, waiting for what she had to say. His consciousness focused on her slim pelvis mere centimeters from his cheek.

"One of our subscribers bled this one off the web," Yolanda said, dangling a sheet of paper by one corner.

"Both your ex-wife and Mrs. Bartlett filed formally through the Archbishop's office with the Mothers of Assassinated and Disappeared," she said. "A representative from the Organization of American States Human Rights Commission is flying in to talk with them and with García."

"It'll get some press back home, that's all," Rico said. "The OAS is noble, but powerless."

"Powerful enough to stop the humanitarian aid García receives from the Mexicans," she said. "That will not improve our image."

"Great!" Rico said. "Somebody's on our side, after all. I just wish it was a bigger somebody than some clerk with the OAS Human Rights Commission. . . ."

The Colonel's fist hit the desktop, and the entire room was silent except for the cocking of a weapon near the doorway, the growl of overhead fans, the shuffling of feet and paper, a cough.

Rico felt the flush of embarrassment on his cheeks. He could not bring himself to look up.

"I am glad that your ex-wife is all right," Yolanda said. "She was good to me and to my children. Do not feel alone. Everyone in this room has felt what you are feeling right now. Everyone here has lost someone to the death squads. Tío was taken himself, and lived."

Rico felt El Indio's hand on his shoulder.

"Now, truly, you are one of us," El Indio said.

"We have to think of the children now," Yolanda said. "They want the children alive, nothing else makes sense. So we know we still have a chance. . . ."

Yolanda was crying, but Rico could conjure nothing but numbness.

"I'm sorry," she said. "I'm very tired."

Rico gestured at the roomful of equipment around them.

"You've got pretty good stuff here," he said. "But no one gets into ViraVax uninvited, and I'm sure that's where we'll find those kids. It's not the tightest security south of the Pentagon, but it's tough enough."

Now everyone was talking at once and Rico wasn't listening.

The guerrillas preferred to think that García was behind everything, because it suited their goals. And García saw the Archbishop's shadow everywhere. Rico had himself to blame; he'd spent years reinforcing this feud under orders. This would not be a tangle he could unravel in a few minutes.

For a moment his mind flashed on Grace, pacing an embassy carpet, agonizing over the disappearance of their son. She would believe what they told her—that Rico did it, that he'd turned double agent. He had brought her only pain for the past few years. Somehow, Rico had thought he could make things up to Grace, that in time he would become someone she could respect, as she had in the beginning. He felt the pump of anger filling his veins.

It's Casey, he thought. *Playing García, the embassy, the Agency, the guerrillas, me. . . .*

He was trembling again, with the cold sweats and the lusts for Yolanda.

What's happening to me?

Taking up with Rachel had been his antidote for these barely controllable urges, but Rachel wasn't here and he knew that he wasn't really in the mood for sex. It was his body, his chemistry. All of his drinking had brought this on and he had to tough it out, get clean and clear, find Harry and Sonja and get them back.

Amid the babble, Yolanda leaned down and whispered, "ViraVax. We have someone inside. She is monitored and can only communicate through the burst. It won't be long, and we will know for sure."

She squeezed his shoulder and hurried back to play the satlinks.

Rico turned to El Indio.

"I want to get a message to the Speaker of the House, Nancy Bartlett's father," Rico said. "We're going to need some cavalry."

"Type your message here," El Indio said, and handed him a set of gloves.

"I'm a keyboard man," Rico said, "and I've barely got the hang of that."

One of the techs cabled him an old warped keyboard and Rico typed an urgent summary to the Speaker's personal Sidekick via his Agency green card. He sent a duplicate to Solaris in the DIA office in Mexico City.

Yolanda returned with news from a cornfield near the Double-Vee.

"Identities not confirmed," Yolanda said. "But an old man says a big black plane pushed a little yellow plane into the ground near his *milpa*. People in spacesuits took away two figures in body bags. They flew towards ViraVax. This was less than two hours after they were reported missing."

"Body bags?" the Colonel said, and stood.

Yolanda placed a palm on his chest to reassure him.

"They were struggling," she said. "That was noted."

"Casey, that sonofabitch!" Rico hissed in English. "What the hell could he be up to? Blowing up the embassy, taking two innocent teenagers, killing . . . killing. . . ."

El Indio's hand was on his arm. "You know now what we have suspected for a time," he said. "The bombing was a typical smokescreen, as you say. But the pattern has been this: keep your government, the García government, and our people busy fighting amongst themselves, blaming each other for this and for that."

"Yes," Yolanda agreed. "This is an example. Many times there have been operations—diversions—that the U.S. or the García government blamed on us. We knew we didn't do it and assumed that one of them did, to arrange blame. It was ViraVax, and those Children of Eden, keeping us at each other's throats so that we would not notice them using our people for their experiments."

Rico flushed with anger and embarrassment. Had the Agency kept him in the field, had he not been so blinded by his drinking and his anger and his dalliance with Rachel, he would have seen how far this had gone long ago. The gall was made more bitter because he'd had his suspicions and he had shut them out of his mind.

None of my business, he'd thought, petulant as a schoolboy left out of a game.

Now Harry and Sonja were paying for his petulance, while Red was dead and a lot of other people weren't that lucky.

And how many sterilized? he wondered. *How many mongolized?*

"Colonel?"

El Indio had been speaking to him.

"Yes, sorry."

"Tell us about their security."

"They are missionaries on a two-year rotation," he said. "Night School trained, well equipped, motivated by the fear of God. Most of their security are concentrated on the ground level and the level immediately below, with a detachment at the dam. No more than a hundred, altogether. But that hundred is very well armed, the perimeter booby-trapped, and if you're thinking of sending your people in there, forget it. You can only get in or out by air, and they are always sealed off below Level Two as a precaution."

"But then they are trapped, are they not?"

Rico smiled. El Indio saw everything in terms of victory.

"Depends," Rico said. "Remember, there are people who have worked the bottom levels without seeing daylight since that place was built. Fifteen years. They have three oxygen-generation systems, plenty of water, and at Level Three they produce enough protein and vegetable matter to feed the entire facility. The topside farming is just a cover. They don't need it."

"You say, then, that they can live down there *forever*?"

"Basically, yes."

Everyone was silent, and Rico visualized the facility again, trying to recall every stage of construction, trying to find a way in. It wasn't difficult. He had protested the difference between the plan and the construction because it essentially negated security. There had been the same problem with the U.S. Embassy, and it had been the same contractor.

He reviewed what he remembered out loud.

"First, we built the dam," he said. "Easy. Narrow canyon, dry season, piece of cake. Next we cleared fifty hectares, which is the existing perimeter, and in the middle of that we dug the hole. Twenty-five hectares on the square, fifty meters deep. Each level is five meters thick, with five meters of fill separating each one. The foundation wall is not the real wall. . . ."

Here he sat upright and scrabbled for his keyboard under a shuffle of papers. He generated a rough 3-D of ViraVax on their central viewer.

"You see, we had to consider earthquakes and repairs," he explained. "The building is actually a box inside a box, with room for maintenance crews to work between them. A latticework of steel members secures them, but there is still nearly two meters of space to move in workers and equipment."

"And is the only access from the inside?" Yolanda asked.

Rico smiled. "That's how it's supposed to be," he said. "But it was built by a very important local contractor who married into the Children of Eden. The same one who built the new embassy compound had married into his contract, built the facility for as little as possible and left a note saying simply, 'Paris is worth a mass.' None of the embassy elevators is secure. My son and I used to have lunch on top of the cars."

Rico sketched out the two apartment-sized decontamination elevators at ViraVax and showed how the two dozen conventional elevators linked with an interior rail system.

"Casey got me out of there as soon as he could." Rico shook his head. "He couldn't bear the thought of an idolator on his grounds."

Rico sketched in the dam above the Double-Vee.

"There had been constant minor damage from quakes. The Corps of Engineers blamed the water load behind the dam, the moon, everything but bad planning. Anyway, the conduit that carries the power lines from the dam to the facility enters that passageway. There are three places topside to enter that conduit at half-kilometer intervals. Other access shafts inside the buildings are covered with ten-ton concrete lids."

He marked them in the graphic.

"So we could get a team inside," someone said.

Rico shook his head.

"A team, never," he said. "Their electronic surveillance is excellent—designed to detect unauthorized exit, not entry, but that's beside the point."

"So," El Indio said, rubbing his uncharacteristic day-old stubble, "you say we can't assault them, and we can't put a team inside. What do we do, then?"

"We *can* assault them," Rico said, and patted El Indio's shoulder, "and we can put somebody inside. I've been there, I know the floor plan, I know the surveillance and I know how their security is trained. One person has a much better chance of getting inside than a team. But a team will assault the dam to draw them. We will also draw García's people."

El Indio snorted a laugh and shook out his hand in the gesture that the Costa Bravans used for "Hot, very hot."

"Then you will die in there," El Indio said, "and we will accomplish nothing."

"So," Rico said, his chin out, "if I can't do it, launch your assault."

"What about diplomatic channels?" El Indio said. "We know the children are there. Can't your government demand that ViraVax give them up?"

Yolanda laughed at that one.

"They would be fertilizer for beans by morning," she said. "Or, worse yet, there would be a cursory inspection by one of the many in your embassy who are of the Children of Eden. Or García himself, who is of their faith. They would look for nothing and find nothing. Your government would apologize; they have more pressing matters facing them at home. The children would remain.

The infection of our people would continue. No, this is no place for diplomacy."

"You always were a warrior," El Indio said.

"And you the statesman," she countered. "The Colonel is right. Someone has to get inside. Someone who knows the complex, someone who can fight. Our contact inside has neither of these advantages. In fact, she believes herself to be in danger as well, and she cannot get out."

"How often can you contact her?" Rico asked.

"Twice a day, at the most," she said.

"I'll give you some questions for her. Any answers would be helpful. Meanwhile, I have a plan. And you, warrior woman, you will get your fight."

Yolanda smiled, and the rest of the room lit up with smiles as well.

Yes, he thought, *it's what we know best.*

Except for El Indio, who was one of the great negotiators of all time, they all preferred a good, tangible fight. But Rico well knew the diplomatic stalemate that inevitably occurred when negotiating with fundamentalist extremists of any stripe. They were right because their god said they were right, and there was no reasoning with that. This had been the lesson of the Crusades, westward expansion, the oil and messianic wars.

"This is what we can do," he began. "And I'm afraid it's the only thing we can do. It helps that sundown begins their Sabbath. . . ."

It felt good to him to be a colonel again, even though he was briefing rebel forces. He indicated four positions on either side of the dam, and one in the center.

"These are the security shacks," he said. "The dam is their weak point, and they keep their best people here. In fifteen years, no one has attacked them, presumably because a ground attack through that terrain and jungle would be easily detected by their sensors and inefficient without heavy weapons. And they know that your forces have never attacked by air. Do you have anyone who jumps? *Paracaidistas?*"

"Yes," Tío spoke up. "I have jumped from the plane."

"And others?" Rico asked.

"Perhaps twenty who have jumped one or two times. . . ."

"*Oye,* Colonel!" a small man, Raimundo, spoke up. "There are those of us who would jump into that nest without the silk."

There was general laughter around the room.

"I have witnessed the bravery and the ferocity of the Peace and Freedom brigades very closely for twenty years," Rico told him. "And I believe you, *compa*. With twenty, we can take the continent. One person to blow their power. Their backup is a set of diesel generators, but it should draw them out nicely. They will be strung out, in the dark, the whole three kilometers from their fence to the dam."

"And what of the children?" Yolanda asked. "And our contact inside?"

"That's my job," Rico said. "I'll drop in first, alone, and get inside. We will agree on time enough to get in, find them and get out while you hit the generators and concentrate their security forces."

"And if you and the children are not out by that time?"

Rico sighed, and massaged a cramp in the back of his neck.

"If we're not out by that time, we wouldn't be coming out, anyway."

El Indio spoke up.

"The things they make in there, the diseases. Won't they escape, too?"

"It's possible," Rico said. "Certain of those elevator shafts, the maintenance perimeter and the conduit to the dam are open and risky. That's why it's better for one who knows the way than many who don't. Besides, letting ViraVax continue what it's doing is infinitely more risky, in my opinion."

"What will they do?" Yolanda asked.

"At any sign of danger they'll seal off completely," Rico said, "shut down all outside support and stay put. Nothing and no one will get out of there."

"What if they release something deliberately?" El Indio asked.

"They already have," Rico admitted. "And they will continue to do so. Which is worse? But they will expect reinforcements from García, so that will not be a first defense."

Yolanda nodded agreement. "Yes," she said through gritted teeth. "Let's finish this now."

"What about U.S. support?" El Indio asked. "When they hear that ViraVax is under attack, they will send your troops up there."

"True," Rico said, "but our nearest troops are another contract station in Tegoose. They hire our advisors to train their people, but the Night School is an Agency strike force that takes an act of Congress to move. We contract a lot of our military movement through their shipping arm. It's cheaper than keeping our own troops here when they're needed so much at home. The ViraVax security are missionaries who get a draft exemption for their service. That way they don't have to worry about fighting their neighbors back in the States."

"If they're trying to hide something up there, they'll wait until the last second to call for help," El Indio said.

"Remember, they have all those young-buck missionaries who rotate civil duties," Rico said. "They might be green, but they're fighting for their god."

Rico explained Casey's Sabbath rituals and his scaled-down operations.

"The missionaries and many of the Innocents attend several functions topside during Sabbath," he said. "They take only bread and ice water and meet in a large, glassed-in structure that allows them to meditate on the jungle around them, a symbol of their goal—to return the earth to its Edenly state.

"The rest of the Innocents usually remain in quarters, as do the few non-Gardeners among the staff."

"That's our chance, yes?"

"Yes. The elevator shafts will be our best bet. If we can hitch a ride on one, fine. We can scale the shaft if we have to."

"We will have to move very quickly, and with precision," Yolanda said.

Rico nodded, and returned to the battered keyboard.

"Meanwhile," he said, "there are still some favors owed me. I'm going to try to cash them in. And there is something else."

He watched the pathways that his fingers traced on the screen, rather than Yolanda's eyes.

"What else?"

"Your bag of tricks, does it include Hypnosemide?"

"The serum of truth?" she asked. "Yes, we have it. Why?"

"When I am finished here, I want you to give it to me." Rico said. "That way, even things that I've forgotten, you will know. And anything that *they* have blocked, I will know."

"But." Yolanda protested, "that will take hours, and afterward you will not . . ."

"Afterward, I will not have to worry about any tricks or traps that they've planted in my brain or my body," he said.

Rico finished bleeding the dam's schematics off the Agency's web and diverted the file to print.

He smiled Yolanda a cockeyed smile.

"Before I blunder about asking for favors, I want us both to be sure who the friendlies are." He took a deep breath, glanced at El Indio and said, "I owe you, I owe my son and I owe myself. Let's get started on that Hypnosemide."

26

THE COUPLE WHO brought Sonja and Harry their meal looked to be in their teens, older than most *deficientes* that Sonja had noticed on the streets of La Libertad. Down's syndrome babies seemed to be everywhere in Costa Brava these days. Her father had been liaison when the delegation from World Health came to study the phenomenon. Her father was the most accessible prime researcher, being the one ViraVax contractee who had off-compound privileges.

Her father had told her about the ViraVax service staff, all brought in through the Church's foster program. Most were Down's syndrome, all of them trisomy twenty-one types. They came from a network of Gardener foster homes around the world, and they were fiercely loyal.

Sonja remembered that her father had laughed.

"Not 'fiercely,' " he corrected. "Say, 'extremely.' I don't think they would be fierce about anything."

The children were screened at various facilities, in the States and elsewhere, all run by the Children of Eden. These were children who would always be children, and therefore they were truly innocent in the eyes of the Church, neither pagan nor gentile.

Nor human.

"Maybe we can get these kids to help us," Harry said. "They aren't part of the religion, are they?"

"We can try," Sonja said. "They're known for being loyal and stubborn, but we don't have anything to lose."

"How did they get them all here, anyway?" Harry asked. "My dad didn't talk about them much."

"The Gardeners run boarding schools for them," she said. "After my dad died, I found a newspaper article in his things. It claimed that one of the orphanages was a place where children were raised like plants for their organs."

"I never heard about that," Harry said. "What happened?"

Sonja continued her pacing, each step in time with a beat from her pulse.

"I tried to call the paper up on the networks," she said. "They aren't in business anymore."

Sonja thanked the Maya martyrs and the gods of Balaam that these innocents made up eighty percent of the work force at ViraVax.

Maybe we can *get them to help us,* she thought.

The children had looked so afraid of her and of Harry.

If they'd do this to us, Sonja thought, *I wonder what they do to those poor people?*

As she paced, Sonja wrung her memory for everything her father had told her about the ViraVax compound and its functions. She couldn't remember much, most of it related to the lift pad and aircraft.

There was a weekly chopper that her father used to ride from the compound to the embassy and back. Under cover of the early hours, a B/M-3 cargo shuttled daily between ViraVax and its airport warehouse, transporting supplies, equipment and VIPs.

The airport warehouse also served as a hangar and, for fifteen meters underground, a bunker. She had flown within sight of the warehouse hundreds of times, getting in flight time, and on a few occasions she had seen the changing of the guard and crew.

ViraVax and the Children of Eden owned the satellite taxiway that led from the runway to the warehouse, and they owned the kilometer square that it sat on. And under.

The B/M-3 was a vertical takeoff and landing airplane—expensive, state-of-the-art and a breeze to fly. It was not much trickier than her little *Mariposa,* both of them kites compared to a helicopter. She'd done three flights in the gimballed Boeing/Mitsubishi and three in one of the embassy's old Hueys as a birthday present from her parents. She didn't care if she ever got into another chopper, but she would love to get her hands on the B/M-3 again.

Sonja put her lips to Harry's ear, cupped her hands around her mouth and whispered, "I've flown their cargo plane. It comes and goes daily three A.M."

Harry nodded, and whispered back.

"Great. Here's the plan. I'll get us past the biological field and the Missionary Rangers and on the pad at two fifty-nine. You fly us out."

She pinched him, encouraged by his humor, even if it was a little black.

"And remember," she added, "we can't run or move fast or we'll roll up into helpless, writhing jellyballs of pain."

"Why is it that those two and Mishwe get in here in spite of the virus hazard?" he asked.

"Maybe there isn't a hazard, for them."

"What do you mean?"

"Maybe they're vaccinated against whatever it is."

"I can't imagine Mishwe allowing himself to be inoculated," Harry said.

"Chill," Sonja said. "You know him so well. . . ."

"If we're that important to them, they don't want us messed up," he said.

"So," Sonja asked, "you claim there's no virus?"

She picked up the cup with the two pink pills, rolled them around, set them back down. This time she didn't whisper.

"What makes you so sure about these?" she asked. "What if you're wrong?"

"If I'm wrong, they'll take care of it," Harry said. "Nothing else makes sense."

Harry returned to his bunk, and Sonja had the feeling that he was hurting more than he wanted her to know.

Isn't this macho stuff ever going to die out?

The hiss of incoming air was no longer scented, but pure and dry. It was not cold, like the air-conditioning elsewhere, but pleasantly warm on her skin.

The peel-and-peek reactivated, showing a full-faced and sweating portrait of the dzee. The dark eyes glittered, and stared from the screen directly into Sonja's soul.

"Your moment is nearly at hand," Mishwe announced. "Soon everything will become clear. You are the Adam and Eve of the new Garden, a Garden which my sword, even now, purifies for your use."

As suddenly as the image had come, it disappeared. The peel became a window overlooking the topside grounds through a thick stand of foliage. It added a voyeuristic feel to the scene. A line of retarded workers, young men and women, shuffled towards another building. Sonja could only see the corner of it, but she could tell it was concrete, painted to look like a metal shop or barn.

"What do you make of *that*?" Sonja asked, still staring at the screen.

"He's one crazy dzee," Harry said. "We are in much deeper shit than we thought."

On-screen, two people in lab jackets accompanied the workers, one in front and one behind. No one appeared to be talking. They held hands like kindergarten kids and formed a double line. There was some shoving and pulling, but most of them went quietly to their afternoon chores. They seemed undaunted by the usual afternoon rain and the mud. One turned his moon face upward and caught raindrops on the pink platform of his tongue, and laughed. Sonja smiled.

She knew that the scene was illusion, yet she imagined she heard the whine of the B/M-3 topside as it settled onto the pad.

She motioned Harry to the screen. His movements were slow, painfully deliberate. Together they watched its final drop and the swirl of dust overhead.

"Do you know this plane?" she asked.

Harry nodded.

"Vertical Vinnie," he answered. "A Boeing/Mitsubishi VT-3. Also called a Bowel Movement-3. Copied after, and improved upon, the old British Harrier. Quieter, faster, more stable. Cargo or combat capacity."

Sonja remained silent, staring after the dissipating dust cloud. They could not see the landing site itself, nor the security around it. Their limited vantage allowed only the barest glimpse of three other buildings at the surface. Sonja knew that there were twelve buildings aboveground, and a small city beneath it.

Ventilation ducts, maintenance passageways, service elevators . . .

She thought there must be a hundred ways to move around the facility without resorting to the usual traffic areas, but she didn't know any of them. She vowed to construct a map for Harry as soon as she could orient herself. Besides her father's talk over the years, she had flown the outskirts of the compound several times and knew that she could recall the image accurately if she concentrated.

She put her lips to his ear again, cupping her hands around them, and whispered.

"Keep track of everything," she said.

"Why do you think they're letting us see this?" he asked. "Wouldn't it make better sense to keep us blind? I mean, look at how much we can see. . . ."

"Yeah," she said, "and we can't get there. Maybe they just want us more comfortable. You know, some kind of psychology, like the pink room."

A scrap of paper caught in a dust devil whirled up, up and out of sight.

"Looks so close," he mumbled.

Harry sighed, and something in that sigh frightened Sonja more than their circumstances. It was a sigh that registered an enlightened resignation, and she knew it for what it was—the enemy.

"They intend to keep us forever," he said. "They don't care what we see, we're not leaving."

Sonja decided she would not pep-talk him now. Their monitors picked up his despair, his resignation.

Good, she thought. *Let them think we're giving up. Between what he knows about security here and what I know about the layout and flying, we just might make it.*

27

MARTE CHANG LOOKED up from her fistful of shipping invoices to the stainless-steel coolers, sealed and stacked at the loading dock. The numbers and dates matched, bringing the agonizing trail she had been following full circle. Mariposa had suspected, but now Marte Chang had the proof:

"Body parts."

Marte barely vocalized the whisper. She blinked a couple of times quickly, but did not move, nor did she take her eyes from the plane. It could leave here, and she could not. She wondered, would she leave now, if she could, with enough evidence to shut ViraVax down? Or would she stay to the bitter end, theirs or hers, to sniff out every macabre project, every perpetrator?

She thought of David, her exuberant guide, and looked once again at the coded reports. Would there be an invoice here for him someday?

Today, watching the loading of the stainless-steel refrigerated cases, she wanted to flee more than she'd wanted anything in her life.

Body parts for transplant, she thought, and shook her head in wonder. *And a genetic immuno-prophylaxis to guarantee compatibility. No more immunosuppressives, no more searching for just the right donor. Too bad such a great idea had this kind of monster birth.*

Marte breathed deeply to quell her fear and her anger. She recalled her only briefing with Mariposa, a long weekend that had brought her over the edge of fatigue. She had wanted to sleep, but the adrenaline of her anger wouldn't let her. Mariposa had told her about the successful transplants, always for highly placed Children of Eden, and her suspicions about the anonymous donors.

Marte was surprised at the sudden and complete sadness that washed over her. She flicked a tear out of the corner of her eye and took a deep breath.

Poor, poor, pitiful me.

Marte checked her messages, and the board led off with a notice from Casey.

Line conf 1530 Fuse update. Code 3.

"Code three," she muttered. "I hate code three."

Marte had participated in two code-three conferences since arrival at ViraVax, and they both gave her the willies. Participation was live, via network, scrambled, and none of the participants was identified except Casey. Casey knew the principals, including his own staff, but some of the questions from anonymous sources gave her the creeps. Some of the questions got her thinking about the "drought and pestilence" charges that had led her here. She was becoming one of them, if only to ensure her cover, and her stomach churned at the thought.

The chronometer in the lower right-hand corner of her viewer read 1530. Big-money buyers from all over the world were waiting, not for what she could do *for* humanity, but for what she could do *to* it.

Promptly her screen cleared, her gut wrenched, and the conference began.

She coded a note for the in-house frequency and shipped it to Casey's mailbox while the introductory data scrolled.

"I hate it when you clear my viewer" was all it said.

Marte hoped that everything that she thought was clearly implied. She dared to hope that she would be deported for her impertinence until the memory of those stainless-steel boxes flashed to mind, and she swallowed hard.

What am I doing here? What have I done?

Casey had handed her a basic architecture and a challenge, possibly a step towards a deeper confidentiality. Out of that architecture, Marte had refined a time bomb for the human body, and a trigger. Now strangers, very powerful strangers, discussed its merits and limitations on her own viewer.

"This animal can stop a body dead in its tracks," Casey's briefing materials informed them. "We've mastered the autoimmune system, and now we can shut off the mitochondria with a whiff of perfume. . . ."

"Which is like shutting off the body like a switch," someone said.

The voice, like all of their voices, was converted to print. Not a hint of accent, gender, age.

Marte could imagine Casey in his office as someone took the bait. In her mind, he couldn't help licking his lips, and his intense eyes bored their gaze into his viewer the way they sometimes bored into her own. At first this intensity had amused her. Now it chilled her.

"Details, please, researcher."

That was her.

Who wants to know? ran through her mind first. *General, President, Oil Baron, King?*

Marte knew that the Master didn't have to bid. He got everything he wanted for free. Casey's tone sounded from her console, prompting an answer.

"It's actually three different animals," she replied.

Her Litespeed translated her speech into typescript so there would be no voice recognition.

"Stage one disarms the immune response. Stage two sets itself up within the mitochondria and, when triggered by stage three, instantly blocks ATP production."

"And how long is it effective in its dormant state?"

Again, the tone prompt from Casey. He would want to speak with her later about her tardy responses.

"For life," she said. "Thanks to our work with monoclonal antibodies, it's resident and undetectable until activated."

Responses in her viewer:

"Won't a pheromone trigger deliver an element of unpredictability?"

"Any chemical, including light, becomes a trigger. Pheromones are only one example."

"So," someone replied, "you could inoculate an entire army to self-destruct at your command?"

"If you wish," she replied, and held her head in both hands.

Marte thought of her viruses as babies and talked to them as she talked to herself while working. Now she could see where it had led her. She understood now how the mother of the killer of her parents might have felt.

Sitting a nest of dragons, she thought.

Always, in the past, her viruses, her babies, thrilled her.

Not anymore.

She kept no duplicates of her notes or procedures, and she vowed to destroy this project, and any others she could get her hands on, before she left ViraVax.

The conference ended at 1600 in a blur. All she could think of was David and the other Innocents. David, who squired her everywhere, always smiling, always having a good day.

What will they do to him?

An image of stainless-steel boxes stacked on his cart chilled her through and through. Even so, Marte was soaked in sweat. She used that as an excuse to stand in her shower for a long, long time.

28

DAVID LEFT HIS cart at the Level One elevators, as instructed, and led the others through the maze that bypassed decon. The Angel Dajaj had a mission for them, and it was David's job to deliver the team safely to the Angel.

"I go back now," Mark said. "Steve be mad, I go back now."

"Dajaj is boss, not Steve," David said. "Dajaj says 'Come,' so we come."

"I work hard," Annie said. "Strong back, good back."

David, too, was restless. He liked adventure and he liked secrets, but it scared him and he didn't like to be scared. On his cart, he knew what he was doing. A red tag on the package meant follow the red line to deliver it. Brown overalls on passengers meant that he followed the brown line to deliver them to the brown area. Always he got home using the white line. Today the five of them were all different colors, and where he was taking them had no color.

"Pic-nic, pic-nic, pic-nic," Tomasina chanted.

She shut her eyes tight the whole way down, letting David lead her by the hand when they changed cars. Dajaj had promised a picnic, but they had to hurry to beat the Sabbath.

The Angel Dajaj did not go to the big room on the Sabbath like the others did. He taught David and some others how to pray to God every Sabbath, and he gave them a picnic. Dajaj was their friend. He helped the great God to love them and to remember them when nobody else would.

The doors slid back at Level Five, and the Angel Dajaj awaited them. A pile of small green backpacks buried his feet, but he threw open his arms in welcome.

"My children," he said, "are you ready to meet the Lord?"

"Yes!" David said.

Heads bobbed all around him.

"Yes!"

"Yes!"

"Pic-nic. Pic-nic."

"We will have our picnic," the Angel told them. "First, we'll go for a walk. Everybody pick up one of these packs and put it on. Here, David, let's show them."

Dajaj fixed the pack on his back and snugged up the straps for him. It was not heavy at all. The pack that Dajaj picked up for himself looked very heavy, and David was glad he didn't have to carry that one.

David helped the others amidst the grunts and thick breathing. The hallway was empty except for their little group, and it was quiet except for some distant barking and the occasional screech of an animal. Topside was always noisy, people jostled people everywhere, so only occasionally did David hear the birdsong and animal cries from outside the perimeter.

Catherine, the youngest, perked up.

"Puppy dogs?" she asked. "See puppy dogs?"

"Not this time," Dajaj answered. "This time we're going outside."

Outside!

David couldn't remember Outside. He knew that if he got Outside alone he would die, he would walk around and get lost and he would die. The missionaries warned them all about it almost every day. Even the missionaries didn't go Outside. His heart jumped at the thought, and his fingers absently stroked the surgical scar down the center of his chest.

The Angel Dajaj led them through a room full of noisy fans, into a crawl space and through another hatch. They were packed together inside a dark, narrow passage that felt like it was full of cables and pipes. David's nose was very sensitive and Catherine didn't smell very good when she pressed against him. Dajaj switched on a hand lamp so they could see, and it was just in time because Annie was already crying.

"Picnic," Dajaj reminded them. "This way."

They had to balance on the pipes and put their hands on the walls to keep from falling. As it was, everyone except the Angel Dajaj fell more than once. David himself slipped twice, wedging himself between the pipe and the wall. Catherine wouldn't help him and Dajaj couldn't get past everybody else, so both times it took him a while to get up.

The passageway was steep, too. Topside, everything was flat and David rode his cart everywhere. Now his thighs burned, he was thirsty, and if Annie wasn't crying enough for all of them, he would have done it himself. He never wanted the Angel Dajaj to see him cry.

Dajaj stopped them all with a palm up and a finger to his lips. He stood on tiptoe and unfastened another hatch overhead. A bright blast of sunlight watered David's eyes.

"Outside!" Mark cried.

"Shh!" the Angel whispered. "It's a surprise."

29

JOSHUA CASEY RAN his hand over his head without mussing his tender scalp. The conference had excited him, though Marte's performance had not. For a moment he had been transported out of ViraVax and the political mess that Mishwe had made of it and into the world he loved best—hustling biological gadgets, making the world a more perfect place, making money for God.

"She's dangerous," Shirley said.

Only when she spoke was he aware of her hand on his thigh. She gave it a squeeze.

"She's marginally acceptable," Casey boomed. "Everyone here has to be ready to sell any portion of their projects at any moment. We've always made that clear."

"That's not what I mean," she said. "She's dangerous because she has secrets."

Casey chilled.

"What secrets? How do you know?"

Shirley's hand worked its way higher on his thigh.

"Remember I said I've monitored everything that comes across her screen?"

"Go on."

"Everything relates to her work," Shirley said. "Her only detectable network contacts are the usual library and data searches related to her projects."

"What do you mean 'detectable'?"

Casey could tell by Shirley's smile that she was quite full of herself. He wished she'd just spit it out instead of dangling it out of his reach. He refused to sit up and beg. He would let her take her time. One day soon, Shirley and her manipulations would be out of his life forever.

"Sometimes a symbol appears on her screen, a butterfly," she said.

Her hand squeezed again. Casey reached down and removed it.

"Get to it," he growled. "I've got the Master and Mishwe to deal with before sundown."

"It's a signal," she said. "Someone is contacting her, bypassing everything we have. Her responses are also blocked. I think she's a spy."

Casey was sure that it was true.

Who?

She arrived the day that Bartlett died, could that be it? And who was Bartlett's best friend in the outside world?

"Colonel Toledo," he whispered.

"It's possible," Shirley said. "The butterflies always appear just before or after your embassy dump."

"Then they're bursting, using our own system and transmissions. . . ."

Casey stood, ran his hand through his hair, sat.

"That new tall guy in Micro, Dwayne, get him on this. If we can't tap her, maybe we can trap her."

"I don't think we can make it by sundown."

"Then stop thinking and start moving," he said. "Tell him we want an intercept, and we want to be able to generate that butterfly on her screen ourselves. Then I want a security shakedown of everybody in this facility."

"Marte Chang's an exception," Shirley said. "An outsider. Mishwe is another exception, he's crazy."

"It wasn't timidity," Casey growled, speaking more to himself than to Shirley, "and it wasn't cultural. She *hesitated*. She was *thinking*. She was *weighing, moralizing*. . . ."

These last he pronounced with a fist to his desktop.

"A morality different from ours is a luxury she can't afford."

"Well, she has impressed you," Shirley said. "In spite of her . . . hesitation, she has produced for you. Produced quickly, elegantly. And so have her assistants. Before she arrived they were nothing more than overpaid dishwashers."

Casey smiled, in equal measures charmed by the economic promise of the new projects, by Marte's naïveté and by the heady prospect of sheer power. Shirley was right. In spite of her moral struggle, her questionable loyalties, Marte was producing. He stroked Shirley's firm thigh absently. Nothing disgusted Casey more than disloyalty, and Marte Chang was proving herself to be quite disgusting, indeed.

The Sunspots were Toledo's Trojan horse, he thought. *Now I have to question everything, details of her mitochondrial project. . . .*

She had not applied to remain on at the completion of her project, and she had not warmed to him, to Shirley, not to anyone. She had appeared loyal, true, but she hadn't ever *felt* loyal to him, even in their lunches on the patio. She was not staying, which meant that the knot was tied and the noose slipped. He caught his hand investigating the tender skin above his collar. He moved it to Shirley's thigh.

Not even Mishwe is a traitor.

Mishwe, yes, was another matter, a much more pressing matter.

"Are you thinking of Mishwe?" Shirley asked.

She repositioned herself under his hand, then repositioned his hand, then guided his unconscious strokes more to her liking.

Casey dampened his fingers and broadened his field of exploration.

"Why?" he asked.

Her pelvis reached up for his fingers, sucked them in.

"Every time you deal with Mishwe these days you look like you're having a seizure," she said. "Wait now . . . oh, shit, oh Jesus. . . ."

"No bad talk," he reminded her.

"No," she said, and pulled his belt buckle free of its clasp.

Casey's security channel beeped its "urgent" notice, and his chief announced in his clipped manner, "We have a Meltdown situation, sir. Three Innocents. One in the ag shop, another on the lift pad and a third in the field. All went up at once. Details on-screen . . . now."

Casey stepped out of Shirley's grip and switched the video from "console" to "council." His wall lit up and a perimeter pickup bracketed, focused, then zoomed in on a brown mass dripping from its skeleton, fouling a forklift. Casey touched a key and the screen split, bracketing two other lumps of flesh. The one at the lift pad shimmered under a blue flame.

"Oh, God," Shirley said. "God help them."

"God help *us*," Casey muttered, "if the Master finds out."

The second figure had already blended into shadow, becoming nothing more than a stain on the tilled earth. The burned stub of a hoe handle and charred clothing punctuated his death.

"Command?" he snapped.

"Yes, sir."

"What do we have?"

"Three individuals in Meltdown, sir. We began Sabbath shutdown, so teams are just now sealing off. . . ."

"Nobody goes near them without full gear," Casey ordered. "I want all residue impounded and sealed, including the concrete from the lift pad, that forklift, the dirt around the field worker. I want to know what set them—"

"Sir," the chief interrupted, "we have two more cooking in Maintenance right now."

"Shut down topside operations," Casey said. "I want their crews in isolation, including missionaries."

"Sir, shouldn't we seal off—"

"*I'll* decide that," Casey snapped. "A full seal-off would cost us weeks of production and it would mean notifying García and the embassy that we've got a problem. I presume you don't want an army holding us in here any more than I do. Proceed as I've ordered."

He slapped the "off" key, but not before he noted how pale the chief looked, and how freely he could sweat.

Already Casey had the feeling he had lost, that something had exploded and swept past him and the shock wave came next.

He reopened one screen to see two spacesuited men give a thumbs-up sign, run a final check on their Colts and armor, then trudge towards the ag shop.

Casey was sure where this investigation would lead.

To Dajaj Mishwe, he thought. *One way or another. Mishwe, Meltdown and a migraine.*

Casey didn't like that combination, particularly with his father in tow.

"Command?"

"Yes, sir."

"What's the status of Mishwe's two newcomers?"

"Decon in progress," the voice announced. "They're Level Five property, sir. You authorized—"

"Put them on hold," Casey ordered. "Bring Mishwe to me."

30

THE THREE MELTDOWNS topside performed perfectly for Mishwe, exactly thirty minutes after their inoculation.

Ice water is the best yet, Mishwe thought.

His other vehicles of infection had proven wildly imprecise for this particular animal, which was why Red Bartlett got all the way to the city before it hit him. The three Innocents disintegrating in the ViraVax compound offered Dajaj Mishwe the cover he needed, exactly as planned. He signaled his helpers topside and shushed them as they blinked into the bright sunlight at the top of the dam.

Mishwe checked his watch.

1739.

The ultraviolet trigger should release in fifteen minutes. Two of these five Innocents should begin Meltdown at 1754, just before sundown. They surfaced behind the sentry's box, a two-story affair that afforded them cover as long as they stayed close to its base. Next to the sentry box stood his goal: the entryway into the turbines.

Mishwe pressed two keys on his Sidekick and triggered a series of impulses from the communications control bunker to the security blockhouse. A pressurized canister released its contents into the guard's air-conditioning. At 1740 a green light on his Sidekick signaled Mishwe that this guard was no longer a problem. The other guard, on the far side of the dam, couldn't see them and, with luck, would never know what hit him.

"Pic-nic. Pic-nic." Tomasina rocked back and forth in time with her chant.

"Okay," Mishwe said. "It's time for our picnic. Let's find a good spot."

He disarmed the sensor on the doorway to the turbines and led his group inside. The size of the turbines and their noise frightened the Innocents at first, but he hurried them along, placing each of their packs at the top of a spillway.

"What are we doing, Dajaj?" David asked, shouting to be heard above the wind and the howl of the turbines.

Like the others, David was out of breath from the unaccustomed rush across the dam and back.

"Getting ready for a surprise," Mishwe said.

Dajaj checked his watch, then spread a blanket from his pack over the concrete floor. He took out a handful of sandwiches, paper cups and a large insulated jug of ice water.

"Here's our picnic," he announced. "Eat fast, we have to get back down before the Sabbath."

The Innocents dug in hungrily and drank up all the ice water right away. The exertion, the heat and humidity, the salt in their sandwiches, all made them terribly thirsty, just as he'd planned.

Mishwe didn't have to check his watch again to know that it was 1754. The two Innocents inoculated with the UV trigger both let out a grunt and slumped to the floor.

"Dajaj! Dajaj, help them!" David cried.

"Don't touch them!" Mishwe warned. "We can't help them now. We have to get back. Follow me. Hurry."

Simple orders during a crisis was the best way to handle the Innocents. They looked back once, from the top of the dam, and saw the skin beginning to slump from their dead fellows. Once he had the remaining Innocents back inside the tunnel, Mishwe allowed himself a moment of praise for Marte Chang.

Great idea, that UV trigger, he thought. *I'll have to try her mitochondria trick next.*

While two of the Innocents clung to Mishwe out of fear, the other one, David, hung back, his eyes widening in distrust.

In a half hour it won't matter, anyway, he thought. *The final trial on the ice water should work by then.*

Each of the Meltdown subjects that security discovered would require full hazard suit-up and decontamination of the site. Mishwe knew he was leaving a trail, but by the time it was discovered to be a trail, neither it nor the security teams would exist.

He thought it too bad, too. Now that he'd tested the UV trigger, he found it infinitely more satisfactory than binding the triggering agent in ice. Inoculation had been performed a few days ago, also via the ice cubes in their daily communion.

Now no one who enters Level Five will dare leave, he thought.

The sun itself will eliminate all witnesses.

He smiled at the poetry of it all—his new arsenal consisted of the two things necessary for life, sunlight and water. Soon Casey and the Master would see that Dajaj Mishwe was not merely a tool, but an architect as well. Of course, they would only have moments to recognize his genius before it overwhelmed them, once and for all.

Next he would teach an important lesson to that know-it-all, Marte Chang.

If I am a tool at all, I am the sword, flaming in the hand of the Archangel.

This Dajaj Mishwe firmly believed.

31

Ex-Colonel Rico Toledo did not fight men in his sleep any-more, he fought viruses. Great skeletal predators stalked his dreams, shifting their protein shells to catch the light. He had allowed Yolanda and El Indio to use the hypnotic on him, for refreshment, but he'd already listened three times, dry-mouthed and incredulous, to the tape he'd made.

There had been much to remember, much that ViraVax, perhaps even the Agency, had tried to block from his mind forever. He was beyond being shocked at how they'd used him, the one Agency officer who should have been above their machinations, beyond their reach.

Nothing is beyond their reach, he thought.

The Colonel was embarrassed and woozy. He felt the drug dissolving in his bloodstream, and the kaleidoscope of visions dissolved with it.

One crystalline monster had Joshua Casey's face. The Colonel snatched at the kingpin that would bring its elaborate structure down. As always, the vital pin reappeared elsewhere, out of reach, and the hard viral shell slammed shut on his arm.

The Colonel woke from the hypnotic to the jarring chatter of an old printer in the next room. His disorientation was momentary, but waking didn't bring him relief, just the awareness that tonight he would face Casey and his forces alone. He hoped he could find a kingpin, like in his dream, and pull Casey's operation apart without destroying the kids, himself and two governments in the process.

Rico rubbed the tension out of his eyes, reached for a sweetened rum beside his chair, then changed his mind. He would be meeting Yolanda soon for the hop, providing she was still willing to let him go. It would probably be the last time he would see her, and

217

he wanted her to remember him well.

Even if he hadn't lived with dignity lately, Rico thought that he could at least die with dignity. He had no illusions for this operation. The only thing that would save the kids would be a full-scale invasion of that facility, and nothing around him looked full-scale.

But I bet we can start one.

Yolanda's new equipment was scattered about him on the bunker floor: code-burst device, locator, a tumbler-sensor lockpick, fiber-optic scanner/encoder. The one item that bulked up his belt was a gift beyond price: the Pulse. The Pulse had been designed to be dropped into the heart of an enemy's command center. It fired three electromagnetic bursts at ten-minute intervals, each one obliterating all electronic activity within a three-klick radius. Ignition systems, computer hardware, radios, security locks, pacemakers, cameras, laser drivers—if it sparked, the Pulse could kill it.

Harry would like these gadgets, he thought.

All of them were available to the special operations unit that he had formed as an adjunct to ViraVax in 1998: the Night School. The Night School had gone from being ViraVax security to being ViraVax hired muscle, and the Colonel objected. The Gardeners changed over to their private security, and saw to it that Rico went nowhere from then on.

Just another bunch of goons.

Rico picked up the code-burst device, rolled the thimble-sized unit between his sweaty palms and clipped it into the socket on his Sidekick. Then he shook his head, sighed and reminded himself that he had very little idea what Harry would or would not like.

I don't know him any better than he knows me.

They looked so much alike that the Colonel expected them to think alike, but that was clearly not the case.

Perhaps, when this free-lance operation was over, Harry would understand, once and for all, that his father was not the monster he imagined him to be.

Or else he'll be convinced of it.

Something stirred in the back of his mind, then elbowed itself to the fore: *And so will I.*

A tap at the door and a cough: Yolanda.

She stepped inside without a greeting and set up a squelch on the dressing table. Their conversation would be secure.

"You're not ready," she said. "That's not like you."

"I'm ready."

"Afraid?"

Rico checked her eyes for intent. No taunt, just fact.

"Yeah," he said, "afraid. Not paralyzed."

"Good. I'm not even going and this scares me to death."

Yolanda dropped her gaze and sighed.

"You're a better man than Casey," she said, "and better men should live."

" 'Should' has not been in our vocabulary before, why start with it now?"

"Are we arguing again?"

"Probably."

They laughed together, and for Rico Toledo it was an exercise of a musculature that had been too many years in atrophy.

The Colonel cinched his belt over the blue maintenance coveralls, loaded his zapper for last. He inserted his green card into his Sidekick, keyed for encryption, then downloaded the file "Someday;you" into a likely juncture on the satellite networks. Only one code could retrieve the file, and that was the photon bubble in the upper left-hand corner of the green card that Major Scholz had passed to Harry. He realized with a pang that he missed the major. She'd been his shadow, his right arm, the kind of second who bordered on clairvoyant. Giving Harry the card had been her idea. Writing up the file had been his own.

If he's as smart as they say he is, he'll find it, Rico thought. Eventually.

And if not?

"Well, we all die sooner or later," he muttered.

"Your usual cheerful self," Yolanda replied. "Too bad so many people die without ever having lived."

"Well, you and I have lived a little."

"Not together."

"No."

"Not my fault."

"No."

His gear was ready. By the slim line of his tool belt, no one would guess that he carried anything more than machete, hammer, screwdriver and wrenches. He glanced again in the mirror at his shaved eyebrows and plucked-out eyelashes. He pulled the bill of his blue cap lower over his eyes and let his mouth go slack. Couple it all with the weight he'd put on and Rico would pass as an Innocent, at least for a moment, and a moment was all he needed.

Yolanda drove him in silence the half dozen kilometers to a squat barn beside a flat pasture. A thin breeze snaked down from the higher canyons and did nothing to quell his profuse sweating.

Yolanda hugged him, then kissed him a long, tender one. Her tongue tapped his once before she stepped back. It took all of his control to keep from throwing her down onto the alfalfa. Now, of all times, was not the time.

"We should have done that years ago," she said.

"There you go again," he said, "spoiling a perfectly good moment with a 'should.' "

"Come back."

"I'll try."

" 'Try,' " she snorted, "that's as bad as 'should.' "

Yolanda folded the antenna of her scrambler and then, as an afterthought, slipped it into his overalls pocket.

"Bring me a present," she said.

"Bottle of Poison?" he asked, and stroked her cheek with a finger.

"You," she said.

Yolanda didn't wait to see the Buzzard lift, but drove off in a dust devil at the *snick* of his door. Rico snapped himself into the chute leaning against the skids, thanked the DEA for their carelessness and climbed aboard.

The Colonel liked the Buzzard for its near-silent flight, high cruise speed and extremely low stall-speed. The gangly little bird was designed as a drone for drug-intercept missions. It could carry up to two observers or extra fuel. It had a nearly undetectable radar profile, and with camouflage was difficult to track visually as well. He knew where the DEA kept two more in mountain hideaways.

The Buzzard was outfitted with standard controls, but Colonel Toledo wouldn't be needing them. He had lifted a drug-interdict flight program and transponder ID from the DEA system. A satellite would be his pilot on a low-topography mission. This mission would stall the aircraft several times en route, mimicking the surveillance techniques of the DEA. One of these stalls would occur at the north end of "ViraVax Valley" in the Jaguar Mountains.

Rico Toledo crawled out of the cockpit onto the flimsy undercarriage of the Buzzard just before its stall over ViraVax. He popped his chute enough to fill it and hurtled the forty meters through darkness into the trees. If ViraVax picked up the Buzzard on any of their sensors, the satellite would feed the phony DEA flight plan into their system with the DEA authorization plastered all over it.

The facility's infrared line didn't start for a kilometer to the south, so he was confident that he hadn't been spotted. The nighttime chirps, shrieks and warbles rippled the jungle air.

The Colonel lay wide awake under a ceiba tree in Costa Brava's lush highlands. He was out of breath, out of shape and doubly thankful that the drop had gone without a hitch. The quick tropical dawn had not yet started its sprint above the horizon and he was already soaked with sweat.

Been out of the saddle too long, he thought.

But he knew, in reality, it was the booze.

Rico felt something flutter past his face and into the dark, something leathery and damp.

Another virus on the prowl.

He shuddered, something he didn't do often, and reminded himself that it was just a joke. Costa Brava always warped his humor, much as it had warped his dreams, his life.

When he thought of the warp of his life, he thought of his son, whom he had tested mercilessly and found to be sound. He could not say the same for Costa Brava, his confederacy of republics, the dream of the free world.

It was necessary for him to hate me, he thought. *This way, he stands a chance.*

Rico Toledo had waited for the day his son would stand up to him. That day Colonel Toledo would be freed to be about the greater business of destroying Casey, ViraVax and everything inside. Now that it had happened, Harry would see what really made his father tick. Then they would all see. . . .

He spun at a rustle behind him. The probes on his zapper framed the quivering nose of a small anteater. He smiled at his own adolescent nervousness and flicked the safety back on. The anteater sniffed his way again, its little black eyes curious, then it backed clumsily into the underbrush.

Rico checked his watch, took a deep breath and let it out slowly. The preliminary to action always had been harder on him than the action itself. This action would have its delicacy. He would destroy Casey, though that was only temporary insurance against the onslaught of artificial viral agents. But his immediate goal lay either topside, near Casey's private quarters where the bigwigs stayed, or in decon. The Colonel was sure that they would not want those children anywhere near the surface. Decon meant the elevators and the elevators were a snap.

Rico Toledo did not know for sure that there was an antidote to any of Casey's special projects, but he presumed so. He presumed that Casey would cover himself in case of an accident, and that some other virologist could duplicate it. He presumed, he hoped, but he didn't know.

In his professional life, the Colonel had seen himself as a virus on the prowl long before real viruses had come into the business. Perhaps that was why the Agency paired him up with Casey nearly twenty years back: both of them thought like viruses.

Find the weakness, gain entry, locate and duplicate the product, get out, he recited to himself.

This was his personal synopsis of espionage, the sentence that boiled his life down to a thick paste of tapes, disks, files. It was supposed to be simple. The enemy was supposed to be "the other side," as though the world were as simple as a laser disk. Rico Toledo stopped counting sides when the world had become a dodecahedron, nearly twenty years back.

He had a standard lecture to the Night School recruits.

Make the enemy your host. Use his own resources against him. Get the product.

That product, information, had been his passion for nearly thirty years. Ironically, it had been this passion that had destroyed everything that he'd made of his life. He intended to see that it would destroy Joshua Casey as well.

"The enemy is anyone that you can't trust," he had warned Joshua Casey in the beginning.

"That pretty much takes in everybody, doesn't it?" Casey had replied, cool, unaware of how much he had given away.

The lift of his eyebrow, the clear gaze, told the Colonel that it was true, that this was a man who was satisfied to be completely alone.

Colonel Toledo had something now that he could entrust to no one, and Casey was at the heart of it. That made the world his enemy, and the world was making him pay. If he told what he knew about Casey and his doctored-up vaccines, the world would tear itself apart. Executioner's axes would pop heads around the globe, beginning with Colonel Toledo's and Joshua Casey's. Casey had inserted new viruses into his vaccines as skillfully as he crafted his cures. The inoculated had become his puppets, ignorant of his tug at their strings. The world had become Casey's lab and half of humanity his deliberately infected mice.

Toledo rubbed absently at his arm. The hypnotic had brought it all back.

You even got to me, you bastard, he thought. *You cost me everyone and everything I loved.*

It wasn't drink that drove him to rage, or pheromones that drove him to lust, but an artificial viral agent that took charge and ground him down. The fact that he had been duped like so many ignorant millions was a hot coal that he refused to swallow.

The Colonel had been more suspicious than wise, but whatever the case he had not allowed his son to receive any of Casey's concoctions. He hoped that Harry would be lucky enough to avoid them now. The encryption that Yolanda had downloaded from her mole at ViraVax explained why, explained the history, explained the ultrasecrecy surrounding everything. But even the mole didn't have all the cards, and the blank spots worried Rico a lot more than the bad news.

A headache pounded the Colonel's skull, reminding him that at least one insidious pet of Casey's still swam his bloodstream, awaiting its cue.

Don't be dramatic, he thought. *It's a hangover.*

The Colonel smiled for the first time all evening, a smile that coincided with moonrise over the great green canopy of the Costa Bravan highlands.

Sabbath evening in Costa Brava, he thought.

In spite of everything, he still believed he had much to be thankful for.

For a last chance at Joshua Casey, if nothing else.

His gray eyes, still sharp at fifty, inventoried the lab complex that sprawled in a park-like hollow about a thousand meters below. A plane traversing the steep hillside might manage a passing glimpse of the farm-like spread, but the "Severe Magnetic Disturbance" warnings on recent charts kept planes away.

This was ViraVax clumped at his feet, and somewhere inside lurked Joshua Casey, the man responsible for his nightmares, his failures, the enslavement of Harry and an unwitting humanity.

Fear and ignorance had been the keys to the world's cooperation. But Colonel Toledo was not ignorant, and now that he was back in the field he knew no fear.

Maybe I march to a greater fear, he thought.

Rico Toledo had lost, given away or driven out everything that was dear to him. He believed that where there was nothing to lose there was nothing to fear.

The idea of his son melting in the wretched death that consumed Red Bartlett—that was his greater fear. His greatest fear was seeing his son become one of Casey's time bombs—an expendable device in his biogenetic arsenal.

If I can't stop it here, at least I won't be around to see it.

He tried to think of something that scared him more. Nothing came to mind; certainly not ViraVax, not Casey.

The Colonel readjusted the tool pouches at his waist. He knew he could penetrate ViraVax security, even though many of them had been trained by his own people in his own methods. He wanted to do this without killing anyone but Casey, if possible. Most of the shipping activity here was at night, so that by day it would look like a sleepy highland ranch with a lot of barns and storage buildings. Casey himself preferred to work at night.

Toledo knew that the Agency would take the heat for Casey's insanity when the time came. No one would believe that one of the world's greatest benefactors would dupe the most sophisticated intelligence agency in the world. No, charges would be quite the contrary.

Bashing the Agency had been a journalistic tradition for four generations now. Colonel Toledo loved the Agency, loved the gathering and analyzing of information, loved the balance it had brought to the world. The inevitable disgrace whetted his hatred for Casey all the more.

Casey had information and the Agency had protection.

A match made in Hell, the Colonel thought.

Casey's brain was the most valuable brain in the world. He kept much of his work stored there, uncommitted to the vulnerability of laser disk or Litespeed. How inconvenient for Casey that his brain happened to reside in one of those vulnerable human bodies.

And how convenient for me.

In the old days, the Agency had been quick to take advantage of a few hijackings to get airport security systems installed worldwide. Drug trading gave them the excuse to install electronic strips inside currency to track the movements of cash. Epidemics, natural and man-made, were now an excuse to inoculate millions of people with a host of foreign agents. The Agency counted it an intelligence and operations opportunity. With a member of each inoculation team worldwide on the Agency payroll, the eyes and ears of America became acute.

At first, the Colonel had had no idea of either the form or the scope of this advantage. Now he knew, and he could not let them cashier him out of the way.

Rico suspected that three others in the Agency had known this secret. Leonard Stalker hanged himself from a stairwell in Alexandria, Virginia, just two months ago. Mitsui and St. John took off last month on a flight to the Philippines but never landed with the plane.

The embassy bombing must have been my turn.

Casey's first tinkerings had been cheap, time-release viral agents that did their work a year or more after injection. Crude but effective, these organic blunderbusses mowed down four million people and effectively ended the messianic wars.

The Colonel had chosen this mountain hideaway himself, and it had served ViraVax well for nearly twenty years. The small dam that the Corps of Engineers had installed at the head of the valley provided the facility with more power than five sixths of the cities in the country.

The Colonel saw the pad lights flash around the simulated corral and he watched a supply chopper swoop in and out. They were fast, black and nearly silent.

This was officially Agency training land—the Colonel had bought it from Costa Brava with Agency funds and dubbed it "The Night School." The Corps of Engineers designed the ViraVax compound and its bunker system, but a yellow-toothed, slick-haired contractor built it and Rico knew the importance of that difference.

His original detachment of two hundred security in this twenty-kilometer-square section of mountains was out of the Agency's own Special Operations Force. Now fewer than a hundred missionaries walked the beat, trained and rotated on a two-year basis just like the techs.

What kind of Christians need to train and outfit an army?

The Colonel's past fifteen years had been hell. The ViraVax project had taxed his skills, commandeered his life and then cashed him out. He no longer wanted to get even. That, he knew, would not be possible. Casey had engineered a new world of slavery. The Colonel had been his muscle. He knew there was a trigger somewhere and he wanted to get Casey before he could trip it. The Colonel knew he had become one of those most dangerous of men—unshakable, resourceful, on a personal mission with nothing to lose.

Jumping into the main ViraVax compound undetected was impossible. The gridwork of sensors would pick up his chute even if he could slip his body through one of the meter-square openings.

No, better to jump outside and have security come to get him. Rumor had it that a few hunters had disappeared over the years, invited all the way to Level Five. He would disable the security patrol, gain entry, send a signal, and ten minutes later all hell would break loose with the guerrillas up at the dam. Then it was a matter of gathering Harry, Sonja and Marte Chang and outrunning the inevitable shutdown.

The Colonel knew what the ultimate price would be long before he peered over the rim of the ridge and surveyed the complex below. He knew that he would die there and that the Agency would make further disgrace of his life to discredit him. But when the Colonel was done, it would not be so simple for anyone to enshackle the world again. In his fantasies, his last word, shouted in the face of death, was "Freedom!"

"You have a death wish, Toledo," an army shrink once told him. "You just want somebody else to do it for you."

He smiled again and enjoyed the feeling. It had been some time since he'd allowed himself the luxury. Such a beautiful moon over ViraVax. The night jungle sounds picked up and the day twitters died down. Colonel Toledo was glad that he got to breathe the thick jungle air on this, his last remaining day.

He yawned just as a troupe of howler monkeys cut loose in the treetops to his left. No matter how often he heard it, their sudden whoops always startled him and got his heart racing. This was their rallying call, probably triggered by the moon. Had they spotted him, they would be flinging monkey shit and urine on his head. He remained still until they finished their ritual and settled into nesting. They, too, had suffered at Casey's hands when some recombined polio got loose, leaving three out of a hundred monkeys alive.

Inside the band of his hat Rico had woven a wire garrote, lockpicks and magnetic strips that the Agency used to override electronic security.

Casey had never been worried about someone slipping *into* the compound; he had wanted full protection against anyone getting *out*. As a military man, the Colonel had never liked this

arrangement. Now it would make his mission much simpler, since
he didn't count on leaving alive, anyway.

Colonel Toledo had considered the Gardeners' strict observance
of their Sabbath ritual and their nepotism to be the weakest point
in the ViraVax defense. Predictability was good in science, bad
in war. This time it worked in the Colonel's favor.

Missionaries and mucky-mucks would be at their worship in
the amphitheater or watching from their habitats. No one outside of a skeleton security and life-support crews worked on the
Sabbath. The handful of techs who were not of the faith could
work in place of the Gardener counterparts, and were required
to do so to get anything done. That's why Red Bartlett never
had a life.

He started to think, *And that's why Sonja loves him: he was a
mystery, not a father.*

But Rico corrected himself, and apologized to his memory of
Red, who, he had to admit, had been a good man.

Life support of lab animals was handled, as usual, by the Innocents, the retarded workers who went to their chores as though
to a game. They also monitored the telltales that monitored the
facility. He had broken into the Double-Vee five times during his
tour, testing his own security, and he was confident of getting
inside now.

Rico made his way easily downslope through the damp underbrush, each step smooth and deliberate. He was out of shape,
but his old jungle habits had not abandoned him. The final fifty
meters to the perimeter was open except for waist-high growth
of greenery. He scanned the perimeter, the valley walls, the
compound. Not a sentry in sight. Two men sat in the shade of
an all-terrain vehicle in the doorway to the machine shop, over
two hundred meters away.

They've cut back, he thought. *They haven't had trouble here
in so long that they're overconfident.*

Rico Toledo got down on his belly to wriggle his way through
when he felt the stings on his hands and face.

Nettles!

They weren't nettles. The leaves on these plants were smooth
and blade-like, not palm-sized and fuzzy. He almost had time to
laugh at his bad luck when something switched off his entire
musculature. His brain, however, remained clear.

Shit! he thought. *I should've known it would be something
like this!*

His head was downslope, and the Colonel hoped that lying downhill would make it possible for him to breathe. The undersides of the leaves dripped white and sappy, and smelled like licorice.

Casey, you bastard!

Rico Toledo remembered those wasps that stung caterpillars, then laid their eggs on the living, disconnected flesh. Ex-Colonel Toledo's mind remained wide awake, while his disconnected body ground to a halt around him.

Ex-Colonel Rico Toledo woke inside the perimeter wire of ViraVax with neither tactile sensation nor motor control. Someone worked a bag-mask over his face and pumped oxygen into his lungs. He was numb, paralyzed, and could only see what crossed his vision as two people grunted and hefted him for the carry into the compound. Both wore protective gear that included gloves and taped cuffs at ankles and wrists. They tossed him onto a wooden workbench like a sack of coffee, and lightning shot through his head.

He revived again to a booming headache.

I'm awake and alive, he thought.

Neither was necessarily good news. Not even his eyelids moved. Curiously enough, he found himself calmer than he remembered being since . . . since . . .

Since I decided to split with Grace.

He pushed that aside now and immersed himself in this feeling of calm, this sense of being right and doing right in spite of his circumstances. He had been a fighter all his life, son of a prizefighter, and he had not realized until this moment what a burden that had been.

The Colonel's thoughts turned briefly to the two fail-safe devices that he had installed in his plan. With one, he could kill himself. To manage that, he needed a little more muscular control. The second was a coded message transmitted upon cessation of his heartbeat. This message triggered a series of relays on several networks. One went to Yolanda, one to El Indio and one to his son, Harry. Two were business, one was personal. Neither of his fail-safes was available to him now.

"Tape his eyes shut," one of the men ordered in English.

"What for, he's not going to—"

"I said tape them shut, Corporal. Don't be a dumb shit. He can't blink, his eyes will dry out. We don't want to deliver damaged goods. And *don't* make me explain an order to you again, understand?"

"Yes, Sergeant. Thank you, Sergeant."

What's a veteran like him doing walking perimeter? Rico wondered.

The answer came almost as quickly as the question: *Because he likes it.*

The corporal who taped the Colonel's eyes shut looked barely older than the Colonel's fifteen-year-old son. He was sweating profusely, his hazard suit amplifying the Costa Bravan heat and humidity. The Colonel could hear, but not well. A large, loud bank of fans drowned out nearly everything. But the fans gave him his bearings.

The heat exchangers, he thought. *I'm in the barn north of cultivation and east of the supply pad.*

That put him about fifty meters from the nearest set of elevators, and that fifty meters was across open ground. These heat exchanger shafts dropped to Level Two before they filtered for the first time. Two of the huge ducts blew hot air and two blew cold—either way it would be a miserable, possibly fatal trip. Those little Colts that security wore made the open a miserable, possibly fatal trip even if he were in the best of shape.

Two bad choices.

It looked like he had plenty of time to make them. Once he hit the elevator and transport system he could move quickly, riding the roofs of their cars. He hoped that the toxin wore off before the Sabbath ended.

Not even the residents knew this complex as well as Colonel Toledo. Casey's biological perimeter defense was new, and had trapped him, but the concrete-and-steel layout of the compound was as familiar to him as his car.

I should have anticipated that, he thought.

He remembered hearing insects, so the toxin didn't harm everything.

I'll bet those howlers that died out there didn't have polio, either.

The slipup was a sign that his retirement had been timely.

The Colonel was sure that whatever else lurked outside the perimeter probably was not known to the residents, either.

The Colonel was one of three people who knew what Casey did to dissatisfied employees.

Now it looks like I'll find out firsthand.

He heard the corporal shedding his hazard suit nearby, let himself be lulled by the respirator and the exchanger fans.

The Colonel heard voices and laughter a few meters away. He couldn't make out details of the conversation and cursed the tape over his eyelids. Then he heard the *clink* of silverware against plates, smelled the unmistakable aroma of processed soy food. It didn't make him hungry at all, but he discovered that he could twitch his nose, then his lip. His headache persisted.

Good Friday, 2015, he thought. *I'm still alive.*

He knew, in spite of everything, that he was thankful.

32

MARTE CHANG WATCHED a pair of security guards come up from the fence line across the compound. They struggled out of the perimeter twilight and into the relative glare of the exterior illumination. Both wore hazard suits and carried something blue between them, something that looked a lot like a limp human body.

That is *a person they're carrying,* she thought.

He didn't look alive, and the security team wasn't hurrying him to the dispensary. They disappeared into one of the barns behind the lab, but by the time she raced down the hallway to a closer window, they were gone. A knot of Innocents gathered behind her to jabber and stare.

"Why you run?" Magdalena asked her. "Why you run?"

"It's all right," Marte reassured them. "I needed the exercise."

"I can essise," Magdalena said, and hopped in place, clapping her hands over her head. "Angel Mishwe taught me."

"*Angel* Mishwe!" Marte muttered.

She glanced down the hallway and noted a line of Innocents pushing stainless-steel carts laden with heavy pots. The pots glistened with condensation.

"What's that?" she asked. "What are they doing?"

"Water," several Innocents blurted at once. "Sabbath water."

The facility was in an uproar over something. Shirley had told her that the Master was arriving today, and at first Marte thought that was what caused all the commotion. Then she heard the emergency claxons sound outside, and watched emergency crews rushing about, some of them in hazard suits.

The yellow caution light winked above her door all afternoon, telling her to stay inside until the all-clear was sounded. No one answered her calls through intercom or the web.

If there was a contamination situation developing, she wanted to be as far away as possible. She also thought she should find out as much as she could to take with her. She wished David were here.

I want out, contamination or not!

The maintenance crews wore blue coveralls, but security took the limp person into the ag area, where the workers all wore brown coveralls. And both security men struggled with the heavy body and with their clumsy hazard suits.

Marte had received a burst from Mariposa that said simply, "Help coming. Locate and verify two possible captives arrived today. Harry Toledo and Sonja Bartlett. Remain topside. Prepare to move."

Marte sincerely hoped that the limp figure in building A-3 was not her rescue party. She also hoped it was not one of the captives.

She had been restless since the weekly shutting-down began for the Sabbath, so checking for Harry and Sonja had been a release for that energy. She had found them, but not through the ViraVax records. She had found them through David, her indispensable David, just before all hell broke loose.

"David," she asked, "have you unloaded anyone from the lift pad today?"

He had looked troubled earlier, but when she'd asked him if he wanted to talk, he shook his head. Now he shut his mouth firmly, breathed hard through his nose a couple of times and said, "Two of them. In those black bags."

"In bags?" she asked, and feared the worst. "Were they dead?"

David shook his head. "No, but they were naked."

"You saw them? Where?"

"In my cart. I took them to decon. They gave the girl a shot but dumped the boy on the floor."

Sabbath procedures had started early, and now there was a Code Yellow. She hoped the Code Yellow was a diversion, and not the real thing. If they went into full shutdown, no telling how long she'd be here.

Months, she thought. *Maybe years.*

Marte suspected that Casey was taking no chances. If Harry and Sonja were as important as Mariposa implied, Casey didn't want anyone to stumble onto these children. Marte had hopped the cart next to David and had him race to the elevators, but the readout at the elevator gate said, "Level Five Decon in Progress."

Level Five was Mishwe's domain, and very bad news, indeed.

Now she worried about David, and hoped that they considered him too ignorant to threaten anyone with what he'd seen. He had been beeped away, and left her at her doorstep like a suitor.

"When I get back, let's walk out in the artichokes," he'd told her. "They're beautiful."

Her restlessness burned, and the yellow light above her door continued its incessant warnings. It had been dark for nearly two hours, but Marte stared out her only window, wishing for sun. Because of the precipitous mountains, Marte would not see the sun again from this window until tomorrow, halfway to noon.

She turned to her terminal and added a note to her morning burst, awaiting the outgoing bureaucratic rushes to the embassy.

"Sentries carried in limp male, dressed in blue, from perimeter at 1855, to bldg A-3, no alarm."

Her burst already informed Mariposa that the captives were out of reach in the confines below. The only thing she had seen crawl out of Level Five was Dajaj Mishwe, and he was hardly a good omen.

If the rebels or the Agency were going to rescue her before the Sabbath ended, they'd better get moving. She wished that her quarters afforded her a better view.

Why don't I just wish myself out of here?

Her window faced east, into the canyon wall less than a kilometer away. The landing pad, the only lifeline to the outside, was directly behind her.

What if they come and go and I miss my chance? she worried. *How much time would they spend looking for me?*

Casey had told her that the elevators were the only access down below Level Two, yet she'd seen Mishwe beat the elevator's mandatory four-hour grind by over three and a half hours. He had a back way, or a trick to override the elevators. Still, if whoever was coming in here wanted the two hostages, they would have to bring them up an elevator, of this she was certain.

But which one? she wondered.

The newcomers had gone down the usual decon route directly from receiving. That was right out of the hangar bay beneath the landing pad. Marte was not allowed to loiter in that area, but on the Sabbath movement was much easier. Access topside and deepside was sealed off in sensitive areas, but still Sabbath was the only day she felt free to take a walk and actually feel the sun.

The "transmit" light on her console winked on, and she reacted promptly, flurrying her fingers inside her gloveware.

"I'll be near the pad" was all she had time to add at the end of her burst.

Marte put in a call on David's box, but he didn't reply. She thought that he might be at the Level Two lounge across from her labs, where he often had tea with her in the afternoons. She stepped off the elevator in time to see his cart at the far end of the corridor, racing full tilt towards her.

Marte and David were the only two in the passageway; already the rest of the crew had quit for the Sabbath. As the cart got closer, it began weaving from side to side without slowing down. Marte recognized the expression on David's pale face as complete terror, and she was not sure that he even saw her.

"David!" she called. "David, slow down!"

He didn't slow down. "Run!" he shouted. "Run!"

David slumped in the seat, pulling the steering handle as he went. The cart slammed against the wall and Marte slipped into a doorway to keep it from hitting her. It whined past her and wedged itself into the next doorway, its hot wheels squealing on the waxed floor and its flashers blinking.

"David, what happened?"

Just as quickly as she touched his shoulder, she jerked away. His face was slack in unconsciousness or death, and his skin had already begun to sag and split under the weight of the contents underneath.

"Help me!" Marte screamed, looking both ways down the corridor. "Help!"

No one responded. She yanked a firebox handle beside the doorway, then pulled David by his overalls to get him off the cart. He left a trail of tissue behind that flickered with the trace of a blue flame as it melted into the rubber mat. She decided not to wait for help, and she did two things that she vowed she would never do if faced with a contamination situation: she had already touched the victim, and now she was going to flee the facility to save herself.

She jumped aboard the cart, backed it out of the doorway and raced for an elevator.

33

JOSHUA CASEY WASHED his father's feet in the old ceramic bowl that his mother had made. Calvin Casey was sweating, in spite of the air-conditioning, and his breathing was wet and labored. His feet and ankles were so swollen that the tops of his socks left an impression that would not rub out. Joshua finished his ritual, then pressed a thumb into the swollen tissue. The thumbprint stayed, and it was white.

"Are you feeling all right, Father?" he asked.

"Can't sleep," the Master wheezed. "Too restless."

"How many pillows are you using?"

"Five or six. Why?"

The Master sprinkled water on the tops of Joshua's feet, then swiped them once with the linen towel. It was the shorthand version of their old ritual, and Joshua didn't care for it. He could tell that it would tax his father greatly to bend down or to kneel, and this worried him. Joshua replaced his father's socks and shoes, tied up his laces and disposed of the water and towels.

"Your ankles are swollen, you can barely breathe sitting up, much less lying flat on your back. . . ."

To Joshua's surprise, his father smiled.

"You're a smart one, Joshua," he said. "I know you dislike the *médicos,* but you've got the touch."

Joshua poured out their ice water and broke the small loaf of dark bread between them.

"Don't worry, Father, it's salt-free," he said.

"Salt's not the problem," Calvin said. "You know me better than that. Anyone who's read my books knows."

"So we know it's congestive heart failure," Joshua interrupted. "What happened that you haven't told me?"

235

Calvin Casey chewed the dense bread, washed it down and poured himself another glass of water.

"Haven't told anybody," Calvin said. "Heart attack, I think. Just after I left here last time."

"You *think*? You mean, you didn't check it out?"

"Didn't have to," Calvin said. "I'm prepared to meet our Lord, and the Children of Eden are prepared to go on without me. So are you."

Joshua Casey had not given much thought to his father's mortality. Until this visit, his father had never looked older than fifty or fifty-five. In two months he had aged twenty years. Today every minute of his seventy-five years showed in his gray, puffy face, his bent posture and trembling hands. This was an old man before him, a very sick old man, and it was clear to Joshua that he would not live much longer.

Too bad he can't know what we've done for him, Casey thought.

"I'm sorry, Father. I've had problems here. The country is blowing up again."

"I know," his father said, a hand on Joshua's knee, "I know when you're preoccupied. And my people keep me abreast of the news in this region. Terrible thing about that Toledo fellow, going south as he did. Would you care to tell me about it?"

He knows! Joshua thought. *As usual, he knows everything but he wants me to tell him.*

Mishwe had gone too far, and if Calvin Casey got wind of trouble inside ViraVax, trouble that related to the political situation, then it wouldn't be long before everybody else got wind of it, too. Joshua Casey trusted his father completely, and valued his judgment, but he did not want to endanger the Master's health any further. He finished his ritual water and bread before speaking.

"One of our best people is insane," he said. "He has endangered our security here. He has visited a scrutiny upon us that we may not survive."

"Dajaj Mishwe?"

Joshua sighed. His father was, truly, an insightful man.

"Yes."

"He has performed well for you in the past," Calvin said. "Has he begun that business with the young women again?"

"No," Joshua said. "It's more serious than that."

Calvin's bushy eyebrows jumped once, twice, then his lips set in a gray line.

"It's hard to get more serious than murder," Calvin wheezed.

"You know that I prefer not to nose into your business here. But give me the details, perhaps I can help."

Joshua told his father what he knew of Mishwe's private agenda.

"Our goal is to make humanity better, just as we are making the earth better," Joshua said. "Mishwe talked about starting over with the Garden of Eden. He wasn't happy improving humans. He wants to start over with the perfect couple—a new, handcrafted Adam and Eve."

"And how would he manage that?" Calvin asked.

"Cloning," Joshua said. "Using our artificial viral agents with sperm as the vector."

Calvin Casey waved an impatient hand at his son.

"I don't follow your shoptalk," the Master said. "I know what a clone is, start from there."

"A clone is a copy of a person," Joshua said. "That's the basics. But as long as you're mucking about in there and cloning, you might as well take care of other business, too. Even viable clones from petri dishes have a lot of defects—basically, from overhandling, exposure to ultraviolet, crude tools or clumsy technique. But our AVAs take away all that hardware and provide a way to get inside the cell, manipulate its map and send it on its way."

"I thought it was illegal to clone humans."

"It's not illegal, it's unethical," Joshua said. "Besides, very little is illegal in Costa Brava these days. I'll hand it to Mishwe, he even kept it from me for years."

Calvin Casey pinched the bridge of his nose, ran his hand over his bald head and asked, "He has done this?"

Joshua swallowed hard.

"He has done it," he admitted. "Sixteen years ago. He informed me well after the fact. Toledo's son, Red Bartlett's daughter."

"The *daughter*?"

Calvin Casey looked perplexed.

"How could it be the daughter?" he asked. "You said cloning made a copy from the *sperm*."

"Yes," Joshua said. "The mechanism was delivered through Red Bartlett's sperm. It did not deliver Bartlett's genetic material, only the appropriate messages to trigger duplication of the ovum. Parthenogenesis."

"Doesn't sound like any part of Genesis to me," Calvin muttered.

If the matter hadn't been so serious, Joshua would have laughed long and hard at this.

"Go on," his father urged.

"You were present for the incident with Bartlett a couple of months ago. Well, Bartlett and Colonel Toledo were longtime friends. He thought that Bartlett's murder might have something to do with his work here."

"And was he correct?"

Joshua shook his head, sorry that he had to lie to his father, the only man in the world that he truly respected.

"No," he said. "It was a break-in of some kind. The man was executed. Toledo had family problems, got a divorce, got drummed out of the service. But Toledo kept drinking and he kept digging. Somebody began accessing our system. Mishwe suspected Toledo and wanted to stop him. Also, Dajaj was afraid that the mothers would take Harry and Sonja out of the country, out of his reach. They are his Adam and Eve, and they are teenagers. He wanted to get control of them before they were . . . contaminated."

"Before they lost their virginity, you mean."

"Exactly."

"So Mishwe engineered all of this political bungling?"

"To draw Toledo into a trap and destroy him," Joshua said. "And to get possession of his two clones."

"Then the two young people are here? With both governments after them?"

Calvin Casey's face had gone from gray to purple, and he was very short of breath. Joshua did not get the chance to answer.

"Security," Shirley announced over his console. "Your package is outside."

"Mishwe?" Calvin asked.

Joshua nodded.

"We'll get to the bottom of this right now," he promised.

Joshua buzzed the doorlocks open, but before security could usher Mishwe inside, Joshua Casey saw his father jerk in his chair as though struck by a fist. A look of complete surprise washed over his face and he pitched forward onto the carpet with a grunt.

Joshua Casey heard a high-pitched, disorienting whine that seemed to come from inside his own head. He tried to rise, but could not make his legs or arms work. A guard walked through the door and Casey tried to speak, but the whine had changed to a very loud rushing sound and he couldn't be sure he was heard over the racket. Eyes wide open and hand over his mouth, the guard backed into Mishwe.

The last thing Joshua Casey saw was Dajaj Mishwe, smiling over the crumpled body of the Master. Faint screams and the rushing of feet came to him from Shirley's office and from the hallway. A small blue flame flickered from his dead father's ear, and Casey knew that it was not the Holy Spirit.

34

HARRY LOOKED BEHIND their peel-and-stick viewscreen and used the handle of his spoon to unscrew the bases of their light fixtures. He tapped and poked every square meter of ceiling. He wanted to find a way out before they were moved to a real room in another part of the facility. The machinery sounds around them had died down.

"They're shutting down for Sabbath," Sonja told him. "We'll probably be stuck here until Monday morning."

The elevator shaft is a straight shot, he reasoned. *If they take us anywhere else, we'll get lost in the maze and never get topside.*

Sonja paced, trying to draw the attention of any observers away from Harry.

"What are you looking for?" she whispered.

"The service hatch," he whispered back. "There's got to be one."

When Harry was five his father stopped an elevator between floors. The two of them were the only passengers, and his father had said, "Let me show you something," then he pushed a red button on the number panel. The numbers went all the way to number 10. Number 5 was lit.

A sudden stop had pitched Harry to his knees, and a loud, clanging bell hurt his ears. Harry had clapped his hands over his ears and did not try to get up. The Colonel had silenced the bell with a screwdriver from his back pocket.

"Now," he'd said to Harry, "look here."

The Colonel had reached up to the top of the elevator, lifted the big, square light fixture up and set it aside with a *clunk* onto the top of the car.

"The elevator is just a box," he explained, "and that's the top. I'll lift you up, and then come up after."

Before Harry could protest, his father had him under the armpits, over his shoulders and through the hole. It was a high, dusty
shaft, cool, and it smelled of oil. Besides the light that lay beside
him, Harry saw light spilling from around the sides of elevator
doors all the way up the shaft.

"Move over," his father said.

Harry scrambled aside as his father heaved himself up, then
through the hole. The Colonel picked up the light fixture, replaced
it, then squatted at a dusty control panel atop the elevator.

"Sit here in the middle," his father warned him. "There are
things coming up and down the walls that will take your arm
off. Stay away from that cable, it's greasy. Your mother would
kill me if you got grease all over you."

A cable as thick as Harry's wrist looped over a framework atop
the car. The Colonel pushed a button, and the bell came on again.
He pushed another, and it went off. The next button he pushed
started the car going up, and Harry saw why it was important
to stay away from the walls. A huge concrete weight whooshed
down its track in the wall and he jerked back, falling against his
father.

"Now watch this," his father said. "Look through the light."

Harry knelt over the light fixture. The bright light hurt his eyes
after the contrast of the darkened shaft, but he could see the whole
inside of the car. His father stopped it, opened the doors, and a
young, long-haired couple stepped inside.

"Do you think it's safe?" the girl asked, looking the car up
and down.

"It's running," the boy answered. "The alarm stopped. It must
be okay. Probably some kid."

He pressed a button and the door closed. The elevator rose one
floor, two floors.

The Colonel did something on the rooftop control panel, and the
elevator eased to a stop. The couple stepped forward as the doors
opened, then stepped back in shock. The elevator had stopped
about a meter short of the next floor.

"Shit!" the girl said, pressing herself against the back of the car.

"Yeah, well," the boy said, grabbing her hand, "let's go. Let's
get out of here before the doors close."

He boosted her up to the next floor, then jumped up himself,
limber as a cat.

The Colonel and Harry laughed behind their hands as noise-
lessly as they could. The Colonel closed the doors in the faces

of the curious bystanders, and they proceeded to the top of the tenth floor. The Colonel threw a switch that shut the machinery down. He pulled out a pocket flashlight and showed Harry the pulleys and counterweights and explained that he could ride the top of the elevator without getting smashed against the ceiling.

"Never use an elevator if there's a fire in the building," his father warned. "The shaft is just a big chimney, the smoke will kill you. Otherwise, remember if you're stuck in a building, there's a way out. At the top of the shaft, there's usually an access door to another floor or to the roof."

The Colonel showed Harry the doorknob, opened it, and there was the bright light of day at the top of the world. He closed the door.

"Remember," he went on, "from an elevator, there's a way into the shaft. From the shaft, there's a way out. If nothing else, you can reach the doors to the floor above you and pry them apart."

Later, waiting out a roadblock on the way home, his father had told him something else.

"Everything is a trap," he said. "Before you leave the entrance to any room, make sure you have an exit. Before getting into a car, make sure it has door handles inside. Remember, every window is an escape if you can break it."

Only lately did Harry realize how differently he and his father saw the world. Harry saw a window as a way of enjoying the outdoors without the bugs. His father saw it as an opening for snipers, a source of deadly fragments, an escape hatch.

"Shit!" Harry said, and snapped his fingers. "Window!"

"What window?" Sonja asked.

That two-way mirror is a window, he thought.

Harry hurried into the bathroom without answering, put his face to the mirror and peered through.

Gone!

The spy crew had shut down and left.

"Harry?" Sonja asked. "What are you doing?"

He put a finger to his lips and shooed her out. Harry inspected the mirror and found that it was installed within the structure of the wall itself—nothing to pry or unscrew. He returned to his bowl in the other room, picked out three balls of rice paste that he'd formed there and handed two of them to Sonja.

"Cover the lenses in here, just in case," he said. "I'll get the one over the bathroom, you get the other two. Make it as fast as you can. Ready?"

She licked her lips and nodded. "Ready."

By the time Sonja covered the second lens, Harry was swinging his chair into the bathroom mirror. His muscles fought back, twitching and trembling. The chair bounced away, cracking the mirror but not breaking it. He recovered his balance and caught a glimpse of his reflection hefting the chair. What he saw made his heart race.

God! he thought. *I thought it was Dad!*

The tousled black hair, the fierce grip on the chair, the hot, focused anger in his gray eyes, all completed the image. This was his young father during their workouts in the gym. Or, later, his drunken father shattering the kitchen cupboards. Harry swallowed hard and hefted the chair again.

This time Harry placed his feet wide apart, took a deep breath, and as he let it out, he swung the chair into his father's twisted image with everything he had.

Two of the legs punched through the laminated glass but Harry's own rubbery legs dropped him to the floor. He reached up and enlarged the holes by pulling out the shards. He got out all the big ones, draped a towel over the sill and squeezed himself through, headfirst. He fell, panting and sweating, between two monitor stations.

He gestured Sonja over and helped her through, and the two of them made it with only a few nicks and cuts.

"Nobody here," he whispered.

"And no alarm," she answered.

"None that we can hear, anyway."

The room appeared to be the workstation of three or four people. All was silent except for the slight whirr of the air-conditioning fan. The little room was crowded with its three terminals and four desks, as though at least half the equipment was there for temporary storage. Harry realized that some of the equipment probably belonged in the room they just left, and it had been stripped for their journey below.

Sonja started for the door.

"Wait," Harry said. "There might be an alarm on the doors. Let's see what we can do from here, first."

"Like what?"

Harry saw the fight-or-flight gleam in her eyes and noted that she was getting better cooperation from her muscles than he got from his. He waved his hand to indicate their surroundings.

"Like get this elevator running to get us topside."

Sonja rolled her eyes. "This thing's the size of a decent house," she said. "You're worried about me opening a door—and you think nobody will notice if you fire this thing up?"

"Any better ideas?"

She pointed to the computer terminals in front of them.

"If it's true that they're shut down for the Sabbath, maybe we can call somebody, let them know where we are. You're the networks whiz, aren't you?"

"Thank you for the recognition." Harry bowed slightly. "First, let's find the access hatch, so we have a back way out in case we're spotted."

"You're right," Sonja said.

She tiptoed to the door, cupped a hand to her ear and held her breath. "Nothing that way," she reported.

"Chill," he said. "Looky there."

He pointed over her head, to the maintenance hatch in the ceiling over the doorway.

"Help me drag this table over there," he said.

It wasn't that easy. The table, like the desks and other heavy furniture, was bolted to the floor with wing nuts. When they unbolted the table and slid it across the doorway, Sonja discovered that the table could be bolted into place to block the door.

"If we can cover that hole we made in the mirror, too," he said, "we can make it mighty tough on anybody who tries to come after us."

Harry set a chair atop the table and coaxed the hatch screws out with the handle of his spoon. Sonja unbolted one of the desks, turned it on end and leaned it against the window.

"With or without alarms, somebody will be on our tails," Harry muttered. "They'll check their monitors, or deliver dinner."

Sonja grunted him an acknowledgment, then slid the remaining desk snug against the first and bolted it down. Only two of the legs lined up with the holes for the bolts, but Harry could see that it would take a superhuman effort to knock her blockade free.

"Nice job," he said with a smile.

"Thanks," she smiled back, dusting off her hands. "How does it look up there?"

"High," he said, giving her a hand up. "Very high. But I suppose a hotshot pilot like yourself won't be intimidated."

Sonja stood on the chair and poked her head and shoulders through the hatch. "You're right," she said. "That's a long way up.

This is *huge*. I'll bet the whole Pan Am Hotel could fit in here."

"If it worked like it's supposed to, it would be impressive," Harry said. "My dad said that they have crews on these things every day because of the contractor rip-off."

"Yeah," Sonja said, "but not on the Sabbath. Sure is black."

She ducked back inside and stepped down from the chair.

"I suppose you want me to carry you up there," she joked.

"Now, *that* thought terrifies me," he said. "I want to try these terminals. We're going to need the cavalry and they need to know where to look."

Sonja pulled on his sleeve.

"Let's just *go*," she whispered. "Somebody will check on us, and I want to be gone when they do it."

"Just give me a minute," Harry said, turning to the nearest console. "If I can get outside, I can get a message to the Agency. If anybody can crack this place, they can."

"All right." Sonja's lips were tight with disapproval. "Do it." Then, as Harry switched on the nearest terminal, she added, "My dad told me that he used me for his password. Maybe my name will work."

When the machine asked, "User ID?" he responded, "Sonja."

"Invalid ID," it responded. "User ID?"

"Try 'Louise,' " Sonja said. "That's my middle name."

"Invalid ID. User ID?"

"I have a number that will get us out," Harry said. "The number Major Scholz gave me. But the dzee might intercept the message. If you're ready to make a run for it, I can . . ."

"Try my birth date," she said. "Let's save ourselves all the running room we can. Use your access if we hear them coming. Try 1/12/00."

That didn't do it, either, but on a hunch Harry typed, "SLB011200."

The voice-box responded, "Hello, Red. Your last access was 18 February 2015, at twelve twenty-four. You have fifty-six files in personal folders. Eleven messages waiting. Go to?"

It was Red Bartlett's personal log.

"Harry, send your message and let's go! They might use gas, like last time, and a pile of furniture won't stop it. . . ."

"Yeah," Harry said, "I know. No problem. Let me try something here."

He saved the Bartlett log to a file called "Out," then navigated himself out of the local network that tied this set of computers

together. In less than thirty seconds he broke through the greater networks of the Level Five system, then into the corporate
mainframe topside. From there, he thought he had a line to the
outside.

If nothing else triggered an alarm, he thought, *this will.*

The viewscreen announced, "Welcome to Telcom. You have
three unretrieved messages and one memo in storage. Read,
Download, Help, Exit?"

Sonja touched the top of the viewer, and Harry saw tears
welling in her eyes.

"If he left a memo, it would be a holo of himself," Sonja said.
"It would have to be right before he died. Show it."

"There isn't time," he said. "I'll get it into the block with his
other files and we'll take it out with us."

Harry dumped the files, memo and messages to block. He
addressed the block to Major Scholz's Agency number and pressed
"send."

The electronic voice reported, "Message sent one hundred
percent error-free. Send another?"

"Got it!" he said, and the first *thump* of a fist hit the blockade
across the room.

Harry unclipped the data block from the Litespeed and tossed
it to Sonja. He typed "Y" to send another message.

"Harry, *please!*"

"Get moving," he said. "I'm coming."

He turned so she couldn't argue and typed, "SOS SOS SB
& HT held fifth level ViraVax up shaft." He hit "send" and
followed Sonja out the hatch as fleshy blows rained down on
the door behind them.

35

DAJAJ MISHWE KNEW that mercy was no survival trait, and it was doubtful that he would have shown the Caseys mercy, anyway. Mishwe was a believer, and he was the sword arm of the Archangel of Wrath. Blasphemy and betrayal had no place in the Garden of Eden, and their agents had no place amongst the faithful. So far, only Dajaj Mishwe had remained faithful to the God of Eden. The Caseys, the missionaries, all of the rest, had sold out to petty politics or cash. They were vermin, barely fit for sacrifice on the sword of the Angel.

Each missionary took possession of twelve Innocents and called themselves Children of Eden. Eden required work, it was a prize to be won. Mishwe had seen how the faithful used those Innocents to stuff the corporate coffers and quench their secret lusts. Selling the labor and the organs of their twelve Innocents was greed in God's eyes, but Casey's eyes never blinked.

Missionaries who forced their Innocents to wait on them were slothful, disgusting beasts hardly worthy of sacrifice. How they would bellow at the burning!

Bartlett had been correct to call it slavery in his memos, while Casey had preferred the euphemism "genetically induced symbiosis."

Mishwe knew all along it would be a Sabbath-day accident, catching the Caseys and their missionaries topside. Mishwe had his plan in force for months, and executed each stage with precision, purified with the sweet scent of sacrifice to the Lord. Good Friday was a time of entombment, and Easter a sign of resurrection of the faithful, a perfect symbol of his intent.

Now that the two Caseys steamed on the charred carpet, and the rest of the staff disintegrated into a stinking muck around him, truly there was no turning back. Within moments the first two levels would be sealed off and rendered lifeless. His precious creations, Harry and Sonja, awaited him, safely sealed off in the elevator on Level Five.

He knew that it was unlikely that Chang would take the sacrificial drink with the others. She was a pagan, in resistance to her indoctrination at the Master's university, and for this good sense he almost admired her. Her work was meticulous, elegant, and Mishwe regretted that she would not live to see the transformation that her Sunspots would bring to his new world order, his Garden of Eden, his Earth.

Even if Chang and some outsiders survive, she'll get the blame, he thought. *And no one topside will survive for long.*

The thought was very nearly a gloat, and gloating lacked dignity. Mishwe breathed deeply, a cleansing breath, and washed the thought away. His every act, his every thought and dream, must be framed in dignity or all was for naught. Adam and Eve lied to the Lord and their dignity fell away from them, leaving them a pair of ignorant grub-eaters in the desert.

At first glimpse, the Lord commanded His Angel to drive those lying bags of carrion from the Garden, cloaked only in the shame of their true nakedness, their lack of dignity, their lie.

Mishwe abhorred the lie as the ultimate cowardice, the seat of all betrayal, God's reason for weeding humanity from His Garden in the first place. Neither liars nor lies would desecrate the new Eden.

It was time for the Angel of Eden to heft his sacrificial sword, his hot blade of purification. Darkness would be his ally, along with the tools and opportunity provided by the Lord Himself.

Mishwe activated the correct toggles within his gloveware, then paused a moment. The pause was not out of reflection upon the immensity of the act he was about to commit, but a moment of appreciation for his hour come round at last.

Thanks to Marte Chang's innovations, Meltdown slept on in the mitochondria of every staff member and Innocent. It hibernated now in the monthly shipment of vaccines distributed to the outside world, a shipment that lifted off from La Libertad's airport just hours ago. Soon a few hundred thousand humans would be infected, to die under the first harsh scrutiny of the sun.

Those who were not infected by the doctored vaccine would perish soon enough, for Mishwe had added a few twists of his own to the brew. The steam from their combustion carried the new infection. This design would prove to be the most highly contagious, quickly moving AVA ever made.

Forty days and forty nights, Mishwe estimated. *Then the soil of the Garden must lie fallow awhile, awaiting my Adam and Eve.*

With his preparations, Mishwe and his two charges could live nicely at Level Five for five years, ten years, even more. His weapon was human-specific, sparing the other animals of the Garden. Only Marte Chang could identify the base, and she would not live to do so.

At the touch of a toggle, the lake behind the dam would be unleashed. The cleansing waters would wash the topside facility to the sea and scour the ground to concrete. The world would presume the entire facility lost. And the world, at least its corrupted version of humanity, would not last the month.

Dajaj knew that he and his Adam and Eve could live forever at Level Five, sealed off in the perfect ecology he had developed. But they would not have to hide forever. In two months the danger would pass. Six months should clear the stench of the dead and they could step out into a world of fresh air and opportunity. Truly, the Garden of Eden.

His sword would have beaten itself into a plowshare long before then. Meanwhile, cradled in the cellular fluids, Meltdown would spark a conflagration that would make Nero look like a child waving a sparkler against the night.

Mishwe imagined the holy moment, now at hand, when everyone at Level One and Two burst to flame, becoming candles to light the way of the Lord. He flicked his right index finger inside his gloveware, and relaxed. The preinfected would die today, killed by ice water with no more sensation than an electrical *snap* in the solar plexus.

Dajaj began the seal-off program for the top two levels, spiraling the precious life support inward, downward, to maintain the core for the Angel of Eden, a support crew of selected Innocents and his Adam and Eve. It was what a body in mortal danger would do, and Mishwe did it methodically, regretlessly.

If his plan went wrong and they dug him out, he would be a hero for his quick action at containment and for broadcasting the proper Mayday messages. All hardware of the world would remain intact, displaying the same discrimination as the old neutron bomb but without the mess. The Garden came with an infinite supply of free tools.

Mishwe wanted to kill Marte Chang and Colonel Toledo himself. Chang, because his plan could not abide her accidental survival. She was a smart one, perhaps even smarter than himself, and he knew she could easily construct a vaccine because she developed the vehicle. No one else would have the luxury of this head start. Toledo he wanted just because it would feel good.

He shook off the feeling, reminding himself of all the histories that went wrong because someone chose the path that felt good over the true path, the well-laid plan. Mishwe reaffirmed that his history would not be one of those.

The body that waits, loses.

He triggered the timing devices at the dam and felt like a sporting figure, come out on the playing field of the gods. Mishwe wondered if he would feel the departure of all those souls, as an amputee feels the limb cramp at night, as a mother grieves over the entombment of her sons.

Did they have souls?

The Innocents, of course, did not. But the missionaries shared in the knowledge of good and evil, the ultimate failing of Adam and Eve. To be soulless, and to sit in judgment on good and evil, that is the ultimate enemy. It must be destroyed at once.

Mishwe had to make sure with Harry and Sonja. He wanted to believe that he'd been faithful to them, his chicks. That he'd thought of them daily, done everything possible to keep them within observation range. He hadn't, and he'd agonized over his remission, and if this rare squander of feeling came to naught, if he created an infidel—worse, a devil—and squandered feeling on it, then surely there was no god merciful enough to save him.

36

THE COLONEL FLEXED his fingers and toes carefully, testing his musculature. He had regained sensation throughout his body, but the slightest movement brought on tremors that punctuated his general weakness. Neither guard seemed worried about him, and neither suspected yet that he was from the outside. Rico's eyes were still taped shut, but he positioned the nearby guards from their conversation.

I'll get the sergeant first, Rico thought. *The other one shouldn't be a problem.*

"They get out once in a while," the sergeant was saying. "Rain washes holes under the fence. This one was probably sent out there to fix it and got himself mixed up. Flip a note to Blue, tell them there's still a hole someplace and this time they should send a brain along. It can wait till daylight."

Rico heard the rapid clicking of fingers in control gloves, then the *beep* that went with transmission. A chair swiveled.

"Seems like it's pretty hard to do," the younger man said. "I don't think *I* could figure a way out of here."

"Well, you could see how bad he wanted back in," the sergeant said. "They don't think like we do. They get afraid of everything. You know that one who brings the bread? Well, he's afraid of paper. Crumpling paper. Puts his hands over his ears and howls like a coyote."

"What'll we do with this one?"

"Give him an hour or so. After bread, we'll take him over to Blue, they'll know what to do with him. We'll have to tie him up in a little bit. That toxin makes 'em pretty twitchy when they come around. Hey, here's Gordon with the grub. Watch this."

Feet shuffled through the double doorway, accompanied by the *squeaksqueaksqueak* of a cart, the clink of ice water and rattle of utensils.

Rico risked a left hand to his left eye. Two straps circled his body at the chest and legs. All of Rico's strength and concentration went to prying the tape loose from his eyelid. He let it hang free so his guards wouldn't notice. After a few deep breaths, he had the strength to loosen the right one. As soon as he did so, his body broke out in a profuse sweat, and tremors rippled through the muscles of his arms and legs. Cramps seized his belly and he was afraid he was going to foul himself.

Relax, he told himself, *just relax. Slow, deep breaths.*

The tremors drummed his heels slightly against the steel surface beneath him, but the sergeant chose that moment to crumple a wad of paper and send the retarded servant into a panic.

The poor man fled without his cart, waddling backwards, hands over his ears and eyes closed, crying like he'd been whipped.

Jesus! Rico thought. *Some fun!*

Rico risked a glance at his guards. The corporal poured out their ritual ice water while the sergeant broke the bread. Both men swept off their caps while the sergeant offered a mumbled grace.

"Too bad we'll miss the Master's sermon this evening," the corporal said. "I've never seen him in person, only on-screen."

"You'll see plenty before your tour's through," the sergeant said, talking through a mouthful of dry bread.

He gulped down a glass of water and poured himself another.

"This is my third tour," he went on. "I like it here. I rode escort for him last time from the airport."

"You get all the luck," the corporal said. "I got to ride with yesterday's shipment and back. What's he like?"

"Like the father you wish you'd had," the sergeant said. "Funny, too, but not like one of the guys. He's different. He sure made me feel good, just riding with him."

Rico craned his neck a little to see if he could spot his tool kit. He didn't see it, but the effort sent his body into spasm once again. This time, it was like a full epileptic seizure except he was completely conscious.

"Shit!" the sergeant said. "We should've cinched that dummy down better. Give me a hand here."

The two of them cinched Rico tight to the gurney, then the sergeant leaned close and removed the loose tape.

"Something's funny here," he said. "This guy doesn't look right."

Oh, shit! Rico thought.

"What do you mean?"

"Look at his eyes," the sergeant said, "the shape of his head."

He held Rico's forehead with one hand, ripped the tape off his mouth and spread his jaws wide.

"Look at his tongue. And where did he get gold in his dental work? Look at those fingers. Shit, I should have paid attention."

The sergeant put the tip of his nose against Rico's nose, and Rico was tempted to bite it off.

"Who are you?" he asked. "Who sent you?"

Rico grunted and shook his head, hoping to rescue the masquerade.

"Hit the intruder alarm," the sergeant ordered. "There might be more than one of them. Then get the chief on the horn, tell him we've got one here dressed like a Triple from Blue. And toss me that tool kit."

The corporal activated the intruder sequence on his Sidekick and tossed Rico's tool kit to his partner. Before he could reach the radio, a series of alarms sounded from the direction of the main office complex, summoning fire, aid and security personnel.

"Disaster drill," the corporal shouted.

"It's no drill," the sergeant shouted back. "And I'll bet our company here knows all about it."

The sergeant slapped Rico across the face.

"Don't you?" he asked.

He slapped again.

"Don't you?"

The man pulled his fist back for a punch when a puzzled expression crossed his face. He gasped a couple of times and the exhalations threw a hot wave over Rico's face. The sergeant staggered back a couple of steps, mouth agape, and dropped to his knees.

"Sergeant?"

The corporal came to help but he, too, staggered and fell. He dropped facedown on the concrete, his face making a heavy, wet *thuck* as he hit. The sergeant toppled onto his back without a word, the only sound a wet popping and crackling. Rico's tool kit was underneath him.

Rico was conscious of a sickly smell that reminded him of rancid bacon in hot grease. He exhaled as deeply as he could and squirmed his left arm free. He unclasped the catch on one strap, then had to lie still for a few moments, fighting the tremors that racked his body.

"Better," he told himself. "Getting better."

Rico didn't know what felled his two guards or what set off the disaster alarm, and that scared him a lot more than the guards themselves.

In this place, it could be anything, he thought.

If it was another bug, he didn't want to get it. He didn't want Harry and Sonja to get it, either.

A thick, liquid sound, something like boiling oatmeal, emanated from the floor beside him. Rico managed to turn his head enough to see what was happening to the sergeant at the foot of his gurney. Rico knew immediately that he was witnessing the manner of his friend Red Bartlett's death. This time it was faster, but every bit as ugly.

Rico felt a heat coming off the sergeant's body, intensifying the odor of hot, rancid meat. His own muscles refused to work, and he was forced to watch the sergeant's body suppurate in its rapid decay. The flesh melted from the bone slowly at first, like cold ketchup from a bottle. Then it became more runny, hotter, and as the tissues pulled away from the bones he saw the first little tongues of blue flame.

Rico looked out the doors and saw other flickers of blue flame there in the darkness. He used the rest of his strength to turn his face away, then a dizziness overcame him, the alarms faded out and darkness swallowed him whole.

37

DAJAJ MISHWE MONITORED the facility-wide panic from the comfort of Casey's inner office. The outer office had been rendered unbearable by the searing stench of the two bodies in full reduction and oxidation. The AVA that Mishwe had sent out on today's shipment carried a further, and very deadly, refinement—steam from the sudden oxidation-reduction spread the active agent further, faster. The vaccine was meant for children, and who could bear to abandon a sick child?

Mishwe had reserved Casey's private elevator behind the office for himself, ensuring his liberation from Casey and all his doomed minions. The scene facility-wide was a triumph of horror and despair, a joy for the Angel of Eden to behold. The fires from the two Caseys sparked a general conflagration in the office complex, unimpeded by the fire-control system which Mishwe himself had disarmed just moments before he was summoned by security. Every monitor displayed the same scene: security, missionaries and Innocents alike bathed in the hot, blue blossoms of their sacrifice.

The "intruder" light lit from the ag security desk, and Mishwe's joy was complete. There could be only one intruder. Only one man would risk all to enter this compound, and he had done so just in time for a warm welcome.

"Colonel Toledo," Mishwe said aloud.

He liked the sound of it, the good fortune, the fateful opportunity to tie up this last end so neatly. Dajaj was a fastidious man, as befit an Angel of the Lord.

"Welcome, Colonel," he said. "And thank you, Lord, for your perfection."

He checked the monitor at the ag station and saw nothing but two empty terminals and a desk. The men had not yet turned on

258 *Bill Ransom*

their lights, so the scene was drowned in shadow. Mishwe rotated the viewer and glimpsed a gurney near the exchanger fans, and someone was strapped to that gurney. The identity was impossible to make out. Smoke and steam from the two charred lumps in the foreground obscured all of the detail in the room. The figure did not appear to be moving.

Should I get him myself, he wondered, *or should I leave him to the flood?*

Mishwe decided it was time to burrow in and activate the final seals. A few million tons of water would finish Marte Chang and Colonel Rico Toledo quite nicely.

38

SONJA KNEW SHE should have followed Harry up the ladder. Now she was ahead of him and the sound of his struggle beneath her scared her as much as the scent of smoke that she'd caught on the air-conditioned breeze.

Brought up in diplomatic circles, Sonja and Harry had dozed through many social briefings and shared many a joke over the elaborate ritual of manners that went with their lives. Yet, when they began their climb he had stepped aside for her, out of reflex, and out of reflex she had mounted the ladder ahead of him. Harry was still burned-out by muscle weakness and spasms, and he couldn't fake it on the ladder, not even in the dark.

"It won't kill you to learn a few manners," her father had told her once.

Sonja believed everything that her father told her—until now. Now she believed that something as ridiculous as manners could kill them both.

"Harry," she whispered, "I'm climbing over you, hold still."

A hissing rumble started above them, and Sonja positioned herself behind Harry on the ladder. She pressed herself against his back, one leg hooked through a rung, both hands gripping hard in spite of the blisters. If he slipped, she could manage him.

What is that noise?

Her spine prickled with static and fear. The fine hair on the backs of her arms rose, and she felt Harry's hair rise from the back of his head. Sonja clung to the ladder and to Harry, the vibration burning her palms and ankles where they gripped the metal.

Something huge passed them with a flash and a whoosh just a meter from their faces. Sonja opened her eyes as the downdraft hit, and watched an express elevator recede into the darkness below. The light inside the car was very bright, clearly illuminating the

259

remains of five decomposing passengers through its Plexi ceiling.

My God! she thought. *What happened to them?*

The bodies on the floor of that elevator had slumped away from their bones, as though they'd been outside in the sun for weeks.

A tornado followed the car down the smaller shaft in front of them, and it was all Sonja could do to keep the hair on her head. Her hand would not come free to begin the climb again.

Sonja had discovered a dead horse one time, in the flats behind Casa Canadá. Bloated and wearing its fly-and-vulture coat, the horse had smelled just like those people in the elevator. She leaned her face into Harry's sweaty tunic and gulped a couple of deep breaths.

"Up there," Harry said.

The downblast of air and dust gritted her eyes, but she saw another landing in the fading light, about ten meters above them. The light seeped through the familiar framework of the immense decon doors, doors that the two of them couldn't budge on the last two floors.

"Did you see . . . ?" she asked.

"Inside the elevator?" He took a deep breath. "Yeah, I saw."

"What if the dzee was right? What if he's saving us from some huge mess they've made up there?"

"Why not just fill us in so we can be thankful and useful and suitably respectful little hostages? He's not saving us *from* something. He's saving us *for* something. I don't want to find out what it is."

Harry shrugged off her grip and resumed his struggle to the next landing.

Far off in the dark, another express car plummeted to Level Five, then another.

"I have a feeling we're lucky that we didn't take one of those," she whispered.

Harry grunted, and swung himself around to the catwalk at Level Two. The shaft was sealed off above them, a precaution.

"There's another shaft close by," Harry reassured her. "It's like the embassy—no one elevator goes all the way to the top in one run. The individual shafts all share this serviceway . . . at least, I hope this is it. . . ."

Sonja joined him and they stood breathing hard for a moment, uncramping their fingers, listening. The thousand cacophonous voices of the machinery of ViraVax rose upshaft around them, battling the downshaft breeze. The smell of smoke and spoiled meat was stronger, much stronger. Most of the noise was swallowed, as if by magic, in the mass of the bunker cap above them.

A blue service light at the end of the catwalk marked an active entranceway. When Sonja pressed the blue indicator beneath it, a panel whisked aside to reveal a lobby bathed in very bright light, and two missionaries struggling into a pair of emergency hazard suits. The oozing bodies of several *deficientes* lay around them on the floor.

"Get back in there!" one of them yelled.

Harry and Sonja stood in the doorway, so the panel couldn't slide shut.

"Stay put," Harry whispered. "Give me room."

Sonja shifted away from Harry, but stayed in the doorway. All she could focus on was the Galil in the missionary's trembling hand. The gun was identical to the one her father bought for her mother years ago. The barrel looked like it could swallow her whole.

"Get back!" the missionary repeated. "You get back to Hell, where you belong."

He waved the pistol and stepped closer. His partner, now fully suited, backed him up. Sonja saw only the one weapon.

Harry has a plan, she thought. *What is it?*

"*No entiendo,*" Harry said in his perfect accent. He shrugged his shoulders in the all-purpose Costa Bravan gesture. "*No hablo ningún inglés.*"

"You understand *this,* don't you?"

The missionary took another step and shook the gun in Harry's face. Harry stood his ground, and Sonja heard him breathe slow and deep.

The missionary took one more step and poked Harry's chest with the gun barrel. That must've been what Harry was waiting for. What happened next was nearly too fast for Sonja to see. Harry grabbed the muzzle with his left hand and snapped it down. The man couldn't fire and instinctively jerked backwards. Harry kicked him in the crotch and, as the guard doubled over, kicked him again in the face. The second man made a lunge for Harry, but the suit was too clumsy and Harry stepped aside. Harry put a spinning back-kick into the man's kidney as he lurched past, and it forced him over the rail and down the shaft. He did not scream.

The first missionary lay very still on the floor, a lot of blood bubbling from his smashed nose.

"Stay here," Harry said.

He dragged the missionary onto the landing behind them, then leaned on the railing and vomited down the shaft. His hands were trembling so violently that he dropped the pistol down there, too. He took a few seconds to catch his breath, then put a hand on Sonja's shoulder. Harry and Sonja stepped through the doorway cautiously, and saw no one else alive.

The panel hissed shut behind them and Sonja heard security seals inflate. After much whirring, another door opened across the hallway. This time the two of them stepped into a grisly tableau of bodies, some charred, some in an accelerated state of corruption. The rising steam and stink spasmed Sonja's throat shut, and she nearly blacked out before she could force a breath.

It was a wait station for transport cars, one of which kept trying to shut its doors around a very large, very dead pair of Innocents. Harry shuffled to the nearest doors and tried to pull them apart. No luck. He tried the next pair, still no luck.

"Okay," Harry said, his breath coming harder, "I guess we take their car."

The two dead men came apart in their clothing as Sonja and Harry pulled them out of the transport. A flicker of blue flame licked the stump of one leg, and the muscle began to melt from the bone. Sonja gagged, but caught the door in its final surge and they tumbled inside. Their car rose immediately without awaiting orders, and by the time Harry found the automatic shutoff, they were topside.

The door opened onto a plaza of hallways, each one littered with bodies of people who clearly had dropped instantly, in midstride, without a struggle. A haze of black smoke hung over the scene and stained the whitewashed walls.

"I sure hope it's not catching," Sonja said.

"Maybe this was the 'guard virus' the dzee was talking about," Harry said. "Maybe it turned on them."

Up ahead, reflected in the Plexi, Sonja saw the real thing.

Outside!

She had wanted to see daylight, and blue sky, but she was greeted by stars and a bright half-moon. Escape meant running the length of the hallway, high-stepping over the dead. Sonja and Harry ran this gauntlet of corruption hand in hand, bent almost double to keep out of the smoke. At the next intersection they faced freedom.

It was a simple, institutional door with a stainless-steel bar, straining against the perpetual breeze of the negative pressure inside. That breeze smelled of hot, wet ground and concrete.

"Come on!" Harry urged, tugging her arm.

Together, they shouldered the door outward enough to squeeze through. It slammed behind them and they stepped blinking and alive into the night air. It was not fresh air. Little gouts of blue flame sputtered around the grounds.

One, two, three steps, Sonja counted, away from that howling place, before she was caught by the silence. Not silence, no. There was night birdsong, and a flight of bats down from the lake behind the dam. No, what she heard was the absence of noise. The guts of the machine that they had crawled through carried off the cries of the dying and added them to the choruses of the dead. She had never imagined such a horrible sound existed, and she knew she could never forget it.

Harry was rubbing his cramping legs.

"I know where we are," Sonja said.

She pointed directly ahead.

"That's south. That's their big farming area, you remember that from the air. This"—she gestured to the building behind them— "is the lift pad. One flight up, top of the hangar bays."

"There is *nobody* here," Harry said, his voiced laced with awe and fear.

Hunched shapes in human clothing glowed blue in the beans and the pumpkins. It had just rained, and now the stars were out full force. Some of the bodies were half-charred, probably saved by the sudden evening shower.

"Maybe it was a gas, or something," she said. "Maybe the rain washed it away."

"It must have got the sentries, too," Harry said. "I don't . . ."

In English, then Spanish, a loudspeaker warned:

"Code Red, Levels One and Two. Code Red, Levels One and Two. Suit and seal. Suit and seal."

"What does that mean?" Harry asked.

"We're lucky," Sonja said. "Levels Three, Four and Five are time-locked *before* the announcement. It's vacuum-packed. Nothing gets in or out for forty-eight hours. . . ."

Whang, whang, whang.

Three heavy metal doorways slammed into place in the building next to theirs. The *hiss* and *snap* of an autoweld preceded its heady, metallic vapor.

"Now Command Central shuts down specific areas in Levels One and Two as needed," she said.

"So," Harry mused, "they're not all dead. Someone is alive."

"Not necessarily," she said. "Once programmed, shutdown proceeds automatically."

The announcement repeated itself in English and Spanish.

"It also means that anybody left on Level Two or surface has one minute to get to a bio suit," she said, "one minute to get it on and one minute to find and seal off a safe area. It's really more to trap them than to save them. My dad said he'd take his chances topside."

Nobody came running. Crumpled shadows littered the landscape under the few yard lights.

Harry's eyes widened at a new horror. Vultures plopped from the sky onto the bloating dead in the garden, one by one.

"I thought they only came out in the daylight," he said.

"Must be a special occasion."

Bolts shot to place in the door behind them, intakes hissed shut and alarms blared from a dozen points around the building. Charges blew directly above them and popped their ears.

"It's the dzee," Harry said. "He's doing all this to make sure we don't get away."

That blast came from the lift pad!

Sonja hoped that shutdown didn't include destroying the aircraft on the pad.

They huddled outside the shipping and receiving area, something she'd identified from the air. The actual lift pad was one story higher.

"I sure hope we've still got something to fly," she said.

Harry yanked her down and hissed in her ear. "Quiet!" He pointed to the far corner of their building.

Two hundred meters away, someone struggled with a locked door under an orange security light.

The woman shouted something at the door that Sonja couldn't hear, then turned and ran towards them. She stopped twice in the two hundred meters to stand on tiptoe, trying to see something up on the pad. Sonja noted the thin smoke-shadows wafting across the moon.

Something's on fire up there.

Her one rope of hope had unraveled to a thread.

"What do you think?" Harry asked.

Sonja didn't tell him what she thought was happening on the lift pad. It was still their best spot, if only for pickup later.

The woman, then.

"She doesn't know her way around very well," Sonja said, "but she knows that's how she came in."

"Yeah," Harry said. "Kind of like us."

Sonja stepped into the moonlight, slowly, so as not to startle the woman.

"Hello," Sonja said, showing her hands. "Can you help me?"

She said it again in English. Harry was motioning her to get back, but she ignored him.

The woman stopped. She was Asian, truly Asian, not one of the Innocents with the so-called mongoloid features. Her features were contorted with horror and anguish. Her gaze, like Sonja's, kept itself carefully from the dead.

"Someone is coming in after us," the woman said between gasps. "We need to get up there, and I can't find a way in."

"Who?" Sonja asked. "Who's coming in after us? And who are you?"

The Asian woman caught her breath. "I'm Marte Chang," she said. "Mariposa is sending someone here to get us. She instructed me to be at the lift pad."

"Mariposa?"

Again, that mysterious figure.

"Is whatever killed these people going to kill us, too?" Harry asked.

"I doubt it," Marte said. "Everyone dropped around me and I didn't feel or hear a thing. You're intact. It was probably something that Dajaj Mishwe infected them with. I'm sure he killed them all."

Sonja held the small young woman as the sobs started. She and Harry had walked through the bodies, but this woman had watched them fall.

"You were here all along?" Sonja asked. "Do you know anything about what's going on?"

"I just know that the people who run this place are crazy," Marte said. "And they're having some kind of family feud. You're in the middle of it."

"Us?" Harry asked. "How?"

"This Mishwe guy had you picked up," Marte said. "Mishwe is psychotic and has been a problem lately. Casey, the boss, was livid. Mishwe killed him, and the rest of these poor people."

"I vote we don't wait for the rescue if we don't have to," Harry said. He jerked a thumb towards the lift pad. "Let's get up there and get gone."

"Right," Sonja agreed. "We don't know whether help is coming tomorrow or next week. This place is shutting down. It might have some automatic defenses rigged, too. The sooner we get off the ground, the better."

"There's no way up there," Marte said. "I've been all around the building. No doors unlocked. No stairs or ladders up the outside."

"Maybe we can find a way up," Harry said.

Sonja pointed towards a huge, bunker-like structure down by the farm. "There," she said. "Some kind of shop. Look in the doorway."

Under the doorway light, she saw a tractor and a forklift. Ropes.

"I want out of here," Marte said. "I don't care how we do it, or who it is. Some of them started . . . burning up. God, I want out of here and now all the doors are shut."

Sonja scanned the grounds. Clear sky, tail end of a rain squall spilling over the mountaintops, no breeze. A perfect night for a lift-off.

Neither big bird was in its hangar bay, so she gathered they were both atop the hangar, and, like Marte, standing on tiptoe didn't get her any closer. All access bays to stairs, elevators, transport and passageways were double-sealed. Warning bells continued their clanging.

More vultures dropped in from their circles—first, to the treetops around the perimeter, then the fencetop, lift pad and finally to the ground at the head end of some faceless human mess.

"Look!"

Harry pointed to a set of running lights on the southern sky that became two sets, three.

"Choppers," Sonja said. "Probably García. He'll send two more and an observer to flank us, probably east because . . . there!"

Out of the moonlight bobbed the other three dots, wavy with heat and distance.

The alarms ceased their mind-numbing clatter. The first sound Sonja heard when the ringing stopped was the *blap-blap-blap* of old rotors, holding off. Harry's glance told her that he'd noticed, too.

"They're not coming," he said.

"They just can't see us," Marte said.

She unfolded a thin, silver rain slicker from her back pocket, opened it with a *snap* and waved at the nearest chopper. It hovered just past the fence line, about five hundred meters south. Sonja felt the *whump* of a concussion underfoot. Then another.

Harry yanked her and Marte under the protection of the hangar's bunker-like roof.

"They know we're here," Harry told Marte. "They want to keep us here. It's a lot more important to keep people from getting *out* of this place. Nobody worries about people who want to get in."

A series of three explosions blew out ventilation shafts in front of each of the nearby buildings. The concrete caps of the shafts pulverized with a flash, and rained chunks of concrete and vegetation all around them. Smoke and steam roiled from the topside elevator and transporter accesses.

"What's going on?" Marte shouted, waving her arms at the voyeurs flying those choppers. "I thought they were coming to rescue us."

Harry gave her the bad news, the news he had been unwilling to believe because it was too logical and it weighed too heavily against them.

"García's forces aren't here to rescue us," Harry said. "They're here to rescue the rest of the world *from* us. The place is sealing off, burying itself. This is the ultimate quarantine."

"They'll have to catch us," Sonja reminded him. "And then they'll take us to some other lab who will study us for the rest of our lives. Or they'll see us as vermin and shoot us," she added. "It's happened before, in Japan and the Philippines."

A blast from the nearest warehouse dropped all three of them to the ground. A buzzard, feeding on a corpse in the doorway, blew out of one of its wings and skidded, quivering, on the concrete in front of them. More blasts followed inside the hangar, though muffled by the sealed-off Plexi and concrete.

"Automatic charges," Harry said. "Let's hope they don't include the aircraft."

All stairwells, ladders, shafts and ventilators leading from the ground level to the lift pad exploded at one-second intervals, beginning at the southwest corner and continuing around the huge, squat building to their position.

Harry jogged towards the warehouse and called back to her.

"I'll find something to get us up there. You two stay under cover."

39

HARRY SPRINTED FOR the open doorway and hoped he could make it before the doors sealed him out—or in. The half-minute sprint left him breathless but alive inside a huge agricultural equipment shed. His cramps had reduced themselves to twitches and he felt himself getting stronger as he caught his breath. Some kind of turbine or fan clanked itself to a stop just a few meters away.

That was when Harry saw the prisoner, trussed-up and struggling on a big stainless-steel cart. He was strapped to the top of the cart, and very much alive. The man had worked his head back and forth against the restraints, bloodying the back of his scalp nearly enough to slip out. His left arm flailed weakly, uselessly at the bloody straps.

Nearby lay the remains of two of the ViraVax security team. One of them, beside the forklift, could have been ground zero of an explosion, except nothing else was damaged. The other could have been dead for moments or months, only his charred uniform lending him any hint of humanity.

Harry scanned the undamaged forklift.

We might get out of here yet.

Harry approached the captive carefully, the man's gray gaze following him with suspicion or fear. Something familiar, something . . .

"Jesus!" Harry said, still out of breath from the run.

He stumbled to the Colonel's side and started unfastening the restraints with clumsy fingers.

"Harry!" his father croaked. "What the hell, boy?"

"Jesus!" Harry repeated, and blinked as though to clear the vision. "I suppose you're the mysterious, superhuman rescue squad."

"That's me," Rico said. "Let's get moving."

269

"Looks like the rest of them are all dead."

Harry tore at the double-taped restraints holding his father to the cart.

Rico rolled his head slowly back and forth to free the spasms in his neck.

"Who's with you?"

"Two more," Harry said. "Sonja and another woman, Marte Chang."

Rico freed his legs and ankles, then tried, unsuccessfully, to stand by himself.

"Shit," he wheezed. "I can hardly walk."

"It'll wear off," Harry said. "Just don't do anything twitchy."

"I've let myself get pretty rusty."

The Colonel reached out to Harry and rested an arm across his shoulders. Harry put an arm around his father's waist and gripped a belt loop. Harry couldn't think of anything to say, except that his father didn't smell of whiskey for the first time in years, but he didn't think it was the time to mention that.

"I thought at first that García took you and Sonja to hold against me," Rico said. "I knew the guerrillas didn't blow up the embassy and I knew *I* didn't blow it. I didn't think of this outfit at first because they're so low-key. Blowing things up is not their style. A lot of people were investigating ViraVax all of a sudden, including my people. There was some interior struggle with this Children of Eden bunch. Didn't think it would go like this."

"How were you getting out?"

"Access shaft to the dam. It's not in the drawings. You?"

Harry pointed to the lift pad atop the hangars.

"Sonja was going to fly us out," he said. "Access to the lift pad was the first to go. I came looking for another way up there. Thanks, by the way."

"For what?"

The Colonel lifted his head in surprise, setting off a new wave of spasm. There had been no explosions for several moments. Harry set his father down for a moment and let the spasms pass. He saw Sonja and Marte huddled inside the hangar doorway, watching.

"No sudden moves," Harry said. "They got me with something like it, too. It wears off fast, once it starts going. Try not to fight it."

"Thank me for what?" his father mumbled.

Harry laughed.

"For fifth grade," he said. "When you used to take me into the elevator shafts at the embassy and the Intercontinental for lunch. I'll tell you about it when we get out of here."

"Seen García's choppers yet?"

"Yeah," Harry nodded. "They got here about five minutes ago."

Another three *whump-whump-whumps*.

The Colonel asked, "The facility is in shutdown?"

"Yeah."

"Well," the Colonel sighed, "you know that García's men will have to shoot you down if you try to leave the grounds."

"*What?* You mean, it's *true*?"

"Yeah."

The Colonel sat up and chuckled, his voice clearing.

" 'Contain everything and everyone within the perimeter. Destroy anything or anyone who violates that perimeter until directed otherwise.' Protocols for the government's response to a shutdown situation—I wrote them myself."

"Great!" Harry groaned. "Now there's no way out!"

"No," his father said, and grabbed Harry's shoulder to pull himself up. "If those doors closed, others will open to us. Helicopters can be distracted or destroyed or outrun. García's men are notoriously bad shots. With a radio to the Gs—"

Small-arms fire *snap-snap-snapped* from the direction of the dam.

"Shit," the Colonel said. "I think I can walk now. Let's get the hell out of here."

Rico shuffled to the body of his guard and gingerly extracted his scorched radio and trank gun from the mess he was becoming.

"My tool kit," Rico said.

He toed some of the charred ooze aside and saw that it was just another part of the mess.

"Forget it," he mumbled.

Rico couldn't quite make the high step onto the tall container loader, so Harry gave him a boost.

Harry jumped up beside him as his father slipped a lever, threw two switches and fired up the sleeping beast. They sputtered across the infield towards the women.

The Colonel signaled Sonja and Marte to wait where they were.

"I should take a look first," the Colonel said. "You just push this lever forward to send me up, pull back to bring me down."

"I can go, Dad," Harry said.

The Colonel put up a hand.

"This is not personal," he said. "We need to see if there's a plane up there, yeah. But there could be a surviving sentry, and he could still be doing his job. Just take that last two meters, very, very slow."

Harry watched his dad's hand signals near the top, and slipped him over the edge smoothly. The Colonel disappeared for a few long minutes, then reappeared at the top, signaling to come down. Harry dropped the forks and braked them at the last instant.

"Kind of frisky with this thing, don't you think?" the Colonel commented with a wink.

Harry accepted it as the first compliment from his father in a long, long time.

The Colonel informed the others: "We have two airplanes up there and no sentries. We'll have to check for charges but I think they didn't have time to set them. Hello, Sonja. Hello, Ms. Chang, and greetings from Mariposa."

The Colonel loaded Harry, Sonja and Marte aboard the forks and lifted them atop the hangar, then tied the lever off to make the trip himself.

Harry gave the Colonel a hand off the moving forks just as a loud *whoomp* and a series of *pop-pop-pops* caught his attention. Towards the dam, a large black plume streaked the sky.

"One chopper down," the Colonel said. "Four to go. Ever fly any runs, Sonja?"

"Just simulations," she said. "These are armed?"

"Nothing fancy," he said, "just a cannon on each one. I don't know how much ammo. We didn't want any of these people to be able to fight themselves out."

Harry was conscious of the casual way his father said this, and the shocked disbelief on Marte Chang's face when she heard it.

"I can handle it," Sonja said.

Freckles stood out like buckshot in her pale face, and her lips tightened into a thin line. Harry had no doubt that she could.

Another chopper left its observation post and sped towards the guerrilla emplacement at the dam.

"Get going!" Rico said, and gave Harry a push towards the B/M-3. "If they spot you up here, they'll shoot you."

Rico turned back towards the forklift.

"Where are you going?" Harry asked.

"I'm going after whoever it is that initiated shutdown," Rico said. "He could get away with this, live down there for years. I want to make sure he doesn't come after us again."

"You can't . . ." was all Harry got out.

His father had already dialed a load on the trank gun and popped it into his thigh. Harry felt equal measures of relief and betrayal and little else. He was aware, but helpless.

His father dragged Harry to the loading bay and Sonja helped him inside. Marte scrambled up beside him and strapped him in.

"They'll hit you as soon as you lift," Harry heard his father tell Sonja. "Just clear the compound and get as high up the valley as you can before you have to set down." He indicated his radio. "You'll have support."

Sonja grunted and busied herself with her checklist. Harry heard the hiss that preceded the whine of the turbine, and his father talking into his radio outside. Then his father leaned down next to his ear.

"I love you, son," he whispered, and left, latching the hatch behind him.

The Colonel had been right about García's choppers. Sonja blasted off the pad, and the ticking of sand and gravel into the fuselage was replaced with the heavier *tick-tick-tick* of machine-gun fire. The plane lurched aloft as though slung by a rubber band. The turbine was loud, but not loud enough to drown out Sonja's expletives from the pilot's seat. It occurred to him that he had never heard her swear seriously in either Spanish or English. Her eloquence in both surprised him.

They teetered left, hard left, and the engine started a *pop-pop, pop-pop* that developed into a *clank-clunk, clank-clunk* just as they pancaked into the hillside.

We're out! he thought, and felt Marte scrabbling for his belt release.

Sonja's face appeared above his own, a laceration across her forehead bleeding freely. She and Marte worked together with hardly more than a few grunts to get him out of the plane. They dragged him a few dozen meters into the brush, set him down, and Marte shrieked. Harry couldn't see what startled her, but he could see Marte and Sonja pale even more.

Both women put up their hands, Sonja weaving slightly, her face awash in moonlight and blood. A well-armed squad of four men and three women stepped out of the foliage and into Harry's view, the muzzles of their weapons scenting the air ahead of them.

"Who are you?" the nearest one challenged.

He was the shortest of the men, and looked the oldest. His well-worn fatigues bore neither rank nor insignia.

"Shut up," one of the women barked, and shouldered past him to take Sonja by the shoulders.

"Sit," she ordered, and Sonja sat.

To the short man, she said, "Give me the bag, Cortés."

Nothing more was said and the rest of them stood uneasily listening to the fight at the dam while the woman shook a Kotex out of its wrapper, pressed it to Sonja's forehead and taped it in place.

"The boy," a bearded man asked. "Is he all right?"

"A tranquilizer," Sonja said. "He didn't want to leave without his father. Ah!" She winced as the tape cinched her dressing tight.

"The Colonel?" the man asked Marte, first in Spanish, then in halting English. "He is not with you?"

"He said he stayed to get Mishwe," Marte explained. "The man who started all this. . . ."

The beard's face paled. He glanced at his watch, snapped his fingers, and another of the women produced a small radio.

"Are those charges secured?" he asked. "The Colonel is still inside."

Static came back, then: "Mercury switches, set to detonate if moved. We pulled the men out. Too late."

Sputters of fighting increased nearby, the small-arms fire punctuated by mortar and the occasional rocket. Harry felt his body returning to him. He sat up, shaky, and faced the guerrilla leader, indistinguishable from the army in his jungle turnouts, except for the beard. Harry didn't like the expression that met his gaze.

"You can . . . you can get him out, can't you?" Harry asked.

His tongue made a mush of the words, but the man understood. Harry could tell by the stricken look in his eyes that the man understood completely.

Suddenly, the ground rocked them to their hands and knees, followed a split second later by a concussion that popped their ears and knocked their breath away. Harry tried to get up but his legs wouldn't hold him.

Water and mud rained down on them through the trees.

"The dam!" the leader shouted, and pointed up the valley. "It goes!"

Harry heard the rush of water before he saw its muddy tongue lick the hillside just a few hundred meters away. The brown snarl of water shouldered trees and tractors alike against the downstream fence at the Double-Vee. Then, in a spurt of muck, the Cyclone fence gave way. At one point all that Harry saw of ViraVax was the top of the lift pad, and his father wasn't on it.

"Goddammit," Harry said, his voice choking. "Goddammit."

40

THE COLONEL SAW that the kids were hit as soon as they lifted off, as he had expected, but Sonja fought the bird around nicely and pancaked into the jungle almost a kilometer up the valley. It took just a matter of seconds. The Colonel stood, blinking, wishing he could see them. He reassured himself that there was no smoke from the wreckage, then scanned the little radio for one of the guerrilla frequencies.

"Mariposa, this is Jabalí," he said.

"I hear you, Jabalí."

"The plane? Did anyone see . . . ?"

"Blue squad leader . . . *static* . . . three people leaving the plane . . . *static* . . . close by, two minutes to contact."

The Colonel estimated the distance across the lift pad to the forklift, then to the maintenance access shaft behind the heat exchangers.

"Toss some charges at the north fence line," he said. "Do not let your people approach the fence."

" . . . *static* . . . *static* . . . get out!"

Rico shook the radio, but all he got was static. He keyed for voice again.

"Repeat, do not approach the fence. Keep those choppers busy. Go."

"Charges . . . *static* . . . *static* . . . at the dam . . . *static* . . . out."

"Toss them in," he said.

A rasp of static drowned out the reply, except for the last, "Go with God, Colonel."

Rico ripped skin off both palms sliding down the carriage of the forklift, then spun the machine around on two wheels and raced for the bunker.

The original access shafts inside the compound were covered

with heavy concrete lids that could only be moved with the ten-ton crane. Like the elevator system that they connected with, the access shafts were a weak point in the ViraVax armor. The contractor had felt free to cut a few corners, and someone else had felt free to cut the contractor's throat while he slept in his retirement mansion in Spain. Still, no one had bothered to upgrade. Existing plans detailed how ViraVax should have been built. Rico's memory carried the secrets of the real thing.

The Colonel knew that the lower level was sealed successfully, according to the original plans. But a half dozen passageways snaked through the inside, one of them all the way to the dam, and these would not be part of the shutdown sequence. The access tunnel to the dam had been his original goal, since it was the only one with a hatch that opened outside the ViraVax perimeter. But Casey's guard-plants had stopped him cold.

Mishwe had to come out eventually—months, years from now maybe. Rico wanted him sooner than that.

I wish I had that Pulse unit of Yolanda's to send down after him, Rico thought.

Then he shrugged a Costa Bravan shrug.

But I didn't have anything else planned today.

The Colonel ripped one of the heat exchangers out of the concrete with his forks to get a purchase on the access shaft lid. The lid was so heavy that it pulled the nose of the forklift down and the back wheels off the ground, and for a moment he was afraid that it had been sealed, after all. With full throttle he bounced his machine and the lid up and down, up and down, finally working it slightly cockeyed on its base.

Rico heard some heavy charges blow, and his pulse picked up its pace. He hoped that Yolanda's team would be satisfied with blowing the fence for him. There were too many surprises in here to risk any more people.

At least it'll be easier getting through that fence this time.

The Colonel had to admit that he had come back here, not to corner Mishwe like a rat, but to die.

A high-pitched whistle rode the growl of something big down the valley towards him. All five floors of concrete sandwiched with five layers of bunker material vibrated, shaking down dust from the rafters and drumming the tin roof.

Earthquake! was his first thought.

Rico looked out the double doors of the warehouse and saw, in the half-moon's light, several columns of black smoke where

the dam used to be. For the first time in this operation, Rico
Toledo was perfectly calm. He knew, now, what they had tried
to tell him on the radio. He wondered who had dealt him this, his
last blow.

El Indio, he wondered, *or Dajaj Mishwe?*

He lowered the forks and pushed the concrete cover further
back from its hole. Rico didn't have the Pulse, but he had a
few million tons of water that might do the trick. He gunned
the forklift to the far end of the warehouse and located a second
access cover.

Rico thought it would be an honorable death, rescuing his son
and Sonja and the Agency woman. He would not have to face his
son's disapproval again, nor the vagaries of politics, nor another
failed relationship.

I won't have to quit drinking, either, he thought, trying for some
self-amusement.

His ego was short-lived. He had to admit that they had rescued
themselves. Harry was using his brains, and their escape plan was
working perfectly without him.

Rico jammed the steel prongs against the second concrete lid
and revved the little methane engine as high as it would go. Blue
smoke from the tires gagged and blinded him, but he felt the lid
give and pushed it aside as the first of the water hit.

It was not the crushing wall of rock and mud that he'd expected.
A satisfying sucking sound came from the throat of the access
shaft. A surf-like tide lifted him out of the forklift seat, outrunning
the mud that must be close behind. This was warm water, from
the surface of the lake, smelling of dirt and crushed leaves, and
it tumbled him the length of the bunker before it spat him out the
other side and pinned him to the fence.

I should've had them blow the south fence, he thought.

A tremendous crush of mud and vegetation squeezed air out of
Rico's lungs and ripped the top of his jumpsuit down to his waist.
A cold, heavy surge collapsed all three fences and rolled him over
and over, slashing his chest, back and thighs with razor wire. A
huge root ball slammed him from behind. He grasped the tangle
out of reflex and kept from being dragged under, but his searing
lungs could not hold. He choked and scrambled up the root ball,
gagging foul bile. He got a pocket of air, then another, then for
the third time in one day everything faded from brown to black.

41

DAJAJ MISHWE DID not check on his Adam and Eve right away; he had his own security to address. His private access had been a shaft that originated in the Level Two sewage treatment room, just behind the medical students' dormitory. Mishwe triggered a switch with a flick of his finger. A blast at Level Two released nearly two tons of dry concrete into the shaft. Water from the flood would do the rest. He felt like a pupa inside a concrete cocoon.

Mishwe monitored the shutdown of the top four levels and the pitiful escape attempts of those who had not yet sipped his special waters. Fists and chairs were no match for concrete and steel. In the eyes of the Innocents, he saw only confusion and terror. They did not fight, but huddled together awaiting direction from their missionaries.

The missionaries, he saw, were frightened at first, then angry. Their anger gave way to an exhaustion framed in betrayal, and then fear. By the time he'd shifted to interior power and shut his topside monitors down, he had seen only one person praying, and that person was an Innocent in a surgical gown.

"Hypocrites," he said, and an Innocent at his elbow repeated the charge.

This Innocent was one of the caretakers for his Adam and Eve. He plucked Mishwe's sleeve, but from an arm's reach.

"Don't be frightened," Mishwe said. "You are with the Angel of Eden, and no harm will come to you."

At that moment, Mishwe felt a rumble under his feet, something too big for the bunker to absorb. The maze of caged animals around him set up an unprecedented clamor of shrieks and barks. Mishwe smiled.

"The dam," he explained to the sad-eyed Innocent. "The dam is gone. We are safe here, forever."

"People gone," the Innocent said.

"Yes," Mishwe replied, and ruffled the man's scant hair. "The bad people are gone. Only good people are left."

"No, no," another Innocent protested. "Adam and Eve people gone."

Mishwe felt the first icy twist of fear to grip his belly in twenty years.

"Adam and Eve people?"

The first Innocent nodded vigorously.

"Decon people gone. Come see."

Mishwe pushed them aside with a snarl and sprinted for the Decon elevator two hundred meters across the lab. As he ran, he thought, *They're here. They're here. They're down here somewhere.*

He reached the large Decon elevator and shoved through a babbling knot of Innocents. The main room was empty, their bowls in place atop the table. Something didn't feel right, a smell on the air that he couldn't place.

Dajaj Mishwe opened the bathroom door and saw what Adam and Eve had done. They had burst the mirror, tried to wall him out. He took a step and fetched a tremendous kick at the desk blocking the shattered mirror. It budged, but only slightly.

The peculiar odor was stronger here and accompanied by a strong breeze that whistled through the shattered glass.

Positive pressure pulls the air out *of this room, not into it!*

The whistle developed into a howl. Mishwe stood atop the toilet and peered through a gap between the top of the barricade and the window. The other door was blocked off as well, but there was no sign of his precious couple anywhere in the small room.

Where . . . ?

Then he saw the open hatch above the far door and understood what they had done. In that instant, Dajaj Mishwe also understood the origin of the strange smell, the increasing howl and force of the wind.

Before he could step down from the toilet or shout a warning to the Innocents crowded behind him, an explosion of muck and water punched through the ceiling and crushed his fragile skull like a bug against the bathroom floor.

42

MAJOR SCHOLZ SHUT down the viewer and everyone in their separate isolettes watched Red Bartlett fade to black. The major had previewed Bartlett's incredible block of data the night before with Trenton Solaris, the DIA chief, who had flown in from Cairo specifically for the occasion. Solaris, the albino, had gone from white to whiter to nearly transparent during Bartlett's display.

Major Scholz gave Marte Chang, Harry Toledo and Sonja Bartlett a moment to compose themselves, then gradually brought the lights up. Harry, Sonja and Marte Chang each occupied a separate, double-lined plexiglass cage that command had the nerve to call a "habitat" or "isolette." They were cages, pure and simple, allowing complete monitoring of their biology and psychology. A gray plastic shower curtain surrounded each tiny lavatory for privacy, and the cubes themselves measured three meters on a side.

Self-contained, they stood in an unmarked warehouse in the industrial section of La Libertad's airport. This warehouse also held the secondary quarantine subjects—a SEAL team, a guerrilla squad and a squad of transportation specialists. Their vehicles, where the subjects had been held pending construction of the isolettes, had already been buried in concrete well out of town, along with every sliver of the remains of the B/M-3.

Marte Chang's face was impassive behind the glass. Her fingers flicked over the toggles in her gloveware as she poured notes into her Sidekick. She pored over the data block that Harry had snatched from ViraVax, in hopes of finding out what the enemy was, and how to fight it. The major had been horrified three times since sunrise at the information Marte Chang was culling from that block.

ViraVax is buried, but is it dead? she wondered.

283

Sonja sobbed with her forehead resting on her arms. The last of the block contained a personal statement by Red Bartlett, recorded the day before his death. It was hard on the Bartlett girl, but the major was glad to see it for personal reasons. This way she wouldn't have to remember Red Bartlett as a smoking pool of waste fouling the carpets.

Sonja's face was swollen and bruised from its impact with the B/M-3's control panel, and the fresh dressing across her forehead had begun to unravel. The major wished she could put an arm around the girl, tuck in the loose ends and make everything all right.

Everything will never be all right.

Harry lay on his back on his bunk with his forearm over his eyes, unmoving, as he had lain since entering the cubicle twelve hours ago. He was sullen and uncooperative, unresponsive to everyone except Sonja Bartlett and Marte Chang.

A small group of visitors, including Major Scholz, sat in a Plexiglas enclosure about five meters from the isolettes. This enclosure served as an observation post and briefing room, with data channels, voice and visuals piped into each isolette.

Solaris, Ambassador Simpson, President García and his four bodyguards—all looked straight ahead and shifted in their seats.

President García spoke first, addressing the major.

"It is my understanding that you have captured that traitor, Rico Toledo, is that correct?"

"My dad is alive?" Harry asked. "My dad is alive and you didn't tell me? You bastards are as bad as those Gardener bastards. . . ."

The major felt her face flush with anger. She raised a hand to Harry, asking him to wait. Her anger was an uncharacteristic loss of composure, and that discomfort made her flush all the more. Out of the corner of her eye she saw Harry fist the wall of his isolette. The major glanced at Solaris, and he nodded his approval.

"Colonel Toledo has been *rescued,*" she said, "that is correct. Fortunately for the Colonel, and for us, a SEAL team was laying over at the airport on its way to Tegucigalpa when we intercepted that SOS sent out by Harry and Sonja. Your people, though on the scene, chose to shoot these three down rather than assist them in their escape attempt. The SEALs found Colonel Toledo entangled in a logjam five kilometers from the site."

"Will your government be prosecuting Mr. Toledo?" President García interrupted.

Solaris, seeing the major's difficulty controlling her emotional state, stood to reply for her. The four bodyguards shifted and the one nearest Solaris unbuttoned his coat and reached inside.

"I do not need to harm this man," Solaris told the bodyguard. "Besides, by the time the day's over, you'll probably kill him yourself."

Solaris turned his attention to an indignant President García.

"We will not prosecute Colonel Toledo," Solaris announced. "As of this morning he has been reinstated with full rank and privileges. If this man survives he will receive a commendation, sir, for his persistence in this most timely, most horrifying matter and I promise you that you will not prosecute him, either."

"This is not the United States," García said, performing his famous sneer. "You have no authority here."

"Obviously, Mr. García, you have learned nothing this morning," Solaris said. "Bartlett set up his computer to automatically intercept every communication between Dajaj Mishwe and Joshua Casey. Thanks to the quick thinking of Colonel Toledo's son, here, you saw a few of those memos for yourself—including Casey's reprimand of Mishwe for 'engineering that embassy incident.' I can't imagine what charges you could bring against the Colonel, even if you remained in office long enough to do it. I brought you here, sir, to show you what we are about to disclose around the world. I suggest you listen carefully, then return to your office and pack your bags."

Solaris accepted García's glare with a curt nod, then returned to his seat. All four bodyguards had begun to sweat profusely, in spite of the air-conditioning.

"You have nothing," García said. "Anyone could write those memos and place them on a screen. The boy himself could have written them. My people say that Toledo bombed the embassy, trying to kill his ex-wife, then conspired with the guerrillas to destroy ViraVax to execute an old vendetta against the Children of Eden. Mr. Toledo is a Catholic. The bomb was in his car. . . ."

"And nearly killed Toledo himself," Ambassador Simpson said. She dismissed the President's accusations with a wave of her hand.

"Surely an experienced agent could do better than that, without threat to himself."

"An experienced agent in his right mind, perhaps," García countered. "Your people have had to clean up after him for years. You did not let him go because of his domestic problems.

You let him go because he was worthless."

A tone sounded from Marte's Sidekick, then a gasp from Marte herself caught everyone's attention.

"Major," she said, "I think we have a problem."

Marte's voice was soft, deathly serious.

Sonja had stopped crying and Harry, his face pasty with anger, snapped, "What is it?"

"Sonja told us in last night's debriefing that Mishwe had bragged about them being his Adam and Eve. He also bragged that the Angel of the Lord would purify the Garden, readying it for their use."

"Yes. Go on."

"Well, the monthly shipment of vaccines went out yesterday, just before the Sabbath shutdown."

The major felt the uneasy prickle of fear on her arms and the back of her neck.

"Yes?"

"They are shipped to the World Health Organization, signed out by Mishwe himself," Marte said. "Enough vaccine for a half million infants, to be distributed in every country of the world. I think his Meltdown agent is in that shipment."

"A half *million* . . . ?"

"What makes you think it's there?" Solaris asked.

Marte continued to scan the readout on her Sidekick. She made another entry, then leaned back in her chair.

"He's altered the artificial viral agent," she said. "The structural change shows up in Mishwe's log. An earlier version was included in one of the bursts I sent your Agency. I didn't have time to analyze everything I sent. I don't know what that particular alteration will do without a lot more equipment than this, but I can guess."

"What's your guess, Ms. Chang?" Ambassador Simpson asked.

"He's engineered it to spread on its own, without an inoculation or ingestion," she said.

Marte's voice trembled on the verge of tears, and the major thought that Marte Chang was one who did not cry easily.

"How would it spread?" Solaris asked.

"Probably by contact with infected tissue or by-products. Based on what he told Harry and Sonja, I think he intends to wipe out every last human being on this planet who is not sealed into the bottom level of ViraVax."

"Can you be sure?" Solaris asked.

"Only by analyzing a sample, and that would have to be under strictest precautions," Marte said. "But the risk, the possibility, is too great to waste time. We'll have to account for every last drop of that shipment. If he's changed it the way I think he has, even one Meltdown could eventually kill us all."

"Can we stop it at the airport?" Solaris asked.

"Too late," Marte said. "It's already in Mexico City for breakdown and distribution. The Children of Eden has its own facilities there, and a network of meeting places and storage units throughout the city."

"Notify WHO and Mexico's airport security," Solaris ordered Major Scholz. "Get our people out to the airport immediately. Nobody opens anything, nobody lets any part of this shipment move."

"What if it's already broken up and shipped?" Harry asked.

Solaris rubbed the back of his neck with his death-white hand, and addressed the major.

"Find it," he said. "And get it back. I don't care if it takes a nuclear strike."

"Yes, sir," the major said.

She relayed the appropriate orders via her Sidekick. President García rose to leave and his guards took up their escort positions.

"You are making a big mistake," García said. "Toledo is guilty. The rest is a sham, a persecution of a peaceful, religious people. My administration will not cooperate with what you call a witch-hunt."

"You won't have a choice," Ambassador Simpson said, and smiled. "By this time tomorrow, you and your goons won't be calling the shots here anymore."

"What do you mean, threatening the President of the Confederation of Costa Brava? This is my country, not yours."

"It's not a threat," the ambassador said, "and you forget who handed you that presidency. We have released the information about Project Labor to the press, along with details of the millions of involuntary sterilizations you have authorized and the related trade in transplantable organs. That information has been documented. Harry, Sonja and Ms. Chang have documented the spontaneous combustion of the personnel of the ViraVax facility. If ViraVax and the Children of Eden are found guilty of nothing else, if this vaccine turns up untainted, you are still the ex-President of the Confederation of Costa Brava. You will be lucky to escape execution."

García's face was livid and his hands trembled at his sides. He clenched and unclenched his fists to gain control, then signaled his men and left without a word.

"What an asshole," Harry hissed.

"Hear, hear," the ambassador replied.

A message beep sounded for Major Scholz. She glanced at her Sidekick and bit her lip.

"Your father is conscious," she told Harry.

"Will he make it?" he asked. "Can I talk to him?"

The major shook her head.

"Still critical," she said. "Our people are with him now. Perhaps he can help us with this vaccine problem. I'll find out how soon you can see him."

"What about García's men?" Harry asked. "They've killed people back home on the White House lawn."

"You won't have to worry about García anymore," the ambassador said. "Besides, we brought in a Night School team to baby-sit your father, just in case."

"I'll make preparations so that you can communicate, Harry," Solaris promised.

The albino's glance met the major's, and she felt relieved.

"I'd like to talk privately with you," he added, "if you don't mind."

"What about Sonja?" Harry asked. "We're kind of a set, if you know what I mean. We won't give each other anything we don't already have. And after all this, we don't have any secrets left, either. No sense starting them now."

Solaris smiled.

"We will see," he said. "What I have to say, Sonja should hear as well. Please give us a private channel, Major, and we will let you all be about your business."

43

RICO TOLEDO WOKE up inside a bubble of Plexiglas. He had IV lines in both arms, a tube down his nose, several machines beeping out of synch and a body that felt like it was skinned. He could only see out of his left eye, and that one was blurry. Rico tried to lift his head to get a look at his body, but he was restrained. If pain was any indicator, all of his parts were still attached.

"Relax, Colonel," a deep voice said. "We'll be here a while."

A black man in fatigues loomed into view, the name "Clyde, J." stitched over his pocket. He wore SEAL and corpsman insignia on his fatigues.

"Where?"

"Joe Clyde Memorial Hospital," the medic said with a chuckle. "We're in the back end of a warehouse in beautiful La Libertad, Colonel. Pearl of the Pacific."

"I'm not a colonel."

"You're reinstated, sir."

"Harry? What about Harry?"

"I'll ask the questions, Colonel, if you please."

The voice came from a speaker above his head and was not the deep voice of Joe Clyde. This was the effete voice of a career bureaucrat.

Rico turned his head slowly and saw his jowly, damp-handed replacement at a console outside the glass. He wore a telephone operator's headset and an expression of complete disgust.

"Okay, Colonel. Please tell us the last thing you remember doing today."

"You tell me about Harry, and I'll tell you whatever I damned well please whenever I damned well please. Clear?"

Something had taken the skin off the inside of Rico's throat, and talking felt like hot sandpaper in his larynx.

289

"Your son's okay," Clyde said. "The girl, too."

"Mr. Clyde," the bureaucrat snapped, "I'll speak to your superior about this. *I'm* conducting this interview. And I decide when, or whether, you get out of there."

"No, you don't, Major," another voice said. "You're relieved. Do not leave the building. I'll speak to you when I'm through."

Rico tried to remember that voice. It was so familiar, and his mind was so unwilling. . . .

"It's Trenton Solaris, Colonel, do you remember me?"

Rico smiled in spite of his torn lips.

"Yes, sir. Vividly, sir."

"Fine. Then I'll brief you if you'll brief me."

"Fair."

"Harry, Sonja and the Chang woman are safe. Grace and Nancy Bartlett are still at the embassy for precautions, but they have talked with Harry and Sonja by phone. You are all in quarantine. We don't know what you may have picked up. How much do you remember?"

Images flashed through Rico's mind, like a stack of transparencies dropped into a whirlpool. He could pick out a melting face here, a burning building there, but nothing made sense. Solaris must have guessed his dilemma.

"Okay, Colonel, what's the last thing you remember clearly?"

"Cleaning out my desk," Rico croaked. "Turning in my keys."

"That was quite a while ago, Colonel. A lot has happened since then. You went on vacation. The embassy blew up, the Jaguar Mountain Dam blew up."

"I remember the dam," Rico said. "The water . . . I was smashed against the fence."

"Do you remember which fence?"

"ViraVax," he said, and the memories started flooding back.

"ViraVax, south fence," he said. "I opened the access hatch covers to let the water in. That prick García shot down Harry and Sonja."

"Very good," Solaris said, and his voice sounded relieved.

"Now, what did you see there at ViraVax? Anything unusual?"

Rico started to laugh, but it hurt too much.

"Unusual?" He coughed as gently as he could. "*Unusual?* People melting off their bones and burning up by themselves, charges shutting down every available entry and exit. Guerrillas blowing up the dam . . ."

"It wasn't the Peace and Freedom people," Solaris interrupted.

"The charges were planted and timers set before they got there. The squad leader says they tried to warn you, but you didn't receive the message."

Rico felt relieved. He remembered that moment of doubt before blackness, when he'd thought that El Indio and Yolanda had betrayed him.

"ViraVax, then," Rico said. "Whoever went into shutdown."

"Exactly. And the man who did it is the one who killed Red Bartlett. He also set up the incident at the embassy to turn our people against you. He kidnapped Harry and Sonja to lure you in. You were a loose end that needed tying up."

"How do you know this?"

"Harry rescued a data block that Red Bartlett set up. It was full of product that the Chang woman couldn't find. You should be proud of Harry. He could have fled and we would never know what we're facing."

Rico's flickering memory focused on Harry, bent over him at ViraVax, helping him to his feet.

"I am *very* proud of Harry," Rico said. "But I don't understand why I'm so important to ViraVax. I was out of their hair. Why go to all this trouble over me?"

Solaris was silent for a moment.

"I'd rather get into that later, Colonel. Right now, it's important that we find something that was shipped out of ViraVax to Mexico City, for distribution elsewhere. We need to know the locations of all Children of Eden clandestine operations in Mexico City. Do you have that information?"

Rico tried to remember, but nothing came up. He couldn't tell whether he simply didn't remember, or whether he had never known at all.

"I don't remember . . . I don't know," he said.

"How about your contacts?" Solaris pressed. "This is something big, something that could take out every human on the planet. We don't have the luxury of playing sides."

"Try Mariposa," Rico said. "She has several hundred people in Mexico City. It's their job to keep track of everything and everybody related to this country. She could do it."

"Who is Mariposa?" Solaris asked. "How do we find her?"

"Get on the webworks and ask," Rico said. "She'll contact you."

"We don't have time for that."

"Then get me a priest." Rico said. "And get these restraints off me. It's bad enough I have to be locked up, I don't have to be tied up, too."

Solaris must have okayed the request. Clyde unsnapped the restraints right away.

"Why a priest?" Solaris asked.

"Because I still don't trust anybody," Rico said. "Make it somebody from the Archbishop's office, somebody I know. I'll tell him how to find Mariposa."

With Clyde's help and a lot of pain, he scooted himself up to a sitting position. Rico's mind, the string of images that made his mind, felt shuffled and misdealt. He did not want to give away someone as precious as Yolanda or El Indio because of a basic miscaution. His superior should understand that better than anyone.

"What are you doing out at ViraVax?" Rico asked. "Are you going to dig it out, find out what happened?"

It was more of a probe than a question. Rico didn't want to take any chances on releasing whatever it was that holed itself up underground.

"Not a chance," Solaris replied. "The Corps of Engineers has already diverted the stream. After what Ms. Chang revealed about their operations, we're going to cement over the whole thing and see to it that nothing and no one ever gets out."

Rico weighed this for a moment. He had never known Solaris to be anything but sincere and direct. He found that refreshing in a superior.

"Do we have a phone in here?" he asked Clyde.

"Phone, console, the works," Clyde said. "Whatever you need, we've got."

Rico addressed Solaris.

"If I get Mariposa for you, I want two things."

"Name them, Colonel."

"Amnesty for Mariposa. And I want to talk with my son."

"Done. You know I've always been good for my word."

"Yes," Rico said. "I know. But before we do anything else, I want to talk with Harry."

"There's a lot to tell you both, Colonel."

"It can wait," Rico said. "This can't. Put him on."

The connection was made through a speakerphone, and Rico hated speakerphones. He preferred to hold something, it gave him a better sense of control. The screen cleared and Harry appeared, looking rested and unafraid.

He looks like me.

Rico had had this thought before, but this time the resemblance was more than striking, it was frightening.

"Hello, son," he croaked. "Good job."

"Thanks, Dad," Harry said. "Same to you. Are you going to be okay?"

"I think so," Rico said. "Feels like I've been skinned, but I think everything's here."

"Looks pretty rough," Harry said.

Silence.

"Harry, I'm sorry about the shot . . . I had to do it, I couldn't let you go back there."

"I know, Dad," Harry said. "If I'd had the gun, I'd have done the same thing. Chill."

"Your mom's okay, Nancy's okay."

"Yeah, we just talked to them. They both say thanks, too."

"Colonel," Solaris interrupted, "we have some pressing business."

"Yes," Rico said, "we do. I'll talk with you soon, son."

"Okay," Harry said, "take care."

The screen went blank as he added, "I love you, too."

44

HARRY LISTENED IN stunned silence as Major Scholz and Marte Chang finished explaining the known pathways of his genetic past. The information did not frighten him; he had lived in his body and felt comfortable there. But the implications of a lifetime of imprisonment frightened him, imprisonment for someone else's crime.

"The memory booster came out of Alzheimer's research," Marte was saying. "You and Sonja both have a subtle learning advantage, but it remains to be seen whether you keep it or not. Perhaps, with aging . . ."

"You mean, this thing that you say boosted our memories might give us that old folks' disease?"

"It's an unknown," Marte said. "Possible, but we can't tell without further research. It hasn't made you brilliant, you know. It simply gave you access to more detailed information within a beefed-up storage area."

She quoted him figures on "glial cell production" and "collateral access."

"Well, what does that mean?" Harry asked. "Is it congenital, like diabetes or something? Can we pass it on? Are we going to burn up like Red Bartlett?"

"Red was a whole different matter," Major Scholz said. "And so were the rest of those people at ViraVax. They all died the same day they were infected."

"You're probably clear," Marte said. "Our guerrilla friends intercepted the entire shipment in Mexico, so we'll know by morning what our infection status is. We won't be in isolation forever."

"*You* won't be in isolation forever," Harry said. "You aren't one of the world's only pair of living clones. We got away from that

295

dzee at ViraVax, but his accommodations weren't any different than this. We're still going to be freaks, locked up and poked at for the rest of our lives. I wish I'd died down there."

The major stood and pressed her hand against the glass.

"I promise you that won't happen," she said.

"Sorry, Major," Harry said. "I don't think you have much say in the matter."

"I promise you," she repeated.

Harry inhaled deeply and let it out slowly.

"Chill," he said. "We'll take all the help we can get."

"Do you have questions?" Marte asked. "Anything to do with the science?"

"We're actually twins?" Harry asked. "Like, brothers?"

Marte's figure on his screen nodded.

"Well, he's your father, too," she said. "That's a role, a social position, as well as a biology. But genetically you're actually identical twins, except for your memory boost. A generation apart, of course."

"What about Sonja?" Harry asked. "How could she be cloned through her dad, when she's a twin of her mom? I don't get it."

"Her dad's sperm was the vector for the cloning agent," she explained. "That's how it was introduced into Nancy Bartlett. It is ingenious, I must say. It excluded all of Red Bartlett's genetic material and triggered Nancy Bartlett's ovum to duplicate its own nuclear material. The only material accepted from Sonja's father was the memory enhancement. You are right, it would be most interesting to find out what each of you passes on, and whether the offspring of the two of you would be, as Mishwe must have thought, superhuman. Quite a lot to study, there. . . ."

"Whoa," Harry said. "Enough. Nobody studies this lab rat anymore. Not until we get some rights sorted out."

"I understand," Marte said. "But you must admit, it's very interesting. Surely you can see why Mishwe was tempted."

"Tempted to watch? Yes. Tempted to kill off everyone in the goddamn world? Not really. What I can see is this—the more of you scientists that know about this, the slimmer my chances of walking out of here alive. And what about Sonja? And my dad?"

"Your father will never be as strong physically," Major Scholz explained. "He has a lot of mind stuff to work out—most of it dealing with you and your mom, but plenty that doesn't. Don't give up on him. He thought he died a hero two days ago. Now

he has to work out some old things before he can be on to a new
life. Give him some time."

The screen in Harry's isolette cleared, and the superpale face
of Trenton Solaris replaced the major.

"I see you have heard the news," Solaris said.

"Fuck the news," Harry said. "I want some sunshine."

"And you'll get it," Solaris said. "Blood tests just came back,
and none of you is infected with Mishwe's Meltdown agent. You
will be free to go within the hour. There is one condition."

"What's that?" Harry asked. "Sign myself into some secret
Agency research farm?"

Solaris chuckled. "No, nothing like that," he said. "Your anger
at the violation you have experienced is normal, but it should
not be ignored. You will all be given access to counseling for
this most unusual situation, and I urge you to take advantage
of it. You share your father's genetics, but you make your own
destiny. Ms. Chang has offered her services to rid him of the viral
curse that Mishwe spun against him. Whatever you offer us for
study, Harry, we will accept gratefully. If you want to disappear,
we owe you that, too."

"Does Sonja know?"

"I talked to her about an hour ago," the major said. "She knows
everything that we know."

"And what did she say?"

"She said she wanted to see you. In person."

"Me, too."

"I don't see why we can't do that now," Solaris said. "Both
Grace Toledo and Nancy Bartlett are on their way. We have a surprise for Sonja that is not quite ready, so please bear with us."

Major Scholz tapped out a sequence in her gloveware and
released the seals in their isolettes. Harry met Sonja in front of
the conference chamber and they hugged long and hard without
speaking. For once, Harry didn't care who was watching.

45

SONJA STOOD WITH Major Scholz at the double doors to a hangar adjacent to the warehouse. They were waiting for the surprise that Solaris promised, while Harry visited with his father. She would have to talk with her mother, too, about what she had learned this morning. She hoped it would not have to be today.

The sun felt hotter than ever, and the brilliance of it hurt her eyes, but Sonja refused both hat and sunglasses. She wanted to feel her freedom through its twin messengers of sun and wind. The steady stream of planes taking off and landing nearby reminded her of the good times she'd had in *Mariposa* and of the little biplane's sad end. The plane had been a big part of her life, but she felt guilty about grieving for a *thing* when she had seen so many innocent people die.

"I'm so sad about all those *deficientes*," she said. "They were . . . funny. You know, curious, and all they wanted was to please. Who could kill them all like that after living among them?"

She couldn't go on.

"Yes," the major agreed, "I understand. The best thing that could happen to him happened, and you don't have to feel bad about that. You helped stop him, and I thank you personally. The research team says we would be dead now . . . *I* would be dead now . . . if you hadn't."

Sonja sighed, and watched Harry exit the side door of the neighboring warehouse. He held his hand over his eyes for a moment. When he saw her, his face became one huge grin and he hurried over.

"There's the embassy limo," the major said. "It's your mother and Grace Toledo."

The major stepped aside as the four of them helped themselves to a tearful reunion. When Sonja hugged her mother and touched her face, her skin, it was as though she touched her for the first time.

We are the same, she thought. *The very same.*

Just then, two airmen rolled back the hangar doors and a small military band stumbled into her favorite Knuckleheads tune, "Skyborne." The glare outside made it impossible for her to see inside the hangar, but she glimpsed something red. Sergeant Trethewey stepped out of the shadows and waved her forward.

"Come on," Major Scholz said, her hand between Sonja's shoulder blades, urging her on. "Take a look."

It was a red-lacquered Gypsy Moth, a little bigger and more powerful than her Student Prince. Solaris stood beside the plane, out of the reach of the sunlight, and he was applauding. The others in the hangar—SEAL team, guerrilla squad, Marte Chang and a few airmen—joined him in his applause.

"What is this?" Sonja asked.

The major pressed her onward, and she sought out Harry's hand for support. He gave it a squeeze and escorted her into the hangar.

"This is a small token of our appreciation for your actions on our behalf," Solaris announced. "Your Student Prince was unsalvageable after the flood. This aircraft is a replica, but I trust you will find some of the auxiliary equipment to your liking."

He handed her a set of keys.

"An electric start," he said. "And a full tank. Why don't you fly it home?"

"All the great women flew Gypsy Moths," she mumbled.

"No reason to break tradition," the major said. "Go ahead, take it up."

"Harry?"

"Chill, eh?" Harry said, running his hand over the fabric. "Sure is pretty."

"Shall we take her up?" she asked.

"*We?* Shall *we* take her up? After what you did to me last time?"

"When you fall off a horse, you've got to get back on and ride," Sonja said. She knew it was a favorite saying of Harry's father's.

"If you won't, I will," Sergeant Trethewey called out, and several of the other men yelled, "Take me!" "I'll go!" "She can fly me *anywhere*." "Anytime." "In any*thing*."

"I'm not as dumb as I look," Harry said, and climbed into the passenger seat.

"Good thing!" somebody yelled, and everyone laughed.

"See you back home!" Nancy called. "Be careful!"

"Oh, Mom!"

Sonja ran through her checklist, called for "Clear," and as she hit the starter she knew that her mother would always be her mother, no matter what their genetic details, and that was just fine with her.

In a matter of minutes, Casa Canadá spread out dead ahead. The Gypsy Moth, though bigger and more powerful, handled much more smoothly than *Mariposa*. Sonja flew a few laps around the city, getting the feel of the machine. She sensed Harry's discomfort—he had never like flying, much—so she tried to be conservative. It was difficult to hold herself back when she had command of such a magnificent plane.

On their flight back to Casa Canadá she took one pass over the devastation that used to be ViraVax Valley. She spotted a flash of yellow sticking out of the muck at the bottom of the valley, and banked in to see what it was.

"It's *Mariposa*," she told Harry, "a piece of elevator."

He didn't answer.

Sonja waggled her wings in a farewell salute and set her heading home. At Casa Canadá, charcoal cooking fires braided their plumes and unreeled their smoke west. Several of the coffee workers squinted up at them, pointing, then ran about rounding up others.

"Perfect wind sock," Sonja said, pointing out the smoke. She quartered, then quartered again to set their nose into it. The embassy limo turned into the drive just as she set the plane down, and she smiled at Harry's sigh of relief in her headphones.

"Glad to be down?" she asked.

"Glad to be home," he said.

She taxied over to the hangar and shut down. Dozens of people had gathered along the airstrip and now they ran up to her, cheering.

"Viva Sonja!" they cried. *"Viva 'arry! Gracias a Dios!"*

Already tarps were spread, food laid out, and as they climbed down from the plane a makeshift band struck up "Siempre la Tierra," a forbidden song of the revolutionaries. García was gone. Everything was possible, even music and joy.

46

IT WAS JUST an island breaking the flow of a small river now. A scattering of green broke up the monotony of concrete, but Rico Toledo could see that not even jungle would completely cover up ViraVax again. The people would not permit it. Already local rituals included personal vigils and pilgrimages, small offerings of incense and blood. Some gloated at the tomb of a mysterious enemy, others simply assured themselves that the cap still held the beast firmly in the bottle. Costa Brava was earthquake country, after all, and Rico knew as well as anyone that that seal would crack, sooner or later.

"If he killed them all immediately, this Mishwe, killed anyone who might compete for anything. If he bred his own food out of his lab animals or his humans. If he killed any competition immediately upon recognizing it." The major pondered for a moment and shuddered. "He'd be the one to do it. By our own design, oxygen generation remains unimpaired. Amusing as it seems, fresh water is available though not from the more obvious source. A series of wells and filters supplies the facility. If he's smart, and lucky, and if he wasn't killed outright . . . well, he could live to be a very old man."

"Fifty years?"

The major smiled. "Maybe more. He was in excellent shape."

"And an earthquake big enough to spring him?"

"Or *drown* him, Colonel," she reminded him.

"Drowning him doesn't worry me," he said. "Springing him, or any of his pets, worries me a great deal."

"An earthquake strong enough to open this thing hits this area every six to ten years. Every year ViraVax took enough damage to keep a repair crew busy full-time. Repairs have been a black hole in the cash flow all along, that's why the Agency backed

out. The Children of Eden got the profits and the Agency got
the expenses—a good deal if you can swing it. With all the
distractions back home, it was no problem. The Agency got
lobbied into it by the Children of Eden and signed on the line,
anyway, knowing that this was unstable ground."

"The last one was four years ago," the Colonel said.

"Five," she countered. "That gives us about a year to wait,
given the average."

"And him all the better chance for survival."

"I'd much rather be me, Colonel," she said. "I wouldn't give
you a córdoba for anybody's chances down there."

"But he has a chance."

She answered with a shrug.

The interim government, headed by the economics whiz Philip
Rubia, and his reconciled wife, Yolanda, quickly dumped a few
thousand tons of cement onto the site while it was flooded.
Anything inside ViraVax was going to stay inside for a good,
long time.

"What about the Chang woman?" Rico asked.

He was restless and wanted to walk, but his legs were not
healed yet and the two canes were clumsy. He did not want to
admit to the vanity that kept him from appearing unsteady in front
of his staff.

"So young and brilliant," the major said. "Mariposa called her
to our attention, as you know. Brilliant . . . well, no need for that
now. She was the perfect detective for genocide. Those Sunspots
that she cultivated and patented were her own design. The world
owes her a debt for that as well as for stopping Mishwe's bugs.

"Casey was eager to make the deal when Solaris offered to
replace the dam, and it was the grace of God that Marte Chang
was ready with her Sunspots. As you know, the dam was seriously damaged in the quakes of '98, '02, '08, and nearly failed
completely in the big one in '10. Casey had always hoped to
perfect a cheap method of extracting hydrogen from water for
his power source, but it never happened. Besides, the dam was
three kilometers away and his most vulnerable point. At least,
with the Sunspots, an attack on his power source wouldn't flood
the valley.

"So, there was never a question that he would accept Chang's
project. He had tried to hire her before she developed the
Sunspots. This project merely whetted his appetite. What was
unknown to us was how she would operate for us once inside

a hostile environment. She was untrained in any of the survival
skills that many of us take for granted. She thought fast on
her feet, and she abhorred the release of any unsanctioned
genetics."

Rico already knew most of this, but he also knew that the major
needed to talk about it. She had been in the thick of it all along,
doing the dirty work for Rico and Solaris, taking no credit, voicing
no complaint. The least he could do was hear her out.

"Chang worked with our Virginia people round the clock to
analyze the data that Harry and Sonja brought back," she said.
"She discovered new horrors about Mishwe and ViraVax by the
minute. There were notes about her, files on everyone, including
you. They included quick-look genealogies, religious connections
and assets."

"How did the product get into that data block in the first place?"
he asked.

Rico already knew the answer, but he was beginning to enjoy
hearing the major talk. He had not had a drink since the ViraVax
experience, and she had found subtle ways of supporting him
in that. He knew that she had quit drinking years ago, and had
quit socializing with Rico and the others at the same time. Now,
perhaps, she had a trick or two to teach him. He hoped so.

"Red Bartlett was not a computer genius," she said. "But he
was persistent, and his persistence paid off. He set up a series
of programs to monitor researchers' logs and interior memos
and apparently succeeded just shortly before his death. These
programs continued to monitor ViraVax after his death, dumping
the product into the block that Sonja and Harry recovered. It's
clear that he indicated to Mishwe his discovery of the Meltdown
agent, and that's when Mishwe killed him. He knew it would be
covered up by ViraVax, and that the Agency would support that
cover-up. He couldn't lose."

"But he did lose, Major."

"I hope so, sir."

Rico watched Harry helping a squad from the Corps of Engineers pull a tarp tight over a fresh pour of concrete. The afternoon
sun threatened to crack the three-meter cap that sealed in the entire
Double-Vee, and no one wanted to chance any cracks. The last
dozen truckloads lined up at the remains of the dam, filling in
the conduit and maintenance shafts that Rico had identified for
them. Harry secured his line to a stake and stood, surveying the
project.

"Boys will be boys. Always playing in the mud."

Sonja's voice behind him was huskier than usual.

The squad members around him snapped to attention, and when Harry turned he saw Sonja and his father, flanked by Major Scholz and Trenton Solaris. Solaris was wrapped like a mummy and hefted his umbrella shield against the enemy sunlight.

"As you were," the major said, and the squad returned to their duty.

Sonja squinted at Harry in that way that meant, "Who is this person, really?"

Hundreds had died on this spot, many before their very eyes. Only two other people knew how that felt—his father and Marte Chang.

"How is this going to change us?" he asked.

"Subtlety is not your strong suit," Sonja said.

Her gaze held his, searched him. . . .

For what?

"No one else could understand what happened here," he said. "I get really nervous when you're gone. I . . . you're *part* of me."

"Yes," she said, "we've changed for the closer. At the last, when you were still in school, you frightened me." She hesitated, a blush coming to her cheeks. "What was happening to you at home frightened me, so I stayed away. So did my mother and father. We would have grown further apart. I can't imagine that now."

He would have cried if she hadn't hugged him in time.

"I have some news that we need to discuss," the major said to Rico. "Let's have a seat in the mess tent. Marte Chang and Yolanda Rubia are waiting for us there. They propose a pooling of resources."

"A private information service?" Rico asked.

"Call it a consulting service," the major said, "or a government corporation. What do you think?"

"I'll hear it out," Rico said. "I have a lot of old business to talk over with Yolanda."

A shadow crossed the major's face, but she quickly recovered. Rico caught her arm.

"Then," he said, "I'd like to talk over some new business with you, Major, if that's all right."

"New business would be fine, Colonel," she said with a smile. "That would be just fine."

Harry turned to go but Trenton Solaris stopped him. The albino removed his right glove, then reached out into the sunlight to shake Harry's hand.

"Congratulations again, Harry," he said. "Your performance was first-class. Your country is very proud of you."

"Thanks," Harry said. "My father taught me a lot more than I realized. We have our differences, but I'm glad he's alive. I'm glad it worked."

Solaris's gaze shifted away from his own, then back. He shook Harry's hand again. The albino congratulated Sonja, too.

"Give some thought to what you want with your lives," he said. "You both have skills that your country—and your adopted country—can use. I urge you to consider making a career out of what you do best—learning, and helping others."

"If you mean working for the Agency, I'm not sure I'd care to be in my father's command," Harry said. "I mean, I've learned a lot, and one thing I've learned is to not press my luck."

Solaris laughed.

"I think you would make a better statesman than an agent, Harry," he said. "But I, personally, and the Agency will support you in anything you choose. And we have many, many resources."

Sonja cleared her throat and said, "I'd like to be part of the Mars colony shot, but with all the trouble in the U.S. it looks like it'll never get off the ground."

"I promise you all of the flight time you want in anything you want," Solaris said, his smile-wrinkles deployed. "That's the first step. The rest is up to the politicians. Good politicians."

Solaris winked at Sonja and nodded at Harry.

"You need somebody like him to get their attention. If you do that, the sky's the limit."

Harry's stomach flipped at the thought of Sonja going anywhere without him, but *Mars* . . . ?

She must have read his mind, or at least his expression.

Sonja laughed, and took his hand.

"Hey, baby," she said, "wanna be Mayor of Mars?"

"Chill," he said, and laughed. "With you? Anytime."

BIBLIOGRAPHY

Agee, Philip. *CIA Diary*. New York: Bantam, by arrangement with Stonehill Publishing Co., 1976.

Angier, Natalie. *Natural Obsessions*. Boston: Houghton Mifflin, 1988.

Bear, Greg. *Blood Music*. New York: Ace Books, 1986.

Davis, Joel. *Defending the Body*. New York: Atheneum, 1989.

Dawkins, Richard. *The Selfish Gene*. New York: Oxford University Press, 1976.

Katz, Jay. *Experimentation with Human Beings*. New York: Russell Sage Foundation, 1972.

Preuss, Paul. *Human Error*. New York: Tor Books, 1985.

Uhl, Michael, and Tod Ensign. *GI Guinea Pigs*. Chicago: Playboy Press, 1980.